Wildfire in His Arms

JOHANNA LINDSEY

Wildfire in His Arms

G

Gallery Books

New York   London   Toronto   Sydney   New Delhi

G

Gallery Books
An Imprint of Simon & Schuster, Inc.
1230 Avenue of the Americas
New York, NY 10020

First Gallery Books hardcover edition June 2015

GALLERY BOOKS and colophon are registered trademarks of Simon & Schuster, Inc.

For information about special discounts for bulk purchases, please contact Simon & Schuster Special Sales at 1-866-506-1949 or business@simonandschuster.com.

The Simon & Schuster Speakers Bureau can bring authors to your live event. For more information or to book an event, contact the Simon & Schuster Speakers Bureau at 1-866-248-3049 or visit our website at www.simonspeakers.com.

Design by Jaime Putorti

Manufactured in the United States of America

10   9   8   7   6   5   4   3   2   1

Library of Congress Cataloging-in-Publication Data is available.

ISBN 978-1-5011-0541-8
ISBN 978-1-5011-0549-4 (ebook)

Wildfire in His Arms

Chapter One

"THOUGHT YOU'D LEFT THE territory, Mr. Grant."

Degan looked down at Sheriff Ross, smiling up at him. He leaned forward to soothe his horse before it reared up. The palomino didn't like strangers standing so close to it. Gunshots it didn't mind, strangers it did.

"I'm leaving today. Just making sure no shots get fired in the church."

"Don't need to worry 'bout that. The feud ended last week, soon as the happy couple agreed to get hitched. So you're coming to the wedding?"

Degan looked at the church at the end of the street. The two families getting joined today, the Callahans and the Warrens, were already inside it. People from town were still heading toward it to witness the happy event—and steering clear of Degan, who was sitting on his horse in the middle of the street. As much as he might like to do something as normal as attend a wedding, he knew what his presence would do. And he'd already said his good-byes.

So he shook his head at the sheriff. "No need for anyone to be nervous on a day like this."

Ross chuckled. "I think folks here in Nashart know you well enough by now—"

"That's the trouble. They know me."

Ross got a little red in the face. It was odd for a sheriff to treat Degan so affably. Usually as soon as a sheriff learned who he was, the sheriff asked him to get out of his town. Ross hadn't done that, likely out of respect for Zachary Callahan, who had hired Degan to keep the peace until Zachary's son's wedding. Of course the wedding wasn't guaranteed to happen when the Warren bride had been raised in the East in the lap of luxury and was to marry Hunter Callahan, a cowboy born and bred here in Nashart, Montana, whom she'd never met. And Tiffany Warren had definitely tried to get out of the arranged marriage. At the Callahan ranch she'd even pretended to be a housekeeper so she could find a way to end the feud between the two families without sacrificing herself on the altar.

Degan had liked Tiffany from the start because she reminded him of home, a home he was never going back to. But he'd guessed she wasn't really a housekeeper. She'd tried so hard not to be prim and proper, but she just couldn't help it. The elegant and sophisticated real Tiffany constantly slipped out, although she'd made him question his intuition when she'd befriended a baby pig and made him her pet. That had really thrown him off. It had tickled the hell out of Hunter, too. No wonder Hunter had fallen in love with his future wife before he knew who she really was.

Degan had been hired to be a deterrent to bloodshed between the two feuding families. It had worked, his job was done. It was time to move on. But the sheriff was getting that same look on his face he'd had a few days ago when he'd gotten up the nerve to ask Degan to temporarily take over his job while he went back East to find a wife. Weddings in town seemed to have that effect on single men, made men who had been looking for a wife want one even more. And unattached young women were hard to come by in the West.

Degan had declined the sheriff's offer, and now he stopped Ross from making it again, remarking, "If I ever became a sheriff, it would have to be where no one knows me."

"But it's your name that will keep trouble away," Ross insisted.

"No, it's my name that will bring trouble. You know that for a fact, Sheriff. Until gunslingers are a dying breed, there will always be fast guns wanting to prove they're faster than me. Now go on or you'll miss the ceremony. I'm just waiting to see the bride and groom leave the church before I ride out."

"Well, you'll always have a home here if you want it, Degan Grant. And my job if you want that, too!"

Degan almost smiled as the sheriff moved off. He'd never had a hankering to settle in one place until he'd come to Nashart. Of course he wasn't usually in one place this long, either. And he definitely wasn't used to being treated like a member of the family as the Callahans had treated him. They'd even given him a seat at their dining table and a bedroom in their house. Usually his employers wanted him as far away from their families as possible. They certainly never socialized with him. He *had* considered the sheriff's offer, briefly, because he did like the people around here and was going to be sorry to see the last of them. But what he'd just told the sheriff was the truth. With Nashart's mining problem settled and the two feuding families joined in marriage now, Nashart was going to be peaceful for a spell, maybe indefinitely. It wouldn't remain that way if he stayed.

Many people thought the term *peacemaker* was a misnomer for a man who could draw a gun faster than anyone else. Yet once drawn, a gun was a powerful motivator. It could keep the peace between warring factions even if it wasn't fired. That's what Degan had been in Nashart—a peacemaker. He hadn't had to kill anyone and had only drawn his gun once to make a point with Roy Warren, before he'd known Roy was one of Tiffany's brothers.

An open-top carriage was making its way down the street accompanied by three men on horseback. Degan had ridden to town with the Callahans and had assumed the Warrens were already inside the church, but apparently not. The bride was riding in the carriage with her parents, her father driving them. Her brothers hung back to keep the dust their horses turned up away from the carriage.

Frank Warren slowed the carriage to a stop, and Tiffany stood and gave Degan a graceful curtsy.

"You're late for your wedding," Degan remarked.

Tiffany chuckled. "Brides are allowed to be late, though I swear I'm not trying to make Hunter worry that I got cold feet. I just wanted to look perfect for him today, and that took a little longer than I anticipated."

"You succeeded. Hunter is a lucky man."

Degan envied his friend at that moment. Tiffany was a beautiful woman, and she looked exquisite today in her fancy Eastern wedding gown and gossamer-thin lace veil.

"Are you sure you won't join us?"

He'd ridden over to the Warren ranch yesterday to say his

good-byes and had told Tiffany he wouldn't attend the marriage ceremony. "I'm just waiting to see you two exit the church as man and wife, then I'll be on my way to California."

"Hunter said his father tried to hire you again, to look up his son Morgan while you are in Butte, but you're not going that way?"

"Too many people know me in Butte. I'll be taking the northern route that passes through Helena instead. But Zachary wanted me to scare his boy home, which is pointless if Morgan still has gold fever."

"Well, I can't say I'm not glad your job here is done." Tiffany grinned. "You made sure no one got killed while Hunter and I were figuring out we were meant for each other, and for that you have my heartfelt thanks."

"And mine," Frank Warren agreed.

"Indeed," his wife, Rose, added. "My boys admitted they were afraid to—"

"Ma!" Roy Warren cut in, abashed.

"Well, restraint on *all* fronts was no doubt a blessing in disguise," Rose finished.

Frank cleared his throat. "I don't think Mr. Grant wants to be likened to a blessing, darling."

"Nonsense," Rose huffed. "*He* knew what I meant."

"We need to get going." Frank pointed toward the church.

Degan glanced down the street and saw Zachary Callahan in front of the church looking around anxiously and gesturing to Frank to hurry up.

Tiffany laughed. "I guess I did make Hunter worry, or maybe just my father-in-law! Be safe in your travels, Degan."

She sat back down. Frank got the carriage moving again

and Tiffany's three brothers nodded at Degan as they passed. Then Tiffany called back at him, "If you ever find this kind of happiness for yourself, bring your wife by so we can meet her!"

Degan almost laughed. Trust a woman to think only a woman could make a man happy. Degan knew he would never find out if that was true because women feared him. Even Tiffany did. And he didn't know how to change that without ruining his reputation, so he wasn't about to try.

"Hey, mister, can't make up your mind where you're going?"

Degan glanced behind him and saw a stranger walking his horse through the center of town toward him. He was wearing a yellow slicker that was pushed back to reveal the gun on his hip, a rather good indication that he was looking for trouble of some sort. As the stranger approached him, Degan could see he was young and slim and his face so smooth-skinned that he could actually be mistaken for a girl.

Degan didn't have to answer the snide question. He could just ride off now and miss seeing his happily married friends walk out of church. But he knew boys of this stamp didn't like to be ignored.

"How old are you, kid?"

"Seventeen, not that it's any of your business, so don't call me kid. Name's—"

"Not interested."

The boy looked disgruntled. "Is everyone in this town as ornery as you?"

Ornery? Degan raised a black brow. He'd been called a lot of things, but never that. And the boy had stopped his roan horse a few feet from Degan's. He obviously had more to say, and no one else was around to say it to with the main street deserted now that everyone going to the wedding had reached the church. Only the shopkeepers were still in town, at least half of them standing at their windows. Strangers didn't pass through town without being noticed.

Degan told himself he shouldn't be so suspicious of every stranger who approached him, gunfighter or not. There were a lot of friendly people in the West and dozens of good reasons for a man to carry a weapon. Not everyone was out to make a name for himself by challenging every fast gun he heard of.

So Degan unbent a little and asked, "Do you need help with something?"

"Yeah, I do. Heard from some miners over in Butte that Degan Grant was living here."

"He was just passing through."

"Then I missed him?"

"Depends on what you want him for."

"Huh?"

"If you want a showdown with him, this is your lucky day. If you want to hire him, this might still be your lucky day. Any other reason, it's probably not your lucky day. Which is it?"

"So you know where I can find him?"

"You've already found him."

The boy smiled, quite widely, making Degan wonder for just a moment if his gut instinct was wrong. It wasn't.

"High noon, tomorrow, right here," the boy said, still wearing a confident grin.

That didn't need any clarification. High noon was when most stand-and-face-your-opponent gunfights happened, a time of day when neither combatant would be disadvantaged by blinding sunlight.

Degan glanced up to see where the sun was before saying, "It's close enough to high noon right now, so if we're going to do this, let's do it now. Come hitch up your horse if you don't want it catching stray bullets."

Degan rode his palomino to the nearest hitching post before he dismounted and tossed the reins over it. The boy followed him and did the same, so he wasn't expecting Degan to come around the horses with his gun already drawn.

Now the boy was glaring at Degan as he slowly moved his hand away from his gun. "How'd you get your reputation if you cheat like this?" he spat out.

"By killing men—not boys. And this isn't cheating, it's saving your life." Degan took the boy's gun and emptied it on the ground between them, then handed it back. "But I guess you don't get it yet. We're still doing this. If you win, you can reload and we'll have another go. If I win, you get to ride off and be glad you're still breathing. Sound fair?"

"Hell no. How 'bout we just do this normal in front of witnesses?"

"Look around, you're being watched. And I'm offering you exactly what you came here for, a chance to see if you're faster than I am, just without spilling blood in the street, and without you pissing your pants in fear thinking you're about to die. This is actually a much better test of who's faster, if you think about it. You'll be relaxed, without fear, without sweaty palms that might cause you to fumble. And you'll still have your bragging rights if you win."

Degan removed his jacket and hooked it over the pommel of his saddle. Just because he lived in the West now didn't mean he had to give up the finer things in life he was accustomed to. Well, he'd had to give up some, but not the way he dressed. His black jacket was finely tailored, the black vest silk, the white shirt made of soft linen. His black boots were highly polished;

the spurs weren't tin but real silver. And his gun holster was custom-made.

He stepped out into the street away from the intersection. He didn't want his friends witnessing this if they came out of the church early. The boy had followed Degan's example and left his slicker with his horse before putting some distance between them. He still looked nervous. Degan wondered if he had done this before or if this was his very first gunfight. It was a shame kids like this didn't learn from their mistakes and just go home. Maybe this one would when they were done.

"You're not going to empty your gun like you did mine?" the boy asked hesitantly.

"No. There are witnesses, remember? I'm not a murderer, just a fast gun. So prove you know how to do this."

A few more seconds passed with the boy's hand hovering just over his weapon. He was still nervous, despite Degan's assurances. Degan could see the boy's fingers shaking.

Degan finally sighed. "I'm giving you an edge, to draw first. Anytime now would be good."

"So you're gonna let me win?"

"No, I'm not." Degan drew his gun, then slid it back in his holster just as fast. "See? Now draw."

The boy tried to, but his gun still didn't clear his holster before Degan's was out and pointed at his chest. "Thing is, kid, I don't miss either. So are we done here?"

"Yes, sir, we are."

Chapter Two

"MAX, WAKE UP. MAX Dawson!"

Dark eyes opened wide, then blinked a few times before locating the pretty lady of the night pouting beside the bed. "You don't have to shout, Luella, especially not my whole name."

"Sorry, honey, but I wouldn't have to if you'd just wake up more easily. It's a wonder you can sleep at all in this establishment with all the moaning and groaning going on into the wee hours."

Max grinned. "As long as you're quiet and you don't mind sharing this exquisitely soft bed, everything else sounds like whispering wind."

"It's a wonder you ain't been caught, sleeping that soundly."

"Your door was locked, wasn't it?"

"Yes, of course."

"And no one's ever climbed in though your window?"

"Just you."

"Well, there you go, perfect safety and a soft bed. This is the only place I *can* sleep soundly. At my camp in the hills, the slightest noise, a twig's snapping, will wake me. 'Sides, no one's looking for me in these parts."

"Then why'd you want me to wake you at dawn before the deputies make their early rounds? By the way, that was thirty minutes ago. That's how long I've been trying to wake—"

"Damnit, why didn't you say so! I hate being in town in daylight."

"But if no one's looking—"

"Not actively looking, but the wanted posters have made their way this far north. I snatch them down when I find them, but the sheriff here keeps putting more back up. He must've been sent a pile of them."

Max slipped out from beneath the covers fully dressed except for coat and hat, which were grabbed now. The gun holster hadn't been removed either. Luella didn't like sleeping next to a long-barreled Colt even though she was used to guns and kept a small derringer tucked away in her small bureau for emergencies. But she minded something else even more.

"You could at least remove your damn boots before you go to sleep," she said, staring at the scuffed boots that had just left her bed.

"Can't, case I have to leave fast—like this." Max opened the window, climbing onto the porch roof that fronted the bordello, then dropping to the ground.

Luella watched from her window. Standing there in her chemise, she heard a whistle from across the street. She didn't try to cover herself. After all, part of her job was to attract customers to Chicago Joe's bordello. Helena had far too many whorehouses, and the competition was fierce.

Too many bordellos, too many millionaires, too many miners, heck, just too many people. But then Helena was the most populated town in Montana Territory, had been since gold was discovered in the nearby gulch back in '64. Eighteen years later folks were still moving to Helena when most towns that had sprouted up because of gold had turned into ghost towns. Even Virginia City, a ways south, was dying, and it had boasted a population of three thousand during its heyday. But Helena, with hundreds of businesses, didn't rely solely on gold for its prosperity. It was also the capital of the territory, and the railroad was heading this way, too. In another year or two it would probably reach Helena, and that would ensure that the town didn't bottom out when the gold did.

Luella thought Helena would be a nice place to settle down if she could find a man who would have her. She'd only received marriage proposals from miners so far, and miners didn't have their own homes or make much money, so they didn't have the means to start families here. Usually if a man had means, he wasn't interested in taking a whore for a wife when he could bed one for a few coins.

Luella looked over at Big Al, the man who had whistled at her. He was out early, sweeping the porch of his saloon across the street. He was one of her regulars and had always treated her with a gentle hand. She'd actually been considering him as a potential husband until the night Max had rescued her and she had fallen instantly in love. So dumb for someone like her to succumb to that emotion.

But with Big Al's being a landowner and a businessman, and single, he was still an option. His saloon was one of many in town that never closed its doors. Luella's place of business never closed either. Josephine Airey, or Chicago Joe as most people called her, owned the bordello and many others like it. Quite the landowner, their madam was, and she believed a man who wasn't put on a time schedule—at least when satisfying his amorous needs—was a happy man.

Big Al was giving Luella a cheeky grin now—and not watching where he was sweeping. Dust flew toward one of his customers who was leaning against the porch post, drink in hand. The man, a fancy dresser, was probably a businessman, she thought, until she saw the gun on his hip and quickly took her eyes off him. She figured Big Al must be wary of him, too, if he'd let him take a drink outside to the porch. Big Al never allowed that. Sheriff's orders, no drinking allowed in the streets. Now Al rushed back inside his establishment before the man noticed the dust on the back of his polished boots.

Luella didn't like gunfighters, though Lord knew she'd bedded a lot of them. Gunfighters frightened her because they didn't throw punches when they got mad; they drew guns instead. Max probably did, too, but Max was different. And what wasn't to like about Max Dawson?

"See you next week, Luella!" Max shouted up at her now.

"Sure thing, honey," Luella called back, and waved, but Max was already galloping out of town.

She closed her window and went back to bed. She hoped the gunslinger hadn't noticed her and wouldn't be paying her a visit.

Chapter Three

DEGAN WATCHED THE KID race out of town. He'd watched him exit the brothel, too. Anyone departing that quickly through a window usually meant someone else would soon appear with a gun in hand and start shooting, but that didn't happen. Instead a pretty blonde in her undergarments had appeared at the window to say good-bye.

The little scene was unusual enough that Degan took in more details than he normally would. Not that he wasn't always aware of what was going on around him. He was, but he usually only focused on what he sensed could be danger-ous. The long coat the kid was wearing over black pants and shirt wasn't a typical rain slicker but an expensive garment made of soft doeskin. His tan, wide-brimmed hat was either new or well cared for because it hadn't been dented yet. Light brown boots that were scuffed all to hell and a white bandanna revealed that the boy had no sense of style. He had dark eyes, short white-blond hair under the hat, and a baby face. Another boy so young that he hadn't grown hair on his face yet, but was sporting a gun on his hip. Why did they court violence at such a young age?

But this one appeared to have a love of life. Degan had seen it in the kid's expression as he'd hopped onto his horse and heard it in the laughter that trailed after him as he raced away. A good night with a comely woman could do that, Degan supposed—or young love. And then one of those details he'd only vaguely noticed surfaced in his mind and he stepped back and stared at the wanted poster tacked to the post he'd been leaning against.

He'd seen it earlier, just hadn't paid attention to it. Whoever had drawn the picture must have known the outlaw because the likeness was uncanny. An outlaw visits a brothel across the street from his wanted poster that offers $1,000 for his capture? Degan shook his head. Boys were far too daring these days. But this one was none of his concern. His gun was for hire but he wasn't about to do the sheriff's job for him.

Degan took his empty glass back into the saloon and stopped at the bar. The only other customer in the room had been sleeping with his head down on a table and still was. Degan wouldn't even have stopped at the saloon if he hadn't ridden all night to get to Helena and the saloon hadn't been the first place he'd passed that was open at this hour. He deplored camping in the wilderness and only did it when he was too far between towns. He didn't like traveling at night either, but he hadn't been tired enough to stop last night, and the lure of a bed and a hot bath had kept him going.

"I'll take a bottle of your finest to go—and a rag for my boots."

The rag was quickly shoved across the bar as the barkeep's face turned red. The bottle had to be searched for. When the man returned, he said hesitantly, "I should warn you, there's a law here 'bout drinking in the streets."

"I wasn't planning to." Degan paid up, then added, "I don't consider your porch the street."

"Fair 'nough." The man relaxed now that Degan hadn't taken offense.

"Best hotel in town?"

"That'd probably be the International. Big brick building. Hard to miss if you keep heading into town. So you just rode in?"

Degan didn't answer. It annoyed him that one question from him tended to open the floodgates to his getting questioned in return. He understood it was a nervous reaction of intimidated people who hoped that if he was talking, he wouldn't be shooting. He grabbed the bottle and headed to the door.

The barkeep called after him, "You might check with our sheriff if you're looking for work, mister. Folks bring their troubles to him first, but he don't always have the time to help them all, even with eight deputies. This is a big town. Plenty folks round here could use a hired gun—if that's what you are."

Degan tipped his wide-brimmed hat at the man, but kept on walking. He wasn't looking for work yet. He had made enough money in the West that he could retire for the next ten years if he wanted to. But to do what? He'd been groomed to take over an empire, but he'd turned his back on that.

This town was far too big for his liking, he realized, as he continued through it. He preferred small towns, where you could see trouble coming from a mile away. But he was just here for a bath, a bed, and a meal before he continued on to California, which is where he'd been headed when Zachary

Callahan had tracked him down and offered him too much money to refuse merely to keep the peace for a few weeks.

It wasn't the first time he'd been overpaid. In fact, it happened more often than not. It was one of the benefits of having a reputation that preceded him. The only other benefit of that reputation was that he could get a job done without bloodshed.

It used to bother him, a lot, that he made people so nervous. He used to assure people that they didn't need to be afraid of him. That assurance only worked until they saw him draw his gun. And rarely could he pass through a town where he didn't need to draw it for one reason or another—if people discovered who he was. So he'd stopped being sociable, stopped talking to people if he didn't have to, stopped volunteering his name. Hell, half the time it didn't matter if they knew who he was. He couldn't even walk into a bank without all those in it dropping to the floor, thinking they were about to be robbed. Now *that* was annoying. Maybe it was time to go back East— just not home.

Degan found the International Hotel easy enough, but he certainly wasn't expecting to run into anyone he knew in the lobby.

"Well, aren't you a sight for sore eyes, Degan Grant!"

Degan winced, hearing his name spoken so loudly. "Keep your voice down," he said as he turned, but then he actually smiled.

He hadn't made many friends in the West, but he could count John Hayes as one of them. John was in his midforties now, but Degan had met him not long after he'd first come West five years ago.

"What brings you this far north, Sheriff?"

"It's US Marshal now." John grinned.

Degan raised a brow. "Does that warrant congratulations?"

"It's letting me see more of the country than I ever thought I would, but, no, I wasn't hankering for the position. I got talked into it by an old friend who's a senator now. The railroads have been putting a lot of pressure on the politicians in Washington to clean up the West. They hired Pinkerton detectives years ago to deal with some of the train robberies, but it's not enough. Now our government is taking action, too. But what brings you to Helena?"

"I just finished a peacekeeping job in the territory."

"Then you aren't currently employed?"

"No."

"Damn, that's a relief."

Degan was amused. "I still abide by the law, John. Did you really think you would need to arrest me?"

"No, course not. But since you're between jobs, I'd like to call in that favor you owe me."

"What favor?"

"For saving your life."

Degan snorted. "I was on the mend. You didn't need to drag me to a doctor."

"You were half-dead and still bleeding."

John had been the sheriff in a town where Degan had been shot. A trio of bank robbers had been trying to shoot their way out of town after the alarm was raised. A lot of people had been on the streets that day. Degan had pitched in to prevent innocent people from getting killed and had ended up catching a stray bullet himself. He'd ridden out of that town wounded. John had tracked him down.

If he cared to admit it, he supposed he could have died that day if he had continued on his way. The wound hadn't hurt that much—yet. So he hadn't known he was bleeding so much he'd been leaving a trail of blood behind him.

"I'll allow your doctor did a good job of stitching," Degan said. "It left barely a scar. What favor do you need?"

"It will just be temporary, mind you. I need at least three outlaws on my long list brought in over the next couple months. I haven't just been tasked with cleaning up the West, I've been told to do it on a damn time schedule."

Degan was a little more than surprised. "You want to turn me into a *bounty* hunter? I'm not a tracker."

"You don't need to be. Most of these boys hide in plain sight in crowded towns like this one, or ones too small to have good sheriffs in them. The pay is good and two of the wanted men have been seen in the area. A third was last seen in Wyoming. If you prefer, you can take your pick of who you want to go after. As I said, I have a long list."

"And why aren't you after them?"

"Because my ma is dying. I got the telegram yesterday. Already bought our stage tickets to leave today."

"Our?"

"My wife and daughters are here with me."

"I didn't know you were married."

John grinned and boasted, "Happily for almost ten years now. Our girls are six and seven, and my Meg is expecting another. Because I have to travel so much these days, whenever I know I'm going to be in one place for a while, I take my family with me. The railroads' extending as far west as they do now makes that possible. This trip to Virginia could take me a couple months because I have to get my mother's estate settled. That could cost me my job if I can't cross off at least three outlaws from my list during that time."

"I'm sorry about your mother."

John nodded. "I knew she was sick, I just didn't know it was this bad."

"I assume you already asked the local sheriff for assistance?"

"Talked to him yesterday, but he's too busy, and I'm not surprised. Hell, who would think you could find a town *this* big in Montana, which isn't even a state yet."

"Gold does that."

"It surely does," John agreed. "So, can you help me out, Degan? I only need three wanted men captured in the next two months. If you finish sooner than that, you can continue on your way. But I will need to make you a deputy marshal while you're acting on my behalf."

"Oh, hell no. If I do this, I won't be wearing a lawman's badge."

John grinned. "You don't need to mention it to anyone if you think it will tarnish your reputation. It would just be in case you need to verify that you have jurisdiction, which knowing you, you probably won't have to do. You'll get to keep the rewards being offered. Some might be more lucrative than your usual jobs."

"I doubt that."

"Well, they will be when you add them up. And it won't be that difficult to find these men. I've gathered a lot of information on these miscreants that I'll turn over to you, much more than is mentioned on their posters—known friends and family members, everywhere they've broken the law, any associates they might have, or if they're loners. I've kept a lot of notes, and I've been doing this for a couple years now. I would just ask that you telegraph me in Virginia each time you bring one of them in, so I can let my superiors know that even while I'm taking care of family matters, I'm still keeping to my schedule."

Degan nodded. "As long as your superiors don't track me down afterward to try and talk me into continuing in that line of work."

John chuckled. "I'll keep your name out of it."

Chapter Four

THE LEATHER SATCHEL JOHN Hayes had given Degan resembled a small, thin valise without a handle, but it had a lock and key. Degan didn't open it when he got to his hotel room after bidding John good-bye. He merely dropped it on the floor with his saddlebags and his own valise. Sleep was his first order of business. But when he lay down on the bed, he didn't drift off right away.

The words *lawman* and *bounty hunter* kept running through his mind. Neither occupation suited his temperament, yet he'd still agreed to the job. Because a friend had asked. No, because while he'd never admit it to anyone, he actually liked helping people. It gave a sense of purpose to his wandering. And John Hayes was good people.

When Degan woke it was midafternoon, too early for dinner, too late for lunch, but he was hungry. He continued to ignore John's leather satchel and went downstairs and found the hotel dining room closed just as he'd expected.

The same clerk in the lobby who had checked Degan in

gave him the names of restaurants nearby, although he wasn't sure if they were open either. Degan's scowl had the clerk quickly adding, "But if you will wait in the dining room, I will have something brought to you."

"To my room instead?"

"Certainly, sir. Immediately."

Degan went back upstairs. His room was nicely appointed, finer than any of the other hotel rooms he'd stayed in since coming West, so he wouldn't mind spending a few days here if he had to. Being able to eat in his room was a nice bonus. The less time he spent in public, the better. He hoped the barkeep he'd met that morning wasn't a gossip. If he was, the sheriff would know by now that Degan was in town. Even though the sheriff wouldn't know his name, that wouldn't necessarily stop him from seeking Degan out.

He stood at the window for a few minutes. It provided a panoramic view of Helena, which was spread out over the low hills that circled the downtown area. The streets, and there were many of them, reminded him of home because they were so crowded in the late afternoon. The West had always been a place where people could start fresh. But much of the region still wasn't safe for settlers. Soon it would be. John's mission to round up the outlaws who preyed on settlers was important. Progress, real progress, was coming to the West with the railroads.

Still waiting for his food, Degan opened John's satchel and spread out the papers on his bed. He counted twenty wanted posters. Each of them had a page or two of John's scrawled notes attached to it. One poster featured Big Jim Mosley. That was convenient. Degan only had to capture two outlaws now. He could cross Mosley off John's list since Degan had killed the man last year in Wyoming. He hadn't known Mosley was wanted for murder, but since the man had tried to shoot him in the back, he wasn't surprised. Apparently the sheriff of that town hadn't been able to confirm his identity either, which was why Mosley was still wanted by the law. It made Degan wonder how many others on John's list of twenty names might already be dead. Men who broke the law couldn't count on growing old.

Baby-faced Max Dawson wasn't dead and would be an easy find, considering Degan had seen him at the brothel this morning. Kid Cade, another on the list, Degan had also crossed paths with in Wyoming. In his late thirties, the kid was no kid any longer and had steered clear of him, so Degan didn't figure him to be a gunfighter, just a thief. John's notes mentioned Cade had tried claim jumping unsuccessfully, stage robbing successfully, and a bank robbery that nearly got him killed when he tried to pull it off alone. He'd avoided getting caught for that, as well as numerous other robberies in which he'd been identified as the thief. He had last been seen in the area of Butte, to the southwest, a few months ago.

Degan didn't need to read any further. He had intentionally avoided Butte and ridden north to Helena thanks to the miners in Butte who had let it be known that Degan was in the area. He wasn't partial to backtracking, but Cade and Dawson were likely the two wanted men John had said were in the area, and the two Degan could apprehend most quickly. He might just be back on his way to California in a week or two.

But then another poster caught his eye, the only other one besides Max Dawson's that offered a $1,000 reward. John's notes explained why. Charles Bixford, alias Red Charley, was known to have killed three women, two children, and fifteen men when he blew up a town hall in Nebraska because his wife was in it. She was one of the women he'd killed, and the two children had been his. But that was only the start of his killing spree, which continued across Nebraska, into Colorado, and ended in Utah, where he'd last been seen. Bixford wasn't known to be crazy, yet he'd murdered innocents for no apparent reason. He'd also killed a US marshal along the way who'd tried to apprehend him and had wounded the next one who'd tried.

And John needed to catch this killer? John, who was married with kids of his own? What sort of favor would Degan be doing for John if he only captured the less dangerous outlaws on the list? He decided to grab the two who were nearby and throw in Bixford as a bonus before going on to California.

Degan was putting the wanted posters back in John's satchel when there was a knock at the door. He opened it, and a young man in a white apron nervously handed him a platter of fancy sandwiches and hurried away. It was more food than he needed and he only ate half of it. Then he made use of the bathing room at the end of the hall after the male attendant stationed there assured him it was cleaned after every use and handed him a fresh towel. A smaller tub was behind a screen in Degan's room, but it wasn't connected to plumbing and he didn't want to wait for water to be delivered.

An hour later he was saddling his horse in the nearby stable, which was where Helena's sheriff caught up with him. A tall man, the sheriff appeared confident with a rifle cradled in his arms. And brave, to have come without any of his deputies to back him up.

"We don't want any trouble here, mister, so I hope saddling your horse means you're leaving our fair town."

Degan didn't feel like standing there explaining himself, so he merely said, "I'm a friend of Marshal Hayes. I believe you know him?"

"I do."

"The marshal asked me to help him with his agenda, so if I bring you an outlaw or two to lock up, I assume you'll have room for them?"

"Certainly. That sort of help is always appreciated."

Degan mounted up, tipped his hat, and rode out of the stable before the sheriff thought to ask him for his name. Possibly his reputation hadn't reached as far as Helena, but he couldn't count on that when people in Nashart and Butte knew that he was in the area. And the sheriff would know as well as Degan did that his name would bring other glory-seeking gunfighters to town. Whether he stayed there or not, they would still come looking for him.

He rode directly to the brothel that Dawson favored. The scantily clad women lounging in the large parlor perked up as he entered. He heard syrupy greetings and salacious promises. Two of them even pushed each other to get to him first. A third was seductively walking toward him when she noticed his demeanor—and his gun—and turned around. Her expression must have alerted the others. The women stopped trying to attract his attention. A few of them hurriedly left the room. He was used to that reaction. Women were more afraid of him than men, and they were less inclined to try to hide it, even women like the ones here whose company could be bought by anyone. And they didn't *know* him, knew nothing about him. Yet one close look at him and their instincts had them averting their eyes.

The madam, who was also in the parlor, was the only exception. Her job was to make sure every man who entered her domain left happy. Yet even she approached Degan nervously, though she didn't sound it when she said, "It's not often I meet a man who makes me regret that I'm a married woman now. They call me Chicago Joe. What are you in the mood for, mister?"

Three blondes were in the room, but none of them were as pretty as the one named Luella whom he'd seen standing at the window that morning bidding Dawson good-bye, and she was the one he was there to see. "I'm looking for Luella."

"One of our favorites!" Chicago Joe smiled. "She's upstairs, but she isn't available right now. Can I offer you a drink while you wait, or perhaps another of our lovely . . . ?"

Degan didn't wait for her to finish. He headed up the stairs. No one tried to stop him. Luella's had been the corner room facing the street. The door wasn't locked, but she was with a customer. At least only Luella was in the rumpled bed. Her customer was still undressing to join her there. Both glanced immediately at Degan as he stepped into the room.

"I only need to have a few words with the lady," he told the man. "You can either wait in the hall for her, or find another if you can't wait. But vacate—"

The man had already grabbed his shirt and boots and rushed past Degan with his head ducked down. Luella got out of bed and put on a thin robe before she turned to say, "A few words, huh? And aren't you the handsome one. Remove that gun and we'll get along just fine, mister."

Degan could tell she was trying to be brave. Women usually did get bold with him once he removed his gun. But Luella was also inching her way toward her bureau, where she probably kept a weapon. Degan moved farther into the room to block her from doing something stupid.

"I'm not here for your charms. You're going to tell me where Max Dawson holes up when he's not paying you visits."

She blinked before her brows snapped together. "No, I won't."

"Are you sure about that?"

She rushed to the other side of the bed to put an obstacle between them. Degan realized he'd terrified her with his tone. Unintentionally. He would have liked to put her at ease, but that would defeat his purpose.

So Degan stated clearly, "If I have to wait around here for another week for Dawson to crawl through your window again, someone is bound to get shot during the arrest, particularly Dawson if he tries to run. His wanted poster doesn't say dead or alive, but it doesn't say he has to be alive, either."

"How'd you even know to—? Oh, that was you across the street this morning. If you want Max, why didn't you just follow him then?"

"I didn't want him then. I do now."

That was met with a few long moments of silence before she asked in a painfully hopeful voice, "You won't shoot Max if you don't have to?"

"No, I won't—if I don't have to."

Degan had guessed that young Dawson had feelings for this girl, but he was surprised that she apparently returned those feelings—or at least, there was more between them than her just wanting to protect a paying customer.

So he added, "If you can point me in his direction and he can be taken by surprise, I can pretty much guarantee there won't be bloodshed. But if I have to capture him when he visits you again, he could end up lying dead at your feet. Either way, I am going to find him. So do you try to save his life or not?"

She sat on the edge of the bed, then looked over her shoulder at him so Degan could see that she was crying. Out of politeness, he managed not to snort, but he sure as hell wasn't gullible enough to fall for tears that could easily be faked. He wouldn't be moved by them even if he thought they were real. You had to feel something for someone to be affected by the person's tears, and he hadn't felt anything like that for a long time.

He still had to wait while she wrestled with her indecision, bit her lower lip a few times, and pleaded with her pretty blue eyes. Pointlessly.

She finally figured that out and even made a small, frustrated sound before she said, "Max found an abandoned shack up in the hills. Some fool miner built it years ago, thinking he could find gold on his own, away from the gulch where everyone else was finding it."

"And how do you know that it was abandoned?"

She glared at him. "Max didn't shoot the miner, if that's what you're implying. There were mining tools left in it, holes dug all around it, even a dirt cave dug out of the hill next to the shack. Max was the one who made the guess, not me."

"So you haven't been there?"

"No, I never get out of town. Max merely mentioned that he found it after we met last month and said he would be using it for a while. Said it's got a nice view of Helena, so I figured it must be higher up, probably in the forested hills on the way to the Big Belt Mountains."

"But you're just guessing?"

"Well, there has to be game nearby 'cause Max brought us a deer last week and a passel of dead rabbits the week before."

"That's how he pays for your services?"

"No, he does it just 'cause he's nice."

"A nice murderer and bank robber?"

Luella thrust out her chin. "Max is innocent of those charges."

"That's for a jury to decide, not you or me," Degan said before he walked out of the room.

Chapter Five

ZACHARY AND MARY CALLAHAN were having coffee on the front porch of their ranch house when they noticed the cloud of dust heading their way.

"Were you expecting company this morning?" Zachary asked his wife.

"No."

"Well, I don't have friends who would come calling in a buckboard. Can you make out who that is in it?"

"They aren't close enough," Mary said, squinting. "But it looks like two bonnets, so I'm guessing it's Rose Warren and her maid."

"Not with guards that aren't Warren men. I'd recognize their horses. And I thought you said Rose visited yesterday while I was on the range?"

"She did, but Tiffany and Hunter will be leaving for New York soon. And Rose did a lot of worrying about their marriage. You can't blame her for wanting to see for herself how well it's working out."

"It's only been a week since the wedding. And those two don't come out of the bedroom long enough for anyone to figure out anything."

Mary chuckled. "Actually, I'd worry myself—if they did. Or has it been so long you don't remember how we were when we first got hitched?"

He leaned over and kissed his wife tenderly. "If I didn't have a ranch to run . . ."

Mary giggled. "I'll remind you tonight that you said that."

Glancing back at the dust cloud, he conceded, "I think you were right. That's a mighty big feather on one of those bonnets. No one in town other than our new daughter-in-law would own a hat like that, except for her mother."

"I've changed my mind. I don't think Rose has even unpacked her bonnets yet. And she never wore them when she lived here before. She prefers wide brims same as I do, to keep the sun off her cheeks."

"Then I give up."

"Good, because if you'll just rein in your curiosity for a few more minutes you'll know exactly who is coming to visit." But when the buckboard stopped in front of the porch, Mary added as she stood up to greet their visitors, "Or not."

The young woman was definitely not from Nashart or any town close by. If the young woman weren't so richly garbed in navy silk, her black hair, blue eyes, and her age, which Mary guessed was midtwenties, would have made Mary think she was the real Jennifer Fleming, whom Frank Warren had hired from Chicago to be his housekeeper, the gal Tiffany had been pretending to be when she was *their* housekeeper. Mary couldn't take her eyes off the young woman's stylish clothing. Three rows of short ruffles ran down each side of the front of her jacket, from shoulders to waist in exquisite detail, with pearl buttons down the center. Another row of ruffles crossed the front of her skirt where it was draped back to form part of the bustle. It was just a traveling ensemble, and yet it would outshine the fanciest apparel at any of the shindigs in Nashart.

This was a lady, a rich city lady, and now Mary's curiosity was more rampant than her husband's. Ladies like this didn't come to Montana without a good reason.

The second woman was older and not as elegantly dressed. The two-man escort who had ridden on either side of the buckboard weren't local boys, either. Wearing city suits, bowler hats—and gun belts—they were definitely guards of some sort. One of them dismounted to help the women down from the buckboard. Zachary rose and walked to the top of the porch steps, Mary following him. Only the young lady and her chaperone walked toward the porch.

"Mr. and Mrs. Callahan, I hope?" the young lady asked.

"There are a lot of Callahans here and more'n one missus," Zachary replied.

The lady seemed delighted despite the indirect answer. "Then I've come to the right place. I'm Allison Montgomery. This is my maid, Denise. We've traveled all the way from Chicago to find my fiancé, Degan Grant. The detectives I hired to locate him traced him to your ranch."

"You're a bit late," Zachary said. "Degan was working for me, but his job here is finished. He lit out last week after the wedding."

Allison looked distraught. "He—he married?"

"He didn't, our son Hunter did," Mary quickly put in. "But Degan never mentioned he had a fiancée."

Zachary actually chuckled. "Nor would he. The man never talked about himself."

Allison sighed. "I can't say I'm not disappointed that he's no longer here. Do you know where he was going when he left?"

"West, but that could be anywhere," Zachary replied.

"Hunter might know more." Mary then added to her husband, "Why don't you fetch him while I get some more coffee. You're welcome to come into the parlor to wait, Miss Montgomery. It's cooler in there."

"Thank you, you are most kind." Allison walked up the porch steps with her chaperone.

Upstairs, Zachary knocked on Hunter's door. "I need you downstairs, boy."

"Go away, Pa, I'm busy!" Hunter yelled from inside the room.

Zachary yelled back, "So get unbusy and bring your wife. We have—"

"Tiffany is busy, too, and I'm not about to interrupt her. Go *away*!"

Zachary put his ear to the door and heard a giggle, then a passionate moan. He rolled his eyes and pounded on the door again. "Degan's fiancée is downstairs and wants to know where she can find him. This really won't wait."

A mere moment later, Hunter opened the door, holding up his unfastened pants, wearing nothing else. "Degan has a fiancée? I don't believe it."

"Come see for yourself."

Once they were dressed, Hunter and Tiffany pretty much ran down the stairs. They came to a halt as soon as the parlor was within view and they saw the women sitting on the sofa. Hunter thought his father had just made up a tall tale to get them out of the bedroom since they'd pretty much been living in it all week. Tiffany knew her father-in-law wouldn't joke about Degan's having a fiancée, so she wasn't surprised by the sight of the beautiful young woman in the room and went in to introduce herself.

Hunter stopped to give Mary a bashful grin and a kiss on the cheek before she set down the coffee tray she'd just brought into the parlor. "Morning, Ma—is it still morning?"

"You'd know what time of day it is if you hadn't decided to have your honeymoon here."

"New York is going to be a hectic shopping spree. We'll get there eventually."

"Well, behave. We have guests."

"So I see." Hunter moved over to sit on the arm of the sofa next to his wife. But he didn't appear the least bit cordial as he stared at Allison Montgomery and said, "If Degan had a fiancée, he wouldn't be selling his gun all over the West. Who are you really?"

"Hunter!" Tiffany exclaimed.

The woman was blushing profusely now, having just been called a liar. "I see I'm going to have to explain."

"Yeah, that might be a good idea," Hunter agreed.

Mary poured her guests cups of coffee, but Allison's was left untouched as she began, "You are right, Degan and I aren't engaged anymore, but we were, and if he hadn't left Chicago, we would be married now. He doesn't know I forgave him."

"Forgave him for what?" Tiffany asked.

Tears welled up in Allison's eyes but she blinked them back. "We were childhood friends and so much in love. But Degan had a bit more than a flirtation with another young woman the night of our engagement dinner. I didn't blame him. We weren't married yet, and, well, I understand such things happen. But my parents weren't as understanding. They made me break off the engagement. I didn't want to do it, but I couldn't defy them. I hoped my parents would relent and Degan and I would reconcile, but he left Chicago before my parents could reconsider."

In a friendlier tone now Hunter asked, "Why have you waited so long to come looking for Degan to patch things up?"

"Everyone said to give him a year or two to sow his wild oats, that he'd be back, but it's been five years! I tried to forget about him. I let other men court me, I tried to fall in love with them, but I just couldn't forget about Degan. He and I were meant to be together. I just need to remind him of that and to tell him that I still love him, that I forgive him."

"I never would have took Degan for being a city slicker," Zachary remarked.

"I guessed," Tiffany said with a grin.

"Takes one to know one, Red," Hunter teased his wife.

"Do either of you know where Degan was going?" Allison asked the newlyweds. "I'm not just looking for him for me, now. His father is ill. Degan *needs* to come home."

"He's going to California via Helena, the northern route," Tiffany volunteered.

"But he could stop anywhere along the way and probably will," Hunter added. "He is a gun for hire, after all."

"So I've been told." Allison smiled warmly. "Thank you so much. If I hurry, perhaps I can catch up with him before he leaves the territory."

"Never would have figured a broken heart for the reason Degan came West," Hunter said as soon as Allison Montgomery had left.

"I can't quite imagine *him* with a broken heart at all," Tiffany said.

Hunter raised a brow at her. "I thought you stopped being so wary of him."

"I did, but honestly, can *you* imagine Degan Grant pining for a lost love?"

"No, but I liked Degan, a lot. If that city gal can make him happy, I hope she catches up with him. Speaking of catching up, I'll race you back upstairs."

Chapter Six

IT TOOK DEGAN FOUR days and five evenings to find a shack
in the hills. He hadn't trusted Luella to steer him in the right
direction. The forest on the way to the Big Belt range was too
far from Helena, a full day's ride that would likely require crossing the Missouri River to get to it. While there might be a ferry
somewhere along the river, he doubted an outlaw such as Max
Dawson would want to spend close to an hour in the company
of the ferry operator who might identify him and notify the
sheriff anytime Dawson visited Luella. And Degan wasn't going
to waste time looking for a ferry. He'd rather wait out the week
in town for Dawson to come visiting again before he searched
in that direction. But some wooded areas were closer to Helena,
so he could look for Dawson there during the day and return to
the hotel at night. The two to the southeast and southwest were
quite extensive, which was why the search was taking so long.

Then two prospectors at different sites he passed mentioned
some old claims farther up a particular hill, which is where
he'd been searching today. But he was beginning to doubt

that information, too, until he came across two log cabins and a cut-wood house tucked away in the trees before he finally found what was obviously a shack at the top of the hill. Late at night as it was, he might have missed it and headed back to town if he didn't briefly catch the moon glinting off the tin roof. As he drew close to the shack, he saw a dim light emanating from the cracks between the boards that served as walls. Was there a lantern inside? He couldn't tell until he got closer, which he did now.

Put together piecemeal from broken-down wooden crates, boards of different lengths, and other scraps of wood, it was barely wide enough to accommodate a small bed and maybe a table and a chair. It certainly wouldn't keep the cold out come winter with so many cracks in the walls. But in warmer months, it might at least keep the rain out. And it was certainly better than camping outdoors.

He almost missed the cave Luella had mentioned, at the end of a slightly sloped path, because it was in the shadow of the trees, about thirty feet away from the shack. He investigated that first. It appeared to be no more than a hole dug in the steeper side of the hill. Black as pitch inside it. He'd be annoyed if that's where Dawson was sleeping. He couldn't imagine what the miner who had supposedly excavated it had been thinking. Clear dirt, then dig down until he hit rock, when there might not even be rock under this hill?

Degan took a box of matches from his jacket pocket and struck one as he ducked his head and stepped inside the cave. It wasn't that deep, just enough to fit a horse for the night. The animal swung his head around and glanced at him, but didn't make a sound, so Degan backed out of the hole and made his way back up the path to the shack.

He walked around the structure and found the entrance. This area had been cleared of trees and brush. He saw the remnants of a campfire, a pan left on a griddle, the fire extinguished for the night. A saddle was on the ground next to it. He wasn't surprised. The shack would block that fire from the view of anyone downhill. The miner had definitely wanted to keep his place hidden.

Degan inched his way to the entrance. If there had ever been a door, it was gone now. The shack was barely as tall as he was. The opening wasn't. He had to duck again to see inside.

Light came from a lantern on the floor, but it was set so low it might as well not have been lit. Still, it provided enough illumination for him to see Dawson lying on the floor asleep. So Luella had tried to steer Degan wrong. Young love, in this case, he thought, was damned annoying.

Nearly an hour had passed since Degan had found the place. He'd left his horse at the bottom of the hill so any sound it made wouldn't be heard. And he'd moved slowly, careful to avoid stepping on twigs, which is what had taken so long. There were a lot of twigs. But the moment he stepped inside the shack, wood creaked. Unavoidable when the floor was made of crate scraps.

Dawson heard it, but he'd been sleeping on his belly, so even though he reached for his gun, he still had to turn to fire it. Before that happened, Degan said, "Your back makes an easy target, not that I ever miss what I shoot at. And don't try what you're thinking of trying. It only takes a second to die, kid."

"Can I at least turn over?"

"Not with that gun in your hand. Drop it, carefully, and lock your fingers behind your head."

The boy might have done as told, but not quickly enough.

He was obviously still considering options that didn't include jail. So Degan moved forward and stepped on Dawson's right wrist until the gun slipped from the boy's fingers and a string of expletives from his mouth.

"Lucky for you I never lose my temper," Degan said casually as he picked up the long-barreled Colt and tucked it in his belt before stepping back. "But I can get annoyed when I'm tired and I'm damn tired tonight, so you might not want to test my patience again—I still don't see those fingers behind your head."

Max had been shaking his right hand to make sure his wrist wasn't broken, but he quickly complied now and locked both hands behind his neck. The kid was probably still swearing, but it was just a mumble to Degan's ears and he didn't really care. He dropped the coil of thin rope that was looped over his shoulder and gave the rest of the room a cursory glance. There was nothing in it other than the lantern, two saddlebags with a rifle propped up against the wall between them, and the tan hat hanging from a peg on the wall. The kid was fully dressed, minus his coat, which he'd rolled up and had been using as a pillow.

"You sleep on a pile of leaves? Really?" Degan said with some amusement.

"Was I supposed to make this rickety crate feel like home? Wasn't planning on staying more'n a few days."

"Yet you did stay longer. Why didn't you just get a room in town so you could enjoy a few comforts? Helena is a big enough town to hide in."

"Not with my face showing up on so many porch posts along the boardwalks."

"So it is you, Max Dawson? Thanks for clearing that up so quickly."

"Well, damn. You weren't sure?"

"Sure enough, but there isn't much light in here, is there?"

Degan corrected that, hunkering down to see if he could get any more light out of the old lantern. He managed to make the light a little brighter.

"There's not much fuel left in that," Dawson warned.

"We'll survive if it goes out. You can sit up now."

Max did so and dusted leaves off his shirtfront before he bent his head and buttoned his leather vest. Other than the vest, he was wearing exactly what Degan had seen him wearing four days ago, including the white bandanna. He looked as if he'd just wallowed in the mud since then. Well, it had rained yesterday as Degan recalled, so the boy might have slipped in the mud up here. It was caked on one of his cheeks, down one sleeve, and on both knees. Some was even in the boy's ash-blond hair, which made it spike up in places.

Noticing the uneven length of the boy's hair, Degan asked, "Where's the knife you butchered your hair with?"

"Don't have it no more."

"If I have to ask again, I'll have to strip you to find it."

Max dug the knife out of his boot and tossed it angrily toward Degan's feet before he glanced up with a scowl. The scowl disappeared and the dark eyes rounded, but not with fear. Fear was easy to recognize, but so was surprise, and that's all that was on the kid's face now.

"Never seen a bounty hunter dressed like you." Max dropped his eyes again.

Degan tucked the knife in his own boot. "I'm not a bounty hunter."

"Never seen a lawman dressed so fancy neither."

"I'm not a lawman, just doing a favor for one."

"You couldn't pick some other time to be so damn generous?" Max spat out.

Degan actually laughed. God, he really was tired to let that slip out. He couldn't afford to show emotions in his line of work. A smile could be misleading. A laugh could remove fear when he might not want it removed. A scowl could prompt someone already afraid to draw his gun. And Dawson hadn't looked fearful yet, just mad. But then Dawson was a kid, appeared to be no more than fifteen or sixteen. Boys this young could be bold beyond good sense. And this one was staring at him again in owl-eyed surprise because of that laugh.

Degan kicked the coil of rope toward Dawson. "Tie the end of that around your ankles. If it's loose, you probably won't like how I tighten it."

Another flare of anger across the brow, tight across the lips, and the boy was taking his sweet time in getting a knot tied. Degan was too tired to push it. As soon as Dawson was hogtied, he'd be getting some sleep.

"Why did you stick around Helena, kid? Because of the girl?"

"What girl?" Dawson asked without glancing up.

"You visit more than one in town?"

Bristling, Max tried to stand up, but couldn't manage it with his feet already tied. "If you hurt Luella—"

"Do I look like a man who would hurt a woman?"

"Hell yeah, you do!"

"When I can find out what I need to know without half trying?"

"Because you look dangerous?" Max snorted. "Looking like it don't mean much out here."

Degan shrugged. "I merely had words with her. She didn't

volunteer much. In fact, she tried to mislead me about where I could find you."

Dawson grinned at that. "She's a good friend—and she knows I'm innocent."

"She doesn't know any such thing, simply believes what you tell her."

"But I am innocent."

No belligerence was in the boy's voice, just a sad tone that struck Degan oddly. But then he guessed this was probably how the boy had convinced Luella and anyone else who might recognize him that he wasn't guilty. He should save the performance for the jury.

"Innocence doesn't show up on wanted posters. Is your ladylove the only reason you stuck around here too long, or were you planning to rob another bank in the area?"

"I was making my way to Canada, but when I heard they mostly speak French there, I changed my mind. I can speak Spanish, but not French. Maybe I should go to Mexico instead."

"Where you're going is jail. You have figured that out, right?"

"I ain't stupid, fancy man," Dawson snarled.

That was debatable. Breaking the law entailed a measure of stupidity—or desperation. At least for men. But boys like this could also do it simply for fun, because they were too young and reckless to consider the consequences. Max Dawson was finally going to figure that out.

"Get up on your knees."

"Why?"

Degan didn't answer, he just waited. It wasn't his habit to talk this much. Ever. The most he'd said in years to one person had been recently to Tiffany Warren when she'd been masquerading as the Callahans' housekeeper. But then Tiffany had reminded him of so many things he'd given up. And she'd been full of questions, despite how nervous she was around him, so it had been hard not to talk to her.

But Dawson had been something of a curiosity from the moment Degan had seen him escaping through the brothel window in Helena, so full of exuberance and laughter. A happy outlaw. But again, Degan figured young love accounted for that contradiction.

The boy finally rolled to his knees. Degan knelt behind him to test the knot that had been tied, then wrapped the rope around Dawson's feet a few more times.

"Your hands now."

A few minutes later he had Dawson effectively hog-tied, with the rope extending from his tied feet to his tied hands, a few loops around his neck, and tied off at his feet again.

"Do you have any idea how uncomfortable this is?!" Max yelled furiously when Degan pushed him over so he could lie on his side.

"Can't say that I do. But then I don't break the law, don't get taken by surprise, and I sure as hell wouldn't be shouting about it like a girl. So shut the hell up, Dawson."

"You're not taking me in right now?"

"In the morning. I've barely gotten any sleep these last four days since I started searching for your sorry ass."

Degan grabbed the boy's rifle before he left the shack to bring his horse up to it for the night. The palomino would warn him if anyone approached, not that he expected company. If Luella had known where Dawson was staying, she would have been up here to warn him long before now.

Reentering the shack, Degan saw the boy was exactly where he'd left him, lying in the bed of leaves, though he'd lifted his feet as high as he could to loosen the pressure of the rope around his neck. He hoped the kid didn't strangle himself before Degan fell asleep. There'd be no danger of that if the kid would just lie still, so Degan wasn't going to loosen those ropes. He sat down and gingerly leaned his back against the wall, afraid the shack might tumble over if he leaned too hard against it. But he was asleep in moments.

Chapter Seven

THE SOFT CREAK OF wood woke him. Degan opened his eyes to see Dawson tiptoeing out the door with his saddlebags in hand, coat donned and hat on. Degan's failing to check the pile of leaves the outlaw had been using as a mattress proved just how tired he'd been after tying up his prisoner. Any number of things could have been hidden under it. Obviously another knife.

"I wouldn't if I were you," he growled.

The boy still did, bolting out the door. Degan swore and gave chase, nearly tripping over the saddlebags that had been dropped just outside the door. He didn't draw his gun even with such a clear target in the moonlight. He'd never shot a man in the back and wasn't going to start now. And he had a feeling Dawson was too desperate to stop for a gun right now, even if it was fired.

The boy didn't head for his horse. Turning the animal around in the small cave where it was hidden would waste too much time. He was simply running down the hill for freedom, zigzagging through the trees, probably hoping Degan would lose sight of him so he could hide, then double back for his mount. It might have worked. There were enough trees to hide behind. But the kid was short and Degan's legs were long.

He got a handful of the long doeskin coat that was flapping behind the boy and yanked on it. That should have stopped him, but Dawson slipped his arms out of it, leaving the coat in Degan's hand while he kept on running. Degan tossed it aside and closed the distance between them again. He got his hand on Dawson's vest this time, but damned if the kid didn't do it again, slipping his arms out of it so Degan was left with just the stiff leather—and the sound of the kid's laughter floating back at him. So Dawson had planned that one, unbuttoning the garment as he ran? Incredible! This was starting to feel like a joke with Degan as the punch line.

He hadn't chased anyone like this since he was a child playing with his younger siblings. Since coming West, he'd never encountered a situation where he *had* to chase anyone. And his gun could put a stop to this nonsense, but he still didn't draw it. But he wasn't falling for Dawson's tactics again when the kid was probably already unbuttoning his shirt for a third slip.

"Give it up, fancy man!" Max yelled without looking back. "You ain't catching me!"

Degan tackled the boy to the ground. It probably knocked the breath out of him, considering their weight difference. The kid was so still now it might even have knocked him out. Or was he thinking up some other trick? Degan was done playing children's games.

Dawson's tan hat had rolled farther down the hill when they'd hit the ground. Degan got off the boy, grabbing a handful of spiky blond hair, pulling Max to his feet. The kid came up swinging his fists. Degan shoved him back to the ground and, getting down on one knee, held him there at arm's length while he searched for the knife the kid had used to cut the ropes. The boy was resisting with fists and knees now. The fists couldn't reach Degan's face and he barely felt them as they struck his chest, but the knees jabbing him in his side were getting annoying. Then Max changed tactics and just tried to get Degan's hand off his belly, but that didn't work either.

"I could have slit your throat while you slept but I didn't!" Max snarled at him.

"Two points for you, kid."

"For your life? That's a hundred damn points if you ask me!"

"I'm not asking."

The knife wasn't in the boy's belt, so it was probably in one of his boots. Degan figured he could either knock the kid out and carry him back to the shack to find it, or risk getting a boot to his face if he removed the boots here. For the trouble Dawson had caused him, he opted for the knockout, and he was in a good position to deliver the blow with one hand still holding Dawson down.

But Max saw the punch coming and used all he had left to avoid it, trying to turn on his side and covering his head with both arms. With the sudden movement, Degan's palm slid up a few inches and touched something soft.

That brought him to his feet fast. "What the . . . ?"

The kid was still cowering on the ground—like a girl. Oh, hell no. There had to be a money pouch or something else strapped to Dawson's chest that would account for what he'd felt. He was *not* dealing with a damn girl.

"Get up," Degan growled.

The kid did with a wary look. Degan clamped his fingers

around the back of Max's neck and, keeping him at arm's length in front of him, walked him back up the hill. Degan didn't collect the discarded garments they passed on the way. His thoughts were bordering on furious, which was pretty damn disconcerting since he hadn't been this angry in years.

He shoved Max into the shack before he let go. The lantern was still burning, and fear was in Max's dark eyes now. About damn time.

"This is what is going to happen now," Degan said in a low tone. "You are going to remove your shirt."

"The hell I will!" Max backed away from Degan until the wall got in the way.

"If I have to do it, there won't be any buttons left on your shirt. If it's the only shirt you've got, too bad. I'm not interested in you, just what's under your shirt."

"So I've got a pair, so what? You don't need to see them when you already felt—!"

"No more pretenses for you or assumptions for me, kid. Show me or I show myself. Your choice."

Degan saw a flash of blue in the dark eyes glaring murderously at him. He might have been startled by the appealing hue if he wasn't so angry and frustrated. If Max was a girl, what the hell was he going to do with her?

The shirt was unbuttoned slowly. If there weren't still murder in her eyes, he'd think she was trying to entice him. She pulled one edge of the black shirt to the side, revealing a breast. It wasn't large, but decently plump and incredibly beautiful to his eyes, which warned him he'd been a fool to go so long without having a woman. She started to uncover the other breast. He must have been staring too long. If she hadn't been trying to seduce him to begin with, she was now. He ought to take her up on the offer, show her what happened when she played with fire. Not that she'd get what she wanted out of it.

He turned around. "Cover yourself."

Whether she did or didn't, she leapt at his back, slamming both fists into it before yelling, "Happy now, you son'bitch? Doesn't change a damn thing and you know it!"

Didn't it? Degan wondered. Maybe not. Max Dawson, female, was still an outlaw wanted for murder and bank robbery. What would John Hayes do under these circumstances? His job, of course, and that was to apprehend and bring in the individual so a court of law could decide the matter of guilt or innocence.

The fists pounding on his back didn't budge him, and since he was blocking the shack's only exit, he didn't turn around right away to confront her. He'd give her time to button up her shirt and himself time to forget what that shirt was covering. When he did turn, she was pacing back and forth across the shack's measly ten feet of space, kicking the cut ropes, kicking the pile of leaves, the only two things on that side of the shack to kick.

The lantern was in the front corner to Degan's right, the coil of rope to his left, but she didn't go near them. She was staying away from him now, as far as she could get. It was a good thing he'd brought a long coil of rope. He was going to have to use the rest of it now.

"Take your boots off."

She stopped to give him another glare before she sat down hard and reached for one of her boots. "Sure! Why not? This shack doesn't stink enough already?"

Two knives fell to the floor when the first boot came off. A third fell with the second boot. Degan shook his head incredulously. He knew one of those knives had been stashed under the leaves. She wouldn't have been able to reach her boots when she'd been tied up. She definitely took precautions, carrying so many weapons.

He looked at her feet and saw dingy gray socks with holes. He wondered if she ever willingly took her boots off. For that matter, he wondered if she ever bathed. He figured she must because she didn't smell bad. But she obviously hadn't washed in the last day since the rain. Her mud-caked face was like a mask, and not a pretty one. Did she know how she looked? Did she even have a mirror?

He could see the two curves under her shirt, now that he knew to look for them. That stiff leather vest of hers acted as a corset, flattening and concealing what was under it. He should go pick up her things that were scattered down the hill and get her back into that vest. Yet he was still having trouble coming to terms with there being a female beneath that rough, muddy exterior. His eyes roamed over her. Her loose black shirt was tucked into loose black pants, leaving her waist and hips undefined. She'd chosen the right clothing to hide her womanly shape. He would never have believed Max Dawson was a woman if he hadn't seen her beautiful breasts.

He picked up the three knives and tossed them outside before he said, "You can put your boots back on, but stay where you are."

"You're all heart, fancy man," she replied scathingly.

He picked up one of the pieces of rope on the floor, one long enough to bind her hands behind her back. He couldn't bring himself to hog-tie her again, but he knew just tying her hands wasn't enough to prevent her from trying to escape again. So he got the remainder of the coil of rope and wrapped it around her arms and torso to keep her arms confined to her sides. Then he hauled her to the back wall and sat her down so she could lean against it.

"I take it back," she snarled. "No heart at all."

"Shut up," he said tonelessly. "It's this or I tie you to a tree outside."

"I'll take the tree if it means I don't have to be in this room with you."

"I wasn't offering a choice."

He started to sit next to her so he could finish securing her with the rope, but he reconsidered. If he tied their ankles together, they would be sitting side by side, and once she fell asleep, she might lean against him and rub some of that dried mud on his jacket. He went outside to get his canteen of water. He offered her a drink first, which she took grudgingly, then removed the white bandanna from her neck and thoroughly wet it. She tried to avoid the cloth as it came toward her face, but she didn't have room to maneuver and fell over to her side. He dragged her back up so he could finish.

"I'll need that back before you take me in."

He held up the bandanna to show her how dirty it was. "It has to be washed first."

"I don't care what it looks like. I have a specific use for it, and it's not to protect my face during dust storms."

"I can guess."

"No, you can't. I use it to cover up the fact that I don't have a lump in my throat like you do."

"Yes, I've already figured that out. And that lump is called an Adam's apple."

"Like I care what it's called? Just put the bandanna back around my neck."

"You can in the morning when it's dry."

He draped the cloth over the peg in the wall. When he turned back to sit next to her, he paused. He'd done his best not to look at what he'd been cleaning, but it was hard to miss now. He didn't castigate himself for not seeing it sooner. He'd come across too many smooth-skinned, late-blooming boys for a girlish face to have warned him, even if hers hadn't been so dirty. Well, maybe not. With the mud and dirt gone, Max Dawson was a little too pretty now.

Chapter Eight

MAX OPENED HER EYES and instantly snapped them shut. She hadn't meant to fall asleep. She had wanted one last chance to escape, not that she had any options left other than to wiggle out of that rope and get her hands on one of the knives her captor had tossed outside. He hadn't woken earlier until she'd almost been out the door. If it hadn't been for those damned creaky boards that were barely nailed together, she would have been free, riding away to Mexico, Noble racing his heart out for her. She *knew* she should have tossed those boards out when she'd moved in, but she was so tired of sleeping on the ground.

She missed the cabin she'd found in Colorado. She'd made herself so comfortable there for the first winter she'd been on the run that she'd stuck around until the fall and would have stayed longer if the owner hadn't returned. She missed home, too. She'd been gone nearly two years, and after the wanted posters had started showing up, she'd begun to think she was never going to be able to return. But this fancy dresser was going to send her back to Texas. To hang. And what the hell was he, dressed like a city-slick gambler? All in black except for a white shirt that looked softer than anything she'd ever owned.

He was a handsome man, maybe a little too handsome. Tall with wide shoulders. His clothes fit him as snugly as if they'd been tailored just for him. He didn't have a beard or a mustache, but some dark stubble was on his face this morning. His wavy, black hair wasn't long, but wasn't real short either. His gray eyes were inscrutable. But she'd heard him laugh that one time, before he'd cut it short, and she'd seen a few frowns, too, but otherwise there had been no sign that he had emotions like normal folks did. But he had the prettiest gun belt and holster she'd ever seen. Silver etching? Who gussied up a gun belt like that unless they just wanted to show off?

The only men she'd ever seen dressed somewhat like him were fresh in from the East, but greenhorns didn't wear a gun the way he did, as if they knew how to use it. This man was too fancy, too competent, and when he frowned, darn right scary. But she was too angry at getting caught to be wary of him.

He was still sleeping next to her, back to the wall, his legs slightly bent. When she tried to get up she saw why. Damn! He'd tied their feet together, must have done it the moment she fell asleep. Her legs were stretched out. He couldn't stretch his without pulling her away from the wall. And he'd wake up the moment she tried to move. Or would he? He'd complained about being tired last night. Judging by the light coming in through the open doorway, the sun was barely up, so he still hadn't caught up on much sleep yet.

She leaned forward to see if she could wiggle her foot out of the boot he'd looped the rope around. The rope was tied tight. She could actually feel it pressing through the leather against her ankle.

"How old are you, Max?"

She flinched slightly, startled by the sound of his voice. "What month is it?"

He snorted as if he doubted that she didn't know. She gnashed her teeth, frustrated that he was already awake. There went her options other than to somehow convince him to let her go. But she wasn't sure she could stop growling at him long enough to do that. He was besting her at every turn. No one had ever done that to her before, not even that old bastard Carl Bingham, who got her into this mess for dying when he shouldn't have died.

She still didn't know how that had happened. She hadn't met anyone she could trust enough to help her correspond with her grandmother until she'd come to Helena. After becoming friends with Luella, she'd finally written to her grandmother and told her to write back to Luella, who would give the letter to Max. She expected Luella to receive her grandmother's reply any day now. But now she wouldn't get it, thanks to *him*!

She was frustrated enough to scream and far too furious to even look at her captor, but since he hadn't said anything since asking about her age and hadn't moved yet, she sat back and volunteered, "If it's July, I reckon I'm twenty. If not, then I will be soon. Don't have a reason to keep track of days, just seasons. And I haven't seen a newspaper since last year. So why don't you keep your skepticism to yourself, fancy man."

"You toss out a word like *skepticism*, yet you butcher the English language. Where'd you grow up?"

"Texas, and if you send me back there, it will be to die. Will your conscience survive that?"

"I'm not sure I have one."

He leaned forward and untied their feet, then stood up.

With her hands still tied behind her back and the rope still tied around her arms and torso, she couldn't stand, not without a lot of wiggling, so she stayed where she was. He grabbed her bandanna from the wall and tossed it in her lap, implying he'd be untying her hands so she could put it back on. But he didn't. He stepped outside instead.

She got to her feet as fast as she could and moved to the doorway. He wasn't in sight. Her knives weren't either. His horse was there, but he'd unsaddled it last night, so she couldn't get on its back without first getting her hands loose. And that coil of rope was still around her. She tried to stretch the rope at her wrists so she could get one hand out of it.

"Why the assumed name, Max Dawson?"

She sighed in disappointment. He'd only gone off to relieve himself. "I didn't assume nothing. I got named after my pa, Maxwell Dawson, since I was his firstborn and there was no guarantee he'd get a son, though he did a few years later. My name's actually Maxine, but my family always called me Max, and the folks in Bingham Hills where we lived only knew me as Max, so that'd be my guess why that name was put on the wanted posters."

"And that's why you're dressing the part? You didn't once think that wearing a dress would conceal your identity better than any hideout could?"

"Yeah, I thought of it. But if it ain't obvious to you, it's actually more dangerous to be a woman alone out here than a man on his own who resembles an outlaw. 'Sides, no one takes a girl who wears a gun seriously. And I like to wear my gun. I'm damn good with it, you know. You're lucky yours was already drawn."

"What about your hair? The poster depicts you with short hair."

"I had it cut short long before I had to leave Texas, but Gran cut it better'n I do. Thought it would make me less appealing so the boys in town would stop sniffing around. But it didn't work."

He nodded as if he agreed that short hair wouldn't have made her less attractive to men. It was a bane to have a face like hers when she didn't want to be noticed. But ever since she'd left home, taking her brother's clothes with her instead of her own, she usually only had to wear her wide-brimmed hat, keep her face smudged with dirt, and introduce herself as Max for people to take her for a pretty-faced boy. Even Luella hadn't guessed and had had to be told on their second meeting.

As if he'd read her mind, her captor asked, "All things considered, how would you meet someone like Luella?"

Max actually grinned. "Obviously not in the usual way. I rescued her the night I first passed through Helena. She doesn't usually leave that brothel, at least not at night and not alone, but one of the girls was sick. She'd been sent to fetch a doctor, and a trio of rowdy drifters thought they could have their way with her in a back alley. I'd been avoiding the main street m'self, skirting around the backs of the buildings. Otherwise I probably wouldn't have heard her crying."

He raised a black brow. "You ran off three men? Or you shot them?"

She snorted. "Didn't need to shoot. I might look like a kid, but I'm as dangerous as anyone with a drawn gun. They took off and I escorted Luella back to her brothel. It was the first time I'd ever been in one, so I was curious enough to follow her up to her room when she invited me there. Didn't know she wanted to repay me in her usual fashion. Now that I think back on it, it was kinda funny how fast I got out of there."

"So she doesn't know you're a girl?"

"Oh, she does now and keeps my secret, but that night she didn't know. I felt bad though, for leaving her without an explanation, so I went back for a visit later that week after I found this shack. Told her who I really was. It was her night off and we talked all night. Never made a friend that fast before. Heck, she's the *only* friend I've made since I left home. And once a week, when she has a night off, she lets me sleep in her bed. I surely do miss a soft bed." Max ended with a grin.

He came to stand directly in front of her. Looming over her is what it felt like. She was tall for a woman at five feet eight, which supported her guise as a boy, but he still had a good half foot in height on her. She wasn't going to give him the satisfaction of looking up at him and backed up into the shack instead.

He followed her in and picked up her bandanna, which had fallen from her lap when she got up. She turned around so he could cut the ropes on her wrists. He didn't. He put the bandanna around her neck and tied it himself, which had her gritting her teeth again. Was he just going to leave her vest and coat behind? She couldn't put them back on with her hands and arms tied like this.

"Why doesn't your wanted poster identify you as a woman?"

She shrugged, but he might not have noticed, standing so close to her, so she said, "That poster comes from Bingham Hills, Texas. It's people there who want me back. Maybe they figured out that offering that much money for a woman would set more'n just bounty hunters and lawmen after me, if you know what I mean. Just a guess, mind you. But I'm glad they left out that little detail for whatever reason—or I might've had to kill someone for real."

"Is that your way of trying to convince me you haven't killed anyone—yet?" he asked, still standing behind her.

"Did it work?"

The man was mighty curious about her this morning, but he didn't bother to answer that. Instead, he asked, "What sort of food do you have on hand?"

She moved farther away from him. "Nothing. I've been hunting for food as I need it."

"You've been subsisting only on meat up here?"

He sounded hungry. Her desperate, impulsive attempt to seduce him with her body last night hadn't worked, which wasn't surprising considering how dirty and angry she was. And thank goodness, because she hadn't given any thought to what would have happened if she'd succeeded. But food! Her gran was fond of saying that the way to a man's heart was through his stomach. She even had some spices left in her saddlebags that she could use to make him something special.

She turned around and gave him a tentative smile. "It's not exactly safe for me to go shopping in town for anything else. But I can hunt up something for us if you're hungry. I sure am."

"You and your rifle have parted ways for good" was all he said.

She was back to gnashing her teeth. She was *not* going to try to get on his good side again, not when he obviously didn't have one. She'd have to find some other way to escape while they were carting her to Texas for the trial. If there would even be a trial. Accused of killing the beloved founder of Bingham Hills, who was also the mayor of the town, who supported half the town and owned most of it—no, she probably wouldn't even be given a trial. They'd send her straight to the gallows. And she didn't even shoot that bastard.

Chapter Nine

UNBELIEVABLE! MAX WAS FUMING. The man was actually pulling her along behind him with that damn rope of his, as if she were an animal! He'd tightened the coil wrapped around her, then tied it off and had the end of it in his fist. He collected her horse first and hobbled it by the shack, then dragged her down the hill with him to collect her coat and vest.

Her hat was nowhere in sight, and after only five minutes he gave up looking for it. Max was livid. He should have gotten her things last night, not waited until the wind blew her hat away!

"What do they call you, fancy man?" she gritted out on the way back up the hill. "I want to know who I'm killing when I get loose."

"Degan Grant," he said without glancing back.

Max almost choked. "Holy cow, the gunfighter?"

He didn't confirm it, didn't reply at all, but who would use that name if he didn't have to? Folks were claiming he was the fastest gun there was, but she reminded herself that gossip like that was rarely true. *She* was fast, likely faster than him. She'd like a chance to prove it.

Back at the shack by the fire pit, he still didn't untie her or even let go of the rope as he saddled his horse, so she still got tugged a little as he did that. All she could do was stand there and watch him. That wasn't entirely unpleasant. With long legs, a lean, hard torso, muscles that pressed against the cloth of his jacket as he worked, Degan Grant was finely put together. Maybe a little too fine. No wonder her impulse had been to try seducing him into letting her go. She might not have minded, after all, if she'd succeeded. A worthy trade—her virginity for her life? She wasn't ready to make that trade yet.

She wondered if he had a sweetheart in every town he passed through. That funny thought had her grinning, because if he wasn't who he said he was, it could well be true. But if he really was the notorious gunfighter Degan Grant, then it might only be true if he kept that information to himself. What woman would want a man destined to die young? Or one as dangerous as this one was reputed to be? Well, she could understand why a woman would be attracted to a man this handsome, but she couldn't understand why a woman would want to fall in love with him. He was what Gran would call a heartbreaker.

"You find something amusing about your situation?" he asked.

"Hell, no. But I'm usually a good-natured sort. Sometimes I even laugh out loud by my lonesome if something funny pops in up here." She meant to tap her head. She made a frustrated sound instead, having forgotten, even only briefly, that she couldn't move her hands. "But you won't be with me long enough to notice, thank our lucky stars."

"So you're still thinking you can escape?" His tone was amused even if his expression wasn't.

"I'm thinking Helena's jail is less than an hour away," she snapped.

"So it is. So what had you grinning?"

She was annoyed enough to give him the truth. "Your name, and your probably having trouble getting a woman once she hears it."

"They don't need to hear it when I reek of death," he said tonelessly.

"Really? Just the look of you sends them running? Now I wouldn't have figured on that."

"Why not?"

"'Cause that's not what would send me running. You, fancy man, are a death sentence hanging over my head. That's more'n enough reason for me to see the last of you."

He started to unwrap the rope that was binding her arms, coiling it back up as he did it. Then he turned her around, she assumed so he could cut her wrists loose, but he didn't. He took his sweet time untying the rope instead. So he could use that piece of rope again? Damned man thought of everything, didn't he?

"Do you need to relieve yourself before we leave?"

She blinked. "You'd actually let me go off in the bushes by myself?"

"No."

She was sure she was going to grind down her teeth from gnashing them while in his company. "Didn't think so," she growled. "So if it's all the same to you, I'll piss my pants. Better'n having you stand next to me for something like that."

"You can use the shack. You won't be coming back up this way, so it doesn't matter."

She was surprised. He was a gentleman beneath that dangerous veneer? But she didn't give him a chance to change his mind. Shaking the stiffness out of her arms almost brought tears to her eyes. She hurried into the shack while he saddled Noble for her. Her chestnut gelding wasn't skittish. Noble only glanced back at Degan once before ignoring him.

When she stepped back outside, she saw her vest and coat draped over the saddle of Degan's horse. Relieved to have her clothes back, she went to put them on, but his horse tried to bite her when she got close to it. Her instinct was to punch its nose, but fancy man probably wouldn't like that, even if she didn't hit hard. So she moved to the animal's head and murmured some soothing words and gave it a few tender rubs until she managed to reclaim her garments.

She put on her vest and buttoned it, then shrugged into her coat. She didn't usually wear the coat at her camp in the summer. She didn't need such a warm garment. She only donned it when she was going to be around other people, and now she was about to be paraded through town. The more clothing that covered her breasts, the better. She still felt naked without her holstered Colt because she'd been wearing it for so long. Even an empty gun could stop someone in his tracks. But Degan wouldn't be giving it back to her.

Going over to her horse, she saw Degan standing next to the shed. She laughed. He'd had his own gun drawn and pointed at her the whole time. "I wasn't going to run off with your horse."

"He wouldn't let you."

"Care to wager?" she asked with a grin.

He ignored that and said, "If you have anything stashed around here, now's the time to mention it."

"Don't own anything worth hiding."

Out of habit, she grabbed the cold pan and griddle off the fire pit so she could stuff them back in her saddlebags, which were already on her horse. Then she realized she wouldn't be doing any cooking where she was going. The enormity of what was going to happen in the next hour hit her hard. Jail and then a cage in which she'd be carted all the way to Texas to hang for a killing she didn't do. She'd seen a prisoner transport wagon on the road down in Utah. The cage was tiny.

She turned and looked at her captor, feeling more desperate than she ever had before. "Don't do this. You don't need the reward, you know you don't. Let me go!"

His gun was still pointed at her, obviously because she wasn't tied *and* was standing next to her horse. "You might have avoided the bounty hunters so far, but you have a US marshal after you now. I found you easily and I'm not a tracker. Marshal Hayes is."

"But I'm innocent!"

"Then you should be glad you'll have your day in court to prove it."

"There won't be a trial, not if Carl Bingham really did die."

"If?"

She snapped her mouth shut. Talking to him was like talking to a jackass, and how was she supposed to explain that a murdered man might not be dead? Degan wasn't going to believe that any more than he would believe that she was innocent. She figured he just didn't care one way or the other. She was just a fat reward to him and a means of settling a favor he owed his marshal friend.

"All right, I'll come along peacefully if you could just do me one favor?"

"I already did you a favor," he reminded her. "I didn't shoot you."

"Well, if you're counting still standing here alive, I didn't slit your throat last night either. But you're going to be getting a ridiculous amount of money for me, so the least you could do is one tiny favor for me first."

She squeezed out a few tears to help her plea, but he merely raised a black brow. "Don't bother, tears have no effect on me."

He didn't display any disgust at her effort to manipulate him. No amusement either. Was he really so dead inside from his line of work that he'd lost the ability to feel? Not her, and she grinned now to show it. "Well *that's* a relief. I detest them m'self. Had to try though, you understand?"

"Certainly."

"But here's the thing. It's been nearly two years since I left home and I haven't heard how my family is in all that time. Nor was I able to let them know I'm still alive. The one time I snuck back, there were deputies at our house, so I couldn't get close enough to talk to my grandmother. I even waited in the woods for my brother to go hunting, but some other men from town showed up instead, so I couldn't linger there when Johnny might not come that way at all. He never liked hunting like I do. I couldn't risk sending a letter with my name on it to Bingham Hills either, or have one sent back to me, and I never met anyone I could trust to do it for me—until now."

Still pointing his gun at her with one hand, he quickly un-hobbled her horse with the other. "I don't stay in one place long enough to receive letters, and you likely won't be in Helena long enough to receive one either. Mount up." He took her reins.

"I wasn't asking for *you* to do it. Luella's the first friend I've made since I left Texas. She sent my letter off well over a month ago. I expected her to have my grandmother's reply the other day when I visited her. She didn't, but she could have it now. Can we at least stop by her place to see if she's got that letter for me—and give me a chance to say good-bye to her?"

He didn't say yes, but he didn't say no either, so she held her tongue as they started down the hill. She was surprised he hadn't retied her for the ride into town and that he thought holding her reins was enough to keep her behind him. Maybe it was, but she was still thinking of ways to get around that. If she spurred her horse forward into a gallop to pass him, the reins would be ripped from his hold—if he was still holding them. He might have tied them to his pommel instead. She couldn't tell with his broad back in front of her. Of course *her* back would make a large target. Or he might shoot her horse instead.

As if Noble could read her mind, she leaned forward to rub his neck and whisper, "Don't worry, I won't do anything to bring bullets our way." She wouldn't mind sending them toward Degan though.

He'd attached her rifle to her saddle, probably because he didn't have a ring for it on his saddle. Gunfighters didn't bother with rifles, and she would bet her horse that Degan Grant had never needed one to hunt his own food. He probably stopped to eat in every town he came to, while she'd had to avoid most towns. She was so sure the rifle was empty that she didn't even bother to check it. But she leaned back carefully to check the saddlebag where she kept her extra ammunition. Her hand came out empty. He'd even thought of that! But she could ride close enough to him to bash him over the head with the rifle . . .

"Get your hat and make no mistake. I'm not going to kill

you, but I don't have the least qualm about putting a bullet in your leg if you try to run again."

Max looked down at the ground and saw her hat lying there between them. She hadn't been looking for it, but he must have been. She quickly retrieved it and remounted. They were nearly out of the hills. The sun had already topped the Big Belt range to the east and she was hungry. She wondered how long she'd have to wait for a meal in jail.

Damnit! She'd done so well avoiding people other than the farmers with whom she'd traded fresh game for vegetables, herbs, and ammunition. Degan might think she only ate meat and berries, but she didn't. She knew how to get by on her own, but it wasn't always so easy to cope with the loneliness that came with it. That was why she'd relaxed her guard in Helena. Because she'd been so happy to make a friend. And she'd stayed there longer than she should have.

Degan rode them into town the way she usually entered it. He might even pass by Luella's brothel. Might. She tried not to get her hopes up. But if he did and he didn't stop, she was definitely hopping off her horse. He might not notice before she was through the door of Madam Joe's.

But he stopped, dismounted, and tied the two horses to the post out front. Incredulous, Max dismounted slowly, too slowly. He grabbed the shoulder of her coat and shoved her through the brothel's front door. She started toward the stairs, but glanced back to see that Degan was still standing by the door. She gave him a questioning look.

He nodded at her. "Five minutes, kid. If I regret this favor, you won't like it."

He was actually going to wait there in the parlor for her? Ecstatic, Max raced upstairs. Escape was just around the corner!

Chapter Ten

MAX DIDN'T CLOSE THE door to Luella's room quietly. She meant to, but she rushed into the room too fast. But at least the noise woke Luella. She rolled over in bed, started to smile, but ended up wide-eyed instead.

"What's wrong? You don't usually—"

"I need to borrow your gun."

Luella nodded toward her bureau. "Top drawer, but where's yours?"

"It got taken—when I got taken. Someone snuck up on me and I only have a minute to get out of here, or he's taking me to jail."

"Oh, God, the gunfighter? He found you?"

"Yes."

"But I sent him toward Big Belt! I was sure he'd be up there for weeks looking for you, so I'd have time to warn you when you visited next week."

"I guess he didn't trust you any more'n he trusts me." Max stuffed the little derringer in her coat pocket.

Luella had leapt out of bed and opened a few more drawers. "At least let me give you a change of clothes. You're a mess."

Max chuckled, picturing herself riding away in her friend's scanty attire. "There's no time, Lue, except for this."

She gave Luella a quick hug that turned into a long one instead. She was going to miss this girl something fierce. And she'd be crying in a moment if she didn't get out of there. With a last squeeze, she turned and headed for the window.

"Don't do anything stupid, Max. That gunfighter looked far too dangerous."

"I won't have to if I'm quick. I'll get the gun back to you when I can, after I'm sure he's left the area."

Max was halfway out the window when Luella called out, "Wait! This came yesterday."

Luella grabbed the letter from her nightstand and rushed over with it. Max stuffed it into her other coat pocket with a big grin. "Thanks. If it's good news, maybe I can actually go home now."

"I'll miss you," Luella whispered sadly, but Max was already sliding down the porch roof.

She swung over it on the side where she usually did, dangled for a moment, then dropped to the ground. And froze. Degan was standing there between her and the horses, less than a foot away. Her last damn chance to get away from him and he had to second-guess her *again*?

"Don't pat yourself—" She was reaching for the gun in her pocket, until she noticed his gun was already drawn, so she finished, "Go ahead then, pat yourself on the back. Just tell me *how* you knew?"

"If you'd spared a little thought before you jumped in with both feet, you would already have that answer. Do you think

I questioned everyone in town to find out which brothel you visit and which window you like to leave from?"

"You saw me?!" she yelled. "Then why didn't you stop me the other day?"

"Because Marshal Hayes hadn't yet called in the favor I owe him. I merely saw a happy kid leaving a—friend."

Embarrassment was added to the other furious emotions churning inside her. "Why'd you even let me go up there alone? Just to test me?"

"I guess I'd be disappointed right about now if that were the case."

"Is that a joke? As if you can feel anything. Tell me you wouldn't have done the same thing in my situation? Go on, tell me!"

"Exiting through an upstairs window wouldn't be my first choice, no, but then I have other tools at my disposal that you don't have."

"Yeah, well, it was my only choice."

"You got the favor you asked for. How about we leave it at that? But you came out of there with more than you went in with. I'll take whatever weapon you collected from your friend."

"I didn't." Max took a step back.

"That's a bad habit you have, lying."

He grabbed her coat and reached into the pocket. She hit him with both fists. He still got his hand on the derringer as well as the undergarments that Luella had apparently slipped into her pocket when they were hugging good-bye. Max didn't blush as he stuffed it all into his own pocket. She landed a punch to his cheek instead, then swore, sure that she'd hurt her hand more than she'd hurt him. But it must have been the last straw for him, because he tossed her over his shoulder.

She was so surprised she was rendered speechless. For a moment. But then she screeched, squirmed, flailed, and punched his back, but her blows didn't seem to bother him, so she gave up and used her hands to keep her hat from falling off.

"If you keep wiggling, everyone will figure out you're a girl," she heard him say in that deep, infuriatingly toneless voice of his.

"Like that matters now!"

"Well, then, you'll just look like a fool, won't you?"

She went still. He must have grabbed the horses' reins because she heard them following him as he walked her down the street like that for what seemed like two, maybe even three humiliating blocks. Every time she tried to lean up to see where he was going, he bounced her on his shoulder so she lost her breath and the will to try again. As if she didn't know where he was going. She wasn't exactly sure where the sheriff's office was, but she couldn't believe he was really going to deposit her there like this.

He entered a building. She heard people talking, then an abrupt silence. Degan slowly slid her down the front of his body, a little too slowly. Suddenly she became aware of him as a man, rather than just an adversary. Feeling all of his muscular chest rubbing against hers as if they were hugging, smelling his hair and neck, she found his nearness highly disconcerting. She wasn't used to being this close to a man.

She gasped as she felt Degan's hands move slowly over her derriere, then the back of her waist. His touch was so intimate her stomach fluttered and her breath quickened. Then she realized what he'd been doing. Checking for weapons!

"You could've just asked," she said as her feet finally touched the floor.

"Asking doesn't work with you." He gave her a nudge backward. Breath suspended, she thought she might land on her backside, but she landed in the chair he'd pushed her toward. She huffed until she glanced around and realized they were in a restaurant. Nine people were there having breakfast. They started talking again, and she noticed they made a point of not looking at Degan. Three of them even got up and hurried out of the one-room establishment. A few of them were staring at her. Oh, sure, nothing to fear about *her*.

She slid her chair up to the table and cheekily asked, "You buying? 'Cause I'm broke."

He hadn't sat down yet. "Take your boots off."

"Again?!"

"You were right, it was a mistake letting you go to your friend's room alone."

"I swear—!"

"It's already been established that you lie. You just did so again when you said you're broke. I saw the money in your saddlebag."

"That's not mine. I could be starving to death and I wouldn't spend that money."

"A bit extreme," he replied drily, then nodded at her feet. "Just remove the boots, shake them out, then put them back on. You don't eat until you do."

She mumbled a few things under her breath but shoved her chair back and did as ordered. She was amazed he was going to feed her before turning her over to the sheriff. She supposed she should be grateful, but she couldn't quite manage to see him as anything but her worst nightmare, and you didn't thank nightmares for tormenting you.

When she slid up to the table again, he walked around behind her and took her hat off. She started to protest but saw him remove his black hat, too, and hook both of them to the coatrack in their corner. The "gentleman" in him was showing again. Her grandmother had always swatted her younger brother's hat off, before letting Johnny sit down to dinner. Max knew her brother only kept it on to get a rise out of Gran. God, she missed those two. They were all she had left in the way of family.

She reached for the letter in her pocket. But as much as she was dying to find out what Gran had written, it was too personal to read in front of this coldhearted gunfighter. It might make her cry, real tears. She was *not* going to let this man know that sometimes she could be—soft.

Degan ran a hand through his dark hair before he returned to the table. Max didn't bother to do the same. She knew her hair was beyond salvation. She didn't even own a comb anymore. Hers had broken long ago and she'd never gotten around to replacing it.

He still hadn't sat down. "I'll take your coat, too."

"Now *that* ain't hap—"

"It's warm in here. And you no longer need to hide what you are, or hasn't that occurred to you yet?"

Considering what he'd just made her feel as she'd slid down his body, she snapped, "Yeah, I do, and don't *you* be thinking of me like that."

"Like what?"

"Like I'm a girl."

He said nothing, but he did roll his eyes. At least she was sure he would have if he could unbend enough to show what he was feeling. But he didn't press the issue and sat down to her right in the chair that faced both doors to the room. Cautious no matter where he was? Or just always expecting trouble? Probably the latter, considering that every inch of him screamed that he was a gunfighter.

He summoned a waiter and ordered for both of them without asking her what she wanted. She didn't care. It had been so long since she had sat down in a restaurant, she'd be happy with whatever was served.

"Tell me why you think you're innocent."

Max went still and stared at him. He'd already implied it wouldn't matter if she was innocent or not, that his job was only to bring her in, not to decide her fate. So why would he even ask that when he didn't believe anything she said?

Chapter Eleven

"**Y**OU TOYING WITH ME, fancy man? We both know you don't give a hoot what set me on this road." Max clamped her mouth shut after saying that. If Degan's upbringing required him to engage in polite conversation at a dining table, he could find some other subject to bedevil her with.

"Is that what you're going to tell the jury at your trial, Miss Dawson?"

"Don't call me that," she hissed at him. "And I told you, there won't be a trial. The people in that town just want me back so they can hang me."

"Why?"

"Because Carl Bingham, the man I'm accused of murdering, was the founder of Bingham Hills, the owner of it, the mayor of it, and everyone's best friend—'cept mine. But with him being the landlord of all or most of the people in town, and a benevolent one to boot, everyone loved him. Actually, even I used to admire him. It took guts to build a town so far from any others and with the closest fort over a day's ride away, then just hope he could fill it up with people. Course Carl advertised back East and didn't go broke waiting for folks to show up. He was already rich when he came to Texas, so he wasn't looking to get richer—maybe he was since he kept building the town bigger. He was looking to leave a legacy behind, a peaceful, self-sufficient town in what used to be a not-so-peaceful place. Most folks think he succeeded."

"So why did you kill him?"

She gave him a pointed stare. "You want to hear this or not?" He didn't answer and his gaze was a lot more pointed than hers was, so she grudgingly continued, "Life was good in Bingham Hills while I was growing up. I had lots of friends, the boys and girls I went to school with, and we had fun hunting, fishing, and riding. I even enjoyed our sewing circle though I was terrible with a needle, but we did more gossiping than sewing and laughed a lot. But it all changed when I turned sixteen because the boys in town wouldn't leave me alone. I'd filled out by then and had long blond hair. I told you why I cut it, but I couldn't do much to disguise my other attributes"—his gaze moved down to her vest, bringing a slight blush to her cheeks—"because Gran insisted I dress properly in skirts and blouses except when I was hunting. The boys were paying me so much attention that my girlfriends got jealous and stopped talking to me. Gran took a broom to the boys more'n once, and my brother, Johnny, would hide in the bushes and shoot rocks at them with his slingshot. Even that didn't stop them from coming around."

"So you didn't always wear a gun?"

"Goodness, no. I never would have dreamed of wearing a Colt over my skirts—then." She chuckled for a moment. "I was the hunter in the family after my pa took off and never came back. I never carried my rifle in town, but I started carrying a small gun in my skirt pocket when Bingham junior became more aggressive than the other boys and began making inappropriate remarks and advances to me after I turned sixteen."

"The mayor?"

"No, his son, Evan. I used to go fishing with him and his best friend, Tom, when we were kids, until the day Evan bragged that I'd be marrying him someday because his pa told him I would. I didn't believe the mayor had said any such thing, but I avoided Evan and his friends after that. Then he started asking me to marry him. That year, he must've asked about eight times. I wouldn't have said yes even if I wasn't courting the new young man in town at the time."

"Doing what?"

She stared at him. "Do I really need to explain courting to you?"

"I think maybe you do."

"I don't mean I would've asked Billy Johnston to marry me, if that's what you're thinking. I'm bold but not that kind of bold. I just let him know I was interested, saved my smiles just for him, that sort of thing. But Billy left Bingham Hills before I was seventeen, and then the mayor himself asked me to marry him. I probably shouldn't have laughed at the old coot's proposal."

Degan raised a brow. "Just how old was this man?"

"Heck, he's older than my grandmother by some ten years. Even she laughed when I told her about it. Carl had Evan real late in life. Rumor is he went through four wives trying for a kid till he finally got one. But after I refused him, he must've figured that compromising me would get Gran to insist on a wedding."

"Did it?"

"I said he figured it would, not that he actually succeeded. But he sure did try, the bastard. He had his puppet of a sheriff take me to his house late one morning. He even got rid of most of his servants for the day 'cept for his half-deaf cook, who wouldn't hear me yelling. I wouldn't have known the cook was in the house if Carl didn't tell me I could stay for lunch after we were done and that the meal would be ready soon. I think he really expected me to be civil afterward, as if his compromising me were just ordinary business for him. But after some tussling on his sofa, I managed to get my little gun out of my pocket so he'd back off. I even shoved it in his gut so he'd know just how serious I was."

"Then you did shoot him?"

"No, but I sure as hell would have. It turned out my brother, Johnny, saw the sheriff dragging me to Bingham's house and followed us. Johnny waited until the sheriff left, then started looking through the windows. What he saw through one of them was Carl trying to force himself on me. But no one died that day. At least Carl was still alive when I left him. And I didn't even shoot him—my brother did through the open window, trying to protect me. But Carl looked down and saw the blood and fainted like a girl. So he probably thought I did fire at him. I was hoping he would think it. I wasn't going to let him have my brother arrested for his good deed. I took off so I'd get blamed for it."

"Which obviously worked."

"Yeah, blamed for a flesh wound on his shoulder, which is all it was and barely bleeding at that. I checked, just to make sure he wouldn't bleed out before someone found him. I was just going to give Carl some time to cool off about the whole incident and come to his senses, maybe marry another young woman, and not blame me for trying to defend myself. But he or his son sent a posse after me. It took me months to lose them. Carl paid well when he wanted something bad. His son, Evan, is just like him. But before the year was out a bounty hunter found me and showed me the wanted-for-murder poster."

"How'd you get out of that?"

The waiter arrived with their breakfast so she didn't answer. She couldn't take her eyes off those plates piled high with flapjacks and sausage and the basket filled with toasted sourdough slices and flaky pastries. She was too hungry not to start eating right away and have her plate half-cleaned before she got around to saying, "I was wearing a six-shooter by then, but the bounty hunter got me to drop my gun. So I convinced him he'd made a mistake by showing him that I was a girl."

"The same way you showed me?"

Her cheeks reddened. She *knew* he'd felt her breast when he'd been about to punch her last night. He hadn't needed her to show him. She flushed with heat every time she thought of it, and the instinctive, seductive way she'd shown off her breasts to him. It was so embarrassing. Which was why she was glaring at Degan when she said, "No, I just had to flirt with the man a little and take off my vest so he could see I wasn't trying to bluff him. My *vest*, not my shirt. Then I asked him nicely to get the hell out of my camp. I made sure he wasn't following me when I took off."

"You're lying again."

She sat back with a huff. "Why would I lie about something I didn't have to volunteer?"

"Showing him you were a girl wouldn't have changed a

bounty hunter's mind when your likeness on that poster is so good."

She grinned cheekily. "It is, ain't it? On this new poster anyway. This whole episode with the bounty hunter took place over a year ago, and the poster he had wasn't nearly as detailed. The sketch looked like every other immature eighteen-year-old boy. But even after I saw the bounty hunter's reward poster, I still couldn't believe Carl had died from that flesh wound Johnny gave him."

"Wounds can fester."

"Yeah, I know, but Carl would have had the town's best doctors taking care of him. Whether he's dead or alive, I can't go back home now because they'll hang me for sure."

"And in the meantime you took up bank robbery to get by?"

"Now *that* was a joke," she grumbled with a snort. "I was packed up, ready to ride out that day. I stopped at the bank to take my own money out of it, all sixty-four dollars I'd earned from selling meat in town to whoever wanted it. Bingham Hills only had one bank. Carl owned that, too, of course. Wilson Cox ran it for him. It was too small for more'n one employee, so when Wilson took a break to eat lunch, there was no one to help the customers. He didn't bother to close shop though. He likely assumed everyone in town knew better than to try to do any banking at noon. But how was I to know that? I didn't go to the bank often. I walked in and asked for my money. Wilson refused to help me. We argued. He wouldn't budge. He was going to make me stand there and wait for a half hour when he was sitting right there in front of the cash drawer!"

"So you robbed the bank."

"*No, I did not!* But I took out my little gun and told Wilson he could stop eating for two minutes and hand me my money. He stuffed it in a sack and threw it at me, he was so annoyed. Like I wasn't furious at his orneriness? It wasn't until a week later when I emptied the sack that I found an extra hundred and three dollars in it. He couldn't just give me what I asked for, no. In his haste he put my money in a sack that contained someone else's money. The mistake was on his part, probably because he just wanted me gone so he could get back to his lunch."

"Is this the money in your saddlebag that you refuse to spend?"

"Yeah, and I'll be giving it back, every damn dollar—someday."

"You were right. It's laughable—if it actually happened that way."

"It did, so why aren't you laughing?"

He didn't answer. Obviously, he didn't believe anything she'd just told him. Not that it would have made a difference if he did. He'd already made it clear that it wasn't his job to decide her fate, merely to turn her over to the law so others could.

He stood and grabbed their hats. "Time to go."

She didn't budge. This was it. The sheriff couldn't be more'n a block or two away. Would Degan shoot her right there in front of witnesses if she tried one more time to run?

Chapter Twelve

"WHATEVER YOU'RE THINKING, KID, stop thinking it. Yes, I will donate a bullet to your leg, and, yes, I will do it right here—in case you were wondering."

"So now you're a mind reader, too?" Max growled up at Degan.

He tossed some money on the table and nodded toward the front door. "We're stopping by my hotel first, so how about you behave and I won't have to put you over my shoulder again to get there."

Another reprieve? Max got up, started to walk to the door, but didn't feel like getting yanked around anymore today, so she stopped to wait for Degan, only to have him bump into her back because he'd already been right on her heels. She heard an aggravated sigh. Oh my God, she'd annoyed him? His emotions *could* get ruffled? She would have grinned if he weren't throwing her in jail today. Fat lot of good it did her to know he was susceptible to some needling when they would be parting ways shortly.

He didn't have them mount up, he just picked up the reins before leading her down the street. It was more crowded in the late morning, mostly with miners, but there were business-men, too, and cowboys riding by. Delivery wagons were being unloaded in front of stores, and women with baskets on their arms were doing their morning shopping. Glancing around, Max noticed that she was drawing no attention, but Degan sure was. People were eyeing him covertly. She chalked it up to human nature that people were so curious about someone as menacing as him.

He stopped at a stable in the next block and paid to have both horses brushed and fed. While that might not take long, Max still viewed it as another delay for her. She was pleased until she realized the jail could be really close now. In fact, she might not be seeing her horse again. Ever. She hugged Noble's neck one last time and whispered her apologies in case that proved true. They'd been through a lot together. He'd gotten her out of a lot of close calls. . . . Damnit, she didn't want to say good-bye to him!

"You think they'll let Noble tag along even—?"

"Who?"

"My horse."

"Nice name."

"I gave it to him for encouragement." Then she added in a whisper so Noble wouldn't hear, "He was a mite clumsy when he was younger. But will they let him tag along even if they stick me in a backbreaking cage for that trip to Texas?"

He handed her saddlebags to her, but paused to stare at her, probably because she'd just sounded hopeful and chagrined at the same time. While she never tried to hide her emotions and was pretty darn clear about what she was feeling, Degan's gaze was as inscrutable as ever. "I believe you're talking about prison transports. You haven't been convicted yet."

"Then how will they take me to Texas?"

He shrugged and tossed his own saddlebags over his shoulder. "By train, stage, or horse would be my guess. You can be shackled while using two of those means of transportation. Worried?"

"I was worried about my back, yeah. It'll be broken by the end of that long trip. You can't stand up in those cages, you know."

He didn't reply because he simply didn't care. Why would he? She was nothing to him but money in his pocket, and a damn lot of it, too. She was going to make him rich today if he wasn't already.

His hotel was across the street from the stable. Stepping into it was like stepping into another world. Suddenly, she was surrounded by plush velvet sofas and chairs, carved tables with fancy flower vases on them, huge paintings, shiny marble floors, lit chandeliers! Max looked around with wide eyes as Degan pulled her toward the lobby desk. She'd thought that she would be making him rich with her reward, but he had to be rich already to stay in an elegant hotel such as this.

"Mr. Grant," the hotel clerk said politely, "a telegram was delivered for you."

The man eyed Max a little too curiously after he handed Degan the piece of paper. She wondered if he'd seen her wanted posters around town, or if he was just too formal and polite to question Degan about his scruffy cowboy companion. She was standing close enough to Degan to be able to read the telegram as he read it. A Pinkerton detective was requesting a meeting tomorrow afternoon about a confidential matter.

"Friend of yours?" she asked, tapping the paper.

"No, it's probably related to the work I'm doing for Marshal Hayes. He mentioned the Pinkertons were investigating train robberies." Degan almost sounded annoyed when he added, "He wasn't supposed to tell his superiors that I was temporarily taking over for him while he's away. It appears that he did anyway."

She grinned. "Or maybe they think you've become a—" He glanced at her so sharply she didn't finish, admitting instead, "Okay, bad joke. Besides, the railroads would go out of business if *you* started robbing—" His look turned so dark she flinched this time. "I'll just shut up now."

She was surprised to hear him request that hot water be delivered to his room, but didn't comment on it. Talking to him was actually more aggravating than not talking to him. And she'd been doing far too much of that. She supposed it was nervous chatter. He did make her a little nervous, but only because she couldn't figure him out. With most folks, you had plenty of warning about what they might do. With Degan Grant, you just got surprised.

But on the way up to his room she began to wonder about that hot water. Was he was going to have a bath *before* delivering her to jail? That would definitely be odd. Or was he that fastidious? Actually, as polished as his appearance was, she wouldn't be surprised if he was the sort who had to have a bath every day no matter what, and he'd probably missed a day or two while searching for her in the hills. So he might just feel he couldn't wait another minute to get cleaned up. She wished he'd said so, so she could've laughed at him.

She *used* to be like that—once upon a time. Now she didn't have that luxury and had gotten used to the grime. But as they neared his room on the second floor, she didn't feel like laughing. She was getting quite nervous. Was he going to strip down in front of her? What if he ordered her to scrub his back? That would mean she'd have to put her hands on that hard, strong, strapping body of his! She couldn't, wouldn't. She'd been disconcerted enough when he'd slid her down his body at the restaurant. What could he be thinking, bathing with her in the room?

Max froze as he opened the door. Now would be the time to run, but as if he'd read her mind, he put his hand on her back and gave her a little push inside. The room was nice, but then it was one of the biggest hotels Max had ever seen, so that wasn't surprising. A large bed with a beautiful burgundy brocade cover, two stuffed chairs in a dark rose material with a low table between them, a small desk, a large wardrobe, and a soft carpet underfoot. If his valise weren't already in the room, she would have thought he hadn't been in it until now, it was so neat and clean. She set her saddlebags down and went over to one of the two windows. They both faced the street, with no porch roof below them for her to hop out on. Damn.

Turning around, she watched Degan stripping the bed of what had appeared to be clean bedding. He crossed the room to drop the whole bundle in the hall outside his door. She raised a brow at him when he turned back around, but he wasn't interested in giving her an explanation. He did leave the door open though. If he would just move farther into the room, she could make a mad dash for it. . . .

Then the water arrived, four buckets carried by two young men, who emptied them in the tub behind a screen in the corner. That was fast, Max thought. But they weren't done. A few minutes later, they were back with another four buckets. She figured the water source had to be closer than downstairs. They left one bucket full for rinsing, then asked Degan if he needed anything else. He shook his head and closed the door after them before giving her his full attention.

"Get undressed."

"I don't think so." She crossed her arms over her chest.

"I wasn't giving you a choice."

Her heart began to pound in alarm as he stepped away from the door. He wanted her to bathe before he bedded her! That's why he'd stripped off the covers, so there'd be no evidence on the bed after he . . .

She made a desperate dash to the door only to feel his arm lock around her waist before she could reach it. She twisted around and started punching him, but fell back on the bed when he gave her a light push toward it.

"If you don't take your clothes off, I'll help you take them off, but one way or another, they're coming off."

Blue eyes wide, she watched him lock the door, shrug out of his jacket, and lay it neatly over a chair, then start walking toward the bed.

Chapter Thirteen

Max only had moments to decide her fate—if she could stop panicking long enough to think. Degan obviously wanted her, so why couldn't she turn this to her advantage and make a deal with him, her virginity for her freedom? She scrambled over the bed to stand on the other side to give herself a few more seconds. Could she do it without his realizing how scared she was? She had to at least try.

She took a deep breath. "I can undress myself," she said with a flirtatious smile as she cocked her hip and began unbuttoning her shirt.

He raised an eyebrow at her. "You're going to try that again?"

Max froze and felt her cheeks turning red. She was so embarrassed she'd misinterpreted his intentions that she was actually speechless.

"The bath is for you," he continued as if he hadn't noticed how mortified she was. "You can get undressed behind the screen."

All this over a bath she would love to have? But he had

to have a reason and not the one she'd mistakenly presumed. "Why do you want me cleaned up? Are you afraid you won't get the reward if you turn me in dirty?"

"Have you looked in a mirror?"

She knew how filthy she was, but she wasn't going to blush again. She lifted her chin stubbornly. "I'm not bathing with you in the room."

He started to come around the bed. She rolled across it again and ran for the screen in the corner. And gnashed her teeth when she heard him say, "Toss your clothes out here before you get in the tub."

She yanked her boots off, leaned around the screen, and threw them at him. Only one struck him in that wide chest of his. But she caught the frown before she ducked behind the screen again.

"Maybe I need to check you for weapons again."

"No! You don't!"

She'd never undressed so fast, tossing each piece of clothing over the screen, even her drawers, socks, and belts. She wasn't going to give him an excuse to come back here to check that she'd done as he'd ordered. It had been over a year since she'd splurged on a room to get a decent bath. She was *not* going to fight him anymore over this one when she would have thanked him for it if she didn't hate him so much. Actually, she didn't hate him at all, she just hated that he'd caught her and was going to be the death of her.

A short, narrow table was next to the little tub. It held towels and jars of creamy soap. No rough, homemade soap bars for this fine hotel. She opened one of the towels to see how big it was and snorted to herself. It was soft, but not even big enough to wrap around her.

She heard the door close and then the distinct sound of a key turning in the lock. She peeked around the screen. He'd actually left her alone in the room. But glancing around the room, she saw that he'd taken everything with him, their saddlebags, her clothes, even his valise, leaving her nothing but tiny towels to cover herself with. But more to the point, he'd left her nothing that she could use to make an improvised rope to aid her in escaping out the window. Now she knew why he'd removed perfectly clean bedding.

He'd taken every precaution, as if he'd done this before, yet he'd said he wasn't a bounty hunter. He was just too damn smart, preparing for all possibilities. And she drew the line at running through town naked even if she could inch her way along the ledge to an open window. But then, she'd probably fall and die in the attempt, so she wasn't going to try.

Instead, she got into the tub and sank down in it with a dreamy smile. At times when she'd been on the move weeks would go by before she found a decent watering hole to bathe in. There'd been a couple of ponds in the hills by her shack where she'd gotten water for her and her horse, but they weren't secluded enough to bathe in, so she'd been riding over to the big lake to the east every few days to bathe and wash her clothes. But it wasn't an ideal bathing experience, especially since she had to ride back to the shack dripping wet.

She scrubbed herself from top to bottom. She couldn't even remember the last time she'd felt this clean. And her head! The soap that she toted around with her might get her and her clothes clean, but it irritated her scalp something fierce, so she'd stopped soaping her hair long ago. But merely dousing her head in water when she bathed didn't leave her hair feeling clean. Not like this. Already it was mostly dry, and the slightest shake of her head had her hair floating around it. She even stood up to watch it float in the oval mirror above the shaving stand. And laughed.

She was feeling a little kindly toward Degan for this gift he'd given her. Just a little—okay, maybe just not annoyed with him for the moment, though she was still wary.

"Did you fall asleep in there?" Degan asked.

Hearing that and her saddlebags slide across the floor toward her brought her back to the hard facts of her situation, that it was time to go—to jail.

Max turned her head toward Degan's voice. "No, I was just waiting for my clothes." But when she saw that the bags hadn't quite made it to her side of the screen, she realized he might try to fix that and quickly yelled, "I'll get them!"

She stepped out of the tub, dried herself fast, and stuck just an arm around the screen to drag the bags back to her. Pulling out her only other set of clothes, she saw her chemise at the bottom of the bag. It was soft, finely made, and delicate, so she didn't wear it often, but in case they confiscated her bag at the jail she wanted to have her best clothes on her.

"I forgot these," she heard Degan say before Luella's undergarments came flying over the screen. She just managed to catch them before they landed in the tub of water. She'd forgotten, too, that he'd grabbed more than the derringer out of her coat pocket. She put the bloomers on, but she was blushing because Degan had seen how silky they were, had even held them in his hands.

She finished dressing and stepped out of the bathing corner carrying her bags and a clean pair of socks. Degan's eyes followed her. She didn't have to look at him to feel it. The rest of her clothes had been laid on the stripped bed, her boots on the floor by it. She grabbed the boots and went over to a chair to put them on. She wasn't sitting on that bed for any reason. Just the sight of it reminded her of what a fool she'd been to try seducing him again. The man was impervious to her charms. So be it. She'd rather escape anyway and thumb her nose at him—after she was gone.

Chapter Fourteen

"IT DOESN'T LOOK so badly butchered now."

Max blushed slightly. Degan's remark about her hair proved he had been staring at her and still was. But she took a leaf from his book and didn't reply.

She had deliberately kept her eyes off him as she crossed the room. She glanced his way now and saw him folding the screen and leaning it against the wall. She found that odd until he stopped in front of the shaving stand near the tub. His hair was wet, so apparently he'd bathed. But he hadn't yet shaved. She realized he'd moved the screen so nothing would be blocking his view of the rest of the room—and her—while he finished grooming himself.

She casually walked to the door while he was busy in the corner. She had to check. When she tried to turn the doorknob and couldn't, she sighed. He'd locked it again. She was sure he had seen what she had just done, but he didn't remark on it.

She paced in the middle of the room briefly before she gave in to the urge and watched him shaving. The man really was a fine piece of work. But there was always a balance, wasn't there, since no one was perfect. His balance was too handsome but too dangerous.

"I used to do that for my pa before he took off," she volunteered. "He liked everything smooth 'cept for the mustache he favored. I'm pretty good at it. Want me to show you?"

His laugh was spontaneous, but so brief she wondered if she'd really heard it. Then she realized that it was his way of telling her what he thought of her getting that shaving razor anywhere near his throat. But she was more interested in his having laughed, even if it was just a scoffing laugh, when he obviously didn't want to.

"Makes you uncomfortable to laugh, doesn't it?" she speculated.

She didn't expect an answer because he seemed to be concentrating on his shaving rather than on her, but she got one. "My profession prohibits emotion."

"Because you kill people?" she guessed.

"There comes a point when you're fast enough with a gun that you don't have to kill. On the other hand, I've lost count of how many men I've had to wound, but they don't usually die from it."

"Then you've never killed anyone, even in self-defense?"

"I didn't say that."

He didn't say any more about it, either. Of course he was a killer. It was written all over him. She quietly watched him for another minute. He was being particularly slow and methodical now about getting the stubble off his face, maybe because she *was* ruining his concentration. She smirked. She could have done it quicker for him and without a single nick.

"So what do you actually do, besides get in gunfights?"

"I take jobs where my particular skill is useful."

"A hired gun? And you've never taken a job to kill someone?"

"That's not a job, that's murder."

She raised a brow. "You actually draw the line? That's good to know."

No comment, so she let him finish what he was doing. She wanted to get some of that soap she liked so much before they vacated the room, so she rummaged through her bags, which were behind him by the tub, looking for her little leather pouch. When she found it, she emptied its contents into the tub.

Degan had turned around to look at her, probably because he didn't trust her that close to his back. "What are you getting rid of?"

"Gold dust." She grabbed one of the soap jars and carefully poured the creamy soap into the pouch. "I panned a little when I first came up this way."

"You'd rather have soap than gold?"

"That dust ain't likely to be worth much. This soap is more precious—to me."

"Why didn't you just take one of the jars?"

"That'd be stealing."

"And taking the soap isn't?"

"Course not. How would they know you didn't use it all up on that big, strapping body of yours?"

"Perhaps because I've been using the bathing room down the hall and the attendant knows it."

"Oh. Well, so they'll charge you a few more pennies. What's done is done." She stuffed the little pouch back in her bag. But then she frowned. "Will they even let me have a bath in jail?"

He'd already turned back toward the oval mirror. "I have no idea. I've never had occasion to see the inside of a jail cell."

Course he hadn't. He'd probably shoot any sheriff who tried to arrest him. She moved away from him and headed straight for her coat. As long as he was currently distracted, it would be a good time to read her grandmother's letter. She took the envelope out of her coat pocket and ripped it open. Tears sprang to her eyes when she saw her grandmother's handwriting.

Dearest Max,

I've been so worried about you! I am overjoyed to hear from you and learn that you are well. I imagine these last twenty months have been even more of a hardship to you than they've been to me and Johnny. We miss you so much. I've been ailing. Please come home. Despite the tragedy that caused you to flee, I know you will be dealt with fairly if you just come home and explain—

Max's heart sank. What did her grandmother mean she was "ailing"? And by "tragedy" did she mean Carl had died?

"There's a satchel in my valise." Degan's words cut into her thoughts. "Get it and tell me if you know any of the men on the wanted posters in it."

Sniffing back tears so Degan wouldn't see them, Max stuffed the letter and the envelope back in her coat pocket. She'd finish reading it when she was alone in jail. She turned around and opened his valise. Removing the thin leather satchel, she saw her Colt under it and picked it up, too.

"Mind if I wear this?" she asked over her shoulder, holding the gun up. "I feel off-balance without the weight of it on my right hip."

"I do mind."

"But you emptied it."

"It's still a heavy weapon."

She made a face. Did he *have* to think of everything? She shoved it back in the valise and took the satchel over to the chair and opened it. She grabbed the stack of papers out of it and rifled through them.

After a moment she glanced his way again. "And why am I looking at these?"

"I need to bring in three of those outlaws before the marshal returns to Montana."

"You planning on collecting us all before you turn us in? That's fine by me." She grinned.

No answer. Figured. She came to her own poster and read the page of notes attached to it. "Says here I had no schooling." She scowled. "That's a lie."

"It's probably just an assumption based on your atrocious diction."

She raised a brow at him. "You know it don't matter to me none if you don't like the way I talk."

"I've already figured that out." His lips curved slightly. She couldn't tell if it was a smile. Probably not. But she'd definitely heard some irony in his tone.

"It also says here I'm only fifteen. This information didn't come from Texas. Your friend must've gotten it from one of the farmers near here that I traded with."

"That's possible since he knew you were in the area."

She read aloud, " 'Max Dawson is more dangerous than he looks.' Now *that's* funny."

"But accurate." Degan rubbed the area on his chest that her boot had struck.

She rolled her eyes and finished looking at the posters. She'd come across two of these men in her travels. Three others she'd heard about. Only one other had a reward as big as hers, Charles Bixford, a vicious killer of fifteen people, who was also known as Red Charley. It infuriated her that she was likened in any way to such a cruel, dangerous man. It didn't make sense, even if Carl had died from that gunshot wound. Why did the people of Bingham Hills want her back so badly? And why was her grandmother telling her to come home when there was such a high price on her head?

"So what's in it for me if I help you?" she asked in a surly tone.

"I haven't decided yet."

What the hell did that mean? Of course he wouldn't say even if she asked, so she didn't ask. But she wasn't going to help him, either, when it was obvious he was going to be the death of her. So she stuffed the posters back in the satchel and tossed it over by his valise. And crossed her arms, daring him to ask her again for help so she could laugh in his face.

Max didn't get the chance to scoff at him. He probably got the idea that she wasn't going to help him from the mulish set of her chin, so he didn't mention the posters again. He simply put his shaving gear away, picked up his things, and *her* coat, then said, "Let's go."

She was beginning to hate those two words. But she didn't budge and held out her hand. "My coat first."

"No." He tossed the long garment over his shoulder. "You're clean. Let's leave it that way for a while." She still didn't budge, so he added, "You don't need to hide that you're a woman when you're with me. Besides, your vest does that well enough."

She hated when he was right. The sheriff was going to find out, or more likely be told, that she was a woman anyway, so there was no point in fighting for a lost cause.

She conceded, but since he appeared to be leaving the hotel for good, she was curious enough to ask, "Are you forgetting your meeting with that detective tomorrow?"

"People I don't know don't get to dictate my schedule. If it's important, the detective can catch up with me. If not, then it wasn't important."

"You really do things your way or no way, huh?"

He didn't answer, but he didn't march her straight out of his hotel. Once again, he stopped at the desk in the lobby. She took her last chance to escape, dropping her things and bolting out the door while he was paying for his stay and maybe leaving a note for that detective. She expected to feel the sting of his bullet at any second. She might even have been shot already and just hadn't heard or felt it because her heart was pounding so hard in her ears. But nothing stopped her so she kept on going.

This town had hundreds if not thousands of places she could hide in until dark. Then she could sneak into the stable for her horse and be long gone before morning. She picked the one place Degan wouldn't look for her, his own hotel.

Racing around to the back of the large building, she made sure Degan wasn't right on her tail before she ducked through the delivery entrance. She took a moment to catch her breath and calm her racing heart, then she grinned. She'd done it! Outfoxed the fox!

"You're too predictable," Degan said behind her.

"You didn't see me come in here!" she accused without turning.

"I didn't need to. I knew you weren't going to run off without your soap."

Did the gunfighter just make a joke? She sensed that he found the situation amusing, which snapped her temper.

Without replying, she whirled around and elbowed him hard and turned to kick him where it would hurt the most. Unfortunately, he deflected that blow, the one that would have enabled her to race off again. He put a steely arm around her shoulders and walked her back through the hotel. She knew there was no getting out of that grip, but she did try, struggling, all the way to the lobby.

She supposed she should be grateful that he didn't give her that bullet he'd promised her. Of course he hadn't actually had her in his sights. Or had he? Maybe he had seen her before she'd rounded the corner of the building, which would have been how he'd guessed she'd reentered the hotel. There was nowhere else in that back alley where she could have hidden. Had he resisted the urge to shoot her? It didn't really matter when he'd caught her anyway. Again.

He let go of her when he stopped at the hotel desk again, but his eyes followed her when she moved to pick up her saddlebags, which were still in the middle of the lobby where she'd dropped them. She gauged the distance between herself and Degan, then eyed the door. So she was the first to see the pretty lady who walked through it. Black hair wound up in ringlets and coils, an adorable little hat perched atop it. Layers and layers of silk and lace, with a coat swept back to form a bustle behind her. She was gussied up fancy enough for a ball. Max had never seen anyone like her.

The young woman stopped in her tracks when she noticed Degan, her blue eyes suddenly as wide as they could get. Max was getting used to that reaction to him. The lady would probably bolt back out the door now. . . .

"Degan?" the lady said. "Degan Grant? At last I've found you, darling."

Chapter Fifteen

Degan couldn't believe his eyes. This was insane! Allison Montgomery in Helena? He was so sure he'd never see her again, but here she was and looking as beautiful as he remembered. Old memories flowed through him, good and bad. But his last memory of her prevailed because it had haunted him the longest. He closed his mind to it and to her, which was the moment Degan realized Max was gone.

He ran across the street to the stable where he'd left their horses. He hoped he'd catch her saddling her horse, but he should have known she wouldn't be that dumb. She wouldn't have risked the time it would have taken when she couldn't count on his being distracted for long, and he hadn't been. But the arrival of Allison Montgomery had shocked him, which had been long enough for Max to slip away unnoticed.

He told the stableman to guard her horse with his life and gave him some extra money to make sure it didn't get stolen. She would want to leave town, so she would try to get to it eventually. She wouldn't steal another. The woman refused to spend money that wasn't hers, so she definitely wouldn't steal a horse. But she could sweet-talk some man into letting her ride with him.

That thought infuriated Degan, but it was nothing compared to what he felt when Allison entered the stable. She shouldn't be there in Helena. He'd come West to make sure they never crossed paths again. More memories came flooding back. Think of Max, he told himself. Max, murderer or not, was a breath of fresh air compared to his past. And where the hell would she hide while she waited for him to stop looking for her?

"You just walk away without a single word to me?" Allison said incredulously. "*Really*, Degan?"

He did it again, walked away from her and the memories. He needed to search Luella's brothel. It was the obvious place Max would go to hide—maybe a little too obvious. He didn't expect to find her there but he still had to check.

"Degan, don't you dare!"

He swung around as he reached the stable door. "I don't know what you're doing here and I don't care. Go home, Allison."

"I'm here for you."

"Then you've wasted your time."

"We were friends before we were lovers. And I'm still your fiancée."

"The hell you are."

"You can't still be holding that one night against me. After all these years that I've waited for you to come home?"

"Waited faithfully for me? Is that going to be your next lie?"

"I searched for you! I hired countless detectives. All they brought back were silly rumors that you had become a pistoleer of sorts and were in the habit of killing men. Utterly absurd. I can't tell you how many of them I fired for such incompetence."

"That's not what it's called out here."

"I honestly don't care what you want to call it. None of us believed it, of course. Well, your brother did. Flint thought it was funny, ironic actually, that you might have taken to wearing a gun when you always hated them. He insisted that confirmed that you were never coming back. But I didn't believe it."

She sounded far too triumphant now. "I'll bite. How did you actually end up here?"

"A friend told me that I was probably going about my search the wrong way. He pointed me to the Pinkers Agency, er, Pinkerers."

"Pinkerton?"

"Yes, those people. And they have men all over the country apparently. The nice man who helped me simply spent a few days sending off telegrams to his associates. Within a week he informed me I could find you in the small town of Nashart in this rustic territory. But by the time I arrived in Nashart, I learned you'd already—"

"Is that who sent me a telegram to arrange a meeting for tomorrow? One of your Pinkertons?"

"Yes, but that was only to delay you from leaving this town before I arrived, and I wasn't at all sure I would. It was such a grueling trip. But the Callahans told me that you intended to continue westward in this direction, so I took the chance that I could catch up to you. And here we are."

That was the last time Degan would ever share his intentions with anyone, friend or not. "I've already said it, Allison, but I guess I need to repeat it. You've wasted your time in coming here."

"But I found you!" she exclaimed. "And not just for me. You *have* to come home before there's no home for you to come back to. Flint is—"

He cut in harshly, "I don't want to hear it. I don't care about anything that happens back there. When I cut those ties it was for good."

She looked appalled. "You can't mean that."

"I do."

Degan saw her gaze moving over him, stopping at his gun belt. "You've—changed."

"You haven't."

"You *used* to listen to reason."

"I used to do a lot of things, be a lot of things, a dutiful son, a loving brother—a devoted fiancé. But you took all that away from me, didn't you?"

"You didn't have to leave!"

"Didn't I? Would you like to know what would have happened if I'd stayed?"

He slowly walked toward her and put his hands on her shoulders. She immediately wrapped her arms around him and raised her face, obviously thinking he meant to kiss her. He shoved her back. Whatever he might have done, saner thoughts prevailed and he simply walked away.

A shot was fired as he reached the stable doors, a bullet hitting the wall next to him, too close to be a stray. His gun in hand, he took in the scene outside as people scattered for cover. An ambush in broad daylight? That sounded like something Jacob Reed would do, and Reed had been searching for him for several years now. The man was so bent on revenge for the death of his brother at Degan's hands that he was willing to die for it.

Allison had heard the shot, too, and rushed to his side. Degan grabbed her shoulder and pushed her behind the wall. "Get down before you get shot."

"What about you? This place is so horrible! This wouldn't happen in Chicago, where you *should* be."

He ignored her and continued to look for the shooter. The rooftops across the way appeared empty but had places to hide. Quite a few open windows across the street, too, especially in the hotel. But the shooter could be anywhere. Or it could just have been a misfire, an accident that no one was laying claim to out of embarrassment. He stepped out of the stable to test that theory, ready for any movement, but there was none. If someone was trying to kill him, he must not be willing to try it when Degan was prepared for it. And he'd wasted enough time when he needed to find Max.

Allison was smart enough not to follow this time. But that didn't mean he could get her out of his mind. He was still beyond surprised to see her in Helena. Why had she, a socialite from one of Chicago's richest families, come all this way to find him? He shouldn't have let her say so much, or maybe he should have controlled his temper and let her say more. What did she mean that he had to go home before there was no home to go back to? Was Flint ruining the family because he didn't know how to handle money? Did that mean Degan's father had died? If that was Allison's news, he wasn't going to let her see whether it affected him. He wasn't sure it would. When he'd left home, he'd expected never to see his family again, or to hear from them. He hadn't cared what happened to them. He hadn't just cut the ties, he'd thrown away the damn ropes.

Before going to Max's favorite brothel, he detoured to send a telegram to an old acquaintance in Chicago.

John's badge came in handy at the brothel, forestalling any protests the madam might have made about her establishment's being searched. It took him a couple of hours because he was thorough. He went through every room, looking under every bed, inside every chest, cupboard, and wardrobe, startling a few customers and many of the women, who were in various stages of undress or were busy getting dressed. But he had been right. Max was too smart to return to the first place he would look for her. So where the hell was she hiding?

Before he started checking the saloons, cafés, and back alleys, he went back to the telegraph office, where he picked up a reply to his telegram. Neither his father nor his brother had died, and both were occupied in the same manner they'd been five years ago. Whatever Allison Montgomery was up to, it pertained solely to her and not his family, or at least it didn't concern his family in any way that mattered to him.

Degan spent the rest of the day searching for Max. His frustration grew steadily because no one had seen her run out of the hotel; no one had seen her going into a saloon or a store or darting into an alley. How was that possible? He stopped showing her wanted poster when two unsavory types overheard him talking with the owner of a stable five blocks away from the one Degan was using. The men thanked him for the tip that Max Dawson might be nearby because they sure could put $1,000 to good use. He didn't like the idea of anyone else capturing Max. She was his prisoner.

When he returned to the hotel that night, he didn't run into Allison, but he saw her guard dogs sitting in the lobby watching him. She was traveling with two of them, big and armed. He didn't give her another dark thought.

The next morning, Degan was up early to search the other

side of town. No one he spoke to had seen Max Dawson, but every one of them seemed excited that an outlaw with such a high bounty on his head had been spotted in town and assured him they'd start looking for Max Dawson, too. By early afternoon, Degan rode out to the closest gold camp to question the miners. And got the same answer: no one had seen hide or hair of Max Dawson. He even rode out to the shack, thinking she might have gotten someone to give her a ride out there. But the place was empty.

Back at the hotel, Allison's guard dogs were still planted in the lobby. The clerk at the front desk handed him a note, but he ripped it up when he saw that it was from Allison. As he ate dinner in his room, he concluded that Max had somehow managed to get out of town fast. She was resourceful enough to have managed it without her horse. He hated to admit it, but he was disappointed. He might not have decided yet what to do with her, but he'd begun to enjoy her company. She tried to be so boyish, but when she'd traded gold dust for soft soap, she'd been all woman.

She didn't have an artful bone in her body, preferred brazen boldness instead. Her first attempt at seduction had been laughable, even though he had been tempted. There were no two ways about it—he was attracted to her. Her gruff bravado and lightning-quick temper that she didn't seem to know how to control were amusing. She was tempestuous—and adorable. Oh, she was more than that. She'd cleaned up far too beautiful for his peace of mind, so he should be glad that he hadn't been able to find her. And yet he wasn't.

He took out John's satchel and started flipping through the wanted posters. He was done wasting his time in Helena. He had to start making some progress on paying back that favor.

He checked out of the hotel early and collected his horse. He stared at Max's chestnut gelding for a long minute. He almost decided to take it with him. But she'd succeeded in eluding him. She'd bested him fair and square. He wasn't going to strand her here just to be ornery—if she was still here. He left her coat there, too, with her saddle. She went to extremes to hide who she was under that garment. He understood that. He'd done the same thing, just with a gun instead.

He had a sack of food from the hotel, enough to last several days, but he needed one more thing before he left town, a bottle of whiskey. He wasn't used to tracking or going off the beaten path, but searching for Kid Cade might require a night or two of camping out. And while the days had been getting uncomfortably hot, the nights could still get chilly, and a dram or two of whiskey could ward off the cold. So he headed straight for the one saloon he knew would be open in the morning, Big Al's.

Before he entered the saloon, he glanced back at the brothel across the street. The windows were all open but the building was quiet, the girls probably sleeping late. Two men stumbled out the door, apparently having spent the night there. They crossed the street to the saloon instead of heading home and appeared to be having a friendly argument.

Degan ignored them and went inside to pay for his bottle, but he paused on the way back out when he heard the men arguing over who was going to have Chicago Joe's new girl first. He turned to one of the men and asked, "When did the new girl show up?"

"Two days ago, mister. There's already a long waiting line for her, and we're at the head of it."

"Have you seen her?"

"No one has yet, but the madam says she's the prettiest little blond whore ever to set foot in Montana."

Degan left the saloon, put his whiskey away, and led his horse across the street. Madam Joe was in the parlor. He wondered if the woman ever slept. She was sitting on a sofa with a cup of coffee in her hand, flanked by two of her girls in their morning attire, which was merely their skimpy underwear barely covered by their open robes.

Joe smiled at him. One of her girls did, too, eyeing him from head to toe. Degan knew that familiarity usually calmed people's nerves, and he'd been to the brothel three times now because of Max—without killing anyone. So the women no longer saw him as quite as big a threat. They also seemed to view him as a lawman now.

"I'm beginning to think you like us, Deputy Marshal," the madam purred. "Pleasure this time, or more business?"

"That depends."

"On?"

"Whether your new girl is wanted by the law or just by your customers."

Joe laughed and winked at him. "That sweet thing is as innocent as they come. If she's guilty of anything, it's being too pretty."

"I'll have her for the day."

"She's not ready yet. She's still in training."

"Then I'll teach her a few things. I'm not inclined to wait."

The madam frowned slightly as if she were about to argue, but changed her mind and shrugged, nodding toward the stairs. "Suit yourself. Second door on the right. But don't complain if you aren't satisfied."

Chapter Sixteen

"**Y**OU REALLY DO NEED teaching, don't you, honey? You're supposed to pull that down, not up."

Max gave up trying to tug the tight, red satin bustier a little higher and glanced at Candy, who was leaning in the doorway, fanning herself with a long, pink feather. Candy loved pink. Her entire wardrobe was pink. The short, ruffled skirt Max was wearing now was Candy's. The dark red bustier belonged to Scarlet.

The girls at Chicago Joe's were like a big family. They laughed and teased and squabbled, but they cared about each other. And they considered themselves lucky. Not all brothels were as nice to work in. Some were rife with in-house fighting and cutthroat competition, but Luella had assured Max that didn't happen here. All the girls had welcomed her, and many insisted that she borrow their clothes until she made enough money to buy her own.

Max enjoyed trying on the clothes. She'd never worn such bright colors or dresses with such high hemlines and low bodices, or foundation garments that emphasized her curves. They made her look like a completely different person, so different from who she really was that she couldn't help but laugh—at herself. Many of the garments were either too tight, too loose, or too short; few of them really fit her. But she reminded herself she only had to wear them for a few days.

The girls didn't only visit her to donate to her wardrobe. They also came by to offer advice on how to handle a man and please him.

"Don't get them mad," Scarlet had warned her in one of those sessions. "Occasionally, that can be interesting, but usually it won't be."

"And compliments!" a short, chubby girl named Sue Annie had added. "Men like to feel special even if it ain't true."

But Candy had snorted, "That can backfire on you, so don't veer too far from the truth."

Max had blushed. And a couple of times she'd blurted out, "Really?" Luella had tried to shoo the girls out of Max's room, insisting she would teach Max the trade. But the other girls were just trying to be helpful because they didn't know that Max was just using the brothel as a hiding place. So she couldn't exactly tell them to leave her alone.

This was not how she'd wanted to hide here when she'd snuck in after she'd escaped from Degan. She'd been afraid he wouldn't be distracted long enough by that beautiful woman who'd called him "darling." But he must have been. Max had been able to slip out of the hotel again, but this time she'd grabbed a jacket from the employees' coatroom, so she wouldn't look the same when Degan started looking for her. Keeping her head down and sticking to the back alleys so no one would see her, she made her way straight to the brothel and entered through the back door and ran up the back stairs to Luella's room.

Max had still been in a panic, certain that Degan would arrive at any minute, looking for her, but she needed to borrow some money from Luella so she could get out of town. Then Luella had started undressing her, telling her to put on a dress because she had a plan: Max would hide where the deputy marshal would never expect to find her—among Madam Joe's girls. Max knew it was risky. But so would be anything else she tried in order to avoid Degan till he left town.

Luella had called in a few of the other girls to meet Max without telling them her plan. Luella timed it perfectly because when she heard Degan coming toward her room, she threw a ruffled dress over Max's head so it looked as if she were in the middle of dressing, and it had worked. All he saw of Max was her legs! He didn't even see Luella ducking behind the girls surrounding Max, so he must have thought it was Luella they were helping. And after he looked into her wardrobe, he moved on to search another room. When he finally left the brothel, Luella finished dressing Max and introduced her to Madam Joe as an old friend who wanted to get into the business. The madam was more than welcoming and even agreed to allow Max a few days of training before she put her to work and gave her one of the extra rooms to use.

With Max feeling so anxious about continuing to evade Degan, and the law in general, she found it disconcerting when the girls walked into her room without knocking as Candy had just done.

"Joe isn't going to wait much longer," Candy warned her now. "She's already got men lined up waiting for you."

Max paled. "I've only been here two days."

Candy chuckled as she sauntered forward and yanked down the red bustier. "There, that's better. And it doesn't take a few days to figure out how to make a man happy. I don't know what Luella was thinking to suggest you'd need that long."

Max had wanted that long. She wanted to make damn sure Degan was gone before she left town herself. Maybe she ought to leave tonight before the madam called her bluff and actually sent a man up to her. But it was a daunting thought. She was going to have to leave on foot—and without any weapons. Even if her horse was still in town, she didn't dare try to fetch him when Degan might have left a guard with him, hoping she would. Damn Degan Grant.

As soon as Candy left, Max looked down at her breasts to see what the girl considered "better" and snorted. Her nipples were almost showing! She pulled the material up once again, hard, annoyed that there still wasn't much give. You would think leaving a little mystery would heighten a man's anticipation, but, no, these girls thought blatantly advertising their wares was the best way to entice a man.

"Don't do that on my account."

Max sucked in her breath. She'd know that voice anywhere. She glanced up to see how angry he was, then drew in her breath softly.

Seeing Degan surprised speechless by that fancy lady at the hotel had been priceless. She'd chuckled to herself every time she remembered it because it had gotten her free. She wasn't chuckling now, even though he definitely looked surprised again—by what she was wearing. And he was slowly taking it all in, her long legs, which were mostly bare since the pink skirt only reached the middle of her thighs. Her arms and shoulders were completely bare. Half of her breasts too. She'd experienced quite a bit of embarrassment the last two days with the girls teasing her and talking so frankly about sex, but it was nothing compared to how she felt now.

So her cheeks weren't just hot because she was furious at getting caught again. But he had to be angry, too, that she'd escaped and evaded him for two days right here in town. He just wasn't showing it because he was too busy undressing her with his eyes. If this weren't *Degan*, she'd swear he'd just turned sensual on her.

She crossed her arms over her chest. "You weren't supposed to come back here."

"Come back?" He slowly entered the room.

She would have smirked if she weren't so angry at him. "You walked right past me the other day when you were searching the place."

He raised a brow. "Where were you hiding?"

She shouldn't tell him. If he had any sort of curiosity at all, it might drive him crazy wondering. But he didn't, so she admitted, "I had a dress over my head. All you saw were my legs."

He glanced down at her long legs. "I didn't know yours were this shapely. You're lucky you weren't exposing your bare breasts because I haven't forgotten what they look like."

Max couldn't deal with feeling mortified and angry at the same time, so she stopped covering her breasts long enough to take a swing at him. That didn't work too well. He grabbed her. She struggled against his hold, still hoping to land a decent punch if she could get a little space between them, but that wasn't working out well, either. Then they fell together on the bed, or he pushed her so she would land there and he just followed her down, she wasn't sure which. But she immediately crossed her arms tightly over her breasts again—and that's where his eyes went.

"No hiding the merchandise I'm paying for."

She gasped. Did he really think she was here for *that*? She quickly told him, "If you want a woman, there's half a dozen down the hall."

"And if I only want you?"

Those words wrapped themselves around her like a warm breeze. It would be too easy to open her arms to this particular man. But he wouldn't bargain! She'd tried that the night he'd captured her, and he hadn't been interested. She'd been ready to cut a deal yesterday morning, and all he'd wanted was for her to take a bath so she wouldn't be dirty when he turned her over to the sheriff!

But she could be just as clear. "Too bad."

She pushed away from him so she could get off the bed. He let her, but before she could turn around, he was behind her, his fingers moving over her stomach in a slow, sensual circular motion, pulling her back against his chest.

"Raise your arms and put your hands behind your head," he directed.

"Are you arresting me?"

"Later. Right now I want full access to your—charms."

Before she could get beyond the shock of those words, his hands slid up over her breasts and stopped there to gently squeeze them. He did it again. Oh, God. Coils of heat shot right to her core, immobilizing her for a moment. Even her knees turned to mush. She had to take a few deep breaths. It took every ounce of will she had to turn around so he would stop caressing her like that, but looking up into his eyes and

seeing the heat there just aroused her more. She stumbled backward and turned away so she wouldn't see such raw sensuality.
Again, he let her.

But then he said, "So you're in training but not practicing
with a man yet?"

She heard the humor in his tone. He *wanted* her to hear it.
He'd just been teasing her? Or rubbing in her choice of hiding
places?

Likely the latter because he added, "This is how you hide?
By letting the madam advertise that she has a pretty new
blonde on the menu?"

She turned to glare at him. "She wasn't supposed to do
that!"

"Why not? It's good for business. But if I actually thought
you were taking up the red light, I'd put you over my knee and
spank the hell out of you."

Now *that* was the Degan she knew, cold and heartless.
"*That's* not one of your options—ever."

"Not your choice, Maxie. But now it's time to go. You can
put your own clothes on, or I'll take you out of here wearing
that. I really don't care which."

"I'll change," she grumbled. "Just step outside for a minute."

"Not a chance. There's a window and a door here. You aren't
going through either one without me."

She'd had a brief respite from gnashing her teeth in the time
she'd been away from him. But now she was back at it. The
little room had no screen that she could step behind to change.
It was a brothel. No one here hid anything. But she refused to
give Degan a show.

She yanked open the little wardrobe and grabbed her hat
and slapped it on her head. She felt like screaming. She'd been

so close to avoiding jail. She'd even decided to leave town. She would have been gone by tonight.

She wondered if a scream would bring Madam Joe's two bruisers upstairs to beat up Degan. They were always on the premises to keep the peace. She could slip away again while he was busy with them—no, he'd just shoot them and he could do that quickly.

Keeping her back to Degan, she stepped into her pants and pulled them all the way up before she unwrapped the little skirt and let it drop to the floor.

"Mind if I borrow that?"

Max recognized Scarlet's voice, and for the briefest moment she thought the girl was actually referring to Degan. But when Max glanced around, Scarlet was already picking up the pink skirt, though her eyes were admiring Degan, even when she whispered to Max, "Good job! When you're done with him, send him to my room."

Max protested, "He's not my customer!"

But Scarlet just chuckled as she sauntered out of the room with the skirt in hand, her eyes *still* all over Degan. Max tried not to gnash her teeth yet again and finished dressing, putting her shirt on over the bustier, then unfastening the tight, red garment and letting it fall, too, before buttoning up her shirt and tucking it in. The rest went on fast now that she was completely covered. She picked up her saddlebags before turning to face him.

"Now *that* was disappointing," he said as he took the bags from her.

More teasing? But dressed in her own clothes, she felt like herself again and wasn't going to be carted to jail without a fight.

But then Luella suddenly rushed into the room, and like a mama hen she stepped between Degan and Max and started yelling at him, "How can you do this? She's not a criminal! You can't let her hang when she's innocent!"

His inscrutable expression didn't change, which might have been why Luella figured out she was wasting her breath. She grabbed Max and hugged her and started crying, so loudly that it drew a few of the other girls into the room. Max tried to comfort Luella, but she was on the verge of tears, realizing she was never going to see her friend again. And the tears were contagious because the other girls started crying, too.

Degan looked pretty exasperated and grabbed Max's arm to tear her away from Luella and lead her out of the room. But all the women followed, crying even louder. Then Max heard Luella shout, "Don't you dare hurt her!"

Degan didn't pause, but his tone was ominous when he said, "Don't worry. Miss Dawson will get exactly what she deserves."

Chapter Seventeen

"WE'RE GOING TO BUTTE," Degan said by her ear.

We? They were a block away from the brothel. Max stopped struggling instantly, but she sure as hell didn't understand what he was up to. And *why* couldn't he have told her that sooner? Like two days ago when they'd left his hotel room? His lack of communication was going to be *his* downfall one of these days.

And he wasn't just feeding her hope to get her to stop struggling. He took her straight to the stable to get her horse. But she only got a moment to hug Noble and to be happy to have him back before Degan grabbed her hands and wrapped a rope around them again. She was surprised he'd waited so long to tie her up. Having eluded him, she knew he wasn't going to trust her out of his reach now. She was still able to mount by herself, and with him holding her reins again, he led her out of town along the southern trail, the one that extended all the way to Utah and was used to freight supplies to Montana Territory from the far west.

She waited until Helena was far behind them before she

let her curiosity loose on him. "You and the sheriff back there don't get along? So you're taking me to another one?"

"We'll be in Butte by tonight."

"That's more'n a hundred miles from here!"

"Maybe half that, give or take a few. If you had read the marshal's notes, you would know that Kid Cade was last seen around Butte."

"So you *are* going to collect all three of us before turning any of us in?"

He didn't answer that one, but she realized, he wasn't answering her other two questions, either. If she had her own reins, she'd stop right there. But she didn't have that luxury. And she was beginning to figure out that talking to him was not only more aggravation but more trouble than it was worth. So she stopped and just enjoyed that, for whatever reason, she wasn't in a jail cell yet.

He had been pacing the horses between some brisk cantering, some annoying trotting, and a little walking, so they were making good time without tiring the animals and didn't turn off the road to rest until midafternoon. Her stomach had been rumbling for the last hour, but she'd continued to hold her tongue and was going to keep that up until *he* got around to asking her something, so *she* could have the pleasure of not replying. Best-laid plans . . .

Degan took them to a small knoll with quite a few shade trees and smaller flowering trees and bushes scattered around it. It wasn't so far off the road that they couldn't still see it below them. They had only passed a few other riders so far, mostly to and from the gold camps that were south of Helena, a few wagons, an oxen-driven cart, and beyond the camps a couple cowboys who looked more like drifters and left the road to go around Degan. Max snickered as she watched them. Degan didn't seem to notice.

After Degan untied her hands, she dismounted and stretched her legs by walking in circles around the knoll so Degan wouldn't think she was about to run off. In the sunny parts, the ground was covered with purple lupines and yellow black-eyed Susans. Max saw a stagecoach racing down the road below them. Luckily, she and Degan had just missed getting doused in its dust. She wondered about the passengers inside the coach. This was a major route for settlers entering the territory. The stage ran between Virginia City to the south and Fort Benton on the Missouri River up north. They'd already passed the little town of Boulder less than an hour ago, which had grown up around one of the stage stops. Boulder had marked the halfway point to Butte, so they just might reach it by nightfall after all, since the sun didn't set until around nine o'clock at this time of year.

Degan was untying a sack from his saddle. She might have offered to hunt up some food if she wasn't still determined not to talk to him anymore. She smelled the fresh bread before he pulled the loaf out of the sack. He broke it in two and tossed her half. He brought out a round of cheese next and broke that in half, too.

"*Don't* toss that!" She moved forward to take it from him.

She waited there to see if anything else was coming out of the sack, but he started eating, so she went over to a big oak tree and sat down there, resting her back against the trunk, and did the same. Plain fare and yet it tasted so good. She rarely got to eat bread and cheese, and she savored every bite.

Degan finished eating first and opened his friend's leather satchel and took out all the posters. He came over to the tree she was leaning against and sat beside her. Their shoulders were nearly touching, but she didn't move.

Sated and lulled by the sounds of the singing birds and buzzing bees, she momentarily forgot her vow of silence. Glancing at the papers in his hands, she asked, "What are you trying to figure out?"

"I told you that I need three of you before I can call John's favor paid and move on."

Max decided it might be to her benefit if he had other outlaws to pick from in case she could still figure out how to talk her way out of being one of the three, so she reversed her earlier decision not to help him and grabbed the papers out of his hands.

Thumbing through them, she pulled out a poster. "This fellow holes up in Colorado. I was in that state long enough to see him more'n once over the course of eight months. He had a young girl with him both times. Seemed like a family man to me, not a bank robber."

"Appearances can be deceiving."

She gave him a nasty look, knowing full well that remark was directed at her, but he was looking at the poster she'd indicated, not at her, so she pointed to another poster. "This Bixford fellow they call Red Charley, I've heard folks talking about him a few times—in fear. The way he kills, by blowing up buildings and everything in them, you don't see him coming, which is why people hope he gets caught before he wanders up this way."

"An unusual method of killing."

With that being Degan's only comment about the vicious outlaw, she pulled out another poster to show him. "Now *this* one actually shared a camp with me early this spring when I was making my way slowly through Wyoming. I stopped before dark to hunt up my dinner, had a rabbit and two trout roasting, which is what drew him my way."

"You fish?"

"Not in the usual way, no, least, not since I left home. I used to carry a little net with me until I had to break camp fast one night and left it behind. But I still had the net that day when I was following a stream teeming with fish. Anyways, this man looked hungry, probably was, since we were so far from any towns, and I had more'n enough to share. Didn't know he was wanted by the law. Didn't recognize his name when he gave it. He seemed harmless enough and was traveling alone."

"So you're in the habit of taking in any stray that comes along?"

She detected a note of disapproval in his voice. He obviously didn't know what it was like to have to avoid civilization, to not see or talk to another person for months.

"Hell no. But as you might have guessed, I like to talk, and I hadn't spoken to anyone but myself or Noble in ages, and Noble doesn't exactly talk back, so I made an exception. I didn't sleep that night. I'm not *that* trusting. But he took off in the morning and I stayed another day in that camp to catch up on my sleep."

"I assume you learned something about him to have mentioned him?"

"These notes say he was last seen in Arizona, but he said he spent the winter in Montana getting a spell of gold fever out of his system. He did approach from the north and headed south when he left. But he said he was heading home to Kansas, that his brother had a farm there. You might want to add that to your friend's notes—unless you think I'm lying about that, too."

He didn't confirm or deny it, just asked her, "Anything else?"

"Yeah. Willie Nolan and his gang aren't hitting the railroads in Kansas anymore. These days, he and his boys prefer the Northern Pacific line over in the Dakota Territory just east of here."

He took the poster from her. "Really?"

"You find that interesting?"

"A friend of mine was robbed on that train on her way to Nashart this year."

Her? So he did have women friends in each town just as she'd guessed? That annoyed her and she wasn't sure why. Of course she didn't need to have a reason to be annoyed with Degan Grant. She'd have more trouble finding a reason *not* to be annoyed with him.

But his mentioning women friends reminded her of the one who had inadvertently helped her to escape. "Who is the fancy lady who was so happy to see you in Helena?"

He finally glanced at Max, but she wished he hadn't. She could almost feel the sudden coldness coming off him. "No one important."

"Really?"

He wasn't going to explain. Instead he asked, "How do you know the Nolan gang is in Dakota?"

"Don't you dare try to pin train robbery on me," she growled.

"It was a simple question, Max."

Now she was touchy? She huffed before saying, "I heard a couple miners talking 'bout it when I went to one of the Helena camps to trade for some lantern fuel. One of them came to

Montana on the Northern Pacific and had to sit through one of those robberies. He used to live in Kansas and recognized two of the robbers as members of the Nolan gang."

"It's Will Nolan who's wanted by the law. Did the miner see him during the robbery?"

"No idea. I only heard him telling his friend who was leaving the territory not to take anything on that train ride that he wouldn't mind losing, or to use a different route instead. And that's why he went into that long story about getting robbed on that train and who did it."

They both heard the posse riding down the road from the north at about the same instant. So much for her stay of execution. One of the deputies must have recognized her as they rode out of Helena.

"Don't look so glum," Degan said as he stood up. "They aren't coming for you."

"How do you know?"

"I recognize that white stallion. Jacob Reed rides one just like it."

"Never heard of him. Who is he?"

"I shot his brother a few years back. It was a fair fight. Jacob was even there to see it was, but he's still got a powerful urge to kill me for it. He tried that day, rode after me on that stallion."

"And yet he still lives?"

Degan shrugged. "He was in a rage from his grief. I wasn't going to kill him for that. I hoped a couple wounds would make him see reason, but all it did was send him back to town for a doctor. I found out last year that he's been looking for me ever since."

"And getting mighty close by the looks of it. Or maybe he ain't following you today."

"I wouldn't count on it. I've been in Montana too long and a lot of people know it. And someone shot at me in Helena. I had a feeling it might be Reed. Get behind the tree." He moved the horses a little farther down the other side of the knoll. "I'd rather not deal with Jacob and his friends while I have you in tow."

" 'Fraid I'll catch a stray bullet?"

"No, afraid I'll have to shoot you when you take advantage of my distraction and run."

She chuckled. "Course I would run. But I could've taken care of your Reed problem if you didn't empty my bags of all my rifle bullets. I could have picked off all five of them as they rode by."

"So you are a killer?"

Did he sound disappointed? *Him?* She snorted. "I hit exactly what I aim at, and a wound to each of them would have sent them back to Boulder for the nearest doctor."

"Or started a shoot-out that could have lasted until dark."

That could have been a possibility if she didn't shoot to really hurt them, so she conceded his point and mentioned instead, "There's a trail near here that will take us through the hills directly south. There's a couple decent-sized lakes down that way."

"How do you know so much about the western part of the territory? I thought you came up here through Wyoming."

"I did, but we're only a few hours' ride from the shack I was using. I couldn't risk going into Helena more than once a week so I kept busy by exploring. It's useful to know where gulches and big rivers and lakes are located. Might take us an extra hour or so before we can wind back toward Butte, but the trail through the hills will keep us from catching up to that bunch on this main route."

"Or we could just wait here a little longer."

"Or you could just go kill Jacob Reed and be done with it. 'Sides, you won't actually find Kid Cade *in* Butte. He knows he's wanted by the law, so he'll be avoiding towns like I do. But if he's around these parts, he'll need to be near water, and there's plenty tween here and Butte, just east of the road your friends are traveling on. Chances are, you're going to end up searching this area anyway. Who knows, you might get lucky and be able to turn both of us over to the Butte sheriff tonight."

"Come mount up."

She glanced around the tree to make sure Reed and his friends were gone before she started toward her horse. But he grabbed her arm and pulled her over to his palomino.

"What—?"

"You can't lead the way if I'm pulling you along behind me."

Ride *with* him? She started to back away, but didn't look behind her first. She tripped on a large rock, fell, and actually rolled a few feet, crushing flowers and getting poked by acorns that had fallen from the oak tree. But that's not all she'd disturbed. She heard the bees before she felt them and panicked at the first sting on her upper arm. She leapt to her feet, slapped at her arms, her head, her legs. She thought she might have gotten them all off her until she felt another sting on the back of her neck and yanked her vest off to use it to swat behind her.

But one more sting on her back had her yell at Degan, "Get it out!" She quickly unbuttoned her shirt and pulled it off her shoulders. "Hurry!"

He pulled the shirt away from her back and looked down it. After a moment he said, "One just flew off."

"Are there more? It feels like I've been stung all over my back."

"The bees are gone, but I see a few red spots and one on the back of your left arm."

"I *hate* bees."

"You'll be fine."

"I'm not so sure. Gran said I had a bad reaction to a bee sting when I was a tyke. I don't remember it, but she always cautioned me to stay away from bees."

"Maybe she should have warned you not to trip over your feet instead."

Was that supposed to be a joke? Or was he just trying to distract her from the burning bee stings? Either way, the remark earned him a glare instead of her thanks.

But she gasped when he added, "The one thing I do know about bee stings is that you have to remove the stinger fast or else more venom will get into those wounds. Drop your shirt."

Chapter Eighteen

THIS HAD TO BE the most uncomfortable ride of her life, Max thought for the tenth time, and not because of the welts on her back and her arm that had developed from the bee stings. Those were still burning, but not as badly as before. As long as her shirt didn't rub against them, she could almost ignore them. Almost. And she hadn't been embarrassed when Degan had removed the stingers for her because she hadn't taken off her shirt. She had merely lowered it and then lifted it so he could get at the spots where she'd been stung. But being this close to him . . .

Seated in front of Degan, she couldn't relax or she'd be leaning against Degan's chest. She couldn't keep her legs from touching his because there was nowhere else to put hers. Although she was supposedly leading them, he didn't even give her the reins to do so! And his arms kept touching hers as he guided the animal where she told him to.

This was *so* unnecessary. The way to go was mostly obvious. Then she started feeling things she shouldn't be feeling. It caught her by surprise. The flip of her heart when his leg moved slightly under hers—like a caress. The tingles when his breath touched the back of her neck as he adjusted the reins. The brush of his shoulder when he turned to look behind them made her flush with heat for no reason. The man needed to sit still!

"Put me back on my horse," she finally demanded. "I can yell at you when you need to turn."

"Luella didn't have your letter?"

Where the hell did that come from? Or was he just trying to distract her from her bee stings? But she did need distracting—from him, so she answered, "She did."

"Good or bad news?"

"Mostly bad, but confusing, too. And I haven't had a chance to finish reading it."

"Then finish it. That might clear up your confusion."

He was right. Even though the letter was disappointing, Gran might have tacked on something hopeful toward the end. Max had taken her coat off when they'd stopped to eat back at the knoll, which was why she'd gotten stung so bad, but she was wearing it now and dug the letter out of her pocket again. A few minutes later she was close to tears. Some of the letter still didn't make sense, but when her grandmother referred again to the tragedy Bingham Hills had had to deal with, the fact that Carl was dead really sank in. She'd clung for so long to the hope that he was alive, that someday she'd be able to go home without having a noose waiting for her. That hope was gone now, and Degan was going to make sure she couldn't avoid that fate any longer.

She stuffed the letter back in her pocket, too despondent to say a word. The rest of letter was about Gran and Johnny and how they were getting on. Johnny had assumed her role as the hunter in the family and Gran's right hand on the farm, but then he didn't have much choice about it. Max and her brother were nothing alike. She took her licks and didn't complain—much. He was a good shot, but he didn't like to hunt or do farm chores. And Max knew Johnny was too sensitive not to be riddled with guilt for letting her take the blame for shooting Carl. She had known her younger brother wouldn't be able to survive alone in the wilderness as she could. So she'd made Gran promise to keep him from making any foolish confessions about his part in the shooting.

Of course, she'd never thought she'd be gone this long. She was the one who should be taking care of Gran. She'd assumed that role as soon as she learned how to shoot, which was right after their pa took off. Johnny had big dreams of seeing more of the world, of becoming a sailor like their father. If none of this had happened, he would probably have left Texas by now. Maybe his wish would come true this year. . . .

"Still confused, or is the bad news even worse?"

The wide path through a gulch had allowed them to ride at a good speed. But deep in thought, she almost missed the easy way out of it, which slowed them briefly to a walk. And why was Degan suddenly showing some curiosity about her situation? Boredom, probably. But maybe she should share the bad news with him. If he had any sort of conscience under his dispassionate exterior, she might at least make him feel a little guilty for being the death of her even if he wouldn't admit it.

"Well, Gran was happy to hear from me since she didn't know if I was still alive. But she wants me to come home because she misses me and she's in bad health."

"I'm sorry about her health, but is that what confused you? That she would encourage you to go home?"

"That's just it, she said that despite Carl's death, she's sure I'll be dealt with fairly if I just come home and explain my actions. That's what doesn't make sense, since she knows I didn't shoot Carl and I made her promise to keep Johnny from making any fool confessions, so she also knows I'll never say Johnny did it. But it also bothers me that she'd even mention her health. She's always been in good health, and even if she did get sick, she wouldn't complain about it."

"So you think she didn't actually write the letter?"

Her eyes flared. "That didn't occur to me. I've been too upset that the news wasn't what I'd hoped it would be."

"Is it your grandmother's handwriting?"

"It looks like it."

"Did she get mail regularly or would the arrival of a letter for her be a special occasion?"

Max was beginning to feel a tiny spark of hope. "That's why I had Luella send my letter, because Gran never gets mail and the whole town would probably know about the letter before it got into her hands."

"Who runs the post office in your town?"

"One of Carl's tenants, of course."

"The discrepancies suggest your letter was intercepted and someone replied with a fake one to encourage you to turn yourself in."

Max turned and looked at Degan incredulously. "Are *you* suggesting Carl might be alive?"

"No, he's dead. Bingham Hills has gone to too much trouble to get you back, offering such a large reward for your capture and tampering with the mail, for it to be otherwise. But my guess is that your grandmother is probably still in good health."

She was relieved to hear that, but annoyed that he'd dashed the tiny spark of hope that had barely formed that a noose wasn't waiting for her at home. But she reminded herself that he was the most skeptical man she'd ever met. She wondered if that skepticism came naturally to him or if he'd honed it for his profession.

Then she realized something alarming. "If you're right, then they know where they can find me now."

"You've already been found—by me."

And how could she forget that!? She snapped her mouth shut and didn't say another word, deciding to concentrate on a different hope she still had—of getting away from *him*.

A while later, Degan said, "You forgot to mention there would be a river in the way."

He sounded annoyed, which got a chuckle out of her. "This is one of two that run through here, both forks of Little Boulder River, but I know where to cross 'em."

Before they came to the crossing they saw a man fishing for his dinner with a pole in one hand and a rifle in the other. Degan rode toward him to show him Cade's poster. The man shook his head but stared at Max, saying, "But you look familiar." Degan rode on and paused again by a miner panning for gold, to show him the poster. Another shake of the head and they kept on going. They passed two Indian women washing clothes on the riverbank, but Degan didn't pause this time.

After they forded the river they were making good time because many beaten trails were on that side. But eventually they had to slow down because they encountered other people on the trails, mostly new miners. With so much ore found around Helena and Butte, the newcomers were persistent in trying to find a claim of their own. Most of them prospected for a few months, and if they weren't successful, they settled into working on someone else's claim or went home.

When they reached the second river, they were able to ride even faster because of the long stretch of trail near it. Nonetheless, Max was beginning to think she'd underestimated the time it was going to take to reach Butte. It was early evening already and they hadn't even reached the first lake. She wasn't going to say it, but she suspected they were going to have to sleep under the stars tonight. Actually, she was dreading having to mention it. Fancy man obviously wasn't a camping-out sort of gunfighter.

When they reached the wide stretch of flat land north of the first lake, Degan let her get back on her horse. She was too grateful to put some distance between them again to point out they still had a few more trails to follow to get back to the road to Butte. But they rode hard enough now that the big body of water came into view within minutes.

Quite a few camps were around the lake, mostly of miners, some still panning while the daylight lasted, some already cooking their dinner. They passed a family of eight, half of them children, who looked like farmers. Some loners, too, were scattered along the lakeshore. Max smiled as she took in the scene. A regular community was forming here. A lot more folks were here than she'd seen the one other time she had come down this way. The smell of food drifted on the breeze, as well as the sound of someone playing a harmonica.

Max wouldn't mind spending the night there. She just had to tell Degan they couldn't reach Butte before nightfall. They probably could if they started toward it right now, but she could lie and say it wasn't possible. It would give her a chance to wash her other set of clothes. And it would give her one more chance to escape—if Degan couldn't swim. If he couldn't, and she got far enough out into the lake where he couldn't see her anymore, she could slip out of the lake a safe distance away from where he was standing. She didn't favor taking off without her horse or her supplies, but she wasn't in a position to be picky.

But when they dismounted by the biggest group of miners, who were sitting around their campfire, she wasn't so sure she could swim herself. She'd forgotten about those damn bee stings while she was riding, but was painfully reminded of them when her shirt scraped across the welt on her arm as she dismounted. Maybe the water would soothe the stings. And maybe she was desperate enough to ignore the pain.

She was debating whether to take the chance when a man said to her, "Ain't you Max Dawson?"

He said it loud enough that more than one of the miners started toward her. She instinctively reached for the gun on her hip, but it wasn't there! But Degan's was. Suddenly he was standing between her and the miners with his gun in hand. He didn't need to say anything. Most of the men sat back down and tried to avoid his eyes. One miner handed him back the poster that had been passed among them, but he did so hesitantly.

And then one of the men volunteered, "Check further down the lake, mister. There was a suspicious fellow that showed up the other day and hasn't left yet, but I can't say I got a good look at him."

"Obliged," Degan replied, and nodded to Max to mount up again.

She did so gladly, only wincing a little as her shirt scraped against the welts again. But so much for staying in *this* area without her gun—or Degan's protection.

He led them to one of the loners sitting at a campfire. She didn't recognize the man from any of the posters, so she was surprised to hear Degan ask, "Kid Cade?"

"No," the man said warily. "And I ain't never heard—"

Degan drew his gun. The man surrendered instantly, arms raised high. "All right, all right, that's the name I go by! Just don't shoot!"

Max rolled her eyes. Did Degan have that effect on most men, or just the cowardly ones such as Cade? She dismounted when Degan did and turned to look at the lake while he tied up Kid Cade. Her plan might have worked, despite the bee stings, but not with the miners aware of who she was. They'd no doubt help Degan fish her out. She sighed.

"Are we staying the night?" she asked.

"No, and make yourself useful and put out his fire."

She moved forward to do that, but whispered at his back first, "How'd you know it was him?"

"His age, his demeanor."

"What do you mean 'his demeanor'?"

"He's not a killer. He's more a bungling thief."

"I can hear you," Cade grumbled.

Max kicked dirt on the fire while Degan saddled Cade's horse. Degan told the man, "You might actually prefer prison to this. Regular meals, a bed that doesn't get muddy when it rains. When was the last time you ate?"

"I ran out of money two days ago. The miners panning along the water were all spread out and fighting over borders like they could stake a claim on a damn lake. But when I showed up, they banded together and started posting a guard at their camps."

"Because you don't look like a miner and didn't come up here with the gear for it," Max guessed. "And you were planning to rob them, weren't you?"

"Well, yeah. But I've been trying it their way instead. Even found a few nuggets, just haven't been to town yet to sell them."

"Some prison time might give you a new perspective," Degan said.

"A new what?"

Max rolled her eyes again. "He means it might help you figure out this ain't a good way to live."

Within minutes, Degan was leading them away, holding the reins of both her horse and Kid Cade's. Maybe she needed a new perspective herself. Now that she knew Carl was dead and the posse from Bingham Hills was closing in on her. But she still glanced back at the lake wistfully.

Chapter Nineteen

"**I** CAN SEE NOW WHY they call this place the richest hill on earth," Max said a little in awe as Degan paused the horses to look down at the huge mining town. "And I thought Helena was as big as it gets up this way."

"You combed the hills north of here but you haven't been to Butte before?"

"I avoid towns, and roads." She shrugged, but he appeared to be studying Butte himself. "What's your excuse?"

"I merely avoided this one. Some miners that were temporarily in the last town I stayed at were from Butte and returned here to spread the word that I was in the area. I've already seen the results of that."

"You mean that Reed fellow and his friends were tracking you here?"

"Among other encounters. Rumors spread too damn fast in the West."

That was a definite complaint. Even if it wasn't said with inflection, it still made her chuckle. "What else do folks have to talk about? You, in particular, make juicy gossip of the exciting sort out here."

He glanced at her sideways. She stared back at him with a grin, daring him to deny it. But then Kid Cade grumbled from Degan's other side, "I'm still starving, lawman. Can we get my ass to jail so I can get fed?"

Degan hadn't tied Cade's hands behind him for the ride, but in front of him. And Degan had given him half a loaf of leftover bread as they'd left the lake. That would have filled Max up, but then she hadn't gone two days without eating. But she was in no hurry to get to the jail herself.

They had made better time getting to Butte than she'd counted on. It was only dusk, but at this time of year that was still long past a normal dinner hour, and she was starting to get hungry, too.

"I don't suppose you're gonna feed us first?" she ventured hopefully.

Degan didn't ask, *Before what?* He just said, "No," and led them into town.

She sighed. Maybe he wouldn't be able to find the sheriff's office. Maybe for once it would be tucked away on some side street instead of in plain sight on the main street. And of course Degan wouldn't unbend enough to ask for directions. Hours could be wasted in the search. She could hope. But this town actually had some signs pointing to places. She stared at one pointing the way to the train station.

She'd been managing to keep abreast of Degan even without her reins. "Didn't know the Northern Pacific train had gotten this far. Luella said Helena wasn't expecting it until next year."

"The Northern Pacific isn't here yet, it's still making its way west from Billings," Degan said. "But the Utah and Northern Railway got here late last year. It connects to the Transcontinental Railroad."

"If you knew that, why didn't you take it to head out of the territory?"

"You don't see much of the country by train, and I'm in no hurry to get where I'm going."

"Which is?"

No answer. She almost laughed. Heaven forbid they actually have a normal conversation that didn't get cut short by his silence. But this time it might be because he'd reached his destination. Max tensed. She hoped the jail here had more than one cell. She didn't fancy the idea of sharing one.

Degan had dismounted and was hauling Cade down from his horse. She got down quickly before he did the same to her. The sheriff or deputy, it was hard to tell which with his badge not showing, had been sitting on his porch, but got up as soon as it was clear Degan was there on business.

"Sheriff?" Degan asked.

"Deputy Barnes." The man tipped his hat. "If you need the sheriff—"

"I don't." Degan handed over Kid Cade and Cade's wanted poster to Barnes. Degan didn't hand over hers. But the deputy was staring at her standing there at the bottom of the steps behind Degan. "You look familiar."

Degan followed the deputy's gaze and answered before Max did. "We hear that a lot, but she's with me."

"She?" The deputy said it. Even Kid Cade said it.

Max could feel the heat racing up her cheeks. But Degan came back down the steps and nudged her back toward her horse before he told the deputy over his shoulder, "I'll come by for the reward in the morning."

Degan mounted up and waited for her to do the same. Rooted in surprise, she needed a few moments to grab her reins and get back in the saddle. Her horse followed his without any urging, already accustomed to it. But she glanced back at the jail as he led them away.

She had no idea what had just happened and couldn't figure it out no matter which way she tried. He hadn't even taken her reins this time!

She moved up abreast of him to give him a pointed look. This was the one time she ought to just keep her mouth shut, but she couldn't. She was too incredulous.

"So why ain't I back there with Cade?"

His eyes were on the street, both sides of it. Looking for Reed? she wondered. Or just trouble?

She wasn't sure he'd even heard her and was about to ask again when he answered, "I haven't decided yet what to do with you."

She waited for more, but as usual, she didn't get it. But she wasn't letting him get away with that this time. "Because you believe now that I'm innocent?"

"No, because you're a woman."

Her eyes flared. Was he kidding? He would turn down a thousand bucks because he used to be a gentleman and putting a woman in jail crossed some invisible line that he still adhered to? How did a man with principles like that ever even strap on a gun?

She shook her head. "So what are the choices you're debating?"

"They aren't up for discussion."

She was surprised he'd even said that much. But as long as he was answering questions, she tried another, "Why did you tell Deputy Barnes I'm a girl?"

"For the obvious reason."

She gritted her teeth. "Obvious to you ain't obvious to me, or I wouldn't be asking."

"Because he's going to remember why you looked familiar to him, but now he'll dismiss it as just a close resemblance to a boy wanted for murder. Or would you prefer he make the connection and come looking for you?"

"Why do you even care?" she mumbled.

"I don't. But I have enough people trying to find me. I don't want eager deputies added to the mix."

She had an immediate urge to turn around and ride in the opposite direction. She even had her reins to do so. Of course he didn't care. He did things for reasons that pertained only to him and no one else, certainly not for her.

But one thing was still keeping her next to him. "I suppose if I ride off without you, you'll still shoot me?"

"Yes."

"So you expect me to just stay with you without any explanation of why I should?"

"For the time being."

She was beginning to figure out that she had to read between the lines with him, or in this case between the words, because his "for the time being" actually said a lot. It said he *might* let her go—eventually.

That was enough to soothe her ruffled feathers, even had her asking in a more amiable tone, "So are we riding out of town now to avoid Jacob Reed?"

"No."

"Why not?"

"Because I don't sleep on the ground when there is a bed nearby."

She blinked. "That's more important than avoiding getting ambushed by five men?"

"Yes."

She started laughing. Fancy man took finicky to a whole new level, he truly did. But now he was giving her a hard look for laughing—at him. "You have something else to say?"

She grinned cheekily. "Not me!"

They had passed a couple small hotels on the way to the jail, no bigger than boardinghouses. He was taking them farther into the town, probably looking for a hotel comparable to that big one he'd stayed at in Helena.

They came to a newer-looking section of town that had brick buildings with various types of businesses. She guessed that there had been a fire here in recent years. Most towns went up fast, and fast meant building them with lumber. But it only took one fire spreading through a town to get folks to want to rebuild with more durable materials that wouldn't go up in flames before anyone could even muster an effort to put them out.

Degan found what he was looking for and headed right for it, a hotel two stories high and big enough that it probably had at least ten guest rooms available upstairs, maybe even another common bathing room. *He* would want a bath even though he'd probably had one that morning before he'd found her. But one a day was a luxury for her, so she didn't need one yet.

He paid for a room and food to be delivered to it, paid for a hotel employee to fetch some medicine for bee stings from the local doctor, even paid to have their horses stabled for the night before leading her to the stairway. She was surprised about the medicine. She thought she'd been hiding her winces pretty well, but maybe not. She was surprised by how many tasks Degan delegated to others that he could do himself. He must have had many servants at his command earlier in his life, and hotels such as this one with a large staff probably reminded him of that. Fancy man really had been a fancy man, so why would he give all that up?

They were halfway up the stairs when a man called out from below, "Are you Degan Grant?"

Degan turned fast, his hand near his gun. He was ready to kill. It was written all over him. The man who had spoken certainly got that message. Blanching, the man threw up his hands and blurted out, "I thought you should know someone was here asking for you."

"Jacob Reed?"

"No, it was a lady. She didn't give her name."

The man ran away. Whether Degan would have apologized for scaring him wasn't clear, but he relaxed now. Max was still a little wide-eyed. Good grief, for such a big man, he could move quickly.

"Another woman friend?" she asked as they continued up the stairs.

"Not likely."

"Someone looking to hire you?"

"I currently have a job, so it doesn't matter."

"Actually, you don't, you just have a favor to finish. One of your normal jobs on the side sounds interesting."

"Interesting for you?"

She grinned. "Yeah. I've only seen one gunfight. Bingham

Hills never had any. We were too far off the beaten trail to have gunfighters visit. The one fight I saw was in Colorado. It was pretty dull, though. One man got shot in the leg, the other in the shoulder. They decided not to try again and went off together to find a doctor. So I wouldn't mind seeing the famous Degan—"

"My usual jobs keep me in one place for a while. That currently isn't an option."

Her grin got wider. "But most of your fights find you, don't they?"

"Is that how you want your freedom? Through my death?"

She didn't see that coming. For the first time, she could tell he was angry. It emanated from him, his eyes gone stormy gray, his jaw squared, his mouth a hard slash. He had to be exhausted to let it show like this, and that was a good guess. He probably hadn't got much sleep the last couple of nights if he'd been searching for her in Helena. Or maybe his guard was down because he'd almost killed an innocent hotel employee.

But she wasn't about to answer him one way or the other when his death *would* actually set her free. He'd never believe her, might even get angrier if she said she didn't want her freedom that way.

Chapter Twenty

By the time they reached Degan's room, his anger was gone, completely roped back in. Max wondered *how* he could turn it off so quickly. Well, it was probably still there, he just wasn't going to let her see it anymore. The man was surprising her too much today. He needed to cut it out or explain himself better. Or was he just so used to being alone that he'd forgotten how to act when he wasn't? But she shouldn't complain. If she was going to be traveling with him, it might as well be interesting. Predictable it wouldn't be.

Max got as comfortable as she could get with what felt like four bee stings on her back and one on the back of her left arm. She draped her coat and vest over one of the two chairs and dropped her belts, socks, and boots on the floor next to it. She wished she could take off her shirt so it wouldn't keep irritating her stings, but she couldn't do that with Degan in the room.

The room's single window was open and faced the front of the hotel, though not much noise was coming through it. Max didn't bother to check if it was an avenue for escape. She would wait for a better opportunity than jumping from a second-story window and breaking her neck.

The room had a bureau and a small desk where the other dining chair was pulled up to, but no other comfortable furniture. It definitely wasn't as nicely appointed as his last hotel. The shaving stand and tub in the corner didn't even have a screen, but then maybe the room wasn't meant for two despite the big bed.

But she glanced at the double bed with a smile. She could definitely get used to Degan's being finicky if it meant she could sleep in a bed every night. But where was he going to sleep tonight?

The food arrived before Degan finished lighting the lamps in the room. Chicken pies filled the plates, which were set on the small dining table along with a basket of biscuits and a crock of butter.

Another waiter came in with a bottle of wine. "Compliments of the hotel, sir, and apologies from the cook. If the fish didn't go bad, we would have had more to offer."

Max reached for the bottle. "I haven't had wine in I can't remember how long."

Degan was removing his jacket to hang it in the wardrobe. "Are you sure you want to drink that?"

She grinned and poured some into the empty glasses on the table. "Unbend a little, fancy man. We're not going anywhere else tonight, right? No gunfights on the schedule? Just to bed?"

He didn't reply as he joined her at the table. Only after she took a sip of the wine did she realize he might have read more into her chatter than she'd meant him to, which led her to blurt out, "I didn't mean *together!*"

He rolled his eyes. He *was* unbending. He just didn't drink any of the wine. She wasn't surprised. Degan wouldn't take the chance of hampering his reflexes for any reason when those reflexes kept him alive. Which probably meant he hadn't enjoyed a good round of intoxication in years. She had. Rotgut was easy to come by, and loneliness was a good prompt to sneak around to the back of a saloon to get some. But she didn't really want the wine tonight, either. As tired as she was, it might put her to sleep before she finished eating.

"Tell me about your family."

She glanced at him, her fork pausing midway to her mouth. "Is it mandatory with you to converse while eating? Does it help your digestion or something?"

"You are the most vocal female I've ever met and now you're objecting to conversation?"

"Hell no, I was just wondering why the only time you're open to it is when you're eating something."

"Only when I have a companion sharing the meal—unlike someone who admits she talks to herself."

She laughed at his joke whether he meant it to be one or not. "Your mama teach you that simple courtesy?"

"It doesn't need to be taught when it's how you're raised. Your family didn't eat in silence, did they?"

"My brother and I were usually fighting at the table. That was a lot of chatter." She chuckled.

"So you didn't get along with your brother?"

"Oh, I did—mostly. But I was a bossy, know-it-all older sister who liked to brag about my accomplishments. He was a jealous younger sibling who didn't have any yet. I love him to pieces, but he knew how to rile my temper. I wouldn't call that an accomplishment, but he was good at it."

"Fighting at the dinner table is usually forbidden."

She laughed. "Says who? But I was talking about when Johnny and I were kids. Just typical childish antics. We wouldn't squabble now that we're older—if I were home."

She wasn't going to succumb to melancholy over how much she missed her brother, but she did fall silent. It might have showed on her face, though, because Degan stopped eating and gazed at her.

Out of the blue, he said, "I knew a pig named Max."

Her brows snapped together. "You calling me a pig?"

"A lady befriended it and named it Maximilian, though she merely called it Max. No, I wasn't calling you anything."

She continued eating. After a few mouthfuls her huff was gone. "A pet pig, huh? I shouldn't be surprised. I fancied a rooster, brought him the best seeds, didn't mind when he woke me earlier than I wanted to get up. I cheered for him every time he challenged the older rooster we had and consoled him every time he lost. But he died in one of those fights. I cried like a baby and almost shot the old bird that bested him, but Gran stopped me and she was right. It's what roosters do and there can only be one boss. But I never got close to another animal after that, except for Noble. I don't like losing anything or any-one I get attached to."

"So you grew up on a farm?"

"A chicken farm. My grandparents built their house away from town, so Carl Bingham wasn't their landlord. They asked his permission first, since he did pretty much own the whole town, and he gave it. But the town grew in our direction, so maybe Carl was sorry he let them build there."

There was another knock at the door. "That should be your medicine." Degan got up to open the door. He took the small bottle the hotel worker handed to him, then locked the door for the night. "If you've had enough to eat, we should put this lotion on your welts."

Max stood up and held out her hand. "I can do it myself."

"Actually, you can't. So come here and lie down."

She stared at the bed. She didn't move.

He added patiently, "I know you are used to fending for yourself, but this is something you need help with, since you can't reach the middle of your back. And while I'm quite capable of wrestling you to the bed—"

"I know you are! You did that this morning," Max couldn't help pointing out, then immediately regretted reminding him of that embarrassing encounter.

"As I recall, you were taking a few swings at me."

She thought she saw his lips curve upward for a moment, but she wasn't sure. "Well, you deserved it," she said, blushing.

"I imagine those bee stings are burning pretty badly by now. Is there really any reason for you not to accept my help graciously?"

Put that way, she would appear utterly childish if she refused. And the stings were bothering her. She moved to the bed, lifting the back of her shirt before she lay down on her stomach and waited tensely for his touch. She couldn't believe she was doing this. She couldn't believe *he* was doing this. Degan's being nice to her felt—wrong.

"Remove the shirt."

All sorts of things raced through her mind, but none of them convinced her to take off her shirt for him. "No," she said adamantly.

He actually sighed. "I'm not joking. Your shirt will wipe off the lotion I'm going to put on you. You can do without it for one night to give your welts a chance to heal."

Did that have to sound so logical?

"Besides, this is a hotel, not a brothel."

Did he have to bring that up again?!

"I've already seen your back, all of it, when I let that bee escape."

Max gritted her teeth. Was he going to remind that he'd already seen her breasts, too?

"It's a very nice back, but I don't have any designs on it other than to put this lotion on it."

"All right! Just put the lotion on my back." She wiggled out of the shirt without sitting up. Degan helped to get it off her wrists, tossing it aside, before he sat down on the bed next to her. She squeezed her eyes tightly closed, preparing herself for the pain that would come when he rubbed the lotion on the stings. But when he touched her, she felt a cooling, soothing sensation, nothing at all painful. She still couldn't relax though, not with him so close and his fingers lightly rubbing her back.

"Where were your parents while you were growing up?"

She felt he was trying to distract her. She didn't think it would work. Nothing would when his touch felt so good, but she answered anyway. "My ma died birthing Johnny so I don't remember her at all. Pa took us to live with his folks in Texas, so I'd have a woman raising me. He didn't stick around though. A few years later he left and was never heard from again. He'd always said the sea was calling him."

"So you don't know if he's alive or dead?"

"No, he died at sea. A package containing his belongings was delivered with a note from a friend of his, saying that he'd drowned." She tsked. "Had such a hankering to be a sailor, but he didn't know how to swim. That was a few months before

Grandpa died, which was when I took over hunting and caring for my gran."

"She's an invalid?"

"No, she's a tough old girl, but I don't want her living alone or doing more'n she has to. Now it's your turn, fancy man."

"I wish it was—but I didn't get stung."

That's not what she'd meant, but she smiled to herself at the way he avoided saying anything about himself. Luxuriating in the delicious sensations of having her pain relieved by the gentle swirling of his fingertips on her back, her neck, her arm, she was too sleepy and too content to insist he divulge something about himself. She was almost asleep when she thought she felt the brush of lips on her shoulder. . . .

Chapter Twenty-One

"THIS TALL," DEGAN TOLD the shopkeeper, holding his hand to his upper chest. "And skinny."

"It would be better if you brought the boy in so he could try the shirt on."

"No, it wouldn't. Just see if you have anything that will fit someone that size."

Degan waited while the shopkeeper disappeared into the back of his shop. A woman came in with a little girl. When the child pointed at the leg shackles Degan had draped around his neck, the woman turned around and walked back out.

Degan removed the shackles and set them on the counter. If the shopkeeper came back empty-handed, Degan could at least get a sack from him for the iron restraints. Not that he was feeling guilty for asking the sheriff for the shackles when he'd picked up his reward money for Kid Cade. He probably wouldn't need them, at least not for Max. Then again, he might. But she needed a clean shirt today so her welts wouldn't get infected, and he wasn't sure if she had one.

Degan finished his business in Butte, which included send-ing a telegram to John to inform him of the Kid's capture, and returned to the hotel. Max had still been sleeping when he'd left, and even though it was still early in the morning, she could be gone by now. He'd left it to fate, tying only one of her wrists to the headboard and, to avoid disturbing her, not as tightly as he should have.

He hadn't gotten much sleep with her next to him, not this time. Not after seeing her in those revealing clothes at the brothel and touching her breasts. Not after riding with her in his lap. And last night, hearing her sighs of pleasure as he'd rubbed the lotion on her back. He couldn't deny how much he'd enjoyed that. He'd let down his guard because she'd been wounded and vulnerable, but it couldn't happen again.

He entered the room and closed the door before he looked to see if she was still there. Although he'd left it to fate, he wasn't sure now that he wouldn't have been bothered if she was gone. But she was still there sleeping. It was incredible how soundly she slept. He'd put more lotion on her a few times last night without waking her. He'd gotten more pleasure from that than he imagined she did, but it seemed to have worked. Most of the swelling was gone from the bee stings.

He put the shackles at the bottom of his valise and draped the new shirt over a chair before he took a deep breath and moved to the side of the bed. He stared at Max for a moment, a long moment. She was still sleeping on her stomach, the sheet draped up to the middle of her back where he'd left it, but her head was turned toward him. She was so lovely. So infuriating. He wasn't surprised that she'd gotten under his skin. The sur-prise was that she'd done it so quickly.

"Wake up," he said as he untied her from the headboard. "Bathwater is being delivered for us."

"Us?" she asked sleepily.

"We'll have to share the tub."

"Share?!"

It was amazing how quickly she could jump to erroneous conclusions and get upset by them. "Separately," he clarified. "We can toss a coin to see who goes first, if you like. Or you can accept the fact that my upbringing leans toward ladies first."

She raised a brow at him. "You really did used to be a gentleman, didn't you? No, I take that back," she added, finally noticing the rope on her wrist. "*Why* did you tie me again? You said you aren't putting me in jail yet, so why would I run off?"

"Because you don't like me. Because you'd rather be on your own. Because you can't be trusted. Because turning you over to the law is still an option. Take your pick."

"All of them," she snarled, and yanked her hand back as soon as it was free. The unruly movement caused the sheet to slip, giving Degan a full view of her breasts. She mumbled, "I must've dreamed that you were being nice to me last night."

Degan smiled to himself, realizing that he could have said the same thing. But he didn't. He watched as she realized she was still wearing nothing above the waist and dragged the sheet off the bed to drape it around her like a cloak before she sat up. How disappointing, he thought. It was too bad her boldness didn't apply to her body.

But recalling her previous remark, he asked, "What would you know about gentlemen?"

"Bingham Hills wasn't a backwater. We had our share of gentlemen, mostly Southerners, though. Families who lost everything in the war and moved West to lick their wounds. What's your excuse for coming West?"

He didn't answer, which had her adding peevishly, "Oh, yeah, I forgot. Nothing personal—from you. And I don't need a bath today."

Was she going to be disagreeable all morning? "You would turn down a bath for what reason?"

"My coat protected me from the dust yesterday." But when he simply stared at her, she grouched, "Fine. I'll go first."

Taking the sheet with her, she got off the bed and stretched her limbs under it, then gave him a long look, noting that he was fully dressed, eyeing his gun belt. "Where'd you go aside from ordering bathwater? Oh, wait, did the woman come knocking at the door?" Then she chuckled. "Which one was it this time?"

It took him a moment to remember why she would ask about more than one. He'd only wondered briefly about the woman who had asked for him here at this hotel. He'd been hired by a few women before, one who just needed his protection on a journey, the other one a new widow with a brother-in-law trying to lay claim to the property her husband had left her. But as he'd told Max last night, he wasn't taking on any jobs right now. And at least he didn't think the woman asking for him had been his ex-fiancée. Even if Allison was fool enough to follow him, it was highly unlikely that she would have gotten to Butte before he did. Actually, stagecoaches traveled pretty fast . . .

That thought annoyed him so much he turned around and walked to the window before Max noticed. He heard her tsk behind him. "That's the most annoying habit I've ever come across."

"What?"

"Your not answering simple questions."

He crossed his arms and faced her again. "There was nothing simple about yours. You were attempting to provoke me. You shouldn't be so obvious about it."

She grinned. "But did it work?"

"A better question would be, why do you want to?"

"Because you aren't as coldly dispassionate as you want people to think. I've seen you slip a few times. And because I *like* conversation, which has already been established. And while I've admitted that I sometimes talk to myself, I'm telling you right now, I don't really enjoy it all that much."

"And your long-winded point is?"

"With you, it seems like I'm always talking to myself," she grouched. "It wouldn't kill you to show the man behind the gunfighter. When it's just you and me and no one else would see if you laughed or run away terrified if they saw you get angry."

"Tell me something—"

"*Not* unless you return the favor."

"Why aren't you afraid of me?"

She stared at him for a long moment before she started laughing. "That's the question you ask after what I just said to you? Really? Or is that just your way of changing the subject?"

"From the first night, you haven't been afraid. You revealed desperation once, but not fear."

She raised her brows. "Do you *want* me to be afraid of you?"

Did he? Actually, no. It had been so long since he'd butted heads with someone, he'd forgotten how aggravating, frustrating, but also, at times, quite amusing it could be. A number of times he'd wanted to laugh at something she'd said, a few times he'd been unable to resist the urge. No, he didn't mind at all that he didn't make her nervous. But it certainly confounded him that she'd never been afraid when everyone else was—at least to begin with.

"It's my business to know people. You don't fall into any of the typical categories."

She threw up her hands. "And now you're calling me strange?"

"No. Either foolhardy—or too courageous."

She chuckled. "Then you haven't given it enough thought. If you want the truth, I'm usually too angry at you to feel anything else."

He shook his head. "Fear isn't an exclusive emotion. You can be angry and too afraid to do anything about it."

"Ha! You know that ain't so in my case."

True. She'd attacked him with her fists repeatedly, kicked him several times, thrown her boots at him, lambasted him vocally, and snarled her rage and frustration at him. She wore her heart on her sleeve, expressing her emotions, but none of them had been fear. Right now her expression showed that she was delighted by his curiosity—which he should have kept to himself.

Her answer hadn't been satisfying. Payback for all the times he hadn't answered her? Or she was learning from him how to avoid a subject she didn't want to discuss.

He turned to look out the window again to let her know he was done with her avoidance antics. He heard the door to the small water closet open and close. He was surprised the room even had one, when it didn't offer a bathing room as well. The hotel was new, so it should have offered that convenience. But perhaps some of the businesses had been hit hard financially when they'd had to rebuild after the fire he'd heard about. The tub didn't even have a screen. That was going to be interesting. . . .

She stepped out of the water closet. "What's taking them so long to deliver the water you ordered?"

"My guess would be that they're heating it," he said without turning.

She came to stand next to him at the window. He glanced down at the top of her head. Her hair had felt like silk when he'd touched it last night after she fell asleep. Best not to think of that. And she was no longer draped in the sheet. She'd found the shirt she'd been wearing yesterday and put it back on. He didn't mention the clean one he had for her since she would be bathing soon.

Then she surprised him by getting back to his question. "You know, I'm not really sure why you don't frighten me, fancy man, but I'll speculate if you like. It might be because you're so handsome I don't see much beyond that. Or it could be because it became clear to me you're not a murderer. There were a few times you could've shot me but you didn't. But mostly it's because you didn't hit me when you started to that night up in the hills, which told me clearly that you won't hurt a woman. My guess would be, that's your answer."

Degan didn't hear much beyond her saying he was handsome and was surprised by how much it pleased him.

Chapter Twenty-Two

Max saw Jacob Reed riding past the hotel. He was alone, and in no hurry, perusing both sides of the street. A lot of people were out there going about their business. He appeared to be glancing at each of them, not that someone such as Degan couldn't be spotted a block away, if that was whom Reed was looking for. And from what Degan had said, she didn't doubt Reed was doing just that. But why was he alone? Or did he think Degan wouldn't remember him? That was a possibility because there wasn't anything distinctive about the man. He had shaggy brown hair and a bushy mustache and was lean, and not very tall. But his white stallion certainly was memorable.

"Your friend appears to be looking for someone."

"He's not a friend." Degan sounded distracted. Was he still dwelling on their conversation? She was still amazed they'd actually had one! Or did her mention of Reed bring back his anger from last night when she'd admitted she wouldn't mind seeing him in a gunfight? She might as well ask.

"Are you done being angry at me?"

"Do I look angry?"

She snorted. As if she didn't know that his appearance offered no clue about what he was feeling—usually. She glanced to the side to remind him, "You shouldn't have gotten so touchy over my wanting to see you in action. It's not like I'm not sure you'd win." Then she grinned. "Except maybe against me."

"Go ahead, get your gun."

"Really?"

"You know where it is."

She was far too delighted to prove her point to wonder why he'd allow it. She rushed across the room to get her gun belt and strapped it on, then dug into his valise for her Colt and slid it into the holster before turning to face him. He'd turned around but was still by the window, bright light behind him, a disadvantage for her, but she could still see his gun and that he'd moved his jacket back to clear it. She was fast, she'd had almost two years to do a lot of practicing. But she'd never been in an actual gunfight, a real showdown, and Degan looked so deadly standing there waiting, cold, utterly dispassionate.

Max actually began to sweat. This wasn't as easy as she'd figured it would be. She *wanted* to be faster than him, but she might not be. And her gun wasn't loaded, while his was. What if he fired out of habit, without intending to? She might be faster but could still end up dead.

"Okay, bad idea. Forget it." She turned around, giving him her back.

"Suit yourself."

She let out the breath she'd been holding and dropped her gun back in his valise. Damnit. Showdowns obviously took the kind of guts she only wished she had, and that hadn't even been a real one! But at least he wasn't rubbing it in, that she'd backed down. She was a woman, after all. He'd probably expected her to do just that.

The knock finally came at the door. Degan let the attendants in. There were four of them this time, so they were likely bringing all the water in one visit.

As soon as they filed back out of the room, Degan told her, "There's a new shirt for you on the chair."

She was surprised. "You bought it for me?"

"To keep your wounds clean until they heal, although most of the swelling is already gone thanks so that lotion."

And his tender ministrations, she thought. That hadn't been a dream. Degan Grant continued to surprise her. She would have thanked him for his kindness if he didn't add, "Five minutes, Max, and I'll be back in here."

He wasn't taking her clothes with him this time? "Ten," she bargained.

"Eight and not a minute more." He stepped out into the hall, closing the door behind him.

Max didn't even look toward the window. She still didn't fancy breaking her neck going out one. But eight minutes wasn't long for a bath, and she didn't doubt Degan was waiting right outside the door. She took off her clothes fast and stepped into the tub. This hotel didn't have fancy creamy soap, but the soap bars it provided were shaped like flowers and sweet smelling, so Max didn't break out her stash of the other soap. She quickly washed from top to bottom.

Stepping out of the tub, she frowned when she realized she was going to have to put on the same pants she'd worn yesterday, but at least she had a clean shirt thanks to Degan. When she donned it, she found that it fit too snugly, which wouldn't do at all. No, it would have to do. She'd just fasten her vest today instead of leaving it open as she usually did.

She needed more clothes, obviously, or less time in hotels and more time in a camp by a lake or river so she could wash what she had. Traveling with someone who would be doing all the leading wasn't going to give her time for the things she needed to do. But she couldn't afford more clothes. Anytime she got money in her trades, she spent it on more ammunition. Besides, she wouldn't be making any money while she was with Degan because he wouldn't let her hunt.

She was still drying her hair when Degan reentered the room and headed straight for the tub. He hadn't relocked the door. She thought that was curious until she saw him place his gun on the towel stand within reach of the tub. So she was back to guessing if he would really shoot her if she bolted while he was buck naked. He should have locked the door instead of tempting her like this!

She watched him as he undressed until he got to his pants. Her eyes widened when she realized he was going to drop them knowing full well she was still looking at him.

She turned away from him. "I should wait in the hall like you did."

"No."

"This isn't appropriate."

"Nothing about you is appropriate. Sit down. Turn around. Pretend I'm not naked."

Her cheeks lit up. *Was* he naked now? Or was he at least sitting in the tub so she could look his way again? She didn't chance it. Instinctively, she knew the sight of him would be branded in her mind forever. She'd seen naked men before, such as the miners she'd encountered at rivers or lakes who had thought nothing about dropping their clothes and walking into the water with other men around. Of course they hadn't realized she was a female. She hadn't been embarrassed then. But she wasn't even looking at Degan now and her cheeks were hot with a blush. It just wasn't the same when it was a man this handsome—when she *wanted* to look!

She looked everywhere but toward his corner, yet she was so flustered that he was undressing behind her that she inadvertently turned and caught a glimpse of him as he added his pants to the pile of clothes behind him. She lost her breath. The sight of his broad, muscular back and firm thighs, and such tight buttocks, brought a wave of heat to her body. For a heartbeat she actually started to put her hand out, wanting to touch him, but she squeezed her eyes shut and turned away. She did *not* just see that big, beautiful body of his naked. She had to repeat that to herself several times. But she didn't let out her breath until she heard the water splash, telling her the tub was hiding at least some of him now.

She still wouldn't look again. But taking deep breaths as she kept her eyes on the other side of the room eventually brought back a semblance of calm. He wouldn't need to shave when he was done bathing. Apparently, he'd done that before he went out while she'd been asleep. She felt slightly relieved, knowing that he'd get dressed as soon as he got out of the tub and not stand there half-naked while he shaved.

"Are we going to hole up here till Jacob Reed leaves town? Or long enough for me to wash my clothes?"

"No."

"But he's out there looking for you right now. You did notice that, right?"

"Yes."

"If he's got any sense a'tall, he'll check the hotels for you next."

"I don't sign registers. And I've already warned the staff to forget they saw me."

"It's big news that you're in town. Do you really think they won't brag that you're staying at their hotel?"

"People don't usually cross me."

She could believe that. Chattering was helping her ignore that he was naked, so she kept it up. "I still need a day to wash my clothes. What's the point of bathing if I have to wear dirty clothes? Any body of water will do if we're not staying here."

"You can turn around now, Max."

She glanced over her shoulder cautiously, then turned. His wet hair was slicked back, but he was dressed again, and his gun was back on his hip where it usually was. It occurred to her that he needed to have his clothes washed, too. His valise might be a nice size, but she'd looked inside it and knew it wasn't stuffed to the brim with clothes.

His gray eyes swept over her before he said, "We need to find a dress for you that you can wear before we enter a town."

She snorted. "I don't think so. I can't wear one on the trail, so what's the point?"

"I said before we enter a town."

She shook her head at him. "Too much trouble, and you still didn't say why."

"To keep you from getting arrested or shot by some bounty hunter."

"I can keep my head down like I always do. No one's gonna recognize me."

"This is my decision, not yours."

She gave him a mulish look. "It ain't your decision if I won't put it on."

"I might find it interesting to do it for you."

She gasped. "You wouldn't!"

"You were hoping things would get interesting, or is my getting shot the only thing you find interesting?"

He *would* dress her. Because he was still mad at her for implying last night that she'd like to see him in action. Or maybe not. Had that been humor in his tone?

He put his hat on. "Let's go."

She gritted her teeth over those same two annoying words of his. "Can you at least add a little something to that? Like, 'Let's go to the train station'? Or, 'Let's go back to Helena'? Or, 'Let's go have breakfast'? Anything that might indicate where we're going?"

"Does it really matter where we're going?"

She raised her chin. "It does when I'm hungry."

"Do you really think I won't feed you?"

That tiny note of humor was there again, just the slightest indication in his tone, and this time she was sure. She gave up, well aware that he'd still managed not to say where they were going.

Chapter Twenty-Three

"THERE ARE A NUMBER of towns between here and Billings. We can pause long enough in one to find a laundress."

Max wasn't surprised to hear Degan finally volunteer that information. They were eating, which was the one time he didn't mind talking.

The hotel restaurant was a little more than half-filled with other guests or townsfolk. Only two tables had emptied when Degan entered the room. Max was delighted to find a variety of choices for the morning meal. She would have liked to try one of everything if she thought she could eat it all. She settled on sausage, eggs, and half a steak.

"Why Billings?" she asked.

"We'll be catching the train there."

"I thought you didn't like riding them."

"I don't when I'm not on a time schedule. Right now there's someplace I need to go, and the Northern Pacific could get robbed while we're on it. It will save me having to search all over Dakota for where Nolan is holed up."

It was beginning to sound as if she was going to be in his company for a long time. It could take more than a week just to get to Billings. But after he got Nolan, if he got Nolan, he'd have arrested two outlaws and would have to decide if she was going to be the third. So she should probably be glad they were going on a long trip. Lots more chances for her to slip away.

"Oh, hell no," Degan suddenly snarled under his breath.

Max was startled to hear some real anger in his voice, even if his expression didn't show a bit of it. At least his ire wasn't directed at her this time. She glanced over her shoulder to see what he was looking at. *Her* again? The pretty, dark-haired woman was dressed just as fancy as she'd been in Helena. But today her dress, jacket, and hat were three different shades of blue. Her adorable little hat had no useful brim that would shade her from the sun. It was purely decorative. Max didn't doubt that every woman in the dining room envied the young woman and wished she could wear something that frivolous and pretty. Max sighed to herself.

The young woman approached their table and sat down. Getting a better look at her, Max realized she wasn't just pretty, she was beautiful. And utterly brazen to sit down at their table without an invitation.

"How far are you going to make me chase you, Degan?" she asked petulantly.

"I'm not making you do anything, Allison. And I warned you, I have nothing to say to you."

"I don't believe you."

"I don't care."

He stood up and nodded at Max to do the same. She gave her plate, only half-empty, a wistful glance, but got up quickly before he yanked her up.

"Degan, wait," Allison said in frustrated tones as he started out of the room. "Your father—"

"Is alive. I've already confirmed it. So whatever game you're playing ends here."

He didn't even stop as he said that, but the woman persisted. "A man doesn't have to be dead not to be who he was. He—"

Max couldn't hear the rest of what she was saying as they left the hotel. But the woman wasn't giving up. She followed him outside and yelled, "Degan Grant, come back here!"

He continued walking to the stable on the corner of the next block, while Max was trying to look behind them. Fancy lady looked fit to be tied. Max wasn't surprised. The lady was too pretty to be used to being ignored.

"Degan, stop!" she yelled again. "You *have* to hear me out!"

Max rolled her eyes. "If no one else knew you were in town, they all do now. Are you really going to let her continue shouting your name like that?"

He didn't reply, but the damage was already done. Max saw Jacob Reed step off the boardwalk up the street and start walking down the middle of the street toward Degan. He was still alone—or was he? He'd had four men with him when they'd seen him on the road to Butte yesterday. Max glanced around quickly but didn't see any of his friends now. Then she did. Reed must have found out where Degan was staying and set his men up for this ambush ahead of time. She *knew* those hotel employees wouldn't be able to keep their mouths shut about such an infamous gunfighter staying in their hotel.

"There's a man on the roof up ahead with a rifle pointed at you," she warned Degan. "This is an ambush."

"I know. I've already spotted two others."

"But that one is out of your range, while you're not out of his."

"It might not matter if I kill Jacob first. This is his fight, not theirs."

This really wasn't the time for him to sound so damn calm or to make guesses. And where was the fourth man? The street was already starting to clear. Two men walking toward each other like this was a dead giveaway of what was about to happen. And "might not" didn't work for her.

"Don't you think it would be better to take cover?"

"You are. Get back in the hotel and do it fast."

She didn't need to be told twice and started running to the hotel. Fancy lady wasn't doing the same. She was *still* following Degan, holding her skirt up daintily just a few inches off the ground, keeping her eyes down to make sure she didn't step in manure. So she probably didn't know what was happening and might not guess until the first shots were fired.

"There's about to be gunfire," Max warned as she passed her.

Max didn't wait to see if the woman turned around. And she didn't enter the hotel to hide. She went straight to the desk in the lobby and told the man there, "Give me any weapons you've got stashed."

"We don't—"

"What you keep for protection. Lie to me and Mr. Grant will be in here shooting up the place in a few minutes."

As threats went, that was a pretty good one. The man bent down and came up with a rifle in his hands. She took it and hid it under her coat, then went back outside to make her way quickly down the boardwalk.

As she passed Degan and Reed, who were within talking distance of each other now, she heard Degan saying, "I didn't kill you last time because you were grieving the loss of your brother. You've had enough time to deal with that grief."

Jacob laughed. "Pretty confident for a man about to die, Grant."

Max kept on going, didn't stop until she was within range of two of Reed's friends, who were squatting on the roofs of two buildings across the street. She knew that as soon as Degan drew his gun, he was going to get riddled with rifle shot. She wasn't going to wait for him to die to get a shot off. But she had begun to sweat. This wasn't like shooting at an animal for dinner. Animals didn't shoot back! But she had no choice. She didn't agree with Degan's thinking that the riflemen on the roof "might not" matter. There was no time to have qualms about shooting the men, but still she was too late.

Shots were fired in the street behind her. With her eyes on one of the men stationed on the roof, she didn't dare look back to see who had won the gunfight. She just fired her weapon the moment Reed's friend leaned up to take aim. She hit his rifle, breaking it and probably taking off a few of his fingers. He dropped out of sight, but she heard him screaming. She aimed at the second man, but he'd already gotten off one shot and was now hiding behind a chimney. She had to wait for him to show himself again.

More shots came from behind her, so she figured Degan must not be dead yet—unless some of the local deputies had gotten involved. She still didn't want to look, didn't know what she'd feel if Degan was dead. Actually, she wouldn't like it. Why else would she still be there trying to help him instead of using this perfect opportunity to escape?

The man behind the chimney left his cover and ran to the edge of the flat roof. Max fired before he dropped to his knee to

take up that new position. Her bullet swung him around and
he lost his balance. She winced as he fell off the roof. He tried
to get up but couldn't manage it, probably having broken a few
bones in the fall.

She steeled herself to look back where the gunfight had
taken place, then let out her breath. Degan wasn't there now.
Jacob Reed was though, lying prone in the dirt. Even though no
one was shooting at the moment, no one was approaching him
yet to see if he was still alive. But Deputy Barnes and another
man were running toward her from the other end of town.

Gun drawn, out of breath, Barnes paused to ask her, "What
happened here?"

She nodded toward Reed. "He and his friends tried to ambush Marshal Grant. There's still two of them unaccounted for."

Just as she said it, a body hit the roof of the porch above
their heads, then rolled off it to the street in front of them. The
man had no bullet wounds, though his nose looked busted up
pretty bad.

"And that just leaves one unaccounted for unless Grant
already took care of him, too," she added, keeping a grin to
herself.

At least she knew where Degan was now. The lawmen
started checking the bodies. Max ran across the street to see if
she could spot the last man on the roofs of the buildings on the
side of the street where she'd been standing, but a movement by
the stable caught her eye first. That would be a good place for
him to hide or grab a horse to flee in case none of his friends
had survived. A few hay bales were on one side of the big stable
doors, and an unhitched wagon on the other side. Then a man
peeked up over the rim of the wagon bed and quickly ducked
down again.

With the stable located on the corner of an intersection, Max worked her way around the corner to the stable's entrance on the other street so she could sneak up behind the unhitched wagon. She already had her rifle aimed as she approached it. She was still sweating due to her darn coat and the darn July weather. She was *not* nervous.

"Get up, mister. Toss your rifle over the side and do it real slow. A rifle shot at this range might tear a hole in you big enough to put my fist through. I'd rather not, but I will if you make any sudden moves."

"Don't shoot!"

He tossed his rifle out of the wagon and then a Colt, before he stood up. Max went around to the front of the wagon to kick his rifle farther away and holstered the Colt. Glancing up at the man, she could see now that he was just a kid, not even as old as she was, and he looked terrified.

"Are you one of Jacob Reed's friends?" she asked as he crawled out of the wagon bed. "Or were you just hiding from the gunfire?"

"Jacob saved my life. I owed him."

She hadn't meant to hand him an excuse like that, but he was too dumb to take it. She tsked. "You should've found another way to repay him a favor, one that didn't include murder. You do know that's what this was, right? What any ambush is? It doesn't get more cowardly than this."

"I think he gets the idea," Degan said from behind her as he lifted the rifle from her hands.

Max swung around. One of the deputies was with Degan and led the kid away.

Degan didn't look as if he'd been in a gunfight, or a fistfight on top of a roof, for that matter. Not a hair on his head was out of place. Still, he had a tenseness about him, as if he hadn't wound down from the fight yet. Neither had she, though her nervousness appeared to be gone, replaced by annoyance.

"Really? The first thing you do is disarm me? No thank-you for saving your life?"

"I reap what I sow, so all consequences are mine to bear. This fight had nothing to do with you. *You* were supposed to be safely inside the hotel."

"Yeah, but something got proved here in case you didn't notice," she shot back.

"That you don't know how to listen?"

That had her gritting her teeth, but she was too curious not to ask, "So is Reed going to heal up and come after you again or did you kill him?"

"A doctor is with him now, but I warned him I would kill him next time. Let's go."

"Famous last words," she mumbled. "I'll remember them for your tombstone."

Chapter Twenty-Four

Max thought it had to be the hottest day of the year. There wasn't even a whisper of a breeze or a speck of a cloud in the bright blue sky. If she were alone, she would have found some shade near a lake or a stream and just waited out the heat before moving on. She didn't think Degan would appreciate that suggestion.

She'd already taken off her coat and laid it on the back of her horse and rolled up her sleeves. That hadn't helped. Now she slipped off her vest and hooked it over the pommel. This was no time to worry about how noticeable her breasts were in the snug new shirt. She even unfastened a few buttons on it. Nothing helped. It felt as if steam were rising from the road, it was so hot and muggy.

Twice they had to move off the road to let a stagecoach pass. If Degan was in such a hurry to get to the train in Billings, he had to realize that a stagecoach could get them there more quickly. The drivers didn't pace their horses, they just traded them out at each stop. He could stable their own horses and pick them up on the return trip. That was if he was coming back this way. Maybe he wasn't. He didn't exactly share his plans.

Degan had to be bothered by the heat, too, because he had removed his jacket and silk vest and rolled up his sleeves. Even without all his formal attire he still looked dangerous. It wasn't his fancy clothes that signaled to people that he was deadly. Clearly, his demeanor told them that he was a man to be avoided, a man to be reckoned with—a man to run from. And she'd saved his life this morning. She must have had a spell of insanity. It had been the worst idea she'd ever had. And she still hadn't received a thank-you.

She was riding with the confiscated Colt on her right hip. He had to have seen it as soon as she'd taken off her coat. There was no way he couldn't have. So he was obviously going to let her keep it. Was this his way of thanking her for helping him in Butte? Or was it because he knew she wouldn't shoot him any more than he would shoot her? She'd rather have her own gun back, but asking for it again might goad him into taking away the one she did have, so she wasn't going to put that to the test.

He hadn't said a word to her since they'd left Butte. Silence, especially unnecessary silence, grated on her nerves something fierce.

Finally she said, "I usually travel through woods and hills. At least there's shade under the trees."

"I prefer roads."

"I don't usually travel when it's this hot, either. Look at the sky, there's not a cloud in sight, which means there will be plenty of moonlight tonight to ride by. I usually hole up on hot days like—"

"We're not. We'll sleep when everyone else sleeps so we don't get surprised."

She snorted. "Everyone else is probably sensible like me and gets out of the heat on days like this."

An hour later she tried again. "We need some water. I'm going to faint if I can't douse myself soon."

"We'll reach the Jefferson River by tonight."

"Not soon enough. I came this way when I was heading north. There's a small lake about a mile south of the road up ahead. You'd pass right by it if you didn't know it was there."

He didn't answer immediately but finally said, "Lead the way."

She did. Concessions from him were too few for her not to jump on one when he made it. He didn't like doing things any way but his way. Well, she preferred to get her own way, too, if she cared to admit it.

According to her belly, it was two hours past lunchtime when she found the deer trail to the lake. White-barked aspens and a few ponderosa pines grew close to the shore with wildflowers scattered among them, but she didn't immediately notice how pretty a spot it was because her eyes were focused on the deep blue water. As soon as they got there, she headed for the lake, dropping her belts and hat on the way and only pausing long enough to take off her boots before she walked right into the water, socks and all. The water wasn't icy cold, but was definitely cool, and exactly what she needed. She leaned back and floated, sighing with pleasure.

Degan didn't do the same, although she knew he had to want to. But cooling off in a lake on a hot summer day would be relaxing his guard too much and heaven forbid he do something like that. He merely led the horses to the water and splashed some on his face and head. Water dripped down his shirt, drawing her attention to where the wet fine cotton material clung to his muscular chest. She quickly raised her eyes to his face.

"Your clothes will dry in no time. Come on in."

He stared at her for a long moment before he said, "Unlike you, I prefer to remove my clothes before swimming."

"Well, don't do *that*!"

He continued to gaze at her but didn't move. She began to picture him undressing as he'd done that morning. Her cheeks started to heat up. It almost felt as if steam were rising around her again, even though the water was perfectly cool. She ducked her head under the water to get the image of his naked body out of her mind.

She wondered if Degan ever did anything spontaneously, anything fun that made him laugh. Who was she kidding? Of course he didn't.

When she came up, she saw that he'd turned away and was opening his food sack. "Toss me my soap, will you? There's a bar in my bags. My clothes, too, for that matter. Now's as good a time as any—"

"No, that can wait until tonight when you'll have time to dry them. Come eat. We're not staying here longer than we have to."

She didn't budge. It felt too good right where she was. And from this distance it let her see all of Degan, without his realizing she was looking at things other than his face.

"Get out of the water, Max."

"No."

"Max."

"No!"

He dropped the food sack on the ground and started un-buttoning his shirt. He would, too. Get completely naked. But he wouldn't come in the water to enjoy himself for a bit, he'd come in just to haul her out.

"You win, fancy man." She laughed and walked out of the water.

She went to her horse and stepped around it before she re-moved her soaked shirt and opened her saddlebag to get a dry one. A dry dirty one. She made a face and pulled out Luella's chemise instead and slipped it on. It wasn't as dainty and fine as hers was and it wasn't as thin, either, so it could probably with-stand a hot day like this.

"I'll be much cooler if you stay off the roads so I can ride in this."

He came around her horse to see what she was talking about. "Like hell you will. You might be cooler, but the sight of you is going to heat the blood of any man who sees you, and I'm not in the mood to do any more shooting today."

She blushed. He didn't sound or look angry, but a definite heat was in his eyes as he stared at her breasts, which were clearly defined by the chemise. Had he been referring to him-self? Was *his* blood already heated? Hers was starting to feel that way.

It was fast, so fast, his drawing her up against him, her feet leaving the ground, her arms wrapping tightly around his neck, his mouth covering hers. She'd never felt such a wild burst of sensations before. Billy Johnston's kisses had been sweet and fun, but full of uncertainty because she made him so nervous. But this was raw passion. This was Degan, a man who probably didn't even know how to be nervous. This was more exciting than she could ever have imagined. The heat, the frayed tempers, whatever had made him kiss her, she didn't want it to stop. He tasted too good and felt even better. He deepened the kiss, thrusting his tongue into her mouth with a sensual urgency that made something unfurl deep inside her, something so incredibly nice that she groaned. But she wished she hadn't! Whether it was the noise she'd made or something else, he put his hands on her waist and set her on the ground at arm's length. Their eyes locked.

"That's what can happen on a hot day" was all he said before he walked away.

Max was dazed for a moment. *Why* did he stop kissing her? Some damn gentleman's code of honor because she was still his prisoner? If so, then he shouldn't have kissed her at all! Her disappointment was still stronger than her embarrassment. And she hadn't even won the argument about what she was going to wear.

But her disappointment had her yell at his back, "This has to be the hottest day this territory has *ever* had!"

"That's because there's no breeze today."

"I don't care what's causing it. We should stay right here where there's shade and water to cool off in until the worst is over."

"No." He pulled one of his own shirts out of his valise and tossed it at her. "Put that on."

She threw it right back at him. "I'd rather wear my wet one. It might keep me cool for about ten damn minutes, before it starts steaming!"

She almost added *too*. But he probably figured that out because he asked, "Why are you angry?"

Oh, God, she didn't know! It couldn't be because he'd

abruptly ended a kiss that shouldn't have happened. It had to be the heat—and his stubbornness. Why did he have to be so dead set in his ways? She was only talking about a brief delay in his journey. But she knew why. The sooner he completed his favor for Marshal Hayes, the sooner he'd be rid of her.

She took a deep, steadying breath before she said, "I'm not. And you don't need to apologize for what just happened."

His lips actually curved a tiny bit as he came back over to her. "I wasn't going to." He held out his shirt. When she still didn't take it, he warned, "You'll get sunburned if you just wear that camisole. Do you want me to rub lotion on you again?"

"No, I—well, that was very—never mind." She was sure that he was teasing her now.

"Then put this on, or I will assist you in putting it on." He added softly, "I really don't mind assisting you."

She took the shirt before he proved it, but as soon as she got her arms into it, he proved it anyway, reaching for the buttons. She didn't stop him. He was confusing her more and more. Suddenly she felt shy with him this close to her. Was he going to kiss her again? Maybe he'd only stopped because he was worried about her skin getting burned.

This attraction she was feeling to him was getting a little too strong. She should be thinking about escaping, not kissing him! Yet she stood there hopeful, letting him button her shirt, feeling all soft inside that he would even want to. She actually liked having him this close and doing something sweet for her. She couldn't deny it, even if this caring side of him puzzled her.

It was taking him three times longer than it would take her to fasten those buttons, but she didn't make a move to take over and do it herself. Was he staring at her breasts or at the buttons he was slowly fastening near them? She lost her breath when she felt the back of his knuckles brush against her skin. A slip of his hand? But it felt so nice! But then his eyes moved up to hers and stayed there. To judge her reaction? She did blush. She couldn't help it.

He left the last two buttons by her neck unfastened, but he turned the collar up, his fingers brushing against her skin again, and said, "That's so your neck doesn't get burned."

Then he walked away, leaving her wondering about the tingling sensations running down her back. But he started doing what she'd done earlier, walking toward the lake, except he was stripping off his clothes. He only kept his gun with him, holding it above the water while he soaked the rest of himself. Fascinated, Max couldn't take her eyes off him this time until he left the water and she saw how well built he really was. Then she turned away, blushing again.

Chapter Twenty-Five

FOR A CHANGE, THERE was no conversation with their quick midday meal. Max didn't try to change that because she was too busy with her own thoughts and castigating herself for falling under a complacent spell. She tried to blame it on the lake. It was so pleasant here and she wished they could stay longer. But it was all Degan. The man fascinated her. He made her feel too many things she shouldn't be feeling. He made her get all girlie and bashful and—hot. But she had to stop thinking about how handsome he was and how much she'd enjoyed kissing him. And he'd been so nice, giving her one of his fancy shirts so she wouldn't get sunburned.

That was another problem. She had to stop thinking that he was *nice* and remind herself more often that he was her captor, that he might still turn her over to the authorities. As much as she was coming to like him, she couldn't completely trust him.

A breeze finally showed up when they got back on the road. It wasn't a cool one though. It floated in as if an oven door had just been opened. It made the mugginess worse for a short while, but finally it seemed to break the heat wave, blowing off the worst of it.

When it stopped feeling as if she were sucking in heat with every breath, Max got around to mentioning, "You've been glancing behind us an awful lot today. Do you hear something I don't?"

"No."

"But you took care of Reed, or are there more men like him actively looking for you?"

"Probably every fast gun in the country."

She had a feeling that was his way of making a joke even though no smile came with it. "I don't mean ones that want to outdraw you so they can crow about it. I meant actual enemies that want to kill you any way they can."

"You can't do what I do and not make enemies. That's one reason I keep moving forward, never back."

"Aren't you backtracking right now?"

"How would you know that?"

She laughed. "Told you, fancy man, you're big news. Even I heard you were in the territory east of here—before you decided to be a thorn in my ass. And you know about the rivers up ahead, so you've crossed them at least once."

"I did a job in Nashart."

Her eyes widened. Had he really just volunteered something about himself when he wasn't eating? "Will we be stopping there?"

"No, the train won't be there long. Maybe on the way back."

Back? Back to what? Had he already decided what to do with her? Back to a jail for her, or back this way so he could capture another outlaw, which would make three? That was if he captured Willie Nolan in Dakota, who would be number two.

Thoughts like that really put a damper on her good mood, so she said no more for the rest of the afternoon. She'd already spotted several rabbits, a possum, and just barely made out the antlers of a buck sleeping in the brush, animals she wouldn't normally have hesitated to kill for her dinner. She was pretty sure they wouldn't be reaching the next town today, so they'd need to make camp.

Before it got dark, she suggested, "If you'll hand me my rifle—loaded—I can get us some fresh meat for dinner before it gets too dark."

He was back to not answering her. He must have more food in that sack of his. Why couldn't he just say so? But ten minutes later without warning he drew his weapon and fired it. Max had her hands full trying to calm Noble, who danced around in a full circle before she could settle him down.

Degan had already dismounted and left the road to fetch the rabbit he'd just shot. He came back and tied it to the back of his saddle, then mounted again, all without a word.

Max laughed. "Bet you've never skinned one."

"You'd win that bet. I'll leave the skinning to the experienced hunter."

He probably didn't realize he was giving her a compliment, but she took it as one. She was back to grinning to herself; her good mood returned. But he continued to glance over his shoulder every so often, and he still hadn't explained to her satisfaction why he was being unusually wary today.

She finally asked again, "Who are you expecting to ride up on us?"

"Someone took a potshot at me in Helena. If it had been

Reed, there would have been a lot more bullets. It was more like a warning shot."

"And you think whoever did it just wanted to run you out of town so they could kill you without witnesses?"

"That's one possibility."

"Or it could have just been a stray bullet."

"That's another possibility."

But he obviously leaned toward caution and being prepared for the worst, which would limit surprises. But she wondered if he'd even be worried about it if he were alone or if her presence made him extracautious. Then he stopped his horse and turned it around. Max pulled up and glanced at him.

"Now what?"

"I thought you might want to take a moment to watch the sunset. Women seem to like doing things like that."

Oh my God, he was being nice again! She hadn't even realized the sky behind them was filling with orange and pink already. It was pretty, but she wondered how he knew women might appreciate such a lovely view—and why he would stop so she could enjoy it.

They didn't pause long, but she still felt warmed by the gesture. The man continued to amaze her with facets one wouldn't expect to find in a hardened gunfighter. It had to be a throwback to the way he was raised, before he took up a gun. She wished she could have met him then. A debonair gentleman? Maybe carefree? Maybe even charming? No, not Degan. She simply couldn't imagine it.

It was dusk before they crossed the first of the three forked rivers, and full dark when they crossed the second one, where they made camp close to the riverbank. A few trees were in this area and a lot of scrub grass, some of it butting up to the water, but they found a patch of bare ground. Max got a fire going while Degan unsaddled and rubbed down the horses.

She paused to watch Degan as he worked. The muscles in his back and shoulders rippled through the damp, thin fabric of his white shirt as he brushed the horses. When he bent down to check one of the palomino's hooves, her gaze moved down to his tight butt and muscular thighs. When it dawned on her that she was watching him instead of getting anything done, she berated herself. She had to stop thinking about how attractive he was. She had to stop liking him! Nothing had changed. She was still his prisoner and she had to keep that firmly in her mind and stop getting so easily distracted by him.

She got what she needed out of her saddlebags: her pan, the iron griddle with short legs, her small pouches of herbs, which she'd been replenishing anytime she found them growing wild. She found a long stick for roasting the rabbit over the fire and a couple of large rocks on which she could brace it. Then she skinned and gutted the rabbit and rubbed it with herbs before setting it over the fire. She watched it for a few minutes to make sure the flames flaring up from the dripping juices wouldn't burn it.

She washed her hands in the river before starting the next chore, washing her clothes. Degan had sat down by the fire, leaning back against his saddle.

"What else is in your sack?" she asked.

"Bread, cheese, condiments, sandwiches, fruit. There might even be something for dessert."

She stared at him. "So we didn't need fresh meat?"

He shrugged. "Not really—but your rabbit smells good."

She looked inside his sack, then shook her head. "If you're going to raid kitchens before leaving towns, you should get yourself a picnic basket to keep the food separated, so it doesn't get all mashed together." Picturing this notorious gunfighter riding through a town with a picnic basket made her laugh. "Never mind. That would *so* tarnish your reputation."

He didn't see the humor in that. "And I prefer to eat at a table."

Yes, of course he did, just as he preferred to sleep in a bed. But they were probably a good thirty miles from the next town, so he was flat out of luck in that regard tonight.

The air had cooled after the sun had set, and she knew from experience that the temperature would dip further during the night, but it was still warm enough to wash in her usual fashion. She could sleep in the shirt Degan had loaned her.

She draped the first set of clothes she washed over a few bushes to dry before she glanced back at Degan and offered, "I can wash yours while I'm at it."

"We'll reach Bozeman tomorrow. I can wait."

He wasn't watching what she was doing, was just staring at the fire. She glanced back at the slow-moving water, which looked so inviting. She'd feel so much better if she could wash her hair and get the dust and sweat off her body. She went behind the horses to remove most of her clothes, leaving on just her chemise and bloomers, then shook Degan's shirt and left it to air out on the nearest bush. Stuffing the bar of soap down the front of her chemise, she went into the water with the pouch of creamy stuff and dunked her head in before she lathered her face and head, then tossed the little pouch back on the shore to scrub down with the bar of soap.

"It's not a good idea to sleep in wet clothes," Degan said behind her.

So he had been watching her after all.

She replied without looking back at him, "I'm going to put your shirt back on as soon as I'm done. I'm not trying to annoy you, you know. I usually bathe in more clothes than this."

"There's one more clean shirt in my valise that you can use to sleep in."

"I will, thanks."

When she finished washing herself, she left the water and grabbed his valise, taking it with her behind the horses to change. When she opened the valise, she saw the Colt. She picked up the kid's gun and opened the chamber to take out the bullets and put them in her Colt so she could swap the two weapons. But there were no bullets in the kid's gun. She almost laughed. Degan must have removed them at the lake when she was in the water and not watching him. So much for thinking he was starting to trust her.

She had to dig deep into the valise to find his last clean shirt. Her fingers touched more metal, and she was curious enough to pull the object out to see what it was. She definitely wasn't expecting to see two iron rings connected to a short, rusty chain.

She lifted the shackles and stepped around her horse to demand, "What the *hell* is this?"

Chapter Twenty-Six

M AX WAS FURIOUS THAT Degan would consider shackling
her now, after she'd helped him this morning in Butte. But obviously he could. Obviously, he had to protect his interests. She
was like money in the bank to him that he didn't want to get
robbed of by her trotting off without him while he slept.

She threw the shackles at him when he didn't answer her
immediately. And missed hitting him, damnit. She stepped
back between the horses to change. It took her a moment to
unclench her fists.

Then she heard, "I'm not going to use them—if I don't
have to."

"But you thought you would?" she snarled over the back of
her horse.

"I thought I would."

The day *had* been eventful enough to make him change his
mind about shackling her. She still wasn't mollified, not even
close.

Wearing just her boots, with her socks pulled up several

inches above them, Degan's large, white shirt that fell to her knees, her gun belt strapped low over it, and her vest, she knew she looked ridiculous. But no one was there to see her except Degan, and he didn't count. So why did she suddenly wish that she'd left home with at least one pretty nightgown? She'd never thought of that before, and for good reason. Alone on the trail, she had to be prepared to leave at a moment's notice, not bed down as if she were safe at home.

She was still bristling when she came back to the fire. She spread out her horse blanket to sit on and draped her coat over her legs so she could sit cross-legged as she finished preparing the meal without being accused of tempting Degan again. She'd even buttoned his shirt up to her neck. She'd had to roll up the sleeves. Even with the cuffs buttoned, they hung down over her hands. She could feel his eyes on her, though, as if he were waiting for her to continue railing at him. Instead, she pretended he wasn't there.

She moved the rabbit away from the fire so it would cool, then rummaged in Degan's food sack and took out a few things, including a couple of peaches. She sliced the bread in her hands, accustomed to working without a cutting board. She could tote only so much around with her, and a cutting board was just too bulky. She laid a few pieces in the pan to warm and crumbled a little cheese on top of them.

She used to have a tin plate to eat from, but these days she usually ate right out of the pan. Like her fishing net, her plate got left behind one night when the sound of a twig's breaking had made her pack up and leave fast. Not used to being alone and camping outdoors, she had been jittery for the longest time. She'd had to force herself to overcome those fears by taking reasonable precautions and adopting a come-what-may

attitude, but she hadn't counted on someone like Degan coming her way, thwarting her at every turn, too perceptive to fall
for her tricks. Yet the snap of a twig wouldn't bother her in
the least with him around. She felt protected, completely protected, when she was with him.

Now *that* was an odd thought, considering that he'd kissed
her and she'd liked it. She wasn't going to let that happen again.
Like hell she would. Kissing a man who had tied her up, who
would have *chained* her up? He was lucky she didn't throw her
knife straight at his heart.

"Stop pouting."

She tossed the knife toward him. "You better take that back
before I find another use for it."

He raised a brow. "Shall I take back the gun you're wearing, too?"

She snorted. "When you already removed the bullets? You
might as well."

He shrugged. "I believe you said that you wanted the
weight of the gun for balance. And I'm well aware that a gun,
with or without bullets, can be a deterrent that you might need
on this trip—just not against me."

She did recall telling him that she missed the weight of the
gun. And he'd glanced behind them enough times today for
her to know he was expecting trouble. He even made it sound
as if she'd be doing *him* a favor by continuing to wear the gun,
as long as it contained no bullets. Because he didn't trust her.
Because she was, after all, his prisoner.

He didn't reach for the knife she'd tossed to him. But he did
pick up the leg shackles on the ground behind him and throw
them in the river. "You had just eluded me for two days in Helena. Don't question my motives again."

For an explanation, that sure was brief. Then again, since he didn't usually provide one, she realized that was a lot. But something had definitely changed between them. Apparently, he wasn't going to define what had changed. Maybe he didn't know.

But she pointed out, "I don't see you tossing your ropes away."

"Ropes have other uses."

Was that his way of saying he wouldn't tie her up anymore either? It was time to back down, yet she pushed her luck. "Will you still shoot me if I take off?"

"Walk away and we'll find out."

No absolute yes this time? She supposed that was an improvement. She was mollified, quite a bit actually.

She ripped the rabbit apart and handed him the bigger piece. For the second time that day, he wasn't initiating a conversation while he ate. For once, she was.

"You never did say how many men you've killed."

"No, I didn't."

He just wasn't going to admit what his death count was up to. Maybe he didn't know. That was possible. He'd said he'd wounded a lot of men, that he'd lost count of how many. So maybe he didn't stick around to see if the wounds he'd caused healed.

"You never said how long you've been solving other people's problems, either."

"You never asked."

She almost rolled her eyes. He was damn good at not answering questions about himself, either with his annoying silence or just simple evasion. "I'm asking now."

He shrugged. "For around five years."

"You weren't born in the West, were you?"

"I grew up in Chicago, attended the finest schools, was groomed to take over my father's business."

Her eyes flared at that much personal information, even though it came out in such a cold tone. "Then what the hell are you doing out here?"

He didn't answer. She waited a few minutes in case he was figuring out how much to say, but he still didn't get around to answering. He was probably annoyed with himself for saying as much as he did.

She tried a different approach. "So you were just a drifter to begin with?"

"I set out to see the country. You could say I'm half-done."

"Been to Texas yet?"

"No, I was saving that for last."

She almost laughed because she could figure that one out. Texas was huge. It could take years to see all of Texas.

Impulsively she asked, "So maybe I can hire you to clear up that mess for me in Texas?"

"You're rich?"

She chuckled. "Told you I'm broke, but I've got other assets," she teased.

He started to get up.

She gasped and scrambled to her feet, quickly saying, "I was just messing with you, fancy man. I'm *not* trading favors for freedom or anything else."

He ignored her. He had only moved closer to the fire so he could reach one of the slices of bread. If she could have kicked herself right then, she would have. She should *not* have reminded him about trading favors. But at least he wasn't going to rip apart what she'd just said. But then he did.

"I recall you intended to do just that."

She managed not to blush, even said cheekily, "That was before you started liking me enough not to turn me over to a sheriff."

He didn't agree with that assessment, merely said, "I told you why."

Yeah, he did, that he hadn't decided yet, and he obviously *still* hadn't decided, or he would have said so right then. She sat back down near the fire to finish the meal in silence. She was already feeling the drop in temperature. It never failed, no clouds during the day, cold at night. But she had her coat and the horse blanket, and her hair was dry already, so she wasn't worried about being uncomfortable tonight.

She was still eating one of the peaches when Degan went to wash his hands in the river. When he came back, he held out his own handkerchief to her. It was pristine white and looked soft as silk, the edges delicately embroidered. Someone had made that with loving care for him. A wife? She was surprised the thought that he might have one somewhere hadn't occurred to her before. He'd been a man when he came West, not a kid, so he could have gotten married first. But that was one question she wasn't about to ask him when he might misconstrue it and think she cared either way. But she had to admit she did.

She wiped her hand on her blanket before she took the handkerchief from him and gave him a questioning look. He was looking at her cheeks when he said, "Your face, even your hair, is glittering with gold dust. While I don't mind, it will draw attention to you when we get to the next town, so you might want to get rid of it."

She laughed. She'd had no idea the soft soap would soak

up whatever dust was still inside the leather pouch. She briskly fluffed her hair with her hands to shake the sparkles loose. But she had to shake out his handkerchief several times to make sure she got all the dust off her face.

She didn't ask him to inspect her face to make sure she got all the dust off, she just handed the handkerchief back to him when she was done. He didn't take it, said, "Keep it."

So the handkerchief had no sentimental value? Max figured it hadn't been made by a wife then. *Did* he have one? Damnit, that question was going to bother her now. Maybe she'd already met his wife. He'd certainly seemed familiar with that woman he'd called Allison. *She* had behaved in a wifely manner toward Degan. Who else would yell at him like that? An abandoned wife would certainly harbor that much anger.

Max tried to put Degan's marital status out of her mind by continuing with her evening chores. She picked up any food scraps that would lure in wild animals, added more branches to the fire so it would last most of the night, and found a thick bush behind which she could relieve herself. When she returned to the fire, she saw that Degan had moved his horse blanket next to hers and was taking a swig from a bottle of whiskey. Both of those things made her nervous.

But he offered her the bottle as she approached. "For the chill."

She relaxed on one count. If Degan got drunk, he could turn dangerous. She started to decline, but she could feel how cool the air was on her bare calves, so she took a swig and managed not to cough. Pure rotgut whiskey. She'd had it before, but she sure didn't like it.

She handed the bottle back to him and mentioned the second count. "You've moved too close to my blanket."

"It's up to you. You can sleep next to me, or elsewhere. But if you choose 'elsewhere,' I'll have to tie your hands."

She gasped, outraged. "You have *got* to be kidding me! After I saved your life!"

"And here I thought you did that because you're growing fond of me. Are you?"

"No," she snarled. "I only helped you because I hate to see an unfair fight."

She got up and moved her blanket away from his, then sat down and stiffly held out her wrists because she definitely didn't want to be near such an exasperating man. He came over and tied her wrists. As soon as he was done, she turned her back on him and curled up next to the fire, her coat keeping her legs warm. If anyone was going to get cold tonight it would be Degan since, apparently, he didn't travel with an extra blanket. She didn't either, but her coat usually served that purpose, at least until winter set in. And she hoped he spent a miserable night shivering!

But the next thing she knew, he was moving his blanket next to hers again. "Not fair!" she protested, glaring at him over her shoulder. "You said—"

"You escaped me in Helena. And your explanation of why you helped me in Butte confirms that I have no reason to think you won't try to escape again. At least I'm not going to tie your feet."

Was that supposed to be a consolation prize? Odious man.

She didn't exactly doze off right away. It was early and she was still bristling. It might take hours. But she wasn't going to talk to him anymore.

So she was actually startled when she heard him say, "If you get cold, you can use my body heat to warm up."

She blushed furiously even though she *knew* he didn't mean that the way it sounded. Then she felt him pull her coat up over her shoulders as if he were tucking her in for the night. She didn't thank him when she could have done that herself if he hadn't put the rope around her wrists.

Chapter Twenty-Seven

MAX SAT UP ABRUPTLY, disoriented for a moment and not sure what had awoken her. She usually slept soundly. Had it been a noise? If so, Degan hadn't heard it. The steady, soft sound of his breathing indicated that he was sleeping. She glanced around the camp. It was the middle of the night, and with the fire having died down, she couldn't see far.

She wondered if she should wake Degan to investigate. But the horses were quiet, not making any sounds of alarm. If it was a noise that had awoken her, whatever had caused it was already gone. Then she shivered, feeling the cold across her chest and back. Her coat had slipped down to her waist when she'd sat up.

She reached for it and got the sharp reminder that her wrists were bound together. Still she tried to pull the coat up, but she was having trouble grasping it, so she stretched her hands toward the fire instead. But the breeze was coming from the east, right across the water, and blowing the heat away from her. She almost growled in frustration. She might as well be naked for all the warmth Degan's fine lawn shirt offered her in the chill of the night.

She looked at the bottle of whiskey Degan had set next to the fire. The bottle was probably warm. What was in it would solve her problem—and probably make her sick. She reached for it anyway, then laughed at herself. She couldn't get the cork out of it! At least the bottle warmed her hands for a few minutes, but she was soon uncomfortably cold again.

She gazed at Degan. He looked so peaceful asleep. He didn't look at all dangerous now, just like a handsome man getting a good night's sleep. While she was wide-awake and shivering. He was probably toasty warm, too. And why was she still resisting? He'd made the offer.

She scooted across her blanket and snuggled against his side, careful not to wake him. Much better. He even served as a windbreak for her. But her coat got left behind. Now her legs were feeling the chill. She tried to get her legs closer to his without touching him.

Suddenly he rolled over. She tried to get out of the way but wasn't fast enough and ended up cocooned against his shoulder and chest. His change in sleeping position provided her with a thick arm for a pillow and availed her of more of his body heat—much more than she'd bargained for. She was about to sigh in contentment when she saw his eyes open.

She quickly said, "My coat slid off me. I'm cold and you said I could use your body heat to warm up."

Degan leaned over her to grab her coat and draw it across her legs before he pulled her closer to him and ran his hand over her arm and shoulder for a few minutes. "Is that better?"

"No, I'm still cold."

He moved his hand to her back and stroked her there. "Are you warm now?"

"That's a little better."

He leaned down and kissed her. His mouth was warm and gentle on hers. She was amazed that such a dangerous, un-emotional gunfighter could kiss so gently yet passionately and stir her up so quickly.

"Are you getting warm now?" he asked against her lips.

Max didn't answer immediately because she was reveling in the delicious sensations that his kiss and his nearness were evoking in her. "That seems to be working, but maybe you should try it again."

He did and began unbuttoning her shirt, too. She started to touch him, but it only brought her bound hands up between them. He paused to untie her without being asked. As soon as she was loose, he was kissing her again.

This wasn't a quick wildfire of passion like the one that had sprung up between them that afternoon. This slow, steady burn seemed to grow hotter and hotter. Yet the same powerful feelings were evoked, that unwinding deep inside her, the sudden racing of blood that made her almost giddy. He even dragged her leg over his as he pressed her even closer. Yet the kissing was gentle! Open, deep, but a slow, tantalizing exploration for both of them. He wasn't taking, he was giving. Her heart still pounded. She raised a hand to his head and ran her fingers through his hair.

Another thing that thrilled her about his kisses was that they weren't spontaneous. They were deliberate, controlled, which meant he wouldn't stop. He would leave that to her. How surprised would he be when she didn't?

His hand was moving briskly along her thigh, over her derriere, even up her back as he kept trying to warm her. He was succeeding—he'd already succeeded with his kisses—but that wasn't the only effect his touch was having on her. Even through the thin fabric of the shirt she was wearing, the movements of his hand over her body felt more like caresses, an intimate stroking that was arousing her.

"You're warm now," he said against her lips. "Shall I stop?"

She moved on top of him in answer, her thighs on either side of his hips. He didn't know yet that she had no drawers on under his shirt. She'd hung her wet ones on the other side of the bush so he wouldn't see them. But what she felt because of that lack of clothing was amazing. A rock-hard bulge was underneath her. She couldn't resist rubbing against it.

Her hands on his neck, her fingers teasing just below his ears, she continued to kiss him much more intensely now, with passion ignited. His hands slipped under the shirt to find her bare skin, creating shockingly sweet, wonderfully hot sensations. She moaned against his mouth as his hands cupped each of her breasts, kneaded them, making them tingle, making her nipples peak. She pressed even harder against him. Breath caught in her throat as the tension built within her.

But suddenly he was holding her face in his hands, forcing her to look down at him. His eyes were turbulent, his voice raspy. "Do you know what's going to happen if this doesn't stop?"

"Show me," she whispered.

With a groan he turned her over onto her back, settled between her legs, and fought with his pants, quickly removing them. Then that hardness was pressing against her for entry, tantalizing her, teasing her, the most amazing thing just out of her reach.

She raised her legs and hooked her ankles together behind his back and pressed them against him, drawing him even closer to her. "Show me!"

He slid inside her. It was as if she were shattered and made whole, broken but now complete. Then he started thrusting within her. Nothing had ever felt so right—or so explosive. It happened within moments, a wave of sweet, hot pleasure that engulfed her whole body, rising up, overflowing, pulsing. She was pretty sure she yelled. She definitely held on to his shoulders tightly, moving with him, not letting go until he felt what she'd felt or something equally amazing. Feeling all of his weight on her for a moment told her he did. She melted like jelly then, her limbs sliding off him, a smile on her lips, ecstatic and proud.

Folks shouldn't keep stuff like this such a secret, she thought. Luella had tried to tell her that being with a man could be real nice, but that was such an inadequate description for something this blissful.

He rolled to the side but took her with him, so she ended up half-draped across his chest. She reached behind her for her coat and pulled it over her legs. She was sure she wouldn't need more than that now. She almost told him that he made a nice furnace, but that would make her laugh. Anything she said right now might make her laugh. She was feeling that good. And his silence was nice for once. She didn't mind it at all.

Chapter Twenty-Eight

Max awoke first. At least, she figured Degan was still asleep since she was still lying snuggled against him. Her cheeks lit up before her eyes were fully open. Did they really make love? If it was just a dream, she wouldn't have such a silly grin on her lips, would she? She tried to set her lips in a straight line, but she couldn't manage it because they kept curving upward. So it hadn't been a dream. She could either be mortified that she'd crossed every line she could cross last night, or she could pretend nothing had happened.

She started to get up, but Degan's arm around her back held her down. "I will marry you, of course."

Max was stunned by his words. Marriage? Then she realized it was the gentleman in him again, offering to marry her because he thought it was what he should do—not because it was what he *wanted* to do. He made it sound like a business deal. Of course! He'd said he'd been groomed to run an empire. Ha! When she married—if she ever did—there'd damn well better be a declaration of love first and a swelling of happiness to go with it, not this businesslike proposal that sounded as if he was honoring an *obligation*.

She pushed away from him, grabbing her coat so she could cover herself, and scrambled to her feet. "Don't do me any favors, fancy man. I needed warming last night. You saw to it nicely. That's all that was, so don't give it another thought and I won't either."

She marched off before she started railing at him. How dare he offer to sacrifice himself on the altar of propriety and try to make her do the same thing? She was still angry when she returned to camp after relieving herself. Degan had gone off to do the same, so she quickly grabbed her dried clothes and got dressed before putting the rest away.

She was chewing on a chunk of bread when Degan returned. His expression was as stoic as usual, not a single one of his thoughts revealed. It occurred to her that he might not even realize she'd been offended by his dispassionate offer. She should probably keep it that way.

"I didn't mean to sound ungrateful," she said, "but marriage to you feels like a shotgun wedding. I'll wait for some good, happy reasons to marry, if it's all the same to you."

No answer, not even a glance, so she added, "Do you ask every woman you sleep with to get hitched?"

"Only the virgins."

That *could* have been an attempt at humor if Degan didn't look dead serious. She still laughed. "I'm not saying I wasn't one, but it's not that big a deal to me anymore, especially now that I'm headed for a hanging. Heck, I was ready to give it up when I was just sixteen."

"But you didn't."

She found it annoying to have this conversation with him

when his back was turned to her, but he'd started saddling his horse and didn't stop what he was doing to talk. "Only because the man I fancied up and left town. The Binghams probably ran him off. They'd had me pegged for one of them even back then."

"So you say."

"You still think I'm lying?"

"I think I'm now obliged to find out."

She stared at him incredulously. The anger was back, but she chomped it down fast. She was *not* going to look a gift horse in the mouth or snarl at it. Hesitantly she asked, "Does that mean what I think it means?"

"We'll head to Texas after I finish in Dakota."

He was going to help her! Max was ecstatic. And all it had cost her was the most incredibly beautiful night of her life. About damn time her luck changed.

She was still smiling when he came for the blanket she was sitting on so he could saddle her horse, too. She got up to kick dirt on the cold fire in case any embers were at the bottom of the fire pit, then grabbed her coat and hat. She didn't put the coat on and wouldn't until they got to town. The day was nice so far, not very warm yet, as early as it was, and there was a little breeze, so she hoped there wouldn't be another blistering day like yesterday.

They got to Bozeman around midafternoon. It wasn't a mining town, so it wasn't likely to vanish once the ore ran out. Soldiers from the nearby Fort Ellis were in town. The hotel was small, but the room they were given was cozy, with homemade doilies on the furniture and vases of fresh flowers on the tables on either side of the large bed.

Degan left her there, merely saying he'd be back in time to

take her to dinner. His taking his valise with him suggested he was going to find a laundress. He didn't even lock the door. He knew she wouldn't run off now, not after he'd dangled in front of her the carrot she wanted.

Max had already resolved never again to wash more than one pair of her clothes at a time. She still blamed Degan's thin shirt and her bare calves for that chill she'd taken last night, which had led her to seek warmth in his arms. Staring at the bed, she wondered what Degan's expectations would be after what happened last night. It wasn't going to happen again. From now on, she'd be sleeping in *her* heavy clothes to make it clear to him that she didn't need or want any warming up.

An hour or so later a package was delivered for her, along with some bathwater. She waited until she was alone to open it, then laughed when she pulled out a skirt, a frilly blouse, and a few different-colored ribbons. What had he done—bought these garments off someone? Aside from overalls and men's shirts, ready-made clothes, especially women's clothes, weren't easy to come by in the territory's general stores. Women usually made their own clothing or found a seamstress to do it for them.

Max bathed and then put on the new clothes before Degan returned and told her to put them on. She didn't mind. The skirt was a pretty pink-and-yellow floral pattern and had room for petticoats she didn't have. The white blouse had a wide, double ruffle that followed the neckline down the V to where the buttons started. She wore her chemise underneath it so she wouldn't need her vest. She picked up one of the ribbons, a red one, and tied it in her hair. The hotel room didn't have a full-length mirror so she couldn't see how she looked, but she actually felt pretty, something she hadn't felt since leaving Texas.

She also washed the clothes she'd worn earlier in the day since there would be time for them to dry before morning. But she was starting to get bored. And hungry. Degan's food sack wasn't there to help with that. He'd told the stableman to dispose of it when they'd arrived in town.

She was about to go looking for him when he opened the door. His gaze swept over her, but all she got was his usual "Let's go."

She didn't mind that either. Degan's helping her instead of jailing her changed everything. She had to be careful now not to do anything that would make him reconsider taking her back to Texas. So she didn't complain that he was late, that her belly was growling, that he'd barely glanced at her or mentioned how pretty she looked in the new clothes, which were *his* idea. He might be helping her now, but one thing hadn't changed at all. He could still be damn annoying.

The little hotel they were staying in didn't have a restaurant, but one was across the street. They waited for two covered wagons to roll past them and then for a cowboy leading a cow to the butcher to pass. Bozeman was prosperous and appeared to be growing. Max saw a newspaper office down the street and even a library. Well, at least the sign above the drugstore indicated that one could be found upstairs. She hadn't seen that very often, a town with an actual library.

The restaurant was crowded. For the first time, Max noticed that people were looking at her as well as Degan. He'd buttoned his jacket, which hid his gun from view, so that could have been why. No corner tables were available. Max knew that was where he preferred to sit so he could keep his back to a wall. If he minded that they were seated in the middle of the room, he didn't show it.

He was back to wanting conversation with his meal, didn't even wait for the food to arrive to ask, "How big is your hometown?"

"Not as big and crowded as Butte, but bigger than this one and more spread out. Bingham Hills was founded back in the forties with just one long main street. It's got over a dozen streets now, five saloons, three stables, two hotels, and a handful of boardinghouses. Carl Bingham took great pride in guiding its expansion. Heck, he even built houses for the tradesmen who wanted more'n a few rooms above their shops to live in. One more reason why that town loves him so much."

"You need to stop thinking the man is alive, Max."

"I know, but I still can't believe he died from that gunshot wound."

Degan made a sound of frustration. "You need to assume he's dead, either by your brother's hand or someone else finished him off and blamed it on you because you fled. There's no other logical reason for your poster to have been distributed across the West."

"Course there is, because they want—"

"Listen to me. Posters are based on facts. The bank robbery might have been a misunderstanding, but you still walked out of the bank with more than your own money. Someone thought Bingham was dead—or about to die—in order to get the US marshal system to send that poster out with both charges on it. His son would want revenge, wouldn't he?"

"Yeah, but—"

"Let me finish. If he's *not* dead, your town would know it, other people visiting would know it, and any other lawmen in the area would know it, so your poster would have been canceled at least within the first year. But it wasn't."

"Unless it wasn't distributed in Texas."

The look she got was so quelling she mashed her lips together. She knew she was deluding herself with wishful thinking now, simply because she *needed* to be right. The alternative was a hanging, and not even Degan would be able to stand against an entire town that would want to see her pay for killing their beloved founder.

Degan obviously hadn't considered that because he continued, "For the time being we're assuming he's dead. We won't know exactly how it happened until we get there. Now, if what you've said is true about what led up to the shooting, there needs to be a reason why the Binghams were so hell-bent on making you a member of their family—and went to such extremes to accomplish it."

Max shrugged. "I just figured they wanted some good-looking babies, since neither Bingham has much in the way of looks."

"That could have been accomplished in any number of ways that didn't have to involve you. Unless one of them was in love with you?"

She snorted. "If they were, they've got a fine way of showing it, putting a target on my back."

"Your wanted poster doesn't say 'dead or alive.' "

"It doesn't say 'alive,' either."

They fell silent when the food arrived. They were both trying the chef's recommended fish cakes, three large patties that filled their plates, fried golden with two different sauces, and glazed carrots on the side.

But as soon as the waiter left, Degan asked, "What else do you have that the Binghams could have wanted?"

"The clothes on my back?" His eyes actually narrowed a little. She chuckled this time. "I don't own anything that a rich family like the Binghams would want."

"You have property standing in the way of the town's expansion, if what you said about the town's approaching your farm is true. Or are there other directions in which the town could be developed?"

She frowned. "There are still other ways to go."

"That are being used?"

"Yeah, I suppose they are. With hills on the back side and lots of flat land on the other side, Carl was mostly making use of the flat land. But there's a quarry to the east he probably didn't want to get close to, and the woods—actually, the only *clear* flat land is in our direction."

"So your family's farm is in the way of Carl Bingham's goal to turn his town into a city."

She grinned. "That ambition is a bit grandiose even for him, although there was talk before I left that he was planning on putting in a railroad spur line to connect Bingham Hills with the Texas and Pacific Railroad at Fort Worth or Abilene. If they manage to do that, yeah, the population of the town could end up doubling pretty quick."

"It might not have been something Bingham originally planned on, but if he's as rich as you say, he would be able to pay any price your family named for the land. Did he offer to buy your farm?"

"It's not mine to sell."

"It wasn't left to your father?"

"It would've been, but he died before Grandpa did, so it went to Gran. And she'll leave it to Johnny."

"Did Bingham try to buy it from your grandmother?"

"If he did, she never mentioned it to us. But she's lived in that house more'n half her life. It's home. She wouldn't sell it."

"Even if she was offered a fortune?"

Max shook her head. "You can't put a price on something you love."

He said no more about it, but he'd definitely opened a can of worms in her mind. She'd thought she was the main focus of the Binghams' interest, her personally. But if it had been about the farm all along, what had made Carl think that having her in his family would give him control of the farm? Why would a man everyone else in town loved and respected turn ruthless over a piece of land? He'd even been prepared to rape her to get that ring on her finger. But for that property to come to him through marriage to her, the rest of her family would have to be dead. Oh, dear Lord, Max thought, had the Binghams hurt Gran and Johnny? She tried to calm herself and think clearly. No, if the Binghams were capable of murder, they would have taken action before she'd left Texas.

Max sighed. Degan had given her too much to think about. She'd been so pleased that he was willing to help her, but now she had to wonder if it might get him killed. She knew he could take on outlaws and gunfighters, but how could he take on a whole town? They were still a long way from Texas, so she wasn't going to mention that now.

Back in their room, she saw immediately that a big, puffy quilt had been delivered and placed on the bed. She supposed it would do for a mattress.

"I'll sleep on the floor," Max said.

"It's a big bed. You can wrap yourself in that quilt so we can share it. If you don't want me to touch you, you only have to say so."

She supposed that would work, but she clarified, "No touching will be necessary. That quilt will keep me warm. Thank you for thinking of it."

He looked as if he might say something else, but he left the room instead so she could prepare for bed. She removed her pretty new clothes and put on her heavy shirt and pants to sleep in. She probably didn't need them with the quilt, but she wasn't taking any chances. She got into bed and wrapped the quilt around her. This was much better than the floor, but she hoped she wouldn't be too hot now.

Chapter Twenty-Nine

Max awoke to find a shirtless Degan propped up on an elbow in bed, gazing at her. She took in the sight of his wide, bare chest—maybe a little too long.

"Have you changed your mind about touching?"

Her eyes rose to his. It would be so easy to say yes, but she couldn't shake her resolve. What had happened the other night couldn't be repeated. Yet she didn't answer him soon enough. He leaned forward and brushed his lips against hers. She raised her hand to push him back, but the moment she touched his bare skin, she ran her fingers over it instead. His kiss deepened. She groaned at how hard it was to resist this man! But she had to.

Gathering her last speck of will, she rolled away from him and right out of bed, then nearly tripped over the quilt on the floor. No wonder he'd thought that she'd changed her mind. She must have been so warm she'd thrown off that quilt in the middle of the night.

She heard him get out of bed, too. Then the door opened. "Next time I'm getting you a cot."

She winced as he closed the door behind him, but it was better this way. No strings that he might misconstrue, no jeopardizing his help, no getting so attached that she couldn't walk away in the end—when he did.

The train ride to Dakota was uneventful, but at least the train didn't get robbed. It was pretty funny to consider that bad luck, but Degan sure did. Max merely enjoyed her first train ride. It was thrilling, moving that fast.

She still hadn't told Degan that his helping her in Texas might not be a good idea. For him. He would likely disagree, so she should probably just take off on him and make her own way home to face whatever awaited her there. Now that Degan seemed to trust her to a degree, he wouldn't be expecting it. But she was still with him. Each time she'd had an opportunity to slip away before they got to the train station in Billings, she hadn't taken it. She wasn't sure why. Maybe because she enjoyed traveling with him. Maybe because Degan might already have a plan to negate her fears and she ought to find out about that first. It was his profession, after all, to solve problems. And maybe she didn't ask him if he had a plan because she just wasn't ready to see the last of him yet. Probably because she knew she had time. But there had been no more chances to escape once they'd boarded the train in Billings, what with their horses loaded in the livestock car. The horses would remain there until Degan reached his final destination.

That location hadn't been determined yet, though Degan was leaning toward a town in the center of the territory. He was questioning every railroad employee on the train and at the stations they stopped at. He had found out that only the westbound trains that carried the railroad's payroll were being hit, which was why the train she and Degan were riding hadn't been robbed and likely wouldn't be. One employee had agreed to show him where along the tracks the last robbery had occurred, but that wasn't going to help much in locating where the Nolan gang were hiding. Soldiers, railroad detectives, and other US marshals had been searching for these outlaws for months, and no one had come close to finding them yet, not even when there had been fresh tracks for them to follow.

"You need a tracker," Max pointed out when they finally disembarked from the train at Bismarck, on the east bank of the Missouri in the Dakota Territory.

Degan led them to the animal cars to wait for the horses to be unloaded. "A hunter who doesn't track?"

Was he joking? He had to be. She snorted. "I can track game, but I've never tried to track people."

"It doesn't matter. A tracker would only be useful right after a robbery. What I need is a scout, or at least someone very familiar with this territory who can suggest places where a group of men might hole up."

"Have you been through here before?"

"Almost."

She peered at him. "Almost?"

"I had to choose which direction to go in when I left home. I'd heard the railroad had gotten pretty far up here. But winter was approaching so I decided to forgo a northern route. And then I decided to forgo trains altogether and just head West."

"It's hard to imagine you as a greenhorn."

"Then don't."

She laughed. "But you were, weren't you?" He didn't answer. Of course he wouldn't. "Did you leave home with the palomino?"

"No. I had a Thoroughbred racer, but he went lame about

halfway through Kansas, stranding me on a road between towns—until an old woman came along driving a wagon that looked older than she was. Adelaide Miller, the most cantankerous woman I've ever come across. Bossy, argumentative, and set in her ways, as different from the women I knew in Chicago as night is from day. It took a while to get used to her."

"Rescued by an old woman. I'll never tell," she teased.

He ignored that. "She took me home with her, promising to take me to town in a week or two when she had to go back there again. Nothing I said or offered would get her to change her mind about that time schedule. It ended up being a month. I figured out pretty quick that she just wanted things done around her place that a man could do easier than she could. At least she was a good cook."

Max chuckled over that point's being important to him. "She lived alone?"

He nodded as a railroad employee handed the reins to his horse to him. She was still waiting for hers. "She raised pigs and a few cows. And had several vegetable gardens. It was a big homestead out in the middle of nowhere, no neighbors in sight, some twenty miles from the nearest town. Her husband had farmed it before he died."

"Don't tell me she had you plowing fields. I'd never believe it."

"No, she only planted vegetable and flower gardens after he was gone. What she could handle on her own. But she wanted some painting done, repairing, fixing, hauling."

As interesting as Max found his tale, simply because he so rarely opened up like this, she began to wonder why he was telling her—until he added, "Learning to shoot."

"She wanted you to teach her?"

"No, she castigated me for not carrying a gun and browbeat

me into learning how to use one. She gave me her husband's Colt to practice with and wouldn't let up until I hit everything I aimed at."

Max started laughing and couldn't stop. An old woman had taught the fastest gun in the West how to shoot? He walked away from her. She grabbed her reins and hurried after him.

"Wait up. You have to admit that's funny, so don't get mad at me for laughing."

"Adelaide did me a favor. It wasn't long before I needed that gun, before I even got out of Kansas. But you pegged it right. I came West a greenhorn. I just didn't stay one for very long."

She was incredulous that he'd told her this. She had a feeling he'd never shared that story with anyone else. Why her? Max couldn't help smiling. Was she growing on him? The same way he was growing on her? That was an interesting thought.

"So are we heading out now?"

"One of the station attendants suggested that the Nolan gang might be hiding in the Dakota Badlands."

She frowned. "Then maybe we should just let them rot there. You know areas like that are next to impossible to travel through."

"I didn't say we were going there."

"Good, because it's no place to live for any length of time. I got close enough to Wyoming's Badlands to know I didn't want to travel through them. Sinking sand, steep crags, no greenery to speak of. I doubt the Badlands here are any different. And the gang has been robbing this line in the warmer months for over a year now, eight robberies in all. They aren't going to camp out for that long, certainly not over the winter."

"I know all that, and that Nolan's gang only targets the trains coming west loaded to the brim with new settlers, or the ones bringing in the railroad's payroll. But the Badlands suggestion was just one man's opinion, and since that area is back in the western part of Dakota, which we've already passed, we'll only backtrack as a last resort. Besides, I'm inclined to believe the gang is more centrally located. It's a big territory, after all, and the robberies have occurred up and down the line."

"I enjoyed riding the train." She grinned. "We could just board one of the trains carrying a payroll and wait for the gang to rob us like you were hoping they would."

"That hope was based on my impatience, and it didn't take into account the possibility that innocent people could get hurt. I'd rather find them myself."

"You do realize that they could be hiding in plain sight like I tried to do. They could even be living here in Bismarck and just acting like normal folks. Who would know?"

"Someone here will. This is the biggest train hub in the territory. Information about what's on the trains from the east comes through here in advance. Someone here is feeding that information to Willie Nolan."

"So you *do* have a plan?"

"Of sorts."

He didn't elaborate. Actually, she was amazed he'd said as much as he did. But then he added, "The first item on the agenda is a bath and a good night's sleep. If I get lucky and find the gang's inside man, we might wrap this up quickly. If not, I want to scout out the outskirts of Bismarck tomorrow."

"You could at least hire a scout for that."

"I was already warned the army employs all the good ones and isn't willing to loan them out."

"So find a bad one. Anyone familiar with this territory is better than no guide a'tall."

Chapter Thirty

JACKSON BOUCHARD WASN'T A scout, but he was familiar
enough with the surrounding areas to be a guide for a few
days. He was a half-breed Indian. At least, he boasted that he
was. Max had her doubts, though, because he looked no different than any other Westerner. He appeared to be in his late
twenties, was not tall, and was stocky. He was handsome with
remarkable turquoise eyes and short brown hair. He didn't
wear a gun on his hip, but he rode with a rifle in one hand and
his reins in the other, and he kept the rifle cradled in his arms
when he wasn't mounted.

He expected to be fed and not have to hunt for his dinner.
Those had been his conditions aside from his fee. He was nosy,
asking a lot of questions. It fell to Max to answer them, or not,
since Degan wouldn't. Jackson knew that she was a woman
because she hadn't tried to hide that after she'd left Bismarck.
That's how safe she felt in Degan's company.

But Jackson didn't know that she was considered an outlaw.
Her wanted poster hadn't reached Bismarck or any of the train

stations between Billings and Bismarck. She'd looked. The last place she'd seen one had been in Billings, back in Montana.

She'd pulled Degan aside yesterday to ask why he'd hired Bouchard if the man wasn't a scout. "Because he knows the territory. He's going to take us to places *he* thinks a band of men could hole up in without notice."

She supposed that was one way to go about locating the gang. Then she'd asked, "So you didn't find the informant last night?"

"I checked a few disreputable saloons, but no one would own up to it. But I have a feeling it's Bouchard. He was too quick to offer his help. He either wants us to find the Nolan gang, or he's going to lead us astray—possibly into a trap."

"So we don't trust him?"

"No, we don't. But in case he wasn't lying, let's see where he leads us."

Jackson was too well fed not to have some sort of normal job in Bismarck, yet he hadn't had to quit one to come with them. He'd been evasive when she'd asked him about his work. In fact, for all the questions *he* asked, he didn't answer many in return, so she was inclined to agree with Degan that he might have ulterior motives.

Quite a few farms were within an hour or two of Bismarck, homesteads established by settlers who'd probably come in soon after the railroad had arrived. But the farther north they went, the fewer thriving homesteads they saw. Most had been abandoned, a few even burned to the ground. Max figured the Indians had still been active in the area when the railroad first came through. Sporadically they spotted cabins, most of which were deserted. Jackson was leading them to the ones he knew were occupied so Degan could stop and question the inhabitants.

They stopped under a lone tree for lunch the first day of their search. Degan's food sack was filled with the usual fare he favored that would last several days without spoiling. They'd been riding hard, so he rubbed down his horse before eating.

Max sat down and leaned against the tree as she ate. She'd removed her coat as soon as the day heated up, so the gun she wore was in view now. Jackson sat next to her, his rifle across his lap.

"You know how to use that?" he asked curiously, staring at her Colt.

Max supposed this was one of those times when it didn't matter that her gun was empty because Jackson didn't know it. All she said was, "Wouldn't wear it if I didn't."

He watched Degan for a few minutes before he said, "You and him?"

She'd been staring at Degan, whose back was turned to them, and Jackson had noticed it. Sometimes she just couldn't keep her eyes off him. She knew what Jackson was implying.

"No. I've hired him to do a job," she lied. "He won't do it until he finishes this one."

"But he's a marshal," Jackson pointed out. "Why would he work for you?"

Not until that moment did she realize that Jackson Bouchard wasn't aware of Degan's reputation as a gunslinger. That surprised her because other people in Dakota they'd spoken to had known exactly who he was. She almost laughed. Not that it mattered. With Degan paying him, Jackson had no reason to be wary of Degan—unless he was exactly who Degan thought he was, which *would* make him wary of a lawman.

"We have an arrangement," she said offhandedly. "I help him with this, he helps me with my problem afterward."

"Which is?"

"Personal."

"Too bad."

That comment drew her eyes to him because she wasn't sure what he meant by it. Was he interested in her? She hadn't sensed that he might be. Until now.

But he got up before he added, "You should go back to town. I can get him where he needs to go."

That was said a little too confidently. She no longer doubted that Bouchard was somehow involved with the Nolan gang, either as their informant or one of the actual robbers. He obviously knew where they were. And his pointing his rifle at her and Degan and turning them over to Willie Nolan could well be his plan. But Degan was prepared for that. Jackson wouldn't get away with it, even though he always kept his rifle in his hand. If he tried, he would be surprised by how fast Degan was.

They slept in a trapper's shed on the edge of a small woods that night. It was mostly empty except for a few metal traps with dried blood still on them. The trapper, Artemus Gains, lived in a small cabin next to the shed. Strung up between the two buildings were lines hung with animal pelts of all sizes.

Starved for company, Gains had invited them to share his dinner and offered them the shed for the night. He knew Jackson. At least they talked as if they were old friends. Artemus even tried to get Jackson to stay for a week or so to keep an eye on his place, so he could go to Bismarck for supplies and to visit his brother. Max couldn't understand why he was so worried that someone would try to move into his little, one-room cabin while he was gone. But Jackson promised to return when his current job was done.

The next morning they rode for hours without seeing any

dwellings. But close to noon they spotted a small ranch in the distance. Cattle were grazing in the fields around it, maybe fifty head. Max saw a pen of horses, a barn, and a few other outbuildings. No one appeared to be working outside, but smoke coming from the chimney suggested food was being cooked for someone.

Max had hung back just enough to keep her eye on Jackson, so she was the first to see him turn and ride hell-bent in the opposite direction. Degan swung his horse about, but he didn't comment on their fleeing guide other than to say, "Now I'm curious about why he would lead us right to Nolan and his gang if he wasn't setting up a trap."

"You think they're at that ranch?"

"Why else would Bouchard take off like that? Looks like you're not the only one who favors hiding in plain sight. A ranch makes a good cover for a large group of men, especially since no one lives nearby to notice if they're working the cattle or not. Come with me."

He rode off the way Jackson had gone. She caught up and said drily, "The ranch is back that way."

"And you're not getting anywhere near it."

She groaned to herself. "Tell me you're not going to ride in there alone."

"I'm not riding in."

She relaxed until he reined in behind a small copse and handed her his saddlebags. All of the ammunition he'd taken from her the night they'd met was in those bags. She laid them across her lap and quickly loaded her rifle and Colt, stuffing the rest of the cartridges in her pockets before handing his bags back to him.

She looked back at the ranch house. "We can barely see anything from here."

"Which makes it a good place for you to wait."

"Degan! I *can* help, you know. At least if I'm within range, which I'm not here."

"For once will you do as I ask?"

"Then why give me bullets if you don't want my help?" she demanded.

"In case something goes wrong and you have to make your way back to town alone."

She blanched at that possibility, and it could very well come true if he confronted the gang alone. And he didn't have to! He had other options that didn't include her. She mentioned the most obvious one. "You're a deputy marshal. You could gather a posse in Bismarck now that you know where the Nolan gang is hiding."

"If there are too many of them I will, but I won't know that until I get closer. There were at least ten of them at the last robbery, though that was the first one that went bad for them. They lost six men that day."

Her panic eased a little. "So you think there're only four of them left here?"

"No, they would have recruited men to replace the ones they lost. Maybe not all, but some. But this isn't going to be a showdown, Max. If I come up with a reasonable head count, I'll circle around behind the house and take them by surprise. Chances are, no guns will need to be fired. And if I find any of them in the outbuildings, I can probably disable a few of them before I even get to Willie Nolan. But I can't do this efficiently if I spend half my time worried about you. So I want your word that you'll wait here out of harm's way."

"Fine," she mumbled, and dismounted.

"I didn't hear you."

"I promise!" she snarled.

"But can I believe you?"

She glared at him. "You've never had a promise from me before because I don't break them. But here's another one. If you die today, I swear I'll never forgive you."

"Fair enough."

Max kicked a clump of grass next to her, thinking about pigheaded mules as she watched him ride off to find a vantage point where he could observe the ranch. He'd be fine. She knew he'd be fine. He was used to dealing with situations like this. She wasn't. She would have caused him to—did he really say he would have worried about her?

Mollified a little and with Degan no longer in view, she decided to get comfortable for a long wait. She took a swig from her canteen, then dribbled some water in Noble's mouth. But she tensed when she heard a horse approaching from the direction they had come. Was Jackson returning? She wished it were him when she looked around and saw two men riding straight toward her. What were the chances of their not being members of Nolan's gang? Slim.

She quickly ran a hand over Noble's dusty flank and then across her cheek and chin, before tipping her hat low. She almost reached for her gun but was glad she didn't when she noticed both men had theirs out and aimed at her. She took the initiative instead.

"Howdy, fellas. I'm Max Dawson. A Mr. Bouchard pointed me in this direction. He said Willie Nolan might have a job to offer a man of my talents. Have I come to the right place?"

"You could have rode in to find out," one of the men said.

"Max Dawson, huh?" the other said, then grinned. "Ain't

you wanted for murder in Kansas? Pretty sure I saw your wanted poster there."

He was probably testing her, but this wasn't something she needed to lie about. "I'm wanted in Texas, but that poster gets around. So do y'all have a job that pays good or not?"

"We might, but it's Willie's decision. Come along and meet him." He rode ahead to the ranch house, while the other man waited for Max to follow so he could keep her in his sights. She hoped Degan wasn't witnessing this and thinking she'd just broken her promise.

She dismounted in front of the porch and saw no sign of Degan coming to her rescue. But she might not need rescuing. Weren't outlaws more trusting of other outlaws? At least one of them knew who she was.

The porch had a roof for shade, but it wasn't raised off the ground, so it had no steps or railings. She *really* wished Degan would come around the corner of this house right then with his gun drawn. She might appear confident, but she wasn't. She'd never had to bluff her way through something like this. And nothing delayed her entry into the house because the man behind her pushed her inside.

She stepped into a large room with a kitchen and a dining table on one side and a sofa and chairs on the other side. A hallway in back probably led to a few bedrooms, but it was dark. Two men sat at the table, playing cards. A young man who looked no older than Max was stirring a pot in the fireplace. Another man who looked enough like him to be his older brother sat slumped against the wall next to him. He looked angry.

Max had a sinking feeling. She counted six men in the

house. Degan wasn't going to be doing any disabling as he'd hoped, not when it appeared that most if not all of the gang were in the house. But she still had to make sure they didn't shoot her in the meantime. She sauntered into the room, maneuvering until none of the men were behind her. If Degan barged in, commanding their attention, she could at least take out a few of them before they remembered she was there. But she had their full attention for the moment.

One of the two men at the card table stood up. He was on the late side of thirty and lanky. He was frowning when he asked, "Who's this?"

"Jackson sent him."

"Since when does Jackson send us men?"

"Since he found out I was looking for a job with a big payoff," Max quickly put in. "And I don't care much how I get it."

"Is that so?" the older man asked, still frowning at her. "And just who are you?"

"Max Dawson. If you haven't heard of me, your friend has."

The one who had recognized her spoke up. "He's wanted for murder and something else, I can't remember what."

"Bank robbery," Max volunteered. "And if you're Willie Nolan, I'd like in on your next robbery."

"I take it you won't mind killing to get your pay? The trains have been doubling up with guards lately."

"Don't mind a'tall as long as there's a big payout. I'm tired of being broke."

"You're not going to get rich around here," the kid's brother who was sitting by the fireplace grumbled.

"Shut up, Bart," Nolan snapped.

This train-robbing bunch didn't sound like a happy crew. Max wondered if she could add to the discord.

She tried by saying, "What sort of split are we talking about?"

"As the newest member you'll get a smaller share of the take until you prove yourself," Nolan answered. "But you'll still be looking at a nice haul—as long as you pull your weight."

The last was added with a disgusted look toward Bart, whose face twisted in anger. Whatever the brothers had done wrong, it appeared the leader of the gang wasn't going to let them forget it. That's when Degan made his presence known.

"Who owns this spread?" he called loudly from the front of the house.

Nolan immediately looked at Max. "This place is getting mighty busy today. Or did you bring someone with you?"

"No, I didn't." She added cheekily, "But I can take care of this if you like."

"Stay here." Nolan started toward the door, but he didn't have to go outside.

Degan appeared in the open doorway. So much for taking the gang by surprise. He'd removed his jacket. With his tooled gun belt and his Colt in full view, and his expression about as unfriendly as it could get, he appeared even more dangerous than usual. But when his eyes lit on Max first, she was afraid he was more interested in getting her out of there than in a show-down. Yet this was going to get ugly if he let on that he knew her, after she'd just said otherwise.

She was about to say something that would disassociate them when he tipped his hat up only slightly and repeated, "Who owns this spread?"

Max let out her breath. Of course. In that brief glance at her, Degan had ascertained that she wasn't a hostage because no guns were trained on her and she wasn't tied up.

"That would be me," Nolan said to Degan. "And you don't look like a cowpuncher, so what brings you out this way?"

"Name's Degan Grant."

"The gunfighter? *That* Degan Grant?" Nolan actually chuckled. "Maybe you're looking for work of a different sort?"

"If you're Willie Nolan, then my job is almost done."

Max winced. That was a little too direct even to her ears, and Nolan no longer looked amused. But he still looked confident. The numbers were on his side, after all.

"I have no fight with you, gunfighter. What do you want with me?"

"Just doing a friend a favor."

"For a measly reward?"

"The reward just covers my costs. You in jail covers the favor. You don't need to die, Nolan. You can come with me instead."

"I'll pay you double the reward if you ride out of here and pretend you never saw me. And that's damn generous, considering the alternative."

"The thing is," Degan said tonelessly, "no one else has to die. Just you—if you insist."

"My brother Jimmy and I didn't sign up for this," Bart said, jumping up and running toward the back of the house.

He didn't even make it to that dark hallway before Nolan shot him. *His own man?* Jimmy, who was still by the fireplace, cried out in rage and drew his own gun. And that's when everyone started firing their weapons.

Max dove behind the sofa before she drew her gun. But with no one else taking cover, the shooting was over in seconds. She stood up slowly and holstered the gun she hadn't even needed to fire.

Bodies littered the floor. Jimmy was still alive and crying over his brother's body. Degan was still standing, thank God, but it appeared everyone else was dead.

Then she heard those famous last words, "Let's go," before Degan walked out of the house.

Incredulous, Max ran after him. But he'd gone straight to his horse on the side of the house and was already mounted.

Max went up to him. "We're not going to bury anyone?"

"Is Nolan dead?" Degan spoke more softly than usual.

"Yeah, shot in the back. Definitely dead. I think the boy did it, the one crying over his brother. You didn't see that?"

Degan didn't answer, just turned his horse around and rode off. That's when she saw the blood on the ground where'd he'd been standing before he mounted.

Chapter Thirty-One

MAX RODE HARD TO catch up with Degan. She tried to assure herself that he couldn't be hurt bad if he could ride. He was sitting up straight in the saddle, his shoulders squared as usual. If she hadn't seen the blood on the ground, she wouldn't think anything was wrong with him.

Actually, that wasn't true. His abrupt departure was odd. She would have thought that he'd want to take Willie Nolan's body back to Bismarck to prove he was dead. But she supposed sending the sheriff back this way would suffice. Jackson, that coward, could lead the sheriff back here—if she didn't shoot the man first. He'd led them to Nolan's lair to be slaughtered, and they might have been killed if that kid Jimmy hadn't reacted to Nolan's shooting his brother the way he did.

She rode a little ahead of Degan so she could look back at him, but she couldn't tell where he'd been wounded. She saw no expression of pain on his face, either. Would a man who never showed his feelings show that he was in pain? He hadn't put his jacket back on and his vest was made of black silk. If blood was on it, she might not see it at a glance.

So she reined up and simply asked him, "How bad are you hurt?"

"Not so bad that I can't ride."

That should have reassured her. It didn't, not when she'd been hoping he hadn't been shot at all. "Stop and let me have a look."

"No." A moment later he added, "If I get off this horse, I might not get back on."

That meant he was badly hurt. A debilitating wave of fear washed over her.

"We should go back to that ranch house. It will only take a few minutes. They've got to have a bed in there. You need a bed!"

"No, I need to get to town. So stop taxing me with your prattle and ride."

He took off ahead of her at a gallop. If he was so hell-bent on getting to town, then he knew he was hurt bad enough to need a doctor. But town was more than a day's ride away. Could he make it that far? Not if he was still bleeding.

When he slowed down again, he was no longer sitting quite so erect in the saddle. Her heart skipped a beat when she saw him sway a little.

"You're not going to faint, are you?" she demanded sharply. He gave her a nasty look, so she quickly said, "I meant pass out."

"If I do, you can find your way back to town, right?"

"Yeah, but I'm not leaving you alone out here, so don't even—"

"You may not have a choice."

Panic was rising up in her. He couldn't be seriously

wounded. Not Degan. What could *she* do to help him? She'd never had to deal with anything like a bullet wound before, just scrapes and bruises, and even then she'd had her grandmother's full arsenal of salves and cure-alls at her disposal. And Gran's knowledge. Gran knew how to fix anything!

"That trapper Artemus Gains can help," she said desperately. "He can take the bullet out of you. He might even have some sort of medicine for emergencies, something to ease the pain at least."

"Who says I'm in pain?"

"Aren't you?"

"Not anymore."

She didn't know if that was good news or really bad news. But she guessed they were no more than an hour's ride from the trapper's cabin, which was on the way to town. Surely Degan could make it that far. Surely he'd agree to stop there. But thirty minutes later he swayed again, this time so far to the side she was afraid he'd already passed out.

"Degan!"

"What?" he growled.

"I thought you—never mind."

"Start prattling again, Max."

"We're almost to that cabin. Don't fall off your horse, damnit!"

She asked him a dozen inane questions, anything that would require an answer from him, and snapped at him when he didn't give one fast enough. Every time he swayed to the left or the right now, her heart leapt. She wouldn't be able to stop him from falling, but she knew if he did, he could end up hurting himself even more.

Frantically she said, "Hold on, Degan. The cabin is in sight now. Just a little farther, then you can faint all you want to."

"I don't—faint."

He stayed on his horse long enough to reach the cabin. But by then he was leaning over the palomino's neck. Max dismounted quickly and yelled, "Mr. Gains! I could use some help out here!"

But Jackson Bouchard opened the door. He didn't ask what had happened, just went straight to Degan, got him off the horse, and lugged him into the cabin and dropped him on the trapper's bed.

Degan made what sounded like a groan. Max pushed Jackson away and hissed at him, "You couldn't be gentle about it?"

Jackson shrugged. "He was about to—he's already passed out."

She peered at Degan. Jackson was right. Degan had lost consciousness. She could see the blood now. The left side of his vest and his pants were soaked in it. She grabbed one of Artemus's blankets and tucked it underneath Degan to absorb the blood.

When she turned, Jackson was handing her a small pouch. "For the wound. An old Indian recipe from my grandmother. She was one of two women my grandfather traded for when he came down from Canada."

"I'm not interested in your family history."

"It draws out poisons."

"Degan's not poisoned."

He shrugged again. "She said it helps infections, too."

Max didn't take it. She didn't trust Jackson. She was furious at him, knowing that Degan might not be wounded right now if this man had stayed to help instead of running off like a coward.

"Where's the trapper?"

Jackson tossed the pouch on the foot of the narrow bed. "Artie took off for town as soon as I returned. He'll probably be gone a week or more."

She nodded toward the door. "You can take off, too. I'll watch his place for him."

"I promised—"

She drew her gun on him. "Get. Your friends are dead."

He picked up his gear. "They weren't my friends."

"But you were working for them, weren't you." She didn't phrase it as a question.

He shrugged once more. "They paid good for information. Too good not to take it—at first. But then they killed someone in one of those train robberies. After that, I tried to end the arrangement, but Nolan said they'd hunt me down."

"There was a reward. Why didn't you just lead the law to them?"

"Because they said they'd take me down with them. I didn't want to end up on the run for doing a stupid thing just because I needed the money."

She raised a brow. "So you hoped Degan would solve that problem for you?"

"Didn't he?"

"You should have helped."

"I don't kill people, good or bad. Never have, never will."

"What about saving them? He needs a doctor. Is there one closer than Bismarck?"

"No, and he won't last long enough for the Bismarck doc to get here, if the doc's even in town."

She shouldn't have bothered to ask when the man couldn't be trusted. "Ride out. Your secret is safe with me. And Degan was only after Willie Nolan, so he won't care."

"Come with me?"

She cocked her gun. He closed the door on the way out.

Chapter Thirty-Two

"YOU GUT ANIMALS, YOU can do this."

Degan startled her. She didn't realize he'd regained consciousness. She wished he hadn't. She'd been standing next to him frozen in place with her knife in hand, staring at the wound, which was still bleeding. It was on the left side of his waist, right above the belt line. She was going to have to dig the bullet out of him. She couldn't just leave it in there. Actually, she'd started to think she could. If she could just get the bleeding to stop, maybe she could still get him to a doctor in Bismarck.

Getting Degan's shirt off him had taken nearly ten minutes because he was dead weight. She'd had to pull it up beneath him to his shoulders so she could then yank it off his arms. That must have woken him, although he'd made no sound or said anything until now.

Max slowly met his eyes. They were half-closed but still staring at her. "I—I've never done this before," she warned him.

"I have every confidence that you'll do fine."

He did? Why didn't she?

She marched outside, gathered their saddlebags and his va-lise, and brought them into the cabin. She found Degan's bottle of whiskey. It was only half-full.

She shoved the bottle at him. "Drink this."

"I don't need it."

"But I need you to drink it. If you start yelling at me, I might slip and gut you for real."

He still didn't reach for the bottle. "Pour some of that on the blade first, and on the wound, then I'll drink some." But before she got out the door, he added, "And wash your hands."

That's what she was going outside to do. It sounded as if he knew more about removing bullets than she did. When she came back in, she poured a little whiskey over the hole on his left side. He merely hissed softly, but it still felt as if a rough board had just scraped over her nerves. She took a swig of the whiskey herself before she handed it to him again. Wincing, he leaned up and took the bottle this time and gulped down a good amount of whiskey.

"Can you see the bullet?" he asked.

She peered at his wound and shook her head. "Too much blood."

"Find it with your finger."

"Hell no!"

"Max."

She sighed. She raised her index finger, and letting it hover over the bullet hole, she squeezed her eyes shut.

"You're making me feel less confident about you."

He was joking. He had to be joking. "I'm making sure nothing distracts me," she growled.

She inserted her finger into the hole. One knuckle, two

knuckles. She was afraid she was going to have to try again with a longer finger when she finally felt it. Degan made no sound, but then she'd been exceedingly careful to follow the path of the hole. She removed her finger and wiped it on one of Degan's clean handkerchiefs and took up the blade that she'd laid on his chest.

"Now would be a good time for you to pass out again."

His eyes were closed but he said, "I'd tell you to hurry up and get this over with, but—"

"But I'd tell you to shut up."

"Something like that."

"*Please* don't yell." She pressed the knife into him.

The wound wasn't shallow. Because she was being as careful as she could be, it took her forever to get the knife in position to start easing the bullet out of him. And then the bullet kept slipping! She was sweating profusely by the time she got it out, even though Degan hadn't made another sound. She glanced at his face to see why and saw that he'd been fortunate enough to pass out again. *Now* she needed to hurry to sew him up while he was out.

She tore through his belongings. He had to have a needle and thread in one of his bags. As fastidious as he was, he'd want to fix any loose buttons or tears in his clothing. So she reasoned, but she didn't find anything. She went through every drawer and container the trapper had, too, but there weren't many. The cabin was small and sparsely furnished with just the narrow bed, one chair at a small table, one cupboard with supplies filling the shelves, and a chest containing both the trapper's clothes and his bedding. He didn't have a needle either. She knew of only one other way to close the wound and stop the bleeding.

She got a fire going in the fireplace and stuck her widest dagger in the fire—and closed her eyes. She didn't know how long to leave it in the fire or how long to press it against the wound once it was hot. She couldn't ask Degan because he'd passed out. But that was a blessing for him, if not for her.

While the blade heated, she ripped up one of Artemus's clean sheets for bandages. She wouldn't be able to replace it. Maybe he wouldn't notice until they were gone. She also got the rest of Degan's clothes off so he'd be comfortable. She would have left him his smallclothes, but the blood had seeped through his pants. She stared up at the ceiling until she got a sheet draped over him. Tempted as she was to give him a full look, she didn't dare get distracted until she was finished with his wound.

She took Degan's bloody clothes outside, put them in a bucket, and pumped water from the well into it so the clothes could soak. She was surprised the trapper had even dug himself a well when a small pond was nearby. But she supposed he hunted by the pond because animals went there to drink, and he wouldn't want his scent all over the place to make them wary. She'd have to test that theory before sundown.

She was delaying a task she didn't want to do, but she knew she had to do it. The blade had to be hot enough by now. She wrapped one of her shirts around her hand before she lifted the dagger out of the fire. It had a leather handle, but metal was underneath it, so it might be hot.

The handle wasn't hot, but she still rushed to the bed and pressed the hot blade against Degan's wound. The sizzling sound and the smell of burning flesh and blood made her gag. Degan's eyes opened wide, and for the barest moment he started to sit up, but then he dropped back, passing out again, thank God. Unable to stand the smell any longer, Max pulled the blade away and ran outside to puke. She prayed that she'd done the right thing and left the blade on Degan long enough to cauterize his wound. If she had to do that again, she would die.

Chapter Thirty-Three

T HAT AFTERNOON DEGAN OPENED his eyes a couple of times but quickly fell back to sleep. Max considered that a good thing. Sleep would help his body heal. And she had a lot to do. She found the trapdoor to a root cellar behind the shed. More dried and salted meat was in it than vegetables, which wasn't surprising considering Artemus's occupation. He would have told Jackson to help himself to the stored food, but she had to feed two, so she would replace some of the meat. But for now, she took what she needed to get a stew started for dinner.

She scrubbed Degan's clothes and hung them to dry. She refilled the water trough behind the cabin where the trapper obviously kept his horse when he was home. He'd even erected a rickety partial roof over it that would only half cover an animal. What was the point of that? Just to keep snow out of the trough in winter? Or maybe he'd just run out of wood to extend it. A long leather tether was attached to the cabin so the horse could graze on the grass back there. She needed two, so she fashioned one for her horse out of Degan's ropes. She left the animals unsaddled and rubbed down back there.

The pond was just beyond the trees, but still quite a distance down the edge of the woods in the direction of Bismarck. She almost hadn't noticed it yesterday when they'd ridden in with Jackson. This morning she'd hoped to slip away and bathe in it, but she wasn't the first one up so she couldn't manage it. She did that now, and to heck with scaring off the wild animals that drank at the pond.

With Degan out cold, no neighbors for miles, and, more important, no riders passing by this way, she stripped down for the bath. Then castigated herself for it afterward. The boy Jimmy might be coming this way to get to Bismarck after he buried his brother. Jackson might sneak back this way, too, for whatever reason. And she didn't know what was on the other side of the woods. There might be dwellings there. She decided to find out for herself.

Dressed again, and with just her rifle, she headed deeper into the woods. With the trapper expecting Jackson to return so he could leave to do his visiting, she figured he had probably removed any traps he had laid in the woods. Still she stepped carefully in case he hadn't. The last thing she needed was to get stuck with a trap on her foot that she couldn't open without help.

A lot of small animals were in the woods, but no signs of any deer. She took careful aim at a plump quail. She'd throw it in the cellar for lunch tomorrow. The other quail scattered. She searched for their eggs and used her bandanna as a sack to carry four of them. She saw a family of wild turkeys, too, but she steered clear of them. Plucking birds that big was tedious, and wild ones usually had tough meat.

She didn't reach the other side of the woods since it stretched farther than she'd figured and was far deeper than it was wide. But she could see no other dwellings. She picked berries on the way back. If Artemus had anything sweet to cook with, she could make a sauce for the quail with the berries—if she didn't eat them all before she reached the cabin.

Although the sun would be setting soon, Degan was still sleeping. She stopped by the bed, moved a lock of his hair off his brow, and just gazed at him for a few minutes. The man was too handsome. Even laid low like this, nothing about him was unappealing. He'd scared the heck out of her today, taking that bullet. She didn't like what it had made her feel. But they would be parting ways eventually. Would he return home to Chicago where the beautiful Allison lived, now that he knew Allison wanted him to return? Max didn't like *that* thought either and thrust it away.

She'd only covered him to his hips with the sheet. Without any salve she was leery of bandaging the wound even though she winced whenever she looked at the blackened skin around it. But the cauterizing had worked. The wound had stopped bleeding, although a lot of dried blood was on his side.

She wet a cloth and warmed it in her hands before she dabbed at the dried blood. She did it slowly and carefully so she wouldn't wake Degan. Nonetheless, he stirred. He even started to sit up before dropping back to the pillow.

"What the hell?"

Max winced at the accusing tone. He'd lifted his head high enough to get a look at his charred flesh.

She quickly said, "I looked for a needle and thread, I really did. Tore through this place and your bags. I almost carved a needle from wood, even started to, until I realized you might get splinters from it."

His gaze swiftly shifted to her. "You're joking, right?"

She grinned. "Yeah."

"It still sounds like I put you to a lot of trouble. You should have just fetched a doctor."

"I thought about it. But it would have taken two days, getting there and back. I'm pretty sure you would've bled out by then."

She glanced back at the wounded area. She'd tried to press the blade only against the bullet hole, but she'd still burned about an inch of skin on either side of it.

"I don't suppose it's still numb?" she asked hopefully.

"Still?"

"On the way here you said you didn't feel any pain. That really worried me."

"Not something you need to be concerned with now."

She winced again, imagining the pain he was experiencing, and turned toward the fire. "Food's hot if you think you can sit up a little to eat it. Or I suppose I could spoon-feed you."

He snorted. *That* was a reassuring sound and one he'd never before made in her presence. It figured he'd let down his guard a little in his weakened condition.

She brought him a bowl of stew and dug into his food sack for the remaining bread so Degan could dip it into the stew. She needed to go through Artemus's supplies to see if he had the fixings for more bread, or if he just existed on meat, fruit, and wild vegetables as she'd been doing. She'd seen a lot of mushrooms and dandelions in the woods. She could bring some of those back tomorrow.

Degan had managed to sit up a little to eat, leaning back against the wall behind the bed with just a pillow to cushion him. The bed had no headboard and just a box frame, but at least he had a mattress. It was better than the floor, which is where she would be sleeping. She had no idea how long it would take for him to recover and be able to ride again. But he was a strong, healthy man, so maybe no more than a week or two. Just seeing him sitting up holding a bowl of stew made her happy.

She got another bowl of stew for herself and dragged the one chair over to the bed so she could eat with Degan. At least he had an appetite. That was a good sign, she supposed.

"What did you put in this?"

She grinned. Conversation! "Plantain, mushrooms, and dried rabbit meat, so don't expect it to be tender. I'll take stock of what's here and make something fresher tomorrow. Already have quail soup planned for lunch."

"You went hunting?"

"Not really. I was just scouting out the woods a little. But I surprised some quail. Got one before they all scattered." Then she took a chance that his guard was down enough for him to talk about himself some. "You think your lady friend has given up on you and gone back home?"

"She's not a friend—anymore."

"But she used to be?"

"My siblings and I grew up with her."

His tone had turned frigid, so she steered away from his old friend Allison. "How many siblings do you have?"

"My sister died in her teens. It's just my brother, Flint, and me."

"Is he anything like you?"

"No, we're nothing alike. We never were."

"So Flint laughs, smiles, and doesn't end up killing folks in his line of work?"

She said it with a smile so he'd know she was just teasing, but he still gave her a nasty look. "He doesn't work."

"Ah, that's right, your family lives in the big city and is rich. What does that make him, a pampered do-nothing?"

"Are you trying to rile me up by asking about my family?"

"No, I just have no idea what that sort of life is like. It sounds boring. Is it? Is that why you came West?"

He didn't answer that. She supposed he found his brother a more palatable subject because he said, "Flint is a charmer. He could survive on that alone, rich or not. He'd make an excellent politician if he had any ambition, but our father never pushed him in that direction."

"So you were groomed to take over, as you said, but he wasn't?"

"He should have been, but, no, he wasn't. Which my father probably regrets now."

"Tell me about your father and why you hate him?"

"I don't hate him."

"You just don't care about him one way or the other?"

"We merely had a falling out."

"About?"

He didn't answer, merely handed her his empty bowl. She headed to the door and the water barrel outside, so she barely heard him say, "He asked something of me that I wasn't willing to do. He was adamant, but so was I. That's why I left."

Just like that? Max thought, perplexed. What kind of disagreement between a father and a son could be powerful enough to make a man turn his back on wealth and privilege— and everything *he'd* been groomed for?

Chapter Thirty-Four

DEGAN WAS KISSING MAX, but he knew he shouldn't be. He'd sworn he wouldn't do that again. He had better resolve than this. What had happened to change his mind? He couldn't think, didn't want to when she was clinging to him so sweetly. But then he smelled the roses mixed with the scent of hay. Max didn't smell of roses. . . .

He glanced up and saw the hay spread out around them and Allison lying beneath him. He shouldn't be making love to her in the stable, but she'd kissed him there and it was the happiest day of his life, the day she'd picked him, so he couldn't help himself.

She was his first love. She was his only love. Flint had loved her, too. Their competition had been fierce but friendly, but it had gone on too long, from the time they were children, when they'd started vying for her attention, to the present, when they both wanted to marry her. She'd encouraged their rivalry because she enjoyed having the two most eligible men in town pursuing her.

Degan and Flint had fought over Allison, even coming to blows a few times. But while they both wanted her, they were still brothers. Their bond was stronger. Degan would have been sorely disappointed but still glad for Flint if Allison had chosen him instead. And Flint had given in graciously when she'd finally chosen Degan to be her husband. Degan had expected no less.

Degan's happiness faded. Adelaide Miller was yelling at him, "If you can't hit it, you die. Pay attention, boy!"

He didn't like guns. The last one he'd held had been his father's dueling pistol. After what he'd done with it, he'd sworn never to touch another gun again. But it was in his hand now. And there it was again, the scream that had caused him to fetch it from the study. He ran upstairs to find out why she was screaming, up the curved stairs, the endless stairs. Why couldn't he get to the top of them? And the heat was everywhere. It felt as if the house were burning down it was so hot. Was that why she was screaming? But no smoke filled the air, just the smell of roses. Her smell. Leading him upstairs. Her scream, and he couldn't get to her no matter how fast he ran! But he had to save her. She meant everything to him, but the damn stairs wouldn't end. . . .

"I wasn't going to use it," a female voice was saying. "Don't trust him farther than I can spit. It could have been poison. But I got desperate when your fever got worse instead of better. Can you hear me? Damnit, Degan, I thought you were waking up."

It was Max's voice, and her endearing annoyance, which made him want to smile. Degan could feel her moving a cold, wet cloth over his chest. He didn't open his eyes. He wasn't sure if he was still dreaming. If he was, he'd rather continue with this dream than that nightmare.

"Don't trust who?"

"Oh, thank God!" Max gasped. "You need to eat this while you can."

He opened his eyes to see her thrusting a bowl at him. "What is it?"

"Turkey and dandelion soup, with some nettle stalks."

He carefully leaned on his side to eat her soup. He still wasn't sure if he was dreaming, and she still looked anxious. "Did something else happen?"

"You wouldn't wake up for two days, Degan," she said accusingly. "Scared the bejesus out of me. Now drink the soup. You need to regain your strength. Having some food will help you to sleep normally."

He did, and thankfully without any more dreams. When he woke again, the cabin was mostly dark, only a low light coming from the fireplace. Max was sleeping on the horse blankets laid out on the floor in the corner. She wasn't covered, for with the windows and door closed, the fire kept the room warm. She was fully dressed, curled on her side, using her coat for a pillow. She was probably worn-out, tending to him. One more thing he owed her for.

Taking the sheet with him, he carefully made his way outside to relieve himself. He couldn't remember ever feeling so weak before. He swayed quite a bit. He wasn't even sure he could make it back to the bed, he felt so drained. And sore. He ached all over, not just on his left side. But Max would be angry with him in the morning if she found him passed out outside, so he forced himself to get back to the bed.

He managed not to wake her and sat for a few minutes staring at her. She should just look adorable lying there so innocently, curled up like a child, her feet bare. But she looked sexy, too, with her bandanna off, her shirt unbuttoned to her breasts, one curve partially visible—and he was never going to get that night they'd shared in Montana out of his mind.

After their first kiss that hot day in Montana, he wasn't at all surprised by what had happened that night. Too much had led to it, too many times seeing her in scanty attire, too many times wanting her even when she was fully dressed. Like now.

It had been the hardest thing he'd ever done in his life, asking her that night if she wanted him to stop. And the next morning she wouldn't let him do the honorable thing, had even gotten angry about his offer to marry her. So be it. It had been a mistake and she wasn't going to let it lead to a bigger one. What had she said? That she'd wait for some good, happy reasons to marry. She was absolutely right. That was the only right reason to marry—because you'd found the person who could make you truly happy and you believed the other person felt the same way about you.

Max had probably saved his life by taking that bullet out of him. She might have saved his life in Butte, too. He owed her a resolution to her problem in Texas, not more complications.

He slept again, and the nightmare returned. But this time he reached the top of the stairs. . . .

Chapter Thirty-Five

MAX WOKE UP DRENCHED in sweat. She probably shouldn't have closed the windows before going to sleep last night. But the flies hadn't wanted to leave Degan's wound alone. It had taken her over an hour to kill them all, and then she'd been afraid the cool night air might bring back his fever.

She headed to the pond with her bar of soap for a quick scrubbing. She wanted to be there when Degan woke up again because she was still worried about him. The past two days had been awful! She'd thought he was going to die on her. She'd never felt anyone that hot before. And when he wouldn't wake up no matter how loud she yelled at him, she'd been terrified. She'd even cried, she'd felt so inadequate to nurse him. She'd almost opened his wound again, had even thought of cauterizing it again. Rubbing his chest and face with cold cloths didn't work either. Nothing helped!

Finally, she'd been desperate enough to try Jackson's powder yesterday afternoon. It had worked faster than she could have hoped. The redness fanning out around his wound had started to recede, and this morning the last signs of the inflammation were gone. And after three days, scabs were forming, so maybe she hadn't burned him as badly as she'd thought.

When she returned to the cabin feeling somewhat refreshed, she found Degan still asleep. She considered heating some water and bathing him with a cloth before he woke. She hadn't wanted to do it last night. With him finally sleeping peacefully, she didn't want to disturb him. That fevered sleep had been exhausting for both of them. He'd tossed, he'd talked, he'd even yelled at one point, all the while delirious. And she'd been afraid to leave his side, had even slept in the chair next to him until she fell out of it and bruised her elbow.

Rubbing him down with a cool cloth when he was in the throes of delirium was one thing. But doing something so intimate when he could wake and his eyes could land on her was a different thing altogether. She decided against it. If he really was better, he could wash himself. So she went to cook instead.

"I need a bath."

Max smiled to herself. Awake *and* sounding normal, he could do some real recovering now. "No baths for you, fancy man. You don't want to get your scabs wet. I'll bring you some water to wash with after you eat this."

She handed him a bowl of corn mush, then grabbed one for herself and sat down in the chair she'd kept by his bedside since the fever had started. "So how do you feel this morning?"

"Tired, like I haven't slept in a month."

"Yeah, fevered sleep isn't restful sleep. I had a fever when I was a kid, but Gran knew how to get rid of it fast. Wish I'd asked her how."

"How long did I have a fever?"

"Nearly three days."

"And I was poisoned?"

"Huh?"

"You said something about poison, or did I dream it?"

"Oh, that. You might recall Jackson was here when we arrived. He helped me get you into the bed and left me a pouch of powder. He said it was good for wounds, but I didn't believe him so I didn't use it—until nothing I did helped. Turns out the powder worked well."

"Is he still here?"

"No, he left. I sort of insisted."

"Why, because he's a coward and a liar?"

"Yeah, he admitted he was the Nolan gang's town man. Said he tried to quit when he heard they killed someone, but they wouldn't let him. He used you to solve that problem for him. He should be paying you for the job, if you ask me, not the other way around."

"Thank you for taking care of me."

She blushed a little, uncomfortable with his gratitude. "Don't mention it." But then she grinned and teased, "I was just ensuring that you stay alive long enough to help me out in Bingham Hills."

"That didn't require such tender care."

She really blushed now. She hadn't been all that tender with him. She'd been so frantic and afraid of losing him that she'd even hit him at one point to make him wake up.

She quickly changed the subject. "So who smells like roses?"

"Excuse me?"

"You said I didn't and I know I don't, so who were you talking to that smelled like roses?"

"When?"

"In your sleep."

"I don't remember."

Did he just lie to her? His guard must still be down if he was so obvious about it. She might be able to get him to talk about himself again if she casually led him into it. And if it wouldn't tax him. His recovery was more important than her curiosity right now.

But he wanted to know, "What else did I say?"

"Not much. You had such a high fever most of what you said was garbled. You said you hated guns. I thought that was pretty funny. You really used to hate them?"

"Where's mine?"

She chuckled as she fetched his Colt and put it on the small crate beside the bed that the trapper had been using as a nightstand. "Don't think you're not answering my question," she warned teasingly.

He stared at her for a moment. She wondered if he was actually debating with himself about answering her. If he was, he probably wouldn't. But then he did. "I never had cause to think about guns in Chicago. They aren't worn or carried in the city except by officers of the law—or criminals. My father had a pair of dueling pistols that he kept loaded in his study, but they were merely for show, a prized possession that had belonged to his own father in the days when dueling for honor was still practiced. Father never had occasion to use them himself. But then my sister, Ivy, was shot and killed, caught in the crossfire of a fleeing thief and the law officer chasing him down a city street."

Max gasped. "I'm sorry."

"It shouldn't have happened. My mother had taken her shopping. Ivy had just stepped out of a store. Mother was right behind her and saw it happen. She blamed herself."

"Why? Something like that is tragic, but—"

"Because Ivy was supposed to ride with Flint and me in Lincoln Park that morning. Mother usually shopped alone, but that day she wanted company and insisted that Ivy join her. I suppose I hated guns because a gunshot killed my sister."

Yet he'd taken them up when he came West, even became notorious because of them, Max thought. So he must have hated something else even more, something that had sent him in this direction to a completely different way of life.

"Is your mother still alive?"

"No, she died less than a year later. She let her health decline, just lost the will to live. She couldn't let go of the guilt."

Max sighed. She would never have guessed that Degan had experienced so much tragedy in his life. No wonder he kept his emotions locked away. Had he done that for so long that he'd lost the ability to feel anything? Well, she knew he could still feel passion. She could vouch for that! But that was more a natural reaction, an instinct rather than an emotion. Maybe she was reading too much into his sister's death. Maybe he didn't show his feelings because of what he'd implied to her before, that he couldn't afford emotion in his line of work.

She took his empty bowl and refilled it. After handing it back to him, she sat down again and said casually, "You mentioned that your father probably regretted not raising your brother the way he raised you. But couldn't he have remedied that by teaching your brother everything he taught you? It's never too late to learn."

"It is when you grow up without taking responsibility for anything and never expect to have any responsibilities. Flint's biggest decisions concerned which party to attend—and who to bed afterward. He shies away from anything more serious than that."

"It sounds like you begrudge him his carefree nature."

"Not at all. My brother and I were close."

"Were?"

"When I lived at home."

"You realize, don't you, that we're not all that far from Chicago now. With the extension of the railroad Chicago is probably no more'n two days away. I wouldn't mind a short delay if you want to find out—"

"No."

She thought she was doing him a favor by suggesting it, but obviously not. She gave him an exasperated look. "I heard what your lady friend yelled at you, even if you didn't, that a man doesn't have to be dead to not be who he was. That sounds like something bad happened to your father."

"Allison is good at exaggerating. You could say it's her forte."

"So that's why you ignored her? Because you just didn't believe her?"

"If my father wanted me back, he would have come and found me, not sent Allison Montgomery to do it."

She rolled her eyes at him, remarking, "You are very odd, you know."

"No, I'm not."

"Of course you are. You have no curiosity as well as no emotions? *Why* didn't you just ask her what's wrong with him?"

"I confirmed he's alive. Anything else is irrelevant since I'm not going back. Ever."

He took his eyes off her and concentrated on eating. She

supposed that was a pretty good clue that he was done talking about his family. It was as if he'd divorced them the way a man would divorce a . . .

"*Are* you married?"

His eyes came back to her slowly. "Would I have asked you to marry me if I was?"

"You didn't ask me. You just said you *would* marry me. *Big* difference there, fancy man."

She marched out of the cabin because she couldn't deal with how frustrating he could be. She walked far enough away that he wouldn't hear her mumbling about it.

Chapter Thirty-Six

Tʜᴇʏ'ᴅ ʙᴇᴇɴ ᴀᴛ ᴛʜᴇ cabin for ten days. Max expected the trapper to return at any time—unless Jackson had found Artemus and told him that he had other guests. He might not hurry back then, might want to wait until he was sure he could have his bed back. She hoped that was the case.

But Degan was already talking about leaving. He was able to walk now at a steady if slow gait. But he was still in pain. He didn't tell her that, but she caught him wincing every so often. Riding was a lot more strenuous than walking. Even if he could keep his horse from trotting, she worried that the jarring motion would rip open his wound. So she convinced him to stay until Artemus returned, or at least a few more days.

It had been a companionable time. They talked about things that didn't strike any nerves, and they'd gotten in the habit of watching the sunset together each evening. Dakota had some real pretty ones that filled up the sky with deep reds and oranges, with no trees or hills to obstruct the view from their location. She would take the chair outside for him, then sit on the ground next to him. He always glanced down at her to catch her smile just as the sun slipped below the horizon, and she would look up at him. She liked the way he looked at her at that moment. For some reason, when their eyes met, she found it more intimate than kissing.

It would have been a good time to warn him that helping her might not be as easy as he thought. She had been counting on Carl's being alive, but Degan was convinced he wasn't, and she could no longer cling to her hope that Degan was wrong about that.

But he didn't know just how revered Carl had been by the people in town, so much that no one there would need a trial to be convinced of her guilt. The moment they saw her, they'd probably drag her to the nearest tree and lynch her, and not even Degan could protect her from an angry lynch mob that numbered in the hundreds. Evan Bingham was going to be flat out of luck at getting a ring on her finger then, wasn't he? Well, at least in the end the Binghams wouldn't get what they wanted, though she wouldn't be around to gloat over it.

But that was a nerve-striking subject, so she continued to avoid it. Still, she'd have to tell Degan before they started south. She didn't want to take him out of his way and *then* convince him to let her go on alone. Or just sneak off. That was still an option, too, and one that wouldn't include an argument.

She'd been giving the latter option more thought. How could she not when now would be the perfect time to slip away? Degan was better. He could take care of himself now. He could even get back to Bismarck, where he could continue his recovery in comfort. She'd like to leave him a note though to thank him for his offer of help and explain why helping her could get him killed. In convincing her that Carl was dead, he'd also convinced her that her plight was hopeless. She wouldn't tell him that, though. Unfortunately, the trapper didn't have any writing materials. In the end, she couldn't bring herself to ride away without leaving Degan a note.

Today she'd exercised the horses by racing them up and down the wide, open stretch that led to Bismarck, and then she'd gone hunting and done some cooking and baking. It was nearing dusk now and she decided to take her horse with her to the pond. After bathing she planned to ride to the other side of the woods to see what was over that way. She'd be real annoyed if she found a town that Jackson had failed to mention.

She'd already served Degan an early dinner: roasted pheasant, stewed mushrooms, and misshaped corn muffins she was able to bake with Artemus's bread tin. But Degan had eaten so much he had fallen asleep before she'd even cleaned up, so they probably wouldn't catch the sunset tonight. She should still be back in time for it in case he woke up.

Max stripped down and entered the pond with her bar of soap. Degan knew where she was bathing every day. He didn't like her going there alone and had been walking her to the pond the last few days—yet another sign that he was getting better, asserting his druthers again and getting away with it. Even without his full strength, Degan could be adamant. He hung back about twenty feet or so from the pond, within shouting distance, so she could have her privacy.

She was wading toward the edge of the pond to get out when she saw that she was no longer alone, and froze. The man was tall, stocky, and already had his gun drawn and pointed at her. He'd come out of the trees from the south. The ones along the western edge shaded him, so she couldn't quite make out his face. Then another man appeared behind him, then a third.

They had their guns drawn, too, and all three were walking slowly toward her.

She had nowhere to run. The pond was too small to help her in any way. One of them could reach her before she got to the other side of it—or shoot her for trying. Without her clothes she couldn't even bluff them into accepting her outlaw persona, much less try to convince them she was a boy. In a moment or two they'd see that she was a woman, if they hadn't already.

She'd brought her saddlebags only because she didn't want to carry the wet bar of soap back in her hands. But they were nearly empty, containing only her ammunition. She'd already removed the clean clothes she'd brought, which were hanging on a bush near the edge of the pond next to her dirty ones. All of her other belongings—her cooking gear, her spices, her creamy soap that she only used every three days so it would last longer—were at the cabin. She also had her money. There'd been no reason to unpack it, which was too bad, since it was probably about to be stolen.

Maybe the strangers would be satisfied with that. Or maybe they wouldn't. They definitely weren't friendly with their guns already drawn. Fear was sneaking up on her pretty fast. She'd probably be dead already if they didn't want something else from her. . . .

She was too far from the cabin for the sound of her scream to reach it, even if Degan was awake to hear it. He'd hear a gunshot, though. Her gun belt was hanging on her saddle pommel, under her vest and coat. But the three men now stood between her and her horse.

Then the closest one to her said, "It's time to go home, Max."

She tensed and peered at the speaker more closely, then

suddenly felt a wave of dread wash over her. "Is that you, Grady Pike?"

He didn't answer, but she recognized him now. Black hair worn longer than usual, probably because he hadn't paused long enough in getting up here to cut it, green eyes drawn close together in a frown. Knowing who it was didn't remove her fear, though; it just added to it.

Grady Pike was Bingham Hills' sheriff and had been Carl Bingham's puppet. Nearing forty, he'd been sheriff for as long as she could remember. Carl had made sure of that. As mayor, Carl had determined when and if elections would be held, and if anyone had started talking about running for sheriff, he had changed his mind pretty quick.

Grady used to be a nice guy when he was younger. He'd toss her a jawbreaker candy whenever he saw her in town, used to keep a pocket full of them. When she was a kid. Before Carl had run into roadblocks like her and had started doing under-handed things to get around them. And all without anyone knowing. But Grady knew.

Grady's deputy, Andy Wager, was the second man. Short, chubby, with curly, brown hair and brown eyes, and around thirty now, he was another who followed orders without question. Andy had led the posse that had chased her all the way to Kansas. He didn't usually have much gumption, so he must have been promised something special to have gone that far, maybe Grady's job when he retired, not that she could imagine Grady ever retiring from a job that appeared to be his for life.

She didn't recognize the third man, who looked younger, maybe twenty-five, with blond hair, blue eyes, and a slight limp in his right leg. A tracker they'd hired? How else had they found her out here?

She asked that first, "How did you find me?"

"Get out of the water," was all Grady said.

Max shook her head. "Not without some privacy to dress."

She was pushing her luck. Grady probably didn't want to let her out of his sight. Yet he signaled the men to turn around and did the same. He was still standing between her and her horse, though, so she quickly got out of the water and dressed.

With her pants and shirt on, she asked again, "How did you find me?"

All three turned toward her again, and Andy answered, "We probably wouldn't have if you weren't traveling with Degan Grant. It's easy to follow him, as memorable as he is."

Degan was right. Gran's letter had been tampered with. They'd obviously followed it straight to Luella. She must have told them that Max was with Degan, or Madam Joe had provided the information. But that didn't explain how they had found her in the middle of nowhere in Dakota. Grady and Andy were town men; they weren't trackers.

Grady was frowning. Apparently, he didn't approve of Andy's talking to her. He waved his gun toward her horse and told his deputy, "Get her weapons," and said to her, "You don't get to ask questions. We didn't enjoy coming up here, and then you weren't even in Helena when we got there. You're more trouble than you're worth, so just keep your mouth shut or you can go home in chains."

She bristled. This was the man who'd dragged her to Carl's house that fateful morning. She had no doubt that he had known what Carl had been up to and had still done it.

"You can at least tell me if Carl's dead or alive," she demanded.

"Maybe you should have stuck around to find out," Grady growled. "Chains it is then."

"All right!" she conceded.

Andy went through her saddlebags. He'd dumped her coat and vest on the ground and looped her gun belt over his shoulder.

Max was fuming as she put on her vest and coat, then sat down to put on her boots. She was glad she had her coat with her. She had a feeling they would be riding hard to put as much distance as possible between them and Degan. Or were they confident because they outnumbered him? Or did they think their badges would keep Degan from killing them?

She decided to test that, asking, "Can I at least get the rest of my things and say good-bye to Degan?"

"Now that's funny, it really is," Andy replied.

He didn't look amused. And she caught him glancing nervously in the direction of the cabin. Had they been watching it and waiting to get her alone? They knew who Degan was, *what* he was. They wouldn't have risked apprehending her in front of him when that might not have worked out in their favor.

"Rich, ain'tcha?"

Her eyes went back to Andy, holding her wad of money. "That belongs to Bingham Hills' bank. Wilson Cox gave it to me by mistake."

"So you kept it all this time to give it back?" Andy asked incredulously.

"Course I did."

Andy snorted. "Yeah, sure."

With her hat and boots on, Max glanced in the direction of the cabin. With most of her belongings still at the cabin, Degan wouldn't think that she had left of her own accord, would he? Or would he think she'd sacrificed her belongings so that he'd waste time looking for her in the woods first?

She couldn't see the cabin through the trees, but if she could just get closer to it, Degan might hear her yell. Or would they shoot her in the back for trying? He'd definitely hear a gunshot, but it wouldn't do her much good if she was already dead.

Still, she had to try. Grady's not telling her what she could expect in Texas could only mean one thing. If they admitted they were taking her home to hang, they would expect her to fight tooth and nail the whole trip, and it was still a long way to Texas. But did they really think she'd be docile not knowing? Maybe. False hope could make you do dumb things—such as ride along peacefully with your executioners.

"You don't want to make me angry, Max," Grady said as he clamped a hand on her arm.

Was he a mind reader now, knowing she'd been about to run? He already looked angry. She supposed she would be, too, if she'd had to travel this far to collect someone. But she'd lost her chance to get closer to the cabin. Grady was now leading her in the opposite direction.

She spotted their horses through the trees about a minute later. A fourth man was standing with them. When he turned, she recognized who had led Grady right to her.

"You son'bitch!" she yelled at Jackson Bouchard.

She charged toward him, ready to rip him apart, but Grady yanked her back.

Jackson looked completely unperturbed. The bastard even shrugged. "You never said you were wanted by the law."

"Sure, I'm a killer and a bank robber. I go around telling

that to anyone who will listen. And if I get loose, I'm going to add you to my list of dead men."

"Shouldn't she be tied up?" Jackson asked.

Andy chuckled. "You were guarding the ropes, Mr. Bouchard."

She did get tied then. But getting gagged, too, infuriated her even more. They rode through the trees for a while until they were so far from the cabin that it couldn't be seen when they left the woods to ride hard toward Bismarck. As they'd mounted up, Grady had said something about getting there before the morning train departed. If they managed that, she knew Degan would never catch up—if he even tried.

Chapter Thirty-Seven

DEGAN WASN'T SURPRISED HE'D slept so long. He was going to get fat and lazy if they didn't leave soon. Eating and sleeping was all he'd been doing here. He supposed his body needed it, but Max made too much food. But then she didn't have much else to do here except cook and nag him to eat and rest. She was good at nagging, and chattering—and enticing him without even trying. He smiled. She was good at a lot of things.

It had been a long time since anyone had taken care of him the way she had. He could get used to it, could get used to living with her. Never a dull moment. A life full of surprises and sweetness and strong passions. Being with Max, in or out of bed, was like holding wildfire in your arms—or trying to. They wouldn't live in a rustic cabin like this, but in a house, in town, any town would do. Nashart came to mind. He wondered, how much trouble would he bring to that town if he accepted Sheriff Ross's offer and settled there?

It was dawn and he lay in bed while light slowly entered

the cabin. There were no sounds, inside or out, except for the early birds singing, which meant Max was still asleep. Usually, she started a fire first thing to get the chill out of the cabin. He could do that for her this morning.

He sat up and immediately saw that she wasn't there. When he went outside to find her, he saw that her horse was gone, too, so he started walking toward the pond. She wouldn't have gone hunting, not this early. Besides, she'd gone out yesterday and had brought back all sorts of game. She'd told him that she'd spotted a lone buffalo, which he'd been relieved to learn she'd left alone. So he knew she wouldn't have to hunt for another day or two. He hoped they wouldn't be here that long. He was sure he could ride now with minimal discomfort. Well, at least he wouldn't fall off the horse because of it.

It was early for her to be bathing, but where else could she be? As he approached the pond, he called out to her. There was only silence. She wouldn't leave now that he had recovered. No, that thought shouldn't even have occurred to him. The woman wouldn't help him as many times as she had, then abandon him when it was his turn to help her. She just wouldn't.

When he reached the pond, he immediately saw the tracks in the dirt that surrounded it, a lot of them, bootprints much larger than hers. One or two men, maybe more. There were too many bootprints for him to ascertain the number. And evidence that a horse, most likely hers, had been led south through the trees. With the ground being dry, these tracks could have been made yesterday before dark.

Degan didn't like what he was feeling. It was alien to him. It resembled panic and dread, emotions that weren't going to help get Max back, so he pushed them aside and returned to the cabin. He gathered his things, and hers, saddled his horse, and ignored what turned out to be a little more than minimal discomfort as he followed the tree line until he found the spot where more horses had left the woods, heading south. He rode hard in that direction.

He reached Bismarck just before dusk. He went straight to the sheriff's office to see if bounty hunters had turned Max in for the reward. But she wasn't in jail, and the sheriff had left a note that he would be out of town for a few days. If bounty hunters had taken her, that could be why she hadn't been turned in yet. They might still be in town waiting for the sheriff to return.

He went to the train station next. It was closed for the night, but the short schedule was posted on the wall. A west-bound train left early every morning, one bound for the east every evening. It appeared he wouldn't find out until tomorrow morning how many passengers had departed today and in which direction. But he could search the hotels in the meantime. If Max was still in Bismarck, he would find her.

He stabled his horse first, which turned out to be a stroke of luck. His horse was familiar with Max's. They nickered at each other in passing, which made Degan examine the chestnut gelding more closely. While her horse wasn't distinctive, it did have a small white patch on the neck just under the mane where it wouldn't usually be noticed. But he'd rubbed down her horse enough times to notice it.

He called the stableman over to him and nodded toward the chestnut. "Who left this horse here, a man or a woman?"

"Jackson Bouchard did."

"Who was with him?"

"No one. He came in this morning with his horse and this one. Mr. Bouchard always stables here. He asked if I wanted to buy the gelding off him, but I didn't. Don't want more horses than I need."

Degan's panic spiked so he reverted to instinct and simply ran to the boardinghouse nearby where he'd been directed when he asked around for a scout after he and Max had arrived in Bismarck. He was afraid she was dead. Nothing else occurred to him as an explanation for why she no longer needed her horse, but then nothing sensible was running through his mind just then, no thought other than getting his hands on Jackson Bouchard. *She* hadn't trusted the supposed half-breed. She knew Jackson had been working with the train robbers. He wouldn't want to leave loose ends like that. But why wait so long to come back for her? Unless it took him that long to find men willing to help him. No, if Jackson had wanted to kill Max, he could have killed her when they'd come back to the cabin and Degan was passing out.

Degan didn't knock, he just kicked Jackson's door in as soon as he got to it. The man was sitting in a small tub naked. No one else was in the room. He'd started to reach for his rifle on the floor next to him, but stopped when he saw Degan's gun was already drawn and aiming at his heart.

"She's not dead!" Jackson blurted out.

"Where is she?"

"On the train heading west."

Degan cocked his gun. "You're lying. She wouldn't leave her horse."

"She didn't have a choice!"

"Talk fast, Bouchard."

"I thought you were wounded."

"Wounds heal. Say something I need to hear while you still can."

"They were lawmen, a sheriff and two deputies. I heard they were asking around town for you and her. I found them and asked why. They showed me her wanted poster. That was a lot of money to ignore."

"So you led them right to us?"

"To her. They didn't want to deal with you if they didn't have to. We rode all night so they could catch the train this morning."

"They're taking her to Texas?"

"That's what they said."

"Why would they go west to go to Texas?"

"They wanted the first train out so they wouldn't be here when you arrived. They figured you would go east."

"Why is her horse still here?"

"They didn't have horses themselves. They came all the way from Texas by stage and train, so they didn't need them and thought they wouldn't—until they got here. Took half a day to find them a few they could rent or borrow. They didn't want to buy them. When we got back to town, they tossed me her reins and said I could keep her horse as a bonus for helping them finish their business without bloodshed."

"You're not keeping it."

"No, of course not."

"I'll take that money they gave you, too. You don't get to profit from this."

"But she's an outlaw!"

"No, she isn't, and I was going to get that cleared up for her. Your interference has done nothing but make me want to shoot you right now. If they've hurt her, I will come back and kill you. Now where's that money?"

"I don't have it," Jackson admitted. "The sheriff wasn't here to help them out with that. And their town doesn't have a tele-graph. But they said they would send the money here as soon as they got home."

"Gullible as well as despicable." Degan turned to leave.

"Hey! What about the money *you* owe me?"

"You're kidding, right?" Degan didn't pause to hear the answer.

Chapter Thirty-Eight

"You're not from bingham Hills, are you?"

It was Max's first opportunity to talk to Saul Bembry alone, well, at least without Grady or Andy within listening range. And they'd finally removed the gag from her mouth. Grady had gotten annoyed pretty quick at her yelling at him so much. He also didn't like her describing how Degan was going to kill him when he caught up with them, so he was keeping her gagged unless she was being fed.

They were at a stage stop on the long stretch east of Bozeman. There had been many stops after they'd left the train at Billings. Not all of them were in towns. Unlike Boulder, which had grown up around a stage stop, this stop only had a trading post next to it. They only had about fifteen minutes to eat and relieve themselves before the stage departed again with fresh horses and a new driver.

Saul had been left to guard her while she was sitting at a table, since only her hands were tied in front of her, not her feet. Grady and Andy were getting them some food.

"Am now," Saul answered her. "Moved there this year with my wife and kids. Never been made to feel so at home in a place so fast. I'm a carpenter by trade."

"Then what are you doing with these two?"

"I moved to Bingham Hills because I heard it was growing, but it wasn't by the time I got there. I tried making furniture for a while, but there wasn't much call for that either."

Max didn't like hearing that. It confirmed that Carl wasn't around any longer, and Evan must not be carrying on with his father's agenda. Evan might even have moved away. Rich now and out from under his father's thumb, why would he stick around? But if the town was stagnating now, everyone would blame her for that, too.

"But I got talked into staying," Saul continued. "Was promised that building was going to start up again soon. And I was offered the deputy job in the meantime. Didn't expect to have to travel for it, though. I miss my family."

She almost snorted at him. He'd been gone less than a month, while she'd been gone nearly two years. *She* missed her family. She wondered if they would let her see Gran, or if they would lynch her immediately.

"Have you met my grandmother? Your wife probably cooks with her eggs."

He grinned. "Who hasn't met Widow Dawson."

"How is she?"

He shrugged. "She was fine the last I saw her."

More proof that her grandmother's letter had been tampered with. "What about my brother, Johnny?"

"Can't say if I've met your brother." Saul glanced at Grady and Andy, then down at the table. "I think you should stop—"

Stop what? Asking? Worrying? Caring? Probably asking.

He obviously had orders not to tell her anything, even about her family. Grady's orders. And with Grady sitting down next to her right then, she wasn't going to be able to ask any more questions of any kind.

She picked up a piece of bread from the plate Andy had put before her, then glanced behind her at the entrance as if she'd heard something outside. She'd started doing that a few towns back. It got results. It made them nervous and they'd started watching the door of whatever canteen or restaurant they were in. It was her little way of getting even, reminding them that Degan might be following them. That *really* worried them.

If he was following them, he wouldn't be able to catch up. Common sense should have told them that, considering they hadn't run into a single delay. If Degan even took the right train, somehow figuring out that Grady was going west before heading south in order to keep him off their trail, he'd be a day behind them. He couldn't outride one. The stages were slower than trains, but still faster than a horse because they didn't slow down to rest their animals, just swapped them out at each stage station. He could outride a stage, but only if he left his palomino behind, swapping for new mounts along the way, and she couldn't imagine him doing that. Besides, he'd have to sleep sometime, and the stages weren't stopping for that, either. At only one stop had a fresh driver not taken over for a tired one. So any way you looked at it, they would still be a full day ahead of Degan—if he was following.

She needed to escape so she could hide out along the road somewhere and wait for Degan to pass, or delay them somehow. But escape didn't look promising. If she wasn't sitting down with a guard next to her at the rest stops, Grady's hand was clamped to her arm, taking her in and out of them. Even in the coach she ended up sitting between two of the three of them. Grady expected her to try something and was making sure she couldn't.

She'd barely finished her meal when Grady stood up. "Get up, it's time to go," he said before he tied the gag back over her mouth.

As Grady practically dragged her to the stagecoach with Andy and Saul following close behind, she tried to come up with a plan. They'd probably reach Butte sometime tomorrow or late tonight and be back on a train again. Butte would be her last chance to escape. She was going to have to feign some sort of sickness in advance of their arrival there, like today. Something that would require Grady to take her to a doctor when they arrived in Butte. If she could make them miss just one train departure, Degan might roll into town on the next stage. But without some obvious symptoms such as a fever or vomiting, Grady wouldn't buy it. She'd been unable to think of anything else except maybe fainting. But she wouldn't put it past Grady to punch her to see if she was faking. That's how despicable the sheriff had become.

Grady got into the stage first, then Andy pushed her up into it. Grady had her sit between him and Andy, and Saul took the last spot on the bench next to Andy. Across from them sat a dark-haired man dressed in trousers and a suit jacket and a woman with a big bonnet and her young son, who amused himself by playing with a big wooden toy horse. They'd joined them at the last stop, and the man didn't appear to be traveling with the woman and the boy. A cowboy joined them at this stop, tying his horse to the back of the coach.

The coach was full now, which might slow it down a little. The dark-haired man mostly slept and didn't say much when he was awake. The older woman had given Max some disapproving glances when she'd seen that Max was gagged and her hands were tied. The little boy had stared at her and asked his mother why the man had a scarf tied over his mouth. "Don't look at him, Tommy. He's an outlaw," the mother had said. Grady nodded.

Now, the cowboy was staring at Max with interest. "Why's he being restrained and gagged?"

Grady merely showed him his badge in answer.

Max wondered if Grady would punch her in front of these witnesses if she tried fainting right there in the coach. It wouldn't be as dramatic as it would be if she were standing. She'd just have to slump over Grady or Andy. They'd have to conclude that something was wrong with her when they couldn't revive her. She'd have time to do it again before they reached Butte just in case they doubted that she was ill.

She was waiting until they were about halfway between stops before she tried it. But someone else had been waiting for that moment, too. The coach slowed and came to a stop. The dark-haired man had already drawn a gun. Grady was looking out one window, Saul the other, to see why they'd stopped. She was probably the only one who had noticed that the gun across from them hadn't been drawn in self-defense; it was pointed at them. They were being robbed from *inside* the coach?

"Drop your weapons," the dark-haired man said.

Max would have grinned if she weren't gagged. With their money stolen and no quick way to get any more, Grady and his men would end up stranded in Butte for weeks! Well, that was, if they remained alive. But from the expression on Grady's face she could see he had realized that, too, and he wasn't about to get robbed without putting up a fight.

He didn't immediately reach for his gun. Saul had already dropped his on the floor. Andy, apparently, had decided to be the hero; he drew and aimed. He got shot for it. Which was when the woman, instead of screaming, hit the dark-haired man, who was sitting next to her, with her purse. And she hit exactly what she was aiming for, too, the hand holding the gun.

The stage robber's weapon didn't fall out of his hand, but it got pointed toward the floor. That was when Grady drew and shot the robber. Grady then jumped out of the coach to deal with whoever had stopped it. Saul quickly retrieved his gun and went outside to help Grady. Andy was slumped forward, still holding his gun, although it was lax in his hand, now lying on the seat. Right next to Max . . .

"I wouldn't," the cowboy warned her.

Well, hell, Max thought. *Now* he had his gun drawn? She couldn't tell if he was with the robbers or just doing a good deed for the lawmen. Probably the latter, since he didn't say anything else. The woman with the lethal purse only gave him a brief glance before she gathered her boy in her arms to shield him from the dead body on the seat next to her.

Max leaned forward to see if Andy was still alive. He was. His eyes were still open and his face was contorted in pain. She looked for the wound, then winced, finding it near his heart. *He* was going to need a doctor—as long as he didn't die before they could get to one.

Chapter Thirty-Nine

THERE HAD ONLY BEEN two stage robbers, and now both of them were dead, their bodies tied to the top of the coach. They would be turned over to the sheriff in Butte for burial.

The failed robbery hadn't delayed them long, only about twenty minutes. Andy passed out soon after the stage starting moving again, but he was still breathing. Saul was pressing a cloth the woman had given him to the wound to stanch the blood flow.

One more stage stop was before Butte, but it was just a house and a stable. Still, Max lowered her gag long enough to suggest they pause there to take the bullet out of Andy. Grady didn't answer, just lunged toward her to put the gag back in place. She did that before he could reach her. Bastard. It wasn't as if she couldn't remove the gag herself with her hands tied in front of her, but every time she did it, Grady tied the gag even tighter. Which hurt.

She finally got the message and stopped trying. But the last time he'd also warned her that he would tie her hands behind her back if she removed the gag again. The only reason he hadn't done that to begin with was because they'd have to untie her and retie her every time they ate, which would have been too much trouble.

They arrived in Butte early the next morning. Andy was taken straight to the doctor on a stretcher. Saul took his bag and Andy's with him and went to find the local sheriff to inform him of the attempted robbery. Grady picked up his own valise and her saddlebags and, with her arm in his other hand, followed behind the stretcher.

On the way, she heard the train whistle blow. Grady swore, hearing it. She would have laughed, was almost tempted to remove the gag so she could. They would probably have *just* managed to catch that train if the stage robbers hadn't shown up and shot Andy.

Grady still went to the train station, dragging her with him once the doctor started treating Andy's wound. That worried her. He wouldn't leave Andy behind, would he, just to catch the next train? He and Andy were friends, had worked together for years. Of course he wouldn't leave him. That would be too coldhearted, even for Grady.

The train schedule was posted. The next one wasn't leaving until tomorrow at 10:00 a.m. Grady bought three tickets. That answered her question. He was going to leave without Andy. But this delay might still be all that was needed for Degan to catch up. If he'd found out in which direction she'd gone in time to catch the next train in Bismarck. If he'd taken the same stages she'd taken after that. If he was even following her. That was too many ifs to ease her anxiety.

They returned to the doctor's office to await news about Andy's condition. When Saul joined them a while later, Grady sent him to get them a room at the nearest hotel. One room. Max started making noises under her gag, a lot of them. She needed a damn bath. She hadn't had one since they'd captured her at the pond a week ago.

Grady finally lowered her gag to demand, "What?"

"I need my own room."

"No."

"Then I need time alone in the room for a bath. You do, too. We all stink."

He couldn't dispute that. He put her gag back in place and took her to the hotel. Saul was still at the desk checking in. Grady left her and the bags with him.

"See that she gets a bath, but don't leave her alone in the room," he told Saul, then left to go back to the doctor.

Red-faced, she followed Saul up the stairs. But he was even more embarrassed than she was. As soon as the water arrived, he got a chair, took it to the window, and just sat there, looking out at the street with his back to her. She could have told him not to bother, she wasn't taking her clothes off. She *did* take the gag off. She ended up dripping water all over the floor, too, when she got out of the tub. She didn't care. Didn't apologize either when Saul used one of the towels to wipe the floor.

"You should change into dry clothes at least," he mumbled.

"I shouldn't be here at all," she mumbled back. "Degan was already taking me home, you know."

"Yeah, sure. Jackson Bouchard said the gunfighter was wounded bad."

"Jackson was a train-robbing liar," she retorted. "Degan had mended enough to travel. We were leaving for Texas the next day. All you accomplished in stealing me from him was to piss him off. Betcha can guess how that's gonna turn out when he finds you."

Saul backed away from her. "Grant won't think we headed west to go to Texas. Grady outsmarted him. I think you should put that gag back on before Grady gets here."

She ignored the suggestion and went to stand at the window, letting the warm breeze help her clothes to dry. It was pointless to lie to Saul. He might be gullible enough to believe her every word, but what good would it do her? Grady was the one in charge, and Grady wouldn't leave her ungagged long enough to let her say anything to him. Nor would he believe her if she did. None of which mattered. The deed was done. She was in their custody now. And Degan would come or he wouldn't.

Chapter Forty

GRADY AND SAUL LET Max have the bed that night. She was surprised until she saw where they were sleeping. Grady stretched out in front of the door despite its being locked. Saul lay down in front of the window. She supposed that was one way to make sure she didn't sneak off while they slept. But if there had been something hard in the room that she could have used to hit Grady over the head without waking Saul, she would have tried. But there wasn't, at least not anything that wouldn't make too much noise when it broke. So she was the first to drift off to sleep, and the last to rise.

Saul took her downstairs to eat breakfast while Grady went to visit Andy. Saul told her Andy was lucky. The bullet had lodged against one of his ribs before it could hit his heart. He had a cracked rib as well as a gunshot wound, but the doctor was optimistic and had assured Grady that Andy would make a full recovery with proper care—which didn't include traveling anytime soon.

Grady obviously did care about his friend, but something

was driving him to get back to Texas immediately, and it wasn't her. Bingham Hills had waited nearly two years to hang her. A few extra weeks wasn't going to make a difference. She suspected Grady's fear of Degan was making him hurry. It had to be.

Did Grady expect to be killed the very moment Degan spotted him, no questions asked? Maybe. But then he didn't know Degan, just that he was a gunfighter, dangerous, and fast. Reputations got exaggerated and tales got tall, depending on who was doing the telling, and Grady could have heard one of the more colorful tales about Degan that included body counts and the names of other famous gunfighters he'd supposedly killed. Either way, Grady wouldn't know that Degan had a code of honor that demanded fair fights, and she wasn't about to volunteer that information. Grady, worried, suited her just fine.

Grady returned before Saul and she finished eating and hurried them out of the hotel. By her reckoning they had about thirty minutes before the train departed. She was running out of time to come up with a plan to avoid getting on it. She gazed up and down the streets, looking for Degan. He'd be so easy to spot. But he wasn't there, and the station was now in sight, the small building that housed the ticket-sales window and the telegraph, the platform where quite a few people were waiting to board or saying their good-byes, and the long train stretched out behind it. Degan wasn't there either, the one place she figured he'd be—if he was in Butte.

She hadn't done much fighting when she was put on that first train because her hands had been tied behind her back and the gag had been so tight. But knowing she was a dead woman the minute she stepped on this train, she yanked off her gag and started screaming and trying to yank her arm away from Grady. People began coming out of the shops to see why. Grady didn't like that. She was making a spectacle of them. He was about to slap her into silence, drew his hand back for it. A shot was fired.

The sound wasn't near them, but it was loud enough to give Grady pause. Max stopped screaming and tried to figure out where the shot had come from. She looked behind them, expecting to see the local sheriff or Deputy Barnes, but neither man was there. Ahead, the people on the platform had scattered and her heart leapt. Degan was stepping off the train. He'd heard her screaming! He'd been on the train making sure she hadn't already boarded it.

She started to run toward Degan, but she'd forgotten about Grady's hand on her arm, which had just tightened. So she swung around and slammed her bound hands toward his head. Damn, that hurt, but his grip went slack enough for her to pull away. She raced toward Degan before Saul tried to stop her. She wanted to throw herself into Degan's arms but stopped short when she actually reached him. She wasn't nuts. You didn't do that to a man like him, especially when he might be getting into a gunfight at any moment. Actually, she was nuts. She couldn't stay away from him and looped her arms around his neck. His arms moved around her and she heard him whisper, "Maxie." Surrounded by his strength, she felt safe and happy.

He lifted her bound wrists from the back of his neck and set her back from him so his eyes could roam over her from top to bottom. They lingered on the gag at her throat that lay against the top of her bandanna. She brought the knot around to untie it. He moved her hands aside and did it for her.

She was grinning now, widely. He'd come for her! And he'd had to travel the same way they had, without stopping for baths or shaving or changing his clothes, without a decent night's sleep. He wasn't his usual spotlessly clean self, either. He was as dusty as they'd been when they'd got off the coach yesterday. He had to hate that, as fastidious as he was, but still he'd put up with it to travel the fastest way possible—to rescue her.

She still wanted to throw her arms around him, but caution prevailed. "I didn't think you'd get here in time."

"Did they hurt you?"

"No."

"Are they legitimate?"

"Yeah, straight from Bingham Hills."

He threw the gag on the ground behind him. His eyes were back on Grady and Saul, who were approaching so cautiously they weren't even halfway there yet.

"Four tickets were bought in Bismarck," Degan said to Max. "Where's the third man who was with them?"

"Andy Wager got shot. He's with the doc here in Butte. They're in such a hurry to get home, they're leaving him behind."

"Did you do it?"

She shook her head. "It was stage robbers, who didn't survive the attempt. I haven't been able to get my hands on a gun since I left the cabin in Dakota. They have mine. I'd like it back. They gave away my horse, too, the bastards."

"But otherwise you're fine?"

"Aside from some chafing on my wrists from the ropes tying my hands, yeah, I couldn't be better—now." She smiled up at him.

"How did they manage to keep you gagged if you were able to reach the gag?"

"With threats of tying it tighter each time I did remove it," she huffed.

"Don't tell me you didn't want to shut her up, too," Grady said to Degan. "She jabbers incessantly."

Max stiffened. She hadn't heard their footsteps behind her. Grady had just sounded jocular. Really? This was how he was going to deal with Degan? She turned. Their weapons weren't drawn. Smart of them. But they had to know they weren't getting her back.

"It's not what you think, Mr. Grant," Grady continued hesitantly when Degan didn't say a word to him. "They want her back in Texas for a different reason. But that's not your concern."

"Isn't it? When you stole her from me?"

"If it's a matter of the reward—?"

"It's not."

"Good, because all charges against her were dropped last year."

Oh, sure, *him* they tell. Max snarled at Grady, "And why couldn't you tell *me* that?"

But Degan pointed out, "You didn't need to take her as you did if that's true."

"No offense, Mr. Grant, but after what we heard about you, we didn't want to butt heads with you out in the wilderness. And I wasn't sure if you'd believe us when I told you that there is no longer a reward for her return."

"I'm not a murderer," Degan said coldly. "And I'd prefer not to become one today. So I suggest you tell me pretty quick why you took her at all—if she's no longer wanted by the law."

Grady started to reach inside his coat. Degan proved how fast he was with his gun. It was simply just there in his hand before anyone even saw him draw it.

Grady threw his hands up in the air quickly, saying, "The document in my coat will explain it."

Degan didn't holster his gun yet. "Get it and give it to Max—after you take that damn rope off her."

With a wary eye on Degan, Saul stepped forward to cut the rope from her wrists. Max was amused that Degan sounded offended that *they'd* tied her when he'd done the same thing himself. But she didn't show it. Both Grady and Saul looked tense. None of this made a lick of sense. The charges against her had been dropped? She couldn't believe it! She was free? Unless Grady was just making a lame attempt to get Degan to simply walk away by feeding him some lies. But he could have done that at the cabin in Dakota if the charges against her had really been dropped. Actually, they had no business even being here if she was no longer wanted by the law.

Grady handed the folded document to her. She opened it and started reading, but didn't get far. Wide-eyed, she looked up at Grady.

"Carl's alive? I *knew* that old fart was too ornery to die!"

"Have some respect for our mayor—and your guardian," Grady said testily.

Max paled. "My gran is dead?"

"No, she's not. But the court ruled her incompetent to raise you."

Max exploded, "Like hell she is!"

"It's true," Grady assured her. "Read the rest of the legal document and you'll understand why. Ella Dawson let you grow up a wild tomboy. No one doubts she loves you, but she still let you do as you pleased instead of giving you proper guidance. She even let you take off on your own. Since there's no male adult in your family, you and your brother were appointed a new guardian by the court. And I was tasked with bringing you home so you could get some proper rearing."

"Why was Carl appointed?" she demanded.

"He was willing to take on the responsibility when no one else was."

Her eyes narrowed on Grady. "Do you even know how old I am, Grady Pike? I don't need a guardian."

"You're not twenty-one years old yet or married. And the law requires you to be in the care of a responsible adult until you are."

Degan took the document from her, but was still staring coldly at Grady. "Wards aren't supposed to be treated as prisoners, Mr. Pike."

"It's Sheriff Pike, and they are when they won't come along peacefully."

"Did you even ask her if she would?"

"He wouldn't tell me a damn thing, Degan," Max put in, "because he knew I wouldn't believe him if he did."

"You would have disappeared the first chance you got if you knew who your new guardian was." Grady turned to Degan. "That document is legal, Mr. Grant."

"The same way those wanted posters were legal?" Degan asked.

Grady turned red with anger and embarrassment.

Max demanded, "Why was I charged with murder when no one died?"

Fuming, Grady said, "You shot a man and he *almost* died." But then he told Degan, "Show that document to the local judge if you still have any doubts. I knew Max would fight it, so we didn't tell her. It's that simple."

"So is this," Degan said. "She stays with me."

Grady stiffened. "We can't go home empty-handed."

"You won't." Degan put his gun away. "I finished my business in Dakota. We would have been on our way to Texas, would have been married by now, too, if I didn't get shot—and you didn't interfere."

"You were going to marry her?"

"I still am."

It was a pretty good bluff, Max thought with a smirk.

But Grady called him on it. "Prove it."

"Excuse me?"

"If she's not married by the end of the day, she comes with us."

Chapter Forty-One

"In case you were wondering, I think your chatter is charming," Degan said with his usual deadpan expression as they walked away from the train station.

Max burst out laughing. The remark definitely eased her tension. She wasn't sure how Degan was going to get them out of this mess, but he must have something planned.

"I have your horse," he added.

She squealed in delight and threw her arms around him again. He put his arms around her and squeezed her briefly, maybe a little too tightly, then let her go. His hands didn't leave her though. They lingered on her waist. She liked the way they felt there. But she knew Grady was behind them, had begun following them the moment they'd left the train station. Degan was just putting on a show for him, no doubt, trying to convince him they were a happy couple. But he couldn't appear too affectionate. He had his reputation to maintain, after all.

When they started walking again, she thought to ask, "How'd you get my horse back?"

"Bouchard was happy to return him."

"Happy?"

"He felt obliged. Also felt obliged to tell me Grady was so desperate to get out of Bismarck he took the early westbound train."

She grinned, but then groaned in disappointment. "But you couldn't bring Noble with you, could you? If you took the stage to get here as fast as you did, you couldn't have brought our horses along. They wouldn't have had a chance to sleep."

"The stage driver solved that dilemma. He suggested attaching a wagon bed to the back of the coach. He'd done it before, just not for such a long distance. But it worked. The wagon only needed to be replaced once because it wasn't as sturdy as the coach. And since I bought all the seats in the coach, there wasn't a lot of extra weight for the stage horses to pull."

Max was amazed that he'd gone to so much trouble and expense for her. It smacked of his being desperate, yet she couldn't imagine Degan Grant desperate.

"I really didn't think you'd get here in time because I was sure you wouldn't leave your palomino behind. I'm glad you figured out a way not to."

"We'll visit Noble after I have a bath."

The church was in sight now and he was leading her toward it. "You were just kidding, right?"

Degan merely said, "I'd like to know what all my options are."

They entered a plain, little church with a white steeple, but no one was there. Max sighed with relief until Degan took her hand and led her to the house next door. Max heard women talking and laughing inside.

Degan's knock on the door was answered by an older

woman, whose eyes widened at the sight of him. "Is this the preacher's house?"

"Yes, it is, but he's not home right now. I'm his wife. Perhaps I can help you?"

Two of the woman's friends had joined her at the door. One held knitting needles and a spool of yarn in her hands. They'd apparently interrupted a sewing circle.

"I need the preacher to perform a marriage ceremony," Degan explained.

"Your names?"

"Degan Grant and Maxine Dawson."

The woman's eyes widened even further, and one of her friends whispered something in her ear. The woman then smiled at Degan. "My husband should be home by five o'clock. I'm sure he'll be able to oblige."

"That's fine, as long as he can marry us before sundown."

Max knew Degan added that for the benefit of Grady and Saul, who were still following them at a discreet distance. Max and Degan continued on to find a hotel. Max directed Degan away from the one she'd stayed at the previous night with Grady and Saul. Degan ordered bathwater. In their room, he sat down to read the guardianship decree. Grady had asked him to give it back, but Degan had ignored him. It was nice to know she wasn't the only person Degan ignored.

But it was too bad his bluff had been called. He wouldn't have been expecting that.

She moved to the window and saw Grady standing across the street watching the entrance to the hotel. Saul was probably around back doing the same thing. She and Degan wouldn't be getting out of there before dark without being seen and stopped.

When Degan set the document aside after reading it, she asked, "Are you going to find a judge to verify that? Is that why you kept it?"

"I studied law at the college in Chicago at my father's insistence. He wanted me to be capable of dealing with his lawyers as well as the ones they dealt with." Degan waved a hand at the document. "I don't doubt that the document is legitimate. But Carl Bingham's means of obtaining it probably wasn't."

She nodded. "Bingham Hills doesn't have a resident judge, just a circuit judge that comes by from time to time. He always stayed with the Binghams. Grady is in Carl's pocket, the judge probably is, too."

"Whether he is or whether he merely did his 'host' a favor is irrelevant. The document needs to be negated, and it specifically states what will do that, your reaching the age of twenty-one or your marrying. So we get married today."

"But you weren't serious about that!"

"I am now."

"Why?"

"It's the safest way to get you back to Texas and find out why Carl Bingham is so determined to control you. Don't worry, it doesn't have to be a marriage in every sense of the word, merely one of legal convenience. I haven't forgotten your prerequisite for marriage—some good, happy reasons I believe you said. Besides, there are ways to get 'unmarried' after we find out what's going on in Bingham Hills."

"You're talking about an annulment?"

"Yes."

He tapped the document with his finger. "This is just another means of getting you under their control. What needs to happen is for Bingham to stop coveting whatever prize it is that you can bring him. The prize needs to become unavailable to him."

"So if I'm already married, that ends it?"

"It should."

"Or it makes you a target instead," she couldn't help pointing out.

But she was incredulous to see him actually smile at that prediction. "I've been a target for a number of years now. I'm used to it."

But she wasn't used to him being one. But the temporary marriage could work, she supposed. Until now she would have been easy to manipulate if either of Carl's schemes had worked. But he'd have to deal with Degan now, and men dealt with each other differently from how they dealt with women. Carl would have to be more cautious.

The water arrived. Degan suggested she bathe first behind the screen while he shaved. He also told her to open his food sack. No food was in it, but she was happy to find her belongings that she'd left at the cabin, including the floral-patterned skirt and white blouse that Degan had bought for her, which she could wear to the church that afternoon.

They had lunch at a restaurant nearby, where Grady and Saul sat down at another table. Those two weren't even trying to hide their surveillance. Degan didn't appear to mind. Max felt he was even amused by it when he said, "Maybe I should invite them to join us."

He didn't, but he extended their lunch another hour with coffee and a second helping of dessert to see if the lawmen would leave first. They didn't.

After the long lunch they stopped at the telegraph office. Degan explained about having to keep Marshal Hayes apprised of the outlaws who could be removed from his list, including her, now that the charges had been dropped. He'd sent John news about Kid Cade before they'd left for Dakota, but he hadn't had time until now to let him know that Willie Nolan and his gang wouldn't be robbing any more trains. Then Max was delighted when Degan took her to the stable to visit Noble.

The gelding appeared to have weathered the trip fine. So had Degan. She'd asked about his wound when he was bathing—and she was trying to keep her mind off it. He'd assured her it caused him barely a twinge now, but she doubted that he would tell her if he *was* still in pain.

When it was nearing five o'clock, they continued on to the church. Max started having doubts about what they were about to do, and those doubts grew stronger when the church came into view.

"Are you sure you want to do this?" she asked Degan.

"I told you, it's just a temporary measure—and it avoids bloodshed."

He'd shoot Grady for her? Well, not shoot to kill, but he probably wouldn't hesitate to disable him.

This certainly wasn't the way Max had pictured getting hitched, with no family present and a gun on the groom's hip. But it wasn't real—well, it was, just not real enough to last. She had to keep that uppermost in her mind—and forget how much this felt like a shotgun wedding.

They couldn't miss the crowd of people outside the church, but didn't understand what was going on until they got closer and heard someone shout, "There he is! There's the famous gunfighter who's getting married today!"

People in the crowd were craning their necks to get a look at Degan and his bride. Max realized Degan was a celebrity to these people after his recent gunfight with Jacob Reed in this town. Even Deputy Barnes was there. Max was stunned by the turnout. Degan seemed annoyed by it and forged ahead, trying to get them inside the church.

But then the reason why they were there stepped forward with his sidekick. "Hold up," Grady said to Degan. "It's occurred to me that you probably need her guardian's permission for this."

Degan turned and drew his gun. "No, I don't."

The crowd gasped and stepped back in unison, but no one left, every eye avidly on Degan. Grady didn't back down. Saul, white-faced, tried to drag him away, but Grady seemed rooted in place.

Which might be why Degan added, "I'm doing exactly what you requested, Sheriff Pike, marrying Max before sunset. And it's going to happen right now—one way or another."

The threat was implicit. It looked as if Grady wanted to say more, but the crowd was suddenly applauding Degan. Max almost laughed. Grady had been a sheriff for so long; he wasn't used to having his dictates, or suggestions, for that matter, ignored. But Bingham Hills was a peaceful town. No one like Degan had ever passed through it. Grady was simply out of his depth in dealing with a gunfighter of this caliber. And he'd certainly never experienced a crowd swayed against him like this, either.

Despite Grady's sour expression, Degan considered the matter settled and escorted Max into the church. Grady and Saul still followed them and pushed their way into a front pew between two women already seated there. One of the women was dabbing at her eyes, exclaiming to everyone around her, "I just love weddings!"

The church quickly filled with people eager to watch the ceremony. Degan shook hands with the preacher, who introduced himself, and then asked, "Why the sudden rush for a wedding, Mr. Grant?"

"My bride has been tied up for the past week; now she's free."

Degan glanced back at Grady as he said that. Max had to bite back a laugh when she saw Grady turn red with fury.

The preacher, unaware of the byplay, began the ceremony. "We're here today to join this man and this woman in holy matrimony. If anyone objects, speak now or forever hold your peace."

Max held her breath, refusing to look at Grady. If he said anything now, she might shoot him herself. But she heard the tussle behind them and glanced back. Grady *had* stood up, but the two women sitting next to him had yanked him back down.

The preacher didn't notice this and continued, "You have the rings?"

Degan didn't reply. Max groaned to herself, catching Grady's smirk because the wedding was going to stop right now. Of course Degan didn't have rings for them. She hadn't thought of it either!

But then an elderly man stood up. "My wife and I are happy to lend you ours for the ceremony. There's fifty years of good luck in these rings."

A collective sigh of relief was released from the crowd, Max's included. While this marriage might not be real, she found herself wanting it to happen more than anything. To put an end to Carl's plans, she assured herself. Then why was she so thrilled when she heard Degan saying his vows?

"I, Degan Grant, take you, Maxine Dawson, to be my wife, to have and to hold from this day forward, for better or worse, for richer or poorer, in sickness and in health, to love and to cherish until death do us part."

After she repeated those vows to Degan, they were pronounced man and wife, and Degan quickly kissed her. Goodness, she could hear all the old ladies gushing over that! Then they got another surprise.

"My wife and her friends would like you to come out back if you would," the preacher said. "Please don't disappoint her or I'll never hear the end of it. Follow me."

The last was said quite loudly, an invitation extended to the whole gathering. Degan and Max saw why when they stepped out of the church's back door. Tables laden with food had been set up in the yard and fiddlers were starting to play. The church ladies had made a party for them!

Max was touched by these strangers' thoughtfulness and generosity, and delighted, too. She'd thought her wedding was going to feel as fake as it was intended to be, but it certainly didn't now. Everyone was talking and laughing, and having fun—well, everyone except Grady. Max even caught him getting his hand slapped by one of the women when he reached for a plate of food. Because he'd been set on obstructing the union of the happy couple, no one there was pleased by his presence.

That's when he came over to her and Degan. Max hoped it was to say good-bye, since he obviously wasn't welcome there and knew it, but she should have known better. With no congratulations, no surprise that they'd actually gone through with it, and still looking extremely disgruntled, he just asked if they would be on the train in the morning.

"Usually I take offense when someone calls me a liar, Sheriff Pike."

Grady started to assure him, "I didn't—"

"But it's my wedding day, so I'll make an exception. I already told you we were going to Texas. Your doubting me *is* the same thing as calling me a liar."

"You didn't say when you were going," Grady grumbled in his defense.

"Because it's irrelevant, and in point of fact it stopped being any concern of yours the moment Max was pronounced my wife. However, I assume she would rather visit her family than go on a honeymoon right away, so in all likelihood we will start south in the morning. But do us both a favor and don't question me again."

Max thought that watching Grady get his hands tied like that was such a nice wedding gift. It was a wonder she didn't laugh out loud. But she didn't doubt that Grady and Saul would still follow them all the way to Texas, despite what Degan had said to Grady. He was too devoted to Carl Bingham and his interests not to.

The merriment continued. Max was sure everyone there had already come forward to congratulate them, but then someone else did. And she heard Degan say, "Well, I'll be damned."

She stared at the man approaching Degan with his hand extended. He was tall and handsome with black hair and powder-blue eyes. She whispered, "You know him?"

The question got answered when the man reached them and introduced himself, "I'm Morgan Callahan."

"I guessed as much." Degan shook the man's hand.

"Yeah, Hunter and I hear that a lot, how much we look

alike. Congratulations on your wedding, but please tell me you're not here because of me."

"I'm not, but why would you think so?"

"I heard from some miners here that you were working for my father. I know he hates that I prefer mining to working with my family on the ranch."

"That's between you and Zachary—and it's not why he hired me."

"So it's true? You actually brought about my brother's marriage to the Warren girl?"

"I'd say Hunter managed that on his own."

"I'm surprised. He really hated having that arranged marriage hanging over his head. I figured it wasn't going to happen unless he was dragged kicking and screaming to the altar."

"Believe me, nothing would have kept Hunter away from that wedding. You'll understand why when you meet his wife."

Morgan smiled. "I'm sorry I missed all the fun, but I struck it rich and will be going home for a visit as soon as I settle a dispute with a rival lady miner. And, no, I'm not asking if I can hire you! But maybe I can kiss this bride since I missed kissing my brother's new wife?"

"Not a chance." Degan put his arm around Max's waist.

Max wasn't sure if Degan was serious or if this was just his way of joking, but Morgan laughed, insisting, "I'm not like Hunter, who charms every woman in sight! But I'm not going to argue with the notorious Degan Grant, either. Have a happy marriage, you two."

As Morgan sauntered off, one of the ladies was bold enough to come over and tell Degan to dance with his wife. Wide-eyed, Max was afraid of his reaction to *that*. But he surprised her by leading her to join the other couples dancing next to the musicians. A Western rendition of a waltz was being played. It was faster than a traditional waltz but not as boisterous as most of the fiddlers' music had been. The tempo slowed a little as they started dancing, and Degan pulled Max close enough that she could rest her head on his shoulder. Her smile turned dreamy. And then she yawned—and laughed at herself.

"You're tired," he said, having heard it.

She'd been through a lot this last week as Grady's prisoner and experiencing the emotional roller coaster of being reunited with Degan and becoming his wife, even if in name only. "A little," she admitted.

"Let's go."

For once she didn't object to those two words. Amid lots of good wishes and happy tears from the ladies who loved weddings and a comment from the preacher's wife about how this celebrity wedding had tripled the size of the church's congregation, Degan led a sleepy Max back to the hotel.

Chapter Forty-Two

"YOUR SHERIFF IS ALREADY suspicious, and with everyone in town knowing we got hitched, we can't risk having a cot delivered to our room."

Max had assumed that Degan had already arranged for one as he'd done at the other hotels they stayed at after Bozeman. But she couldn't fault him for forgetting after everything that had happened today.

"I can sleep on the floor," she offered.

"We can share the bed—as long as you stay on your side of it."

She recalled what had happened that morning in Bozeman when she'd awakened to find him bare chested and watching her. And the kiss . . . She wished now she hadn't remembered that. She'd probably think of nothing else now.

Yet he'd pretty much just implied it might happen again, so she reassured him it wouldn't by teasing, "You think Grady will break in here in the morning to inspect the sheets?"

"I don't think he has a death wish, no."

"I don't know, Grady can be damn determined, especially if he gets it into his head that our marriage is only a legal convenience." Max yawned, but continued to tease, "I'll guard the sheets with my life. I'll even take them with me in the morning. But I should probably strip down a little more than I usually do, just in case he does have that death wish—or climbs up to peek through the window in the middle of the night, which we probably wouldn't hear."

"Are you trying to make me laugh?"

She grinned. "It's not working, huh?"

"Stripping down sounds interesting."

Was *he* teasing her now? Or had the same thing that had occurred to her occurred to him—that no one except them would know if they did actually make love? The marriage could still be annulled. They'd just have to lie a little. . . .

Yet he was walking toward her and looked a bit more determined than usual. Not at all sure what he was about to do, she took a few steps back until she ran out of space and her back was pressed to the wall.

"You know you're not afraid of me, Maxie, so what are you doing?"

Did he really just sound amused? "You don't usually want to get this close to me."

"There's a good reason for that."

"Then what are *you* doing?"

"Making an exception to give you what you missed at the church—a wedding kiss."

"But you did kiss me."

"I wasn't sure you even noticed, it was so quick. And that one didn't count with that unfriendly witness present. I thought you might like a real one for this first marriage of yours."

Reminding her that this wouldn't be her only marriage in the same breath that he wanted to seal it with a real kiss? Was he kidding? He probably was. She should know better than to tease him. He got even.

She put a hand up to his chest. "We can leave it the way it's supposed to be—a fake marriage."

"It's as fake as you want it to be, Maxie," he said quietly as he leaned in a little closer. "But you're still getting this kiss. Consider it a memento."

As if she could ever forget anything having to do with him. But she couldn't dodge his mouth. She didn't try very hard. And quickly, she found out that this kiss wasn't the kind he could have given her in a church. Not even close.

He lifted one of her legs and wrapped it around his hip as he leaned in even closer. His tongue was in play immediately, swirling around hers, tempting a response from her. No coaxing was necessary. Her body responded to him as it always did with the sensual stirring that flipped around as if it were trying to find him but couldn't. Her hands could. She put one behind his neck and quickly moved it up into his hair. The other she slipped under his jacket, but his vest was still in the way. Would he stop long enough to let her get rid of it?

He stopped longer than that. He stepped back so fast she almost stumbled.

Heat was in his eyes, and yet his voice was as toneless as it usually was when he said, "There. In case they're up on the roof across the street looking this way."

Max blinked. "That was just for show?"

"Of course."

She felt like hitting him. "I'm too tired to play any more games today!"

She pushed away from the wall and pulled her blouse off over her head and threw it on a chair. She yanked her boots and socks off next. That took some hopping, but she was too frustrated to sit down to do it. She unfastened her skirt and just let it pool at her feet before she marched to the bed and yanked the covers down. Then she crawled to the center of the bed and stretched out as if she were waiting for him to join her. But she sure as hell wasn't—until a bare-chested Degan lay down beside her.

"That was for Grady," he said softly. "This is for us."

Max sputtered, "What—what do you think you're doing?"

He kissed her before he said, "Relax and turn over so I can rub your back."

As tired as she was, that sounded too nice to refuse. She rolled over for the massage, but it felt so divine she got more and more drowsy until he turned her onto her back and started kissing her again. His mouth moved lower and he nibbled at her neck, sending pleasant tingles rippling through her body. He kissed her shoulder as he touched her breast, running his finger around her nipple ever so lightly until she gasped. But he didn't stop. He kept stroking her as his mouth moved lower again, leaving a trail of kisses until his tongue was flicking at the tip of her other breast. She groaned as heat rushed through her, running her fingers through his hair, rubbing the back of his neck. Degan was kissing both of her breasts now, directing his attention to first one and then the other, his hands caressing her, too.

His mouth kept moving lower, kissing her midriff as he stroked her hips and thighs. What was he doing? Was he going to kiss her all the way down to her toes? She couldn't think beyond that, all she could do was luxuriate in the pleasure his hands and mouth were giving her. The sensations got so intense she had to take deep breaths and close her eyes. But when he gently pushed her legs apart and kissed her thigh, her eyes flew open. And when he reached the most sensitive spot on her body, she climaxed.

She was totally shocked, amazed, delighted, yet too exhausted to grasp what had just happened. As she drifted off, she thought she heard Degan say, "Good night, Mrs. Grant."

Chapter Forty-Three

Cole callahan rode hard to get back to the ranch. He didn't have his mother's bonnet, which he'd been sent to town to fetch. Ever since that Allison Montgomery woman had paid his parents a visit, Mary had been pining for a pretty new bonnet like hers and had ordered one from back East. And he'd been sent to town every day to see if it had arrived. That Eastern lady had made quite an impression on his parents. He wished he'd been home that day to meet her.

His parents had just ridden in from the range for lunch. He caught them leaving the stable for the house and hopped off his horse next to them. Mary looked disappointed when she didn't see a hatbox tied to his saddle, but he knew he could fix that with his exciting news.

Grinning, Cole exclaimed, "I've got a telegram from Morgan!"

Zachary humphed as he took the sealed telegram from his son. "After this long that boy finally lets us know he's still alive?"

"You were worried he wasn't?" Mary asked.

"Course not, but he didn't know that."

"I *knew* I should've just opened it," Cole said impatiently. "Pa, what are you waiting for?"

Zachary opened the telegram, but his eyebrows shot up after reading the first line. "Well, I'll be damned. Morgan struck it rich." Then with a sigh he said, "I was hoping for better news."

Cole was laughing. "What's better than that?"

"That he's ready to give up this mining nonsense and come home for good."

"Pa, striking it rich means he won't be doing the mining himself anymore, he'll have crews to do it for him."

But Mary wanted to know. "What else does he say?"

Zachary read further. "I think he's gone daft. 'Who knew thorns could be so nice?' What does that mean?"

Mary snatched the telegram out of her husband's hands. "Some thornbushes must have led him to his ore discovery," she guessed.

"Or he's in love with someone who annoys the hell out of him," Cole said with a grin.

Mary scoffed, "Morgan in love? That would be wonderful, but I highly doubt it. He's been too single-minded in this mining obsession of his. When would he have time to fall in love?"

"Well, someone we know did," Zachary said with a grin of his own. "Read the last line, Mary."

She did, then exclaimed, "Oh, my! Degan got married!"

"Sounds like Morgan knows Degan was working for me. Why else mention his wedding?" Zachary said.

"Are you kidding?" Cole put in. "Anything to do with

Degan Grant is big news and worth sharing, which I'm going to do right now." He mounted his horse and started off toward town, yelling back, "Don't wait on me for dinner!"

"I liked that Allison girl," Mary said as she and Zachary continued walking to the house. "I'm so glad she was able to catch up with Degan."

"Did your eyes stop on the word *married*?" Zachary teased. "Morgan says Degan married a pretty blonde, which Miss Montgomery isn't."

Mary's brows went up before she sighed. "I suppose I should hope now that Allison doesn't catch up with him. Whatever is that gunfighter up to, marrying someone he barely knows instead of his long-lost love?"

Max had lost interest in the scenery the train was passing and it was only their first day of the trip to Texas. With this being her third train ride now, after the trip to Dakota and back, the thrill of riding so fast had passed. She even thought about taking a nap, though she wasn't tired.

At least she didn't have to be alone with Degan. She still blushed when she thought about what had happened on their wedding night. The girls in the brothel hadn't told her about that. Degan had sensed her embarrassment this morning and had said, "There's no need to blush about what happened last night. That's what married people do. I told you this marriage can be as fake as you want it to be, and that's how it will be until you tell me otherwise."

The train they were riding wasn't fancy with private compartments; they were seated with all the other passengers and would be day and night. Grady and Saul were on the train somewhere. She'd seen them board it in Butte. They'd just made sure to sit in a different car. Or maybe Degan had seen to that.

This first leg of the trip was much shorter than Max had figured it would be. They would be reaching the main junction in Ogden, Utah, later that night, where they would switch to the train going East that would eventually connect with a Texas-bound train.

But over dinner in the dining car that evening, Degan told her, "We may have some trouble with our friend Pike tomorrow."

She snorted. "He's no friend of ours. But why? Those two have been avoiding us."

"They will expect us to catch the eastbound train tomorrow, but I'm thinking about spending a few days in the Ogden area instead of continuing on immediately."

"Why?"

"I need to finish some business."

She wasn't letting him get away with such a brief explanation. "What business?"

"John Hayes sent me a telegram in Butte, saying he got word from the US Marshals Service that Charles Bixford was spotted near Ogden. He's one of the outlaws John needs to apprehend."

"I remember the notes on Red Charley."

"They haven't been able to get a marshal out there yet, and the local sheriffs are reluctant to confront Bixford on their own."

"So you're going after him?"

"Yes."

Degan's changing their plans didn't please Max at all. She was in a tearing hurry to see her grandmother and to get

Johnny out from under Carl's thumb, which was where she imagined he'd been since the signing of that damn guardianship decree. She hadn't expected this delay in getting home.

She stewed over what Degan had said, but as soon as they finished the meal and returned to their seats in the passenger car, she mentioned other options. "I know you still need to capture one more outlaw to pay back your friend, but why would you go after the worst of the lot? As I recall, there are a couple in Wyoming, which we'll be passing through on the way to Texas, and a couple more in Colorado, which we'll also be passing through. Why Red Charley?"

"I don't need to go after any more of them. Three have already been crossed off."

"Because they dropped the charges against me?"

"No, because one of the two outlaws in Wyoming is already dead."

She didn't ask how he knew that. He had to have witnessed it or been involved himself. But now that she knew he didn't have to go after the worst of the lot, she was even more perplexed by his decision.

"You didn't tell me why," she reminded him.

"Because Charles Bixford kills just for the heck of it, and he's already killed one marshal who tried to apprehend him. And because John has a family. He'll be going after Bixford if I don't."

And Degan didn't have a family? No, of course not. She didn't count, and the family he'd left behind didn't either. A family man such as John Hayes counted. A friend. She got it, she just didn't like it.

She said, "Grady used to be a real sheriff before he became Carl's 'do anything' man. Maybe he can help."

Degan leaned his head back and closed his eyes. She recognized that as his answer. He was done discussing it. If she thought they were going to stay together any longer than it took to get to Texas, she would make an effort to break him of that irritating habit. Yet, she had to admit that Degan had changed since she'd met him. The time they'd spent alone in Dakota had opened him up some. They didn't converse only over a meal. And he didn't often clam up like this anymore, at least not with her—only when she said something dumb such as implying that he could use some help.

Chapter Forty-Four

"REALLY? NO BATH FIRST?"

Degan was leaving the hotel room they'd just entered so he could do some questioning in town. His forgoing a bath first gave her the impression that he was hoping to finish his business here today so they could go on to Texas tomorrow.

"Ogden is a big town," he added, "but I should know before dinner if Red Charley is here. And lock the door."

She would have snuck out and done some questioning herself to help him if his remark about locking the door didn't remind her that Grady and Saul had checked into the same hotel right after them. Although Grady had witnessed the marriage ceremony, she wouldn't put it past him to snatch her away if he caught her alone. Carl had ordered Grady to bring her back. Letting her waltz into Bingham Hills with Degan would indicate that Grady hadn't done his job. This was the first time she and Degan had been apart since he'd rescued her in Butte.

She took a bath and then stood by the window, hoping to see Degan on his way back to the hotel. But seeing no sign of him up or down the street, she considered sneaking out to help him. She had her gun back and had been wearing it since they'd left Butte. She could handle Grady as long as he didn't surprise her. But she didn't leave the room because she didn't want Degan to return and find her gone.

Then she spotted a big mountain of a man who could actually be Red Charley. He had red hair, a rat-nested bush of it sticking out all over his head and a full red beard to go with it. His teeth gripped a short, fat cigar, and he was wearing a tattered jacket over farmer's overalls that looked so well worn they might have been the same ones he'd been wearing when he left Nebraska. He was just walking down the middle of the street, laughing when people scurried out of his way.

A man of that size wouldn't be easy to apprehend. Shooting him might not stop him, either. With all that excess flesh, he probably wouldn't even feel a bullet. And Degan was too straightforward. He'd expect a man to go down if he had to shoot him, not come charging at him in rage, which is how Max imagined the big redhead would react.

She hoped the man wasn't Red Charley. She hoped Degan wouldn't think he was if he spotted him. But he did. She saw Degan step out from under the porch of a building down the street from the hotel. He called Bixford's name. Max gripped the windowsill when the big man in overalls stopped and slowly turned.

Degan already had his gun drawn. Charley didn't appear to be wearing one, with no belt of any sort needed for his overalls. He didn't look the least bit concerned about Degan. Everyone else was wary around Degan, but not this man. He just casually took a fresh cigar out of his pocket and replaced the short one with it, lighting it with the stub—and tossed it at Degan. It landed at Degan's feet. That's when Max realized the cigar had a short fuse attached to it.

It was a stick of dynamite! Degan dived toward a water trough across the street. But the explosion occurred too quickly. She blanched, not knowing if Degan had gotten behind the trough in time or if it even mattered since the trough blew up. The porch posts behind it were also blown away, causing the roof to collapse. The windows of the shop had shattered, too. And that mass-murdering bastard just continued down the street with his barrel laugh floating behind him.

Frantically searching the debris with wide eyes, Max didn't breathe until she saw Degan slowly getting to his feet. Water had flown everywhere, dousing him, but incredibly, the back of the trough was still standing, though the other three sides weren't. And Degan's gun was still in his hand.

His first shot hit the fleshy part of Charley's leg. All that did was turn him around again. The second shot hit the hand reaching for another stick of dynamite. That only kept the hand out of his pocket. But the big redhead reacted the way Max had imagined he would. Red Charley charged toward Degan. The third shot hit his other leg at the knee. That had to hurt. It still took another long moment for him to topple over when that leg buckled.

Degan should have just shot him in the head. Max would have. Who would miss a killer like that? But Degan had effectively disarmed Bixford with the shot to his hand, keeping him from setting off any more explosions. And Degan wouldn't kill an unarmed man even if no one would thank him for letting this one live.

Max raced downstairs and out into the street. She didn't hesitate to throw her arms around Degan when she reached him, despite the crowd of people that had gathered there, including the local sheriff and the Texas lawmen.

She arrived in time to hear Grady grumble, "It would have been nice if you'd mentioned you're a marshal." He'd obviously just noticed the badge Degan was wearing today.

"Why?" Degan replied indifferently. "It makes no difference to your task, or to mine."

The local sheriff said, "Bixford blew up a mine down in Coalville to the south that killed five men, but I wasn't sure it was him. I confronted him, but he denied it, so I couldn't lock him up. Had him watched, though, to make sure he didn't leave town. A witness was coming to identify him, but I've been waiting three weeks now for him to get up here. Guess I can let the sheriff in Coalville know we don't need him now. We had no idea he was wanted for so many killings elsewhere. Appreciate the help, Marshal."

There was more talk. Max stopped listening and just kept her ear to Degan's chest. His heartbeat was so soothing to her right then. She was surprised he didn't set her away from him, that he was even keeping one arm around her back. She had to be embarrassing him, hugging him in public with half the town showing up to talk about the explosion. But no one seemed nervous around him right now.

Everyone was thanking him, which he probably wasn't used to. She had a feeling no one around there knew who he was and maybe it wouldn't matter if they did, not after what he'd just done for this town. Max felt Degan could probably fit in anywhere once people found out how nice it was to have him around, but also felt he'd never stick around anywhere long enough to learn that.

"I've gotten you wet," Degan said as he led her back to their hotel, his arm still around her.

"Is that all you've got to say? You were nearly blown up! You should've shot first and asked if he was Red Charley later, not given him time to throw dynamite at you."

"You were watching?"

"Yeah, I saw it happen. And that is *not* how you're getting rid of me, by dying. So don't do it again."

She knew how silly she sounded, but she wasn't taking it back. And she wasn't mollified when he said, "I'll keep that in mind."

Chapter Forty-Five

Three days later when they got off the train for a one-night layover in Council Bluffs, Iowa, and entered a hotel for the night, Degan pointed out in one of his quieter tones of voice, "If you want your own room, then we need to let your friends think that we're having a fight." Then even more softly, he added, "So slap me."

"Like hell I will."

"Just do it, and before we leave the lobby. We can make up in front of them after the last layover before we get to Texas."

Max couldn't bring herself to hit him when she didn't want to. She was getting annoyed by his willingness to humor her and concede to her wishes. In fact, Degan had pretty much been acting like a husband since they got married, in all ways but one, whether they had an audience or not. She could even detect his humor now. She was getting good at recognizing the signs of his amusement. No turning up of the lips, but a softening of his tone and the expression in his usually cold gray eyes. She'd bet he was laughing inside. She sure wasn't.

But she clamped her mouth shut and glared at that hound dog Grady, who was standing at the entrance to the hotel, watching them check in. Grady had his doubts that their marriage was real, and he was going out of his way to prove it. It hadn't just been a far-fetched possibility that their room—and what they did in it—might be watched. In Ogden, she'd spotted Saul asleep on the roof of the building across the street from their hotel, a spyglass in his hand. She'd pointed him out to Degan. He'd just shrugged. He'd probably been amused by that, too. But then he hadn't seemed to have just spent a hellish night sharing the bed, as she had.

She'd thought sleeping together without touching each other would bother him as much as it bothered her. But he'd gotten through that night in Ogden just fine, and he wasn't the least bit out of sorts about their having to share a bed again tonight. No, he was amused that she'd even suggested getting her own room.

If the nights weren't so warm that they needed to leave the windows open, and the curtains weren't so thin that any breeze could blow them out of the way, they wouldn't still have to sleep in the same bed. But she supposed she was jumping the gun this time. This hotel might have thick curtains, unlike the last one.

They didn't go straight up to their room so she could find out; Degan just had their things sent up to it. The plan was to take the horses out for a ride before getting cleaned up for dinner, and she'd been looking forward to that.

The animals were getting shortchanged on exercise. They'd taken them out for a long ride while they were in Ogden, and he wanted to do that again today before they caught the southbound train tomorrow. They'd had to come so far east to connect with the trains that would take them all the way to Texas, but riding the Transcontinental Railroad, it had only taken a few days. Max was glad to have a chance to see Council Bluffs, the town that had made history because it was where the cross-country line began, extending the eastern lines that had reached Iowa all the way to the West Coast. She didn't mention to Degan that they were once again only about a day's train ride away from Chicago. She was sure Degan realized that. If he ever did plan to go home again, he wasn't saying. But it wouldn't be before he finished her business. Of that she was sure.

Riding the horses was fun and had a bonus. It worried the heck out of Grady since he couldn't follow them because he didn't have a horse. They stuck to the roads. Too many farms were in the area to do otherwise.

When they slowed down to turn back, she mentioned, "We could get off the train at one of the watering stops in Texas before it reaches Fort Worth. It might only take one extra day to ride the rest of the way instead of catching the stage for the last leg of the journey home."

"Your friends will, too."

"I wish you'd stop calling them *my* friends. But they don't have horses so they can't follow us."

"Pike is a Texas sheriff. He'll borrow mounts or confiscate the stage horses."

"You really think he'd do that?"

"Yes. And I'd prefer not to camp out with them within yelling distance."

"The alternative is to ride the stage with them. That won't be pleasant."

"Then consider that problem solved."

She grinned. "You're going to shoot them before we catch the stage?"

He didn't deign to answer that, but she did get one of his hard looks. She just laughed and raced him back to town.

Back at the hotel, Max discovered that the curtains in their room were thin. But on the positive side, the room had its own bathing room with running water. Of course it would this far east, she realized, but still it was a nice surprise.

Then she got another surprise. After they cleaned up, Degan took her shopping. He found a store that sold basic clothing and accessories for both men and women, even some ready-made clothes, though those were just for men and boys.

Seeing that, he remarked, "It's too bad we won't be here long enough for you to visit a seamstress."

"I have lots of perfectly fine clothes at home. I don't need more when I'll be home soon."

"We may have different ideas of what constitutes 'perfectly fine.'"

She wasn't sure what he meant by that until she remembered his friend Allison and how she'd been dressed. She rolled her eyes. No, she definitely didn't own clothes like that. In Bingham Hills, she would've stood out like a sore thumb if she'd dressed like that.

She ended up buying new socks and a new bandanna, then gazed for a few minutes at a hat tree that was filled with pretty bonnets. Degan started to reach for one, but Max shook her head and walked away. She didn't need anything frivolous that she wouldn't use. But she laughed when a while later he plopped a wide-brimmed hat on her head, a black one like his, just not as fancy. Then he found a thin, ropelike chain to wrap around the crown and pinned it in place with a pretty cameo brooch. His improvising was amusing, turning a wide-brimmed cowboy hat into a bonnet, yet she was touched that he would do that.

The bigger surprise was when he slipped a wedding band on her finger before they left the store. He even brought her hand up to his lips and kissed the ring on her finger, which was when she noticed he'd bought one for himself as well. Flustered, she looked around for Grady or Saul, but they weren't there, so he wasn't doing this for their benefit.

"You didn't have to," she said, looking down at her gold band.

"I know. But now your enemy will see at a glance that you're married. You shouldn't have to dig your marriage certificate out to prove it—and too many men glance your way when you're not trying to hide that you're a woman."

She burst out laughing. "You're trying to make me think you're jealous?"

"It didn't work, did it?"

"Oh, I don't know—maybe a little."

They had dinner afterward in a restaurant away from the hotel, a fancy one that offered French cooking, something she'd never before had. Grady and Saul didn't show up, which made it even nicer. Max went through half a bottle of wine, hoping it would help her sleep tonight. Degan only had one glass and only drank half of it. He never relaxed his guard. And *he* never had trouble sleeping.

But she didn't think she'd have that trouble tonight either. She was feeling quite mellow after such a nice day. When they returned to their room, she even opened the curtains wide and thumbed her nose in case Saul was out there somewhere with his spyglass. Grinning, she stripped down to her underclothes and got into bed. She was almost asleep by the time Degan joined her.

Then she was wide-awake. The mattress was too soft. It had dipped when Degan lay down on it. She almost rolled right into him. She swore under her breath and gripped her side of the mattress.

"If you want something, just ask."

No, he didn't just say that, she told herself. "I'm fine."

"You're sure?"

"Yes!"

So much for sleeping. It was already happening, that tense sense of anticipation stirring within her as if her nerves had just been shredded. She'd felt Degan's body heat for the barest second before she turned away, yet she still felt warm. Her imagination went crazy when she was this close to him. Was he almost naked again? She hadn't been watching him before he got into bed, and she wasn't going to turn over to look now. He'd turned the lamps off, but the light from the town's fancy streetlamps filtered into the room.

An hour later she was still staring at the ceiling, still trying not to clench her fists. A walk might help. She needed to do *something*, but she'd wake him if she got out of bed. He was like that, instantly up at the slightest sound or movement, which was why she was resisting the urge to toss and turn, though she might just scream pretty soon if she didn't. Was he even asleep? She couldn't tell when he was this quiet, this still, as if he was waiting for something.

She finally turned over and nudged him. "Will you just make love to me already? This is driving me—!"

He was on her so fast she didn't get to finish. If she hadn't just imagined him doing exactly that a dozen times, she might have been surprised by it.

"No stopping this time," she warned.

"Yes, ma'am."

He was grinning at her. He was actually grinning at her! It caused her to give him a beautiful smile and the tightest hug. It caused something else, a wonderful warm feeling that seemed to drain her frustration away. Most of it.

As their mouths touched, she locked her arms around his neck. That made it a bit difficult for him to get her underclothes off, but he managed. He just took his time now, caressing her as he did it. He seemed to want to touch her everywhere, down her arms and even her fingers, along her side and the full length of her leg, which she had bent against his hip. He didn't even ignore the foot he could reach. His hands made a slow, tantalizing path up and down her body, both soothing her and arousing her further.

She was reminded of the night he'd tried to warm her up by rubbing her body, an attempt to soothe that had gotten out of control. Was that what he was doing now because he'd sensed she'd been about to burst? No, his touch was more sensual tonight. He was trying to relax her yet not letting her forget for a moment what was coming. And he never stopped kissing her. His mouth could be deeply stirring one moment, then gently nibbling at her lips the next. He seemed to be taking his time so she would know there was more to this amazing intimacy they shared than an explosion of passions.

But the passion still built steadily, as if it had a life of its own. Her breaths deepened. Her hands trembled as she caressed him. When his hand slipped between her legs, he ignited hot desires that ran through her body the way a flame devours

dry brush. She groaned from the onslaught of pleasurable sensations, then half laughed because she hadn't meant to. But
she also arched her body toward him. She didn't mean to do
that, either. Or maybe she did. Degan must have figured she
did because he responded with exactly what she wanted, badly
needed. He braced his arms on either side of her as he hovered
over her, and it was sublime, feeling him enter her as he looked
at her face, watching her reaction. Then she realized that as
much as he wanted to see what he made her feel, he was letting
her see what she made *him* feel. He was going to let her watch
his climax—oh, God! She went right over the edge, and so
did he.

Chapter Forty-Six

Max didn't want to get out of bed. She felt so peaceful, so—happy. Really? It had been so long since so many good feelings had bubbled up in her this way that she wasn't sure. She guessed it was the lovemaking that had rid her of all the jittery frustration that had been haranguing her. The lovemaking was nice, well, better than nice with Degan.

Last night had been the most special night of her life, almost like a real wedding night. She didn't think she'd ever feel or see anything that wonderful or blissful again. And since she'd crossed the line in starting it, she wasn't going to step back over the line. She and Degan wouldn't be together much longer. Why jump back into hell when she could enjoy paradise with him for the time they had left?

He might have other ideas though. She'd have to wait to see if he apologized for last night. Or maybe she should apologize—no, she wouldn't. If he hadn't figured out that she'd enjoyed what they'd done last night, she'd spell it out. But damn, that would be embarrassing.

He was in the bathing room but had left the door open. It sounded as if he was shaving. She quickly dressed and moved over to the doorway, but her cheeks lit up a little before she got there, and a wave of shyness came over her when she saw him. He was only half-dressed in his pants, boots, and gun belt. His chest was bare.

"Are you ever going to let me do that for you?"

He glanced at her. "Probably not." But then he added, "Not that I don't trust you."

"Then why not?"

"Because one of us won't be thinking about shaving, if you get that close."

There it was, he did still want her, and he wasn't apologizing for last night. She would have smiled if it weren't such a touchy subject. This attraction they had was powerful, maybe a little too powerful, especially when it got out of control. He wouldn't like that, when he *always* had to be in control. But he hadn't complained about it last night. Behind a locked door, he could let down his guard a little.

"So that"—she sort of nodded toward the bed—"didn't change anything, right?"

"A little."

"I mean, we're still getting the marriage annulled? Even though you'll have to lie now?"

He continued shaving. "You needn't worry about that. I'll lie for you—if that's what you want."

He was doing it again, humoring her, conceding to her wishes, making it seem as if it were only up to her whether they stayed married. She supposed it was. He did offer to marry her after their first slip, and he was honorable enough to make the best of it now, if she wanted to stay married. But she couldn't do that to him. It wouldn't be fair if it wasn't what *he* wanted.

"Then I remove my objections to bed sharing—in case you were wondering."

She turned away as soon as she said it, her cheeks bright red from a blush. But he stopped her from moving any farther by placing a hand on her shoulder. Gooseflesh and a pleasant arousing sensation tingled down her arm. For crying out loud . . .

"You don't need to be embarrassed with me, Maxie," he said softly. "You've never had trouble speaking your mind. I like that about you."

He did? But then there was mind speaking and being too bold, and she'd just been the latter. But he obviously didn't want her to be embarrassed about it.

She was about to put her hand over his when he moved his hand up into her hair gently, in a caressing way—until he suddenly fluffed it. "We have time to find a barber for you."

He definitely had a knack for putting her at ease when he wanted to. She turned with a laugh. "They tend to shave you bald if you don't keep a close eye on them. I can wait till I get home. Gran does a good job cutting my hair." But she started backing away before she added with a grin, "You might want to let her take the scissors to you. I promise she won't cut off anything you don't want her to."

He actually laughed. She stared at him wide-eyed. "Stop it," he said, but she could still hear the humor in his tone. "That's not the first time you've heard me laugh."

"Two times ain't much."

"I laugh a lot, you just don't see it."

He walked back into the bathing room to wash his face.

She turned around smiling. Her husband was definitely relaxing his guard—with her.

Max thought her return to Texas would be more poignant, more emotional. After all, it was her home, what she knew, what she'd yearned to go back to. She was sure she'd be overwhelmed by emotion when she saw her family again, but she'd been gone from Texas long enough not to consider it anymore the only place to live. It was her family she'd missed, not Texas. Despite the excitement of the pending reunion, she was also feeling a little despondent the closer they got to Bingham Hills.

Her problems might soon be put to rest if Degan was successful in dealing with them, but she wasn't sure she wanted to live there anymore. She had a lot of good memories of that town, a lot of people she liked there, but she had bad memories of it now, too. And how would she be able to stay once Degan left? Wouldn't she go right back to facing the same dilemma of Carl's scheming to get what he wanted from her? That actually didn't worry her as much as that she'd be parting ways with Degan pretty soon. That was the real reason for her despondency. The reason why a tight knot had settled in her chest and wouldn't go away.

But she had to ignore it and pretend she was just fine. Degan watched her too closely. He'd know something was wrong if she wasn't herself. So she still teased, still joked, still tried to make him laugh with her usual lack of success. But it was hard to do when she didn't feel cheerful.

It was sweltering hot during the day, but they had to light the coach brazier for the night ride. When Degan had said she should consider the problem of getting stuck in a stagecoach with Grady and Saul solved, she never figured that he would buy up all the seats so they could ride alone. She couldn't stop laughing about it. But knowing Grady, he'd probably only be about half a day behind them, maybe less, since Degan had convinced the driver to extend their last two stops so their mounts could rest.

But it wasn't that long a trip from Fort Worth to Bingham Hills, less than two days. They left the stage a few miles out from Bingham Hills so they could circle around on their horses and get to the farm without passing through town. She wanted a peaceful reunion with her family before Carl found out she was home.

Then she saw it—the house she'd grown up in. She'd never realized how dilapidated it looked from a distance, which was how Degan might be viewing it. But it wasn't. It just needed a fresh coat of paint that she hadn't been there to see to.

Built mostly of lumber, only the front of the house had a stone facade, which had been added after Carl had set up his quarry right near town. One story but decent-size, the house faced the woods and the rest of the property on which her grandfather had never gotten around to planting crops. On one side was Gran's vegetable and herb garden, and on the other side was a small stable that housed their three horses and the buckboard her grandmother used to go to town to sell her eggs. Max had always preferred to walk when she did the deliveries, even before the town had grown and edged closer to the farm.

The chicken coops were at the back of the house, facing the road into town. She could see now why Carl might get so annoyed by the sight of the coops that he'd want to do something about it. Maybe Degan was right that Carl's interest in her stemmed from his desire to get his hands on her family's farm—so he could get rid of it. But that just meant someone was going to end up unhappy. She still couldn't see any resolution to the problem that would satisfy everyone.

Then she saw her grandmother in the backyard on her way back to the house with her basket of eggs in her hand, a sight Max had seen hundreds of times before, so familiar, so heartwarming. She didn't see any deputies posted at the house, but then Carl thought he'd won when he'd gotten that guardianship decree, so they were no longer needed.

"Are you crying?" Degan asked, standing beside her.

"No." She laughed as tears of happiness rolled down her cheeks. "But I'll race you home."

Chapter Forty-Seven

"GRAN! GRAN, I'M HOME," Max shouted as she ran to her grandmother.

Ella was so surprised to see her that she dropped the basket of eggs in the yard and rushed toward Max with tears running down her cheeks. "Finally! I wasn't sure if this day would ever come."

"Me either. I've missed you so much!" Max cried as she held her grandmother tightly in her arms. God, she'd missed the smell of this woman, her gentle touch, her boundless love.

"Thank the Lord you're home. I've been so worried about you!"

Max's tears wouldn't stop, neither would Ella's, yet they were laughing, too, as Ella led Max through the back door into the kitchen. Ella immediately went to the stove to pour them coffee while Max sat down at the kitchen table. She glanced around the room. She'd missed this house, too. It was filled with everything her grandparents had collected over a lifetime. Every wall was covered with pictures Ella had painted. She used to paint a lot before Max's grandpa had died. She didn't find much time for it after that.

Ella was only in her early sixties. She'd married young, had her kids young. Of her children, only Maxwell had survived to give her grandkids. Her blue eyes were still sharp, her hair only just starting to turn gray, which was hard to see since her hair was ash blond like Max's. But she looked thinner than Max remembered And had more frown lines than before Max had left. These last two years had taken a toll on the Dawson family.

Ella joined her at the table, bringing a slice of peach cobbler for Max to go with the coffee. Max smiled. Ella was a firm believer that food wasn't just good for the body but also for the soul. She always had some sort of pie or pastry ready to serve. Grandpa might not have wanted to farm here in Texas, but he'd still planted a lot of fruit trees for his wife.

"How long can you stay?" Ella asked.

"I'm not going anywhere."

"Didn't Sheriff Pike bring you back?"

Max grinned. "He tried to. But I have a good friend who's helped me to get around the mayor's newest scheme." Then she whispered, "Degan Grant married me to put me out of Carl's reach—but it's just temporary until we find out what Carl really wants."

Ella's eyes flared, then started to water. "You're married? And I didn't get to witness it?"

They were holding hands across the table. Max squeezed Ella's tightly. "It wasn't a real wedding . . . well, it was, but we did it knowing it wasn't going to be permanent. We may have to wait until I'm twenty-one to annul it, though, if Carl won't give up."

Ella sighed. "I know what the mayor wants, but I didn't when you left. It had been so long since he tried to buy the farm that it didn't occur to me yet that he was trying to get it a different way—through you. I realized it after I got summoned to court for those ridiculous incompetency charges. I didn't even get to say a single word in my defense. I just had to sit there listening silently to what a terrible parent and grandparent I was."

"You were no such thing!" Max said hotly.

"It doesn't matter now. You figured out a way to ruin his plans. Rumors were swirling around town that Carl distributed wanted posters for you outside of Texas in order to get you back here. But no one had the gumption to confront him about it." Ella shook her head. "I've lost respect for a lot of people in Bingham Hills. I confronted him about those posters, but he told me I was crazy and then he filed those charges against me."

"It's true, Gran. Carl turned me into an outlaw with a thousand-dollar price on my head."

"I despise the man, but I'm so proud of you, Max, for surviving on your own and figuring out a way to best him."

"It wasn't my idea to marry, it was Degan's, but, yeah, Carl won't like it that he got outsmarted by a simple clause in the document he finagled to get drawn up. But how does his being my guardian get him the farm?"

"It gave him the power to marry you to whoever he wanted, including himself or his son, if he ever comes home, and it wouldn't matter what you had to say about it."

"Wait, what happened to Evan?"

"He left town shortly after you did for parts unknown. I believe he really cared for you, Max, and hated what his father was doing to you. Anyhow, once one of the Binghams married you, Carl would be the oldest male in our family, which would give him the legal right to make decisions for all of us. No one would bat an eye if one of those decisions was to tear down this place."

"That's *not* going to happen, Gran. Degan is now the oldest male in our family."

"Where is this temporary husband of yours?"

Max knew Degan was giving her some private time for her homecoming and to explain why he was with her. "He's seeing to the horses. You'll meet him shortly." But then she warned, "He's a gunfighter, Gran, but you don't need to be nervous around him."

"Is he capable of butting heads with the mayor?"

Max chuckled. "Dealing with trouble like this is his line of work, Gran. But why did you never say that Carl tried to buy the farm from you? When was that?"

"You and Johnny were still children. It was right after your grandfather died. Carl offered me a decent price for the farm, then a higher price, then a ridiculous price."

"You never considered it?"

"I love this house, but more—"

Ella didn't get to finish. Degan appeared in the doorway, all six feet three inches of him filling it. He tipped his hat to Ella before removing it, then to Max's amazement, he smiled at her grandmother. Max quickly introduced them, but it still took a moment for her grandmother to find her voice. Even with that smile, at first glance you just knew he was a dangerous man.

But then Ella ordered, "Sit. For whatever reason you're helping Max, you have my gratitude."

Max grinned. "He's probably going to want a bath first, Gran."

"You read my mind," Degan agreed.

"Second door on your right, and we have pumped water for the tub, just not hot," Max told him. "But I'll heat some for you now."

She got up to do that while Ella suggested, "You can put your things in my grandson's room, Mr. Grant."

Max swung back around. "He's not going to share a room with Johnny."

"It's fine, dear. Johnny sleeps elsewhere."

"Degan shares with me. We have to keep up appearances, Gran."

Degan backed out of the room, merely saying, "Let me know what you decide."

Max glared at his back before he disappeared. He obviously wanted no part of this explanation. She put her arm around Ella's shoulders and whispered, "It's okay. We had a wedding night."

"Maxine Dawson!"

Max winced and decided lying might be the quickest way to end this embarrassing conversation. "We had to. Grady was spying on us. If Carl finds out this marriage isn't real, then I'm going to get stuck under his thumb and he wins—everything." But then Max admitted in an even lower whisper, "Besides, I—I like sharing a bed with my husband."

"So you're keeping him?"

"No, but—"

"You're keeping him," Ella cut in with finality.

Max rolled her eyes. She was never good at butting heads with Ella. Max could explain later, after Degan moved on, why keeping him hadn't been an option.

Right now she wanted to know "Where *is* Johnny?"

"At the mayor's house, I reckon. He likes it there. The mayor's got him bamboozled with fancy new clothes and servants waiting on him, and talk of sending him to school in the East come fall."

"That's really his choice after he shot that man for me? He's not being forced to stay there because of that dumb guardianship decree?"

"It's a change for him, Max, and I don't begrudge him that. He was so lonesome and bored after you left. All he ever talked about was going to sea like his pa."

Max frowned. "He wasn't going to leave you here alone, was he?"

"No, he was waiting for this nightmare to end, for you to come home—one way or another. The mayor assured him you'd be here before he left for school. And he still comes by every day to help me with the chores, so you'll see him tomorrow if not sooner."

"But he can come home now. Degan's being a part of our family negates that damn guardianship decree for both of us."

"I'm not so sure Johnny will want to come home. In fact, if he thinks you're back for good, he'll probably head for the nearest port."

Unlike her father and her brother, Max had no desire to visit other countries. She'd already seen far more of her own country than she'd ever wanted to see. But Johnny had told her about his dream to see the world. So she wasn't all that surprised by Ella's speculation.

"Whatever he decides, he's old enough to be on his own, so you won't have to worry about him, Gran."

"I'll always worry about the two of you," Ella grumbled. "Habit." Then she tsked and headed for the sink. "And you haven't even started that water for your man."

Her man? How was she going to convince Ella that Degan wasn't when Max wished he were?

Chapter Forty-Eight

"GRAN IS MAKING SOMETHING special for your dinner. She went out to get two chickens for it. I suspect she thinks you're a big eater."

Degan turned as Max joined him at the end of the porch, the side that caught a view of town. He thought she made a much better view. She'd changed into one of the dresses she'd left behind, a blue-and-green gingham that brought out the blue in her eyes. She looked beautiful, even in an old dress, even with butchered hair, but he'd like to see her in silk, just once, before . . .

He didn't finish the thought. Usually he looked forward to moving on, but not this time.

"Your grandmother reminds me of Adelaide Miller."

"Are you calling her cantankerous?"

"No, just bossy."

Max grinned as she put her hands on the porch railing next to him. "Maybe a little. But she'll grow on you."

The way Max had grown on him? She'd definitely gotten

under his skin. She'd broken down his barricades, too, which wasn't necessarily a good thing. He couldn't remain aloof anymore. Not with her.

He looked back toward town and the house on the hill behind it. Like a lordly manor, it had full views of the domain the man inside it ruled. Was he a flawed leader or an ironfisted tyrant? Degan would be finding out soon. He nodded toward the house. "I assume that's your mayor's residence?"

"He calls it a mansion."

"I wouldn't."

"He does, just 'cause it's got more'n five bedrooms in it. Gran said he just kept adding to it over the years, spreading it all over that hill." But then she warned, "You need to have eyes in the back of your head while you're here, Degan. There's no telling what Carl will do when he finds out you thwarted him."

"Do I look worried?"

She glanced up at him. "*Would* you look worried? Ever?"

He didn't answer. He fluffed her hair instead. "She hasn't cut it yet."

"Give her time, we just got here. And she did notice. She picked up a lock and humphed. I expect she'll come after me with the scissors tomorrow."

They both saw Grady Pike riding toward them from town. Max leaned a little closer to Degan. He put his arm around her shoulders. He didn't like the way Pike made Max nervous, didn't like the way the man had treated her, either, all in the name of Bingham's trumped-up law. It was a wonder he hadn't shot the man. He'd certainly had the urge to and still did.

Grady pulled up his horse below them at the side of the porch. "The mayor would like a word with you, Mr. Grant. You've been invited to dinner at his house."

"Do you like being an errand boy, Pike?"

"This is official business," Grady insisted.

"No, it isn't. And I'm having dinner with my wife's family tonight. But I'll pay your mayor a visit afterward. You can tell him I'm looking forward to it."

Grady gave him a hard look before he yanked his horse around and rode back to town. Beside Degan, Max said determinedly, "I'll go with you."

"No, you won't. You don't have the temperament for this meeting." Then he lightened his tone before adding, "But if I end up in jail, you can rescue me."

"He wouldn't dare!" she growled, but after a glance at him, she snorted. "Oh, you were joking."

"I'm actually not discounting any possibility. But then all I know about Carl Bingham is what you've told me, and you're known to exaggerate. And you have another visitor."

She followed his gaze and then squealed, "Johnny!" She ran down the porch steps to meet her brother. Degan leaned against the railing, watching them as the young man lifted Max and swung her in a full circle around him before giving her a bear hug. It was easy to tell they were siblings. They both had the same ash-blond hair and the same bone structure, which made one beautiful and the other quite handsome. While the boy might be younger by a few years, he was now the taller by a half foot.

Max remarked on it. "Look at you! You sure sprouted, baby brother."

"You've been gone a long time."

The censure in the boy's tone earned him a punch in the arm. "Not by choice!"

Abashed, Johnny said, "I know, it's just been horrible

around here without you. I expected you back last year when the mayor became our guardian."

"I didn't know about that, and if I did, I would have been running even farther in the opposite direction. He might've dropped the charges against me, but how was I to know when he didn't bother to have the wanted posters canceled?"

As they approached the porch, Johnny caught Degan's eyes on him. "Holy cow, it's true? You brought a husband home with you?"

"Who told you?"

"Carl sure didn't," Johnny complained. "I heard his servants gossiping about it after the sheriff visited."

"Gran said you were planning to go off to college in the fall. Was that your idea?"

"Yeah, not that I really want more schooling. But I figured it would prove what a fraud Carl is if he refused to send me. But he didn't, and it's better'n staying in Bingham Hills. Anywhere would be better'n here."

"Then you didn't like living in Carl's house?"

"Are you kidding?"

Max rolled her eyes. "You sure fooled Gran. She thinks you like it there."

"I put on a good show for her. I don't want her to worry about me."

"We'll figure things out, Johnny, I promise. I don't think Carl can still claim guardianship of you now that we have a new head of the family. Come and meet him." Then she added in a whisper that Degan still caught, "Don't be afraid of him. He's on our side."

Chapter Forty-Nine

DEGAN RODE HIS HORSE up the hill. It was steep enough that it would be a tiring walk for someone Bingham's age, which was probably why a buckboard and two horses were left out front. The man had wanted to be up high enough to easily survey the town he'd founded, but he hadn't considered how inconvenient that would be. His two-story house was built of stone and had a wide front porch that ran the length of the house.

Degan was shown to a grand parlor. It could have been a parlor in Chicago. Not very tasteful in decor, a little grandiose, but obviously every piece of furniture had been freighted in from the East. It probably didn't get much use and had likely been decorated for show, to impress the locals. Degan wasn't left there long. Another servant appeared and escorted him to the mayor's study. Bingham was already there.

He wasn't as old as Max had led him to believe, possibly approaching seventy, yet still robust with few wrinkles on his face. He had a full head of white hair, side whiskers, and light green eyes that showed no malice. Degan found it hard to credit that this man had ever frightened Max. He appeared utterly harmless, but Degan sensed it was an illusion, the man's public persona, not his true nature. No wonder he'd fooled this town for so long.

"I assume we can dispense with introductions?" Carl said, waving a hand toward the comfortable chair across from the large desk. "You might be notorious in the rest of the West, Mr. Grant, but down here, we haven't heard of you—until now, that is."

"Does it matter?"

"I suppose not. Whiskey?"

"No."

The bottle and two glasses were on the desk. Carl still poured one for himself. As long as the mayor kept his hands above the desk, Degan would keep his gun holstered. Threats would be pointless. They wouldn't last after he rode out of Bingham Hills. But one thing still needed saying.

"If you had raped Max, this meeting would be for a different reason. You know that, right?"

Carl was only discomposed for the briefest moment before he replied confidently, "You wouldn't kill me."

"Yes, I would."

Confidence gone, the man's true colors showed when he complained hotly, "She shot me!"

"Self-defense. You were in the wrong, Mayor, she wasn't. But I'm here for an explanation. I want to know why she had to leave home for close to two years because of you."

Carl sighed and sat back, a glass in his hand though he didn't drink from it. "I'm used to getting what I want. That's why I founded this town so long ago and built it into what it is today. And someday, in my lifetime mind you, it will rival Fort Worth. This is my town. I control what happens here. I thought Max would be thrilled to marry my boy once she was old enough. She'd have servants waiting on her hand and foot, all the fancy dresses she could've wanted, anything her little heart desired. Not once did I think she'd thumb her nose at all this." Carl waved a hand to encompass his house. "You know I could've done worse things to get rid of that eyesore farm of theirs, but I didn't. I'm not as ruthless as she seems to think I am. I might've gotten a little carried away, trying to compromise her to the altar, but I was desperate at the time."

"What warranted desperation?"

"The gal had turned into a beauty. Half the men in town were in love with her. Someone else was going to snatch her up before much longer."

"You're wrong, you know. Force her to do something she doesn't want to do, and she'll fight you tooth and nail. And that's a fact I've seen verified."

"Well, stubbornness runs in that family. I offered Widow Dawson a fortune for that farm of hers. I even offered to take it down piece by piece and put it back up anywhere she wanted, and she would've got rich to boot. That woman isn't reasonable. She wouldn't even discuss it. But my offer still stands."

"In the time Max has been gone, you could have whittled down some of your hills to the south or turned your woods into a park and built around it. Did none of that occur to you, Mayor?"

"Of course it did, but that farm is still going to be an eyesore, butting up against town as it is now. It's standing in the way of progress. This affects the whole town, not just me. I love this town, there isn't much I wouldn't do for it."

"Including forcing Max to marry you or your son."

"She would've been happy in the end. All women are enamored of wealth."

Degan shook his head at that reasoning. "Then you would have forced her to get her grandmother to sell to you?"

"I wouldn't have had to do any such thing. Max in *my* family makes me the head of hers."

"A position that is now mine."

Carl actually chuckled. "Let's face it, Mr. Grant, this town is too peaceful for a man of your talents. And we both know you aren't going to take up chicken farming."

Degan laughed to himself. "No, I'm not."

"I don't just want the Dawson land, I still want Max. Maybe I haven't made that clear, Mr. Grant. I need someone with her courage and spirit in my family. Damn, the gal survived almost two years in the wild on her own. Max can give me the kind of sons who will carry on my legacy."

Degan forced himself not to reach for his gun. "You have a son, don't you? What happened to him?"

"The damn fool left. Said he didn't want to be pinned down here, said I was asking too much of him." Carl waved a hand in frustration. "I'm prepared to pay you any amount you name to sign these divorce papers I've had prepared—"

Degan stood. "Max isn't for sale. If you ever suggest again that she is, or if you ever go near her again, you'll not only see how fast I can draw a gun, you'll feel it."

His face red with anger, Carl stood, too. "Then what are your intentions?"

"I have a proposal for you." Degan handed Carl a piece of paper on which he'd written the price he thought Ella should ask for her farm.

Carl looked down at the paper. "Are you crazy?"

"That includes compensation for Max for your robbing her of two years of her life and endangering her with those phony wanted posters you sent out."

Still fuming, Carl said, "If I agree to this, you'll get the hell out of my town and never come back?"

"I plan to take Max out of town for a while. Other than that, I have no intentions that would concern you."

"I hope you're taking your womenfolk with you—*all* of them."

"There are only two."

"I believe he was including me in the number," Allison Montgomery said peevishly from behind Degan. "I seem to have worn out my welcome here."

Degan closed his eyes. Not again . . .

Chapter Fifty

"A**REN'T YOU TIRED, BABY** girl, after traveling all day to get here?"

Max didn't turn as her grandmother came up beside her at the end of the porch. Max wouldn't take her eyes off the path from town by which Degan would be returning. And dusk had fallen. He'd already been gone longer than she figured he would.

"Tired, yeah, but there's no way I'll sleep until we know what happened with the mayor. Degan went there without any options to lay on the table. He can make threats and that might be enough to work while he's here. But once he leaves, Carl could go right back to scheming."

"Unless he gets what he wants."

She glanced at her grandmother sharply. "*That's* not an option. Carl doesn't get to win, not after everything he put us— me through."

Ella put an arm around her waist. "Will you leave when your husband does?"

"I haven't thought that far ahead. Because of Carl, there's a time stamp on my marriage, at least for another year."

"Because of Carl, you met your husband."

Max started, hearing that. She supposed it was true. But then she sighed. "I'm not so sure that can be considered a favor, Gran."

"Nonsense," Ella scoffed. "You've already admitted you desire Degan, and that's a special thing, you know. It's what tells you a man is right for you. It's what tells you love might be growing."

"Really?"

"Well, not always, but most of the time it does. You could want a man you don't like, but that just opens up a nasty can of worms, so it's better to hope that doesn't happen. But you like this fella?"

"Yeah. I always feel like laughing when I'm around him. And it drives me up-a-wall crazy how much I want him. And I get scared for him, really scared, when he's facing danger, like he's family, like—"

"You love him."

That tight knot swelled in Max's chest again. "I hope not, Gran, 'cause it's not that nice a feeling."

Ella chuckled. "If it's not returned, yes, it can be awful. But if it is returned, it can be the most wonderful thing in the world. So be sure about it, honey, before you let him go."

"I don't think I'm going to have much choice in the matter. I can't imagine a man like Degan settling down in one place, and he isn't going to want me tagging along as his sidekick indefinitely. I'm like a job to him, and when he finishes a job, he moves on."

"How does he feel about you?"

Max rolled her eyes. "Funny you should ask. Degan's a closed book that might as well have a lock on it. No one ever gets to read those pages, myself included."

Ella kissed Max's cheek. "I'm going to make a fresh pot of coffee. If your man doesn't return soon, we'll need it."

"I think I'm going to go find out what's taking Degan so long."

"Then take Johnny with you. I don't want you getting near Carl Bingham alone."

Max nodded and went to her bedroom to strap her gun belt on over her dress, then grabbed her rifle, too, for good measure. Johnny was waiting for her at the front door. He laughed when she handed him her rifle.

"Feels like old times, Max," he teased.

"Let's hope not. I just want to make sure Carl hasn't thrown Degan in jail."

"How the hell did you know I was coming here?"

It had taken Degan a moment to absorb the shock of seeing Allison in Bingham Hills and apparently a guest of the mayor's. Carl didn't bother to correct her statement that she was no longer welcome, he just cleared his throat and hurried out of the room. Leaving them alone in it.

"The private guards I hired are good," Allison said as she moved closer to him. "Though one might be a little overzealous since he fancies himself in love with me." Degan merely stared at her without comment, which apparently disappointed her enough for her to explain, "If you must know, he foolishly thought that shooting at you in Helena might chase you home to Chicago as I wanted. I was furious with him, of course. He might have hit *me* that day!"

"Or was it your idea?"

"Don't be absurd. I still love you, darling. I would never hurt you."

"It's too bad you didn't always feel that way." He ignored her blush. "Just get to the part about how you managed to get to this town before I arrived."

"Well, while one of my guards stayed with me as protection, Miles, to make amends for that Helena fiasco, promised to track you—at a safe distance, of course. He followed you to Dakota, where he lost you, but he picked up your trail when you returned to Butte. I was back in Chicago when I got the telegram from Miles stating that you were bringing an outlaw home to Bingham Hills. I was able to catch the train to Fort Worth and arrive a few days before you. Though I wish you had gotten here first. Waiting here, even for just two days, has been deplorable."

"And how did you get invited to the mayor's home?"

"Without trying. He was agog that someone of my stature would visit his small town. They only have *one* hotel here, you know, if it can even be called that. So I wasn't adverse to accepting his hospitality for my short stay when he offered it."

"Have you really worn out your welcome?"

She shrugged. "I might have complained a little." At his raised brow, she added, "Very well, a lot, but you can't believe how boring this town is, and that pompous old man was determined to impress me, as if anything here could."

"So the mayor knew I was coming before I got here?"

"You, just not *you.*" Then she laughed, realizing how odd that sounded. "I was amazed how easy it was to have you followed. People don't only notice when you enter a town, Miles told me they notice when you leave it, and in which direction you're headed. They're happy to share that information. Apparently, you are quite infamous—except down here in Texas. I did give Mayor Bingham your name when I told him I was here to meet a friend, but he didn't recognize it and I didn't feel inclined to enlighten him. I just didn't know he was waiting for your prisoner until I heard him speaking with the sheriff earlier today."

"She isn't my prisoner, she's my wife."

Allison's mouth dropped open in shock. "You married her? How could you marry someone like her? I didn't believe it when Miles told me there was talk that you got married in Butte!"

"Go home, Allison, and start a new life," Degan said before walking away.

He left the house, but Allison followed close on his heels. "Degan, please, I can't live without you anymore. You belong in Chicago—with me."

He didn't stop. "No, I don't."

"But we were so good together. You know we were. And we can be again." She rushed in front of him so he would stop. "You *have* to come home!"

"You can't believe I'm still in love with you. What's your real motive, Alli, for tracking me down like this?"

Several emotions crossed her face, frustration, regret, even anger, but then she sighed. "Our families have always had ties, and the scandal has touched us all."

"That can't still be a topic of gossip, that we didn't marry."

"Not that. It's your father. I tried to tell you but you refused to listen. He's become a laughingstock. He hasn't left the house sober in years, yet he thinks he can still go on as before. It's cost him his business, clients, even property that he failed to make payments on because he was too drunk to remember that payments were due."

"He has Flint."

"Flint did try to take over for him. I'll give him that. He made the effort and tried to fill your shoes. But he has no head for business, as you well know. All he did was make it worse, and now he's also become a pathetic drunkard. Two peas out of the same pod, those two. And all because you turned your back on your family."

"How do I get blamed for this when *you're* the reason I left?"

"That's just it, you didn't *have* to leave. It devastated your father. You were his pride and joy. You were his legacy. With you gone, he stopped caring about anything important, and now his empire is falling into ruin. Only you can fix this, Degan. *Now* do you see why you have to come home?"

Degan believed she was exaggerating. She'd always been melodramatic. "As I said before, I cut my family ties permanently, including my ties to you. No more pathetic attempts to rekindle a dead love, Alli. You made your choice when you—"

Allison exploded, "I tried to reason with you! I tried to persuade you nicely. But obviously the only thing you understand these days is guns!"

She took a derringer out of her dress pocket and pointed it at him. She looked furious enough to use it.

"And what do you intend to do with that one?"

Two shots were fired. Glass shattered. Allison screamed and dropped her gun while Degan drew his. She was staring in shock at the side of the house. Still facing down the hill, Degan saw Max running up it with her gun drawn and smoking, her brother right behind her. He swung around to see whom Max had shot, afraid it was Carl Bingham. But the man rolling on the ground clutching his hand in pain was young. A Colt had already fallen from his bloody hand, likely the cause of the second shot.

"He was aiming at your back!" Max said as she reached Degan. "And what the hell is *she* doing here? Trying to kill you now?"

"God, no!" Allison swore, horrified.

But that's when Carl came out on his porch, drawn by the gunfire, to demand, "What's going on? Who shot my window?"

But when he noticed Max next to Degan, his bluster turned into a big smile. Grady, having followed Carl outside, put his hand on Carl's shoulder and cautioned him, "Careful, she probably came here to shoot you again."

They all heard that, but the second Max saw Carl, she couldn't control her fury. Waving her gun at Allison and the wounded man, she shouted at her nemesis, "You've been wanting a hanging for two years, Carl Bingham! Now you can have two!"

Chapter Fifty-One

CARL WALKED DOWN THE porch steps and headed for Max. "I want someone to tell me what all this shooting is about and I want to talk to you, Max."

Degan hadn't put his gun away yet. "I told you, Mayor, I would shoot you if you ever went near her again. Want me to prove that?"

Carl's face contorted in anger but he stopped. Still, he directed his words at Max. "Who did you shoot this time?"

Grady had gone over to the wounded man and helped him to his feet. Max saw that he was big and young, dressed like a city slicker in a suit and string tie. "Him!" she spat out, pointing at the man. "He was about to shoot Degan."

"Miles, how could you?" Allison cried, looking angry now. "How dare you shoot my friend?"

"I saw you pull the derringer on him. I was just defending you. He would have drawn his gun on you. You don't need him, Allison." Miles tried to pull free of Grady's grip and get closer to her, but Grady held him back. "He's a no-good gun-slinger! I can take care of you. I love you!"

"No," Allison shook her head. Sobbing, she stepped closer to Degan and almost collapsed, but Degan caught her.

"What's going on?" Johnny asked Max.

Max couldn't tell him because she didn't know, but she felt a sharp pang of jealousy as she watched Degan talking softly to the distraught woman in his arms.

Carl's servants had come out on the porch and were asking him if there was anything they could do. As Grady led Miles away, Max heard Grady say to Carl, "Looks like his bullet went astray and hit one of your windows."

"Put him in jail for now," Carl ordered. "We'll figure out later when to kick him out of town."

With his arm still around Allison, Degan walked over to Carl. "You better take your guest inside."

"She's not staying here," Carl protested. "She was about to shoot you."

"Yes, she is, and, no, she wasn't. She was just trying to scare me."

Max saw Carl raise an eyebrow skeptically. Even Grady must have heard that because he turned his head and rolled his eyes.

"I'm not pressing charges against her and her guard," Degan continued. "She's agreed to take the first stage out of town to-morrow. See that she gets on it."

Carl grumbled, "You bet I will. I should have known she'd be trouble." He gingerly took Allison's arm, but his gaze strayed to Max.

Degan must not have liked the yearning look in Carl's eyes any more than she did because he said, "That's the last look you're ever getting at Max Dawson, Bingham."

Carl glared at Degan and took Allison back to the house.

Degan turned to Max and Johnny and said, "Let's go."

Max was glad to hear him say those words.

Johnny quickly rode back to the farm ahead of them to keep their grandmother from worrying. Degan insisted that Max mount up with him on the palomino, which she did, but at least she was the one holding Noble's reins this time.

"You seem to be making a habit out of saving my life," he remarked quietly.

"I thought Carl, not your lady friend and her guard, would try to get rid of you."

"So that's why you came to Carl's?"

"You were taking too long."

"Because I didn't expect Allison to be there. She figured out where I was going before we got here. Bingham offered her his hospitality, but he was quick to regret it. Apparently Alli can be quite a snob when she's out of her natural environment."

"You didn't know that about her?"

"That she's not adaptable or the least bit tolerant? No, I didn't."

"And smells like roses?"

He actually frowned a little. "It was her favorite scent, but why—?"

"You dreamed about roses, remember? And apparently of *her*."

He leaned closer and she felt his breath against her ear. "You sound jealous."

She snorted. "Of *that* bloodhound?"

"A good comparison. But if you're interested, she's my ex-fiancée. If I dreamed of her during that feverish delirium in

Dakota, it was a nightmare. That's all she is to me now, a nightmare that I wish would go away."

Max was amazed that he'd finally got around to mentioning his previous relationship to that woman, but her curiosity was still going through the roof. "Did she end it between you two, or did you?"

"She did—when I walked in on her being unfaithful before the wedding."

She winced for him, offering the lame rejoinder, "Better before than after."

"That's one way to look at it."

She tried to sound blasé when she asked, "So you don't have any feelings left for her?"

He raised a brow. "*Now* you think I can feel?"

She rolled her eyes. "You know what I meant. And you can't convince me you were always made of stone. I think we've already established that your lack of feelings is job related. So do you still have feelings for her?"

"Other than disgust and the occasional spark of leftover anger, no. In fact, if she's not in the same town, she ceases to exist, that's how rarely I think of her anymore."

That definitely said a lot. Max had to fight not to smile quite happily, aware that he wouldn't appreciate it with the woman's still being such a bad memory for him.

"Allison foolishly pulled that gun on me because she's desperate to get me back to Chicago for some reason. She suspected her guard had become infatuated with her, but she was as surprised as I was when he took a shot at me."

Max wondered if that was true, but she just said, "You have no idea why she's hell-bent on getting you back to Chicago?"

"No, but you've nagged me enough to—"

"I don't nag," she sputtered. "I suggest. Big difference, fancy man."

"Very well, you suggest. But in either case, I had already decided to take you for a visit to Chicago when we were done here—to get you a new wardrobe."

She laughed. "You surely do like wasting your money, don't you?"

"Why? You might decide you like it there and want to stay."

"Me in a big city? Would you be staying?"

"Probably not. I'm no longer suited to that life. But I suppose I can check on my family while we're there."

Probably not wasn't a *no*. Everything could change once he got there and saw his family again. *She* was the one not suited to his old life, not him. Maybe she should have left well enough alone. . . .

They reached the farm and put their horses away. Walking to the house, Degan asked, "Do you think your grandmother is still up?"

"I'm sure she's dying to find out what Carl had to say."

Max was, too. With everything that had happened at Carl's house, she still didn't know what he and Degan had said to each other about the hunt for her, the guardianship decree, and the farm.

Reaching the porch, she said, "I bet she's in the kitchen with Johnny. Come."

She started toward the door and extended her hand to him. It was a natural mistake. She was in her home, back with the people she loved. It's what she would have done with them. She didn't even realize she'd done it until Degan put his hand in hers.

It embarrassed her, how easily she was treating him like family, like a husband—and how easily he was accepting that role. She didn't want him to feel trapped by his gallantry. He didn't expect to stay married to her, he'd made that clear before the wedding. Then why was he taking her to Chicago? She'd like to think it was because he didn't want to part company with her yet, but clothes shopping was a silly excuse. Unless they all needed to get out of Texas before more shooting started. His meeting with Carl could have gone badly. No, he would have said so immediately if it did.

She let go of his hand in the kitchen when Ella rushed toward them. "I'm so glad you're both safe! Johnny told me about the shooting. But I still want to know, is Carl going to leave us alone?"

"That remains to be seen," Degan answered as they sat down at the table. "I told him nothing definitive. It's not my place to make decisions for you. But from a business perspective, I understand his motives. You are a roadblock for him. If a town doesn't expand, it eventually dies. But you were also right, Max. Carl did still have hopes of turning you into a Bingham and even offered me a bribe to divorce you. The man is despicable."

"You won't hear any argument about that at this table," Ella said.

Max turned to her grandmother. "Degan told Carl he would shoot him if he ever came near me again." Ella smiled widely and Max added with a grin, "Yelling at that man tonight felt really good."

"I doubt he wants to marry you any longer after seeing tonight how well you can shoot," Degan said. "But he is still desperate to have this farm. I didn't promise him that you would sell it, but I told him what I would advise you to ask for it, including financial recompense for Max for what he did to her. I can get you enough from him to build a new farm anywhere you want, any size you want, or to live wherever you please. It will be enough so you can be more than comfortable and never have to work again."

"That might be nice," Ella said. "As long as Max is with me or nearby and Johnny has a room for when he comes home to visit."

Max shot to her feet to protest, "But you love this place, Gran!"

"I love you and your brother," Ella corrected her. "And, yes, even the stuff that's in this house that I've collected over a lifetime. But not the wood surrounding us, baby girl. The fact is, when the mayor first offered to buy me out all those years ago, I expected you to get married here one day and be living close by, and *that's* why I told him no. I wasn't going to move way out in the countryside where I'd barely see you anymore after you got hitched. Besides," Ella added bitterly, "over the past two years I've lost my love for this town. So if you want to leave, just tell me when and I'll start packing."

Incredulous, Max turned to Degan. "I guess that settles that."

He didn't seem surprised. "You can come with me to Chicago to see how the other half of the country lives. There are many pleasant farming towns outside of the city you might like. I can also suggest other locations. I've come across some nice towns in my travels, some that are even quite peaceful."

"You mean after you've passed through them?"

He actually chuckled. "And that don't have mayors with grandiose schemes running them."

Johnny concluded with a chuckle of his own. "Sounds like a plan."

Chapter Fifty-Two

THE MAYOR ACTUALLY ENLISTED a good portion of the town
to come over and help them pack up. Max saw it as Carl's wanting them out of town as quickly as possible. Ella saw it as his
attempt to make amends. At least he didn't come to bid them
good-bye as most of the townspeople did. As long as Max didn't
have to see Carl Bingham again, they could depart without
further incident. She went to the bank and gave Wilson Cox
back the money he'd erroneously given her, as well as a tongue-
lashing. The ornery coot took back the money but otherwise
ignored her. Still, getting that old irritation off her chest left her
in a good mood for the trip.

There were some tears. Ella's. She'd come to Bingham Hills
when there had been no more than one short street. She knew
everyone in town by name, and that was a lot of names these
days. Max started to have misgivings about taking her away
from the place where she'd lived for so long, until Ella hugged
her and whispered that she was excited about living someplace
new and getting to visit a city as big as Chicago was reputed

to be—and she was looking forward to painting again. Which made Max guess that Ella might not want another farm after all, not after Degan had mentioned she was rich enough now never to have to work again.

When the stagecoach reached Fort Worth, they had to spend an extra day there to wait for the two wagons to catch up. Max had thought they would need more than two, but Ella had decided to leave all her furniture behind, giving it to a young family who had been especially kind to her during Max's absence from home.

Not until that overnight stay in Fort Worth, when Max was sharing a room with her grandmother instead of Degan, did it finally hit her—the threat from Carl Bingham had ended. She didn't have to wait until she was twenty-one to get her marriage annulled. Degan was probably going to take her to a lawyer to get the process started as soon as they got to the city.

She cried herself to sleep that night. She managed to do it silently so Ella wouldn't know. Somehow she got through the rest of the trip without letting on just how miserable she felt. Johnny's excitement helped. Degan had apparently taken him aside for a talk and convinced him that he could go to sea any-time, but now was the better time to further his education if he had any inclination to do so.

Chicago was amazing. It was like nothing Max could have imagined—the bustle, the endless stream of people, and the buildings, some five stories high! Degan took them straight to a hotel. She was disappointed. She'd thought she was going to meet his family while they were there. Then she was surprised to see that Degan was going to stay in the hotel, too, but *really* surprised when he escorted her to her room and came inside to put his valise down in it.

"I think I would have changed hotels if I couldn't get three rooms this time," he admitted.

"This time?"

"We had to improvise in Fort Worth. They had only two rooms available."

Max felt relieved and happy. She'd thought he hadn't slept with her in Fort Worth because he wanted to quit being her husband right then. But they were still married in more than just the legal sense, and she was going to enjoy every minute of it until they weren't.

But then he headed toward the door again.

"Where are you going?"

"*We* are going to take your grandmother to a bank to set up an account and find you both a seamstress."

"But we just got here!"

"It takes time for clothes to be made. And thieves in the city aren't as easy to spot as they are in the West. I'll feel better when Ella's money is safely deposited, and I'm sure she will, too."

Max laughed. "I don't think she knows you carried it here."

"I wasn't going to leave it in Bingham's bank. While the sale was legal and the documents are signed, he still paid a hundred times over what that property is worth. He might regret that eventually, if he doesn't already."

"Just desserts and small recompense for what he—"

"Did you *want* me to kill him?"

"Would you have?"

"You already know the answer. He is a politician and a businessman—who doesn't carry a gun."

"And you are armed with a business education." She laughed. "Possibly a more deadly weapon to use against him. I bet he wasn't expecting that from a gunfighter."

"No, he wasn't."

They went to the bank first. For such a huge city with thousands of people in it, Max was dumbfounded that every single employee at the bank greeted Degan by name. All of them were deferential, a few were even friendly, too, but none of them were nervous even though he hadn't yet put his gun away or changed his clothes to look more citified.

"I take it you used to come here often?" she asked as they walked through the large building to the manager's office.

"Yes."

Then the manager rushed forward, exclaiming, "Thank goodness you're home, Mr. Grant. Your father hasn't attended a board meeting for years, and your brother has so little interest in them that he simply accedes to the majority vote." And then in a whisper: "I don't think he realizes that he *is* the majority vote."

"I'm not here for a board meeting, I'm here to set up an account for Mrs. Dawson. Attend to it for me."

"Certainly, sir."

"And quickly."

"I understand."

Max pulled Degan back as the manager escorted Ella into his office. "You *own* this bank?"

"It's one of several my family founded, yes."

"You couldn't warn me?"

"Why? Would you have picked another? This one is solid. And despite the apparent lack of leadership recently, the board members have a vested interest in keeping it that way."

It sounded to Max as if Degan had been needed here, though he didn't appear surprised to find that out. Allison

Montgomery must have told him something about his family that he hadn't shared with her. And now Max was more curious and interested in meeting his family than ever. But she ended up spending the rest of the day at the elegant shop of a French seamstress who had a small army of assistants.

Degan left her there with her grandmother, telling her, "Follow their advice. They know exactly what is needed."

Needed by whom? Certainly not by her. This was a frivolous waste of money as far as Max was concerned. But Ella was having fun, and although Max wouldn't admit it, she was, too, after a while. They were even served lunch! A cart was rolled in from a restaurant across the street, and the waiter actually remained to serve them. She had so many choices to make, though she didn't realize it could have been much worse if she had been taken to the stockroom. Instead, swatches of material were brought out to her, only a few per dress. But an argument ensued when the seamstress suggested that velvet only be used as a trim. Max fell in love with that material and wanted all of her new clothes to be made of it.

The seamstress flatly refused. "It is for winter, madam. Return in the fall and we will show you all of the velvets."

"What if I'm not here in the fall?" The seamstress didn't have an answer to that, so Max added, "Just make me one velvet dress or I'm leaving."

She won the argument, but Ella tsked at her as soon as the woman left the room. "She's right, you know. You will swelter in a velvet day dress in this weather."

"I was wearing doeskin and leather in this weather just a few weeks ago, Gran. Anything is cooler than that. But why did she concede to use it for nightwear? I don't want to sleep in it."

"An evening gown isn't for bed. Relax, baby girl. City folk are accustomed to wearing clothes for each part of the day, morning gowns, day gowns, walking gowns, evening gowns."

Max masked her surprise and simply said, "How silly."

And then the bonnets arrived. . . .

Chapter Fifty-Three

THE NEXT FEW DAYS in Chicago were a whirlwind. Degan kept Max so busy she didn't have time to wonder when he was going home or if he'd already been there. He drove her around the city in an open carriage, pointing out sites of interest. She was sure she could live there for months or more and still not see everything there was to see.

He took her to restaurants that featured foreign food that she refused to comment on, though at a few of them she had to drink a lot of water after the meal. They rode through parks he used to frequent, even went to a horse race at a large track, though they didn't stay for all the races. Too many people recognized him and plied him with questions he wasn't willing to answer. He got good use out of the word *undecided* that day.

Was he really undecided about going home, about staying in Chicago, about taking her to a lawyer? He still hadn't mentioned any of that, and she was hesitant to bring it up when they were sharing the same bed again and not just sleeping in it. Max looked forward to lying down beside him every night, feeling the warmth and strength of his big body, looking up in the darkened room and seeing his face so close to hers. She loved touching him and the way he touched her, and all the kissing they did. Inevitably, it got both of them hot and led to lovemaking that still surprised her with all its different kinds of sensual delights. She couldn't bear to think about giving all that up. But they were going to have to talk about it, and soon. Ella had already confided to Max that she was enjoying her first trip to a big city, but she'd be uncomfortable settling down here. Max felt the same way, but she would stay if Degan was going to stay—if he wanted her to stay.

The new clothes had begun trickling in as well as boxes of shoes. Max hadn't even noticed that her feet had been measured at the seamstress's shop. And one round box for each of the bonnets was delivered. She'd bought them all! The dresses she could hang in the small wardrobe—well, until the rest of them arrived—but the hotel room was still getting crowded with all the boxes.

Degan didn't mind, but he did say, "We may have to move to my home just so you can have a room for all your purchases. Some dressing rooms are as big as a bedroom."

"No one needs *that* many clothes. I'll manage just fine. But are you ready to go home?"

He nodded. "We will visit my brother today. By now, he must have heard that I'm in the city. I don't want him to think I'm avoiding him."

"And your father?"

"He will likely be home, but I'd rather not subject you to that meeting. According to Allison, he's developed an addiction to drink. While I've spoken to a few of his old friends, they didn't confirm it, but they did say they rarely see him anymore, and one said he'd gone daft, obsessed with some business venture that couldn't possibly turn a profit. So I'm not sure what to believe."

Max wanted to hug him so bad, but was afraid he'd see it as pity. She still said hesitantly, "I'm sorry. This should have been a pleasant homecoming for you."

"It was never going to be that. I only hope it's not too late for my father to recover. But come here. Before you meet Flint, I should explain why the meeting might be hostile."

He was sitting in one of the two armchairs. He'd just put his boots on. She was already dressed in one of her new walking gowns, which Degan had had to fasten for her because the buttons were in the back. She'd planned to tell the seamstress not to make her any more like it until Degan had finished fastening the gown with a kiss on her shoulder. Maybe she wouldn't mind asking him for assistance after all.

The dress was made of lovely lavender silk and was accessorized with a stylish purple jacket that formed part of the bustle, a lacy, purple parasol that she wasn't sure how to open, and an adorable bonnet with a fluffy lavender feather on it. It was hard to tear herself away from the full-length mirror where she was admiring herself. If Bingham Hills could see her now, they would *not* recognize her!

But she walked over to Degan, who drew her onto his lap. She wasn't expecting that, and as usual when she got this close to him, her body began to respond, her thoughts flying away, and . . .

"It's not pleasant to remember what ended my engagement to Allison."

That name was like a dousing in cold water. "You don't have to tell me if it's still painful."

"It's not and it hasn't been for a long time. I thought the anger was gone, too, until Allison turned up like a bad penny and reminded me."

"Wasn't she merely concerned about your family? That *is* the impression she gave for coming after you."

"Yes, I just haven't figured out why. But the night that my world fell apart, I arrived late at the small dinner party my father had arranged at our home to celebrate my and Allison's engagement to marry. I found out later he had been detained at the bank by business, and Allison's parents had left early, angry that both my father and I weren't present. I had no excuse for arriving so late."

"Then why did you?"

"To be honest, I simply forgot about the dinner. And if I hadn't had a few drinks with a friend before I got home, that night might have ended quite differently."

Max went very still. She was guessing ahead and realizing that Allison must have been angry, too, that he could overlook something as important as their engagement dinner. But to retaliate by cheating on him? Wasn't that spiting herself more than him? Unless . . .

"Good grief, you didn't actually *tell* her you forgot, did you?"

His sigh was drawn out. "No, when I arrived home, it was later than I thought. The dining room was empty. Most of the servants had already gone to bed. And then a scream echoed down the stairs. I panicked, thinking it was Allison, that she'd waited for me, but someone had broken into our house and was hurting her. It wouldn't have been the first time we were robbed at night. So I grabbed one of my father's pistols and raced upstairs and shot the man who was attacking her. I thought I was saving her, but I wasn't. Her screams had been from pleasure."

Max put her arms around his neck and squeezed tightly. She hated that he was reliving this.

"It occurred to me after I'd left Chicago that I didn't really love her. She was merely a prize I'd competed for and won, and Father wanted a Montgomery in the family. He didn't care which of us married her. But at the time, I was devastated."

"But your anger cooled eventually, so why didn't you come back sooner?"

"Because I shot my brother that night—in the back. He might have died. He nearly did die. And I felt such rage at him, at both of them."

Max leaned back, eyes wide. "It was your *brother* Allison was unfaithful with?"

"Yes. But then my father made it even worse when he insisted I still had to marry her. Our engagement had been announced. He didn't want the scandal. I'd felt betrayed by both my father and my brother, the two people closest to me, the two I thought I could depend on. The only thing I *could* do was leave, before I hurt someone even worse."

"Time hasn't really healed this wound, has it?"

"On the contrary. I've recovered, but they apparently haven't. I do wish I'd known sooner how they reacted to my defection, but once I left, I never looked back."

"*You* were the one betrayed, on all fronts. You have nothing to blame yourself for."

"You consider that a wifely duty, don't you? To defend me?"

She ignored the rare smile he was giving her and said

honestly, "You really think I would do that if you didn't deserve it?"

"Yes."

She snorted, but more at herself because maybe she would. But in this case she said, "I stated a fact based on what you just told me—unless that wasn't everything?"

"It was. You know as much as I do. . . . Shall we go? I want to catch Flint early."

He stood up and set her on her feet, but didn't remove his arm from around her waist as he walked with her to the door. He did that a lot lately, maintaining contact with her in one form or another. It seemed husbandly to her. Though she refused to let it go to her head, it still left her smiling on the inside.

Chapter Fifty-Four

THE GRANT HOME WAS in a pretty neighborhood away from the noise and bustle of the crowded downtown. Max had expected a mansion, but it was just a stately town house, no different from the others lining the street. But when the butler let them in, Max realized the house's exterior was deceptive. It looked like a mansion inside. The butler didn't appear to recognize Degan, but he didn't ask them whom they were there to see, as if he had been told to expect callers. Max stared at the grand curved staircase at the end of the huge, well-appointed foyer, imagining Degan as a young man running up it with a pistol in his hand. That one night had changed his way of life. But he was back now. He could fit right back in if he wanted to, and she still didn't know if he did want to. For all her brazenness, she was afraid to find out what his plans were for himself—for her.

The butler led them to a formal dining room. It was early enough that the family might still be having breakfast, but only two people were seated at the dining table, Allison

Montgomery and a young man who looked so much like Degan that Max knew he had to be Flint Grant. He was casually dressed in trousers and a brocade robe with no shirt under it.

Allison, elegantly attired as usual, was peering at Max and said cattily, "You clean up nicely—for an outlaw."

"I left my gun at the hotel." Max replied. "Should I have brought it?"

Allison actually laughed before turning her attention to Degan. "Excellent timing, Degan. You've managed to catch him before he has a drink in hand."

"My father?"

"No, your brother."

"Degan," Flint said stiffly, then saw the gun holster Degan was wearing. "Come to shoot me in the back again?"

Degan ignored that and, with a nod toward Allison, demanded, "What's *she* doing here?"

"Where else would my wife be? Though I frequently damn her to Hades, she just won't go."

Degan's gaze swung toward Allison. Max's swung toward Degan. He didn't like surprises. While some of the old friends and acquaintances Degan had run into since he'd returned to Chicago had told his family that he was in town, none of them had bothered to mention to him that his brother had married his ex-fiancée. Max figured those people had assumed he knew about it.

But his tone was only a little terse when he said to Allison, "You could have said you were my sister-in-law instead of implying otherwise."

"So I lied a little. I was willing to try or say anything to get you to return to your responsibilities here—and telling you that

I had married your brother would have been rubbing salt in the wound."

"That wound has healed."

She huffed, "That wasn't the impression you gave when we were in that awful stable in Helena and you looked like you wanted to kill me."

"She does inspire that emotion in a man, doesn't she, brother?" Flint sneered.

Allison tsked. "What happened that night wasn't planned, Degan. Flint and I had too much to drink while waiting for *you*. But if you want the truth, I'm glad now that it happened because you and I never would have gotten along. You would have been like your father *and* mine, all business, rarely home, never available for the social functions I need to attend. I was drawn to you or I wouldn't have said yes to your proposal, but as soon as I did agree to marry you, I began to have doubts. Flint was the one I needed, not just to make me happy but to keep me happy. I realized that soon after we married. But then everything went from bad to worse because *he* started doubting that I love him."

Flint snorted at that declaration. Degan didn't appear impressed by it either. Max decided to pretend she wasn't avidly listening to the conversation and helped herself to a plate on the sideboard, which held enough food to feed an army. She didn't sit down, though. Taking food that was going to go to waste wasn't as rude as sitting at their table when she hadn't been invited to.

"Where is father?" Degan asked.

Flint shrugged. "He's rarely home anymore."

"*Why* didn't you put a stop to this, Flint?"

"Tell *him* what to do? Is that a joke, brother?"

"No. He needs help, not tolerance. I shouldn't have had to come home to see to it."

"That isn't fair," Allison said, defending her husband. "Flint has been overwhelmed trying to fill your shoes when they don't fit him!"

"It wasn't necessary for him to try," Degan replied.

"Of course it was," Flint mumbled. "But I wasn't raised to take over, I was raised to marry well and sire children."

"You have children?"

"No, that would require two people who actually *like* each other."

Allison flinched. "Flint!"

The younger brother ignored his wife. "Father forced me to marry her, you know. Claimed we'd wronged her. Blamed me for seducing her when it was a mutual damned thing. And now her family isn't doing so well, which is why she's fighting so hard for this one."

"I fight for this one because I *love* you," Allison insisted. "If you'd stop feeling so guilty for driving your brother away, maybe you'd figure that out."

"If you loved me, you'd *listen* to me," Flint said angrily. "I forbade you to locate Degan, but you did it anyway."

"You were just too riddled with guilt to face him. But it's not as bad as you thought it would be, is it? I was trying to help, for *you*, so you'd stop tormenting yourself, because you're not alone, Flint. Whether Degan straightens this mess out or not, you are not alone."

"For what it's worth, Flint, I believe her," Degan said. "And I forgive you—both of you. So don't use me as an excuse not to mend your fences. As for Father, he can either be restrained here until his addiction passes or—"

Flint cut in, "What addiction?"

Degan looked directly at Allison. She gave him a look of exasperation rather than contrition. "I *told* you I lied a little."

"A little?"

"It got you here, didn't it?"

"So he's not a drunkard?"

Flint started laughing.

Allison tsked. "He might as well be for all the attention he pays this family. He is obsessed with his silly new venture to the exclusion of everything else. And it's not even profitable! All his old businesses have suffered because of it, because he simply has no interest in anything else. *That* wasn't a lie."

Degan looked at his brother again. "What about you?"

"What about me? Oh, did she claim I'm a drunkard, too? I'm not surprised since I tend to head for a bottle as soon as she enters the room. But, no, I might drink a tad more than I used to, but with good reason. I suppose you were looking forward to having me restrained as well?"

"You should know better than to say that."

Flint sighed and even offered a conciliatory half smile. "I'm sorry, that was uncalled for. I still seem to be defensive, a habit I've acquired that I truly deplore."

That was the first indication Max had seen that Flint might be the charming man Degan had described to her. Then Flint rose and went over to his brother to give him a hug. That seemed to remove the last of the tension from the room. Max thought it would stay that way if Allison kept her mouth shut. For the moment, she seemed content that the Grant brothers were on better terms.

"I've missed you, Degan," Flint admitted.

"We'll see if you still feel that way after I give you a quick education in dealing with the rest of Father's empire, in case he really has retired for good to pursue other interests. He was always hands-on. He expected me to be hands-on. But, in fact, his empire can run itself with the right managers in place. Responsibility can be delegated, Flint. You and I don't *need* to be hands-on."

"You aren't staying, are you?" Flint guessed.

"What I just said applies whether I do or don't."

Max was quick to note that a perfect opportunity to learn what Degan's plans were had just flown by. He wouldn't even tell his family? That made her realize the only reason he could be keeping those plans such a guarded secret was because she wasn't going to like them. He was going to just ride off into the sunset without her or send her packing down the trail. Like hell he was.

She knew what she had to do, but not while he was having this reunion with his family. He closeted himself with his brother for a couple of hours, and they came out of the room laughing. While the men were in the study talking business, Max got to have lunch with Allison. That was quite uncomfortable. Although they were sisters-in-law for the moment, they had absolutely nothing in common other than the men they were married to.

Max had to stew a little longer about her own future since Degan had to make one more stop after they left the Grant home. Flint had given Degan the address of their father's new business venture. When they got out of the carriage in front of it, she was surprised.

"*This* is what Allison disdains?" Max said with a laugh as she read the writing painted on the window advertising the publisher's latest western novel.

"She obviously assumes dime novels can't possibly turn a profit."

"Then she doesn't know how popular these little books are. Or maybe she's just not good with math."

"Dime novels have been around for a while. What surprises me is that my father is devoted to publishing only those set in the American West."

"Did Flint tell you that?"

Degan nodded. "And that Father knows where I've been these past five years. I would have thought he would despise anything to do with my new life, including where I'm living it."

Max frowned, feeling nervous and not knowing what to expect as they entered the publishing offices. She'd never met a publisher or a financier before, let alone a man who was both. And this was Degan's father! Would he be as intimidating as his elder son? Or even more so?

A young man neatly dressed in business attire was seated at a desk in the front room. "May I help . . ." His eyes widened.

"I'd like to see Robert Grant," Degan said.

The young man scrambled around the desk. "Yes, sir. Of course, Mr. Grant. Please follow me."

They were shown to a back room, where Robert Grant's name was tastefully painted in gold on the door. When the young man opened it, a deep male voice barked, "New submissions go on the fifth pile, not on my desk!"

The young man gestured for Degan and Max to enter, then left, closing the door behind him.

The older man didn't even look up from the pages he was reading. Thin, brown-paper packages littered his desk, with more arranged in piles all over the floor. With mussed black hair turning silver at the temples, his shirtsleeves rolled up, and spectacles perched on his nose, Robert Grant didn't look the way Max expected a wealthy banker to look.

"I can count at least fifteen piles in here," Degan remarked drily, "but I can't tell, which is the fifth?"

Robert looked up, amazement spreading across his face, and slowly rose to his feet. He removed his spectacles. "Degan! Degan Grant, the most infamous gunfighter of all," he said proudly. "Welcome home, son."

Degan was obviously disconcerted, especially when his father came around the desk to hug him. Max stepped back to give the two big men space.

"You know how I've been living, not just where?"

"Of course I do. I've wrestled with my pride many times," Robert said in a softer voice, "and, sadly, my pride always won. I didn't think you'd listen to me if I contacted you myself and asked you to come home after the way we parted."

"You were furious."

"I know, and I am truly sorry for that. I never should have tried to force you to marry Allison or take over at the banks for me when you obviously wanted a different sort of life. I sent detectives to find you that first year after you left, and several times more since then to keep me informed of your welfare. I can't tell you how proud I am of you for striking out on your own, becoming a man of adventure, and thriving in such a tough, dangerous environment. You're quite famous now."

"Not here I'm not." Max couldn't believe her eyes. Was Degan actually blushing?

"You would be if you let me publish you." Robert grinned.

Degan snorted. "I'm not a writer."

"I've had twelve submissions about you since I started this business three years ago. There *are* people already writing about you, Degan, fascinating, exciting stories of danger and daring, heroism and courage, on the frontier. I don't know if they are all based on actual events, since writers do tend to embellish, especially the author of this latest one that arrived yesterday that depicts you marrying a female outlaw. But while I would love to publish every one of them, fact or fiction, I wouldn't do that without receiving your permission first."

"I did marry an outlaw."

Max grinned and stepped forward. "That would be me, recently wanted for murder and bank robbery, erroneously, of course."

Robert's eyes lit up. "This is delightful! And I thought Calamity Jane was the only woman having adventures out West."

"Who?" Max asked.

"Martha Jane Canary?" But when Max still looked blank, he said, "Never mind, you're going to have to tell me all about yourself!"

Max enjoyed the visit with Degan's father much more than she did the one with his brother. Allison had certainly exaggerated about Robert Grant. He might be overzealous about his publishing business and spend all of his time reading submissions for it, but he obviously loved what he was now doing.

But by the time Max and Degan returned to the hotel later that day, she hadn't changed her mind about what she was going to do about her marriage. It was far too important to wait any longer.

In their room she immediately removed her jacket to get rid of the bustle so her gun belt would fit. Degan raised a brow at her as she buckled it on.

"What are you doing?"

"We're having another showdown."

"I thought you agreed that wasn't a good idea."

"It is now. And there are stakes on the table. If you win, we go find a lawyer and end this. If I win, we stay married for good. Are you ready?"

"No."

She heard the humor in his tone. He expected her to back down again, but she wouldn't this time. This time was too important.

"Then get ready," she warned. "Wait a moment."

She paused to empty the bullets from her gun. She wasn't going to let a sweaty finger shoot him by accident. He wouldn't have that trouble. *He* didn't get nervous.

Sliding her gun back in its holster, Max shook her hands briefly before positioning her right hand just above her gun. She could do this. The rest of her life depended on it. "Okay, I'm ready." She finally glanced at him. He hadn't just sounded amused, he looked it, too.

"This isn't—"

"One."

"—necessary."

"Two."

"Max."

"Now!"

For once, she was pretty damn fast, but that's not why she ended up wide-eyed. He drew on her like a tinhorn, about as slow as it was possible to be. Her smile lit up the room. He wanted to stay married!

She dropped her gun and raced across the room to leap at him. And sighed in bliss when he wrapped his arms tightly around her.

"*Why* didn't you tell me?" Max exclaimed as she sprinkled kisses over his face.

"Because you had stated conditions that hadn't been met yet. It didn't matter that I love you, Max. I still would have let you go if you didn't have your happy reasons for staying married."

"Oh, my God, I love you so much! How could you not figure that out, fancy man?"

"I was fooled once before. Understanding a woman's heart is not something I wanted to guess at ever again. But I would have courted you as soon as my family issues were settled. I wasn't going to give up on you easily."

She held his face gently. It was still hard to believe that this man, hard and cold on the surface for everyone else, had let love in for her. "You'll never have to guess again—well, unless I'm teasing you. But you like being teased, don't you?"

"No." He sounded serious until he added, "But I like making you happy, so I'll put up with it. As long as you don't mind the consequences."

"Oh?" He swept her up in his arms and carried her to the bed. Max laughed as he dropped her on it. "I'm going to have to tease you more often."

They spent the rest of the day and the night in bed. Degan caught a maid passing in the hall and ordered food to be brought up to their room before the hotel kitchen closed for the night, and they ate that in bed, too. Then an unexpected knock came at the door. Degan put on his pants to answer it. Max burrowed under the sheets. But she wasn't at all pleased to hear Allison's voice.

"Flint is sleeping peacefully for the first time in years. I thought you might want to know that."

Degan didn't open the door enough to allow entry. "It could have waited until tomorrow."

"I wanted a chance to speak to you alone."

"I'm not alone."

"I know your wife is here. I meant without Flint hearing me. I just wanted to assure you that your brother is going to be okay now. He never believed that I loved him. That was half of his difficulty. The guilt for betraying you was the other half."

"Was he the real reason you wanted me here—at any cost?"

"I'm sorry for the lies, I truly am. Not that your father *hasn't* gone batty," Allison added with a laugh.

"He's hardly that. He merely turned in one way of life for another, just as I did. And he's happy doing what he's doing, which is really all that matters."

"I suppose, though we still worry about him. You know he gets so engrossed in reading those stories that he loses track of time and even sleeps in his new offices half the time. And he won't even talk to his old friends anymore, since all they do is ridicule him about this venture. He's become a laughingstock, which *is* scandalous."

"I really don't think he cares, nor should you."

Allison tsked. "Exactly why I didn't tell you any of this to lure you home. It amuses you, doesn't it?"

Degan laughed. "A little."

Allison sighed. "I didn't come here to argue about your father's odd hobby. I was sure you wouldn't help me with the real problem if I told you that single indiscretion five years ago was still ruining our lives, which was why I resorted to lies instead. Flint wouldn't admit he loves me when he hated himself so much for driving you away. Thank you for forgiving him. It's made a world of difference for him."

"We're not going to be staying, Alli. But we won't be so far away that we can't visit from time to time."

"Thank you, Degan, for fixing this."

Max smiled to herself as Degan closed the door on his ex-fiancée. He was good at fixing things, even broken families. But she wondered, "Where are we going that we won't be so far away?"

He returned to the bed and pulled her close again. "Nashart, Montana, I think. I already know the people, and there's actually a job waiting for me there. I always figured by the time I got around to seeing Texas it would be time to decide if there was anywhere in the West I might want to settle, or if it was time to head back East."

"Do you *want* to stay here?"

"No, not any longer than we have to. I don't feel like I belong here anymore. I might have missed fine cuisine and sleeping in a soft bed every night instead of once a month if I got lucky, but cooks can be hired. I did miss having a permanent residence to come home to. And my stay with Zachary Callahan's close-knit family this year made me wonder if I was ready for one of my own. Then I met you and it all simply fell into place perfectly."

"What do you mean?"

He hugged her closer. "I stopped wondering. I knew."

Chapter Fifty-Five

"**H**UNTER TOLD ME ONCE that a house could be built here in a day if everyone pitched in. I didn't believe him, certainly not a house this size."

Standing next to Degan with his arm around her, Max admired her new home, but she was as surprised as he was that it was almost done. It seemed as if every time she blinked today, another room was finished. But the whole town had turned out to support their new sheriff. When Degan had told her he had a job in Nashart, she'd thought he meant one of his usual in-and-out jobs, not a permanent one such as sheriff.

"They should break for the day," Max said. "It's not as if we can move in tonight. And the food is almost ready."

Zachary Callahan had donated a cow for the barbecue that was set up in the yard. Long tables had been carried over to hold the fixings other townsfolk had brought.

"I know," Degan agreed. "The artisans won't arrive for another day or so anyway to put on all the finishing touches. And it still needs to be painted and wallpapered, carpets laid, furniture moved in. I figure by the end of the week we'll have our first dinner here."

They'd spent a few extra days in Chicago buying furniture and picking out colors and patterns for the walls and floors. She would have liked to have had more time with so many choices to pick from, but Degan had assured her she could change anything she didn't like later, as often as she wanted to. She'd thought that was one of his jokes, but it wasn't. He wanted this house to be just right for her. It already was, simply because it was theirs.

Five bedrooms: one for Ella, one for Johnny when he got school breaks, and a couple more for the children they hoped to have eventually. Until then they would serve as guest rooms. Degan's father had warned them at a big dinner party he had hosted for them in Chicago that he planned to visit often. Flint had expressed interest in visiting them in Montana, too, but Max doubted that Allison would ever come West again. And after Max sent off a telegram to Luella to let her know where Max could now be reached, she'd gotten a reply. Luella had actually married Big Al and was now the co-proprietor of Big Al's Saloon. She promised to visit, too. Maybe five bedrooms weren't going to be enough, after all.

But the house was built on the edge of town, so they could expand if they needed to. The yard was a decent size, too, in case Ella wanted to putter around in a garden. Degan had also included an extra room whose walls were mostly windows just so Ella would have good lighting when she did her painting. Ella was delighted with Nashart and with Degan.

Max was delighted with Nashart, too. It was a nice, peaceful town filled with friendly people where she could ride for miles if she wanted and go hunting whenever she felt like it.

Though she'd heard all about the Callahan-Warren feud that had ended earlier this summer, having met both families, she found it hard to believe that they'd ever been enemies. The young men in both families behaved as if they were the best of friends. And Tiffany and Hunter, whose marriage had ended that feud, were so in love Max couldn't help smiling whenever she saw them together.

But Hunter Callahan took some getting used to. Max had never met anyone who teased and laughed as much as he did. She took to his wife, Tiffany, right away. Despite their different upbringings, Max already considered her a good friend.

"I used to be so nervous around Degan when he and I were staying with the Callahans," Tiffany had confided. "That was prior to Hunter's finding out I was his promised bride. But Degan fairly reeked of danger. Weren't you scared of him when you first met him?"

Max grinned. "No."

"Really?"

"He wondered about that, too. I'd like to think that I knew, deep down, that he was the man for me. But I didn't. I just knew he wouldn't hurt me."

"He's changed," Tiffany marveled. "*You've* changed him. Goodness, I even saw him laugh yesterday!"

Max had smiled. Degan did that a lot lately. The gunfighter wasn't guarded around her anymore, and he'd let his guard down here, too, with these people, because he considered them friends. Already, he thought of this town as home. Max knew it made a big difference when you felt you belonged.

A few days after the house went up, they learned that the carved moldings that Degan wanted at the top and the bottom of every wall, in every room of their house, were going to take longer than they'd figured, even though the craftsman had brought two assistants with him and the local carpenter had pitched in, offering his shop for them to work in. But with everything else done, they moved in at the end of the week anyway and invited the Callahans to dinner to celebrate their first night in their new house. The cook and his assistants, as well as the two maids that Degan had hired in Chicago, weren't due to arrive for another week, so Ella had volunteered to cook with Max's help.

Degan had brought so much here from the East, even servants, that Max worried he was only settling down in the West for her sake. Until he told her about the scarcity of women in Montana and if they wanted servants before the next century . . . She got the idea.

Sam Warren and John Callahan had both applied to be Degan's deputy. He hadn't made up his mind yet which one he was going to choose.

"You could just hire them both," Max suggested.

"The town doesn't need that many lawmen."

"Or you could hire me instead." She batted her eyes at him.

He swatted her backside. "You might be good with a gun and intimidating as all hell—"

"I am not!"

"—but I can't protect the town if I'm protecting you instead. Besides"—he drew her into his arms for a long kiss—"you're far too distracting."

She'd been on her own for so long that she knew it was going to take time to get used to having someone else looking out for her. But she adored Degan's protectiveness. She adored his strength and tenderness. She adored everything about her husband.

As for deputies, while Degan probably didn't need any help, she'd feel better if he had it, since she felt as protective of him as he did of her. Luckily, the town was peaceful, though it might not stay that way for long. She knew Degan expected trouble to find him here. She thought he must have confided the same thing to Hunter when the cowboy stopped by the day after the dinner party and she joined them on the porch, catching the tail end of their conversation.

"You worry too much," Hunter was saying. "Once it gets around that you turned lawman, and it will get around, the glory hunters will stop seeking you out. They'll be afraid you'll just jail them instead of giving them their showdown." But then Hunter spotted Max behind them and exclaimed, "Maxie! I don't think Killer here is very happy."

Hunter got back on his horse, laughing as he rode away, and she frowned. "What are you not happy about?"

Degan rolled his eyes. "He wasn't referring to me. He was talking about his housewarming gift for us. At least he didn't bring us a pig!" Degan grinned as he handed her the puppy in his arms.

"Oh, how sweet!" Max cooed in delight, and yelled after Hunter, "Thanks, Callahan!" Then in a whisper to Degan: "But we're changing his name."

"I agree since it's a female."

She laughed. "Your friend is ornery."

"No, he's just happy. But so am I. I never thought I would end up with everything I could want in this life. Thank you for loving me, Maxie."

"I didn't have a choice, fancy man."